TWO COMPLETE
IN ON

THE FANGS OF MORNING
FIRST TIME IN PAPERBACK

Washington, DC, was the crime capital of the country, but even cynical homicide detective Avery Morgan had never seen anything like the Mall Murders. One by one, victims started turning up among the historical monuments—each drained of blood, his or her life brutally ended. Dedicated, driven, and determined, Morgan was the best man to hunt down the vicious killer. But the city would know a new terror altogether when the hunter was corrupted by the very evil he stalked—and turned on the innocent people he once protected.

THE ALCHEMIST
"Fast paced and exciting...masterful."
—*Washington Post Book World*

To Martin Dobecker, alchemy was just a diversion, a way to blow off pent-up aggression. But the government lawyer soon learned that some very important people in Washington, DC, took his hobby a lot more seriously. Amid a chilling milieu of sorcery, sex, and satanism, Dobecker had to fight those who wanted to use black magic to satisfy their lust for power. If he won the battle, he might escape with his life; if he lost, he'd end up damned for all eternity.

LESLIE H. WHITTEN

THE FANGS OF MORNING

THE ALCHEMIST

ACKNOWLEDGEMENTS

I am grateful for the editorial help and other support of John Littel, my son, Leslie H. Whitten III, and Gerard Brisman.
An Diabolus possit facere ut homo uere resurgent?

Book Margins, Inc.

A BMI Edition

Published by special arrangement with Dorchester Publishing Co., Inc.

THE
FANGS
OF
MORNING

A terror-laden countryside
That mortal eyes will never see
Still haunts me now at morning tide
And, far and vague, enraptures me....

I wake! Through fire-filled eyes, I stare
At my foul lair, my living hell!
And cursed guilt begins to tear
My soul with fangs I know too well....

—by Charles Baudelaire
(L.H.W. *translation*)

Chapter One
Brothermen

The nighttime rally brought together 1500 angry and frightened white and black students and faculty at George Washington University, not a multitude compared to the sixties, but extraordinary for the passive nineties.

But the events that led to this demonstration in the Nation's Capital were themselves extraordinary: four unsolved murders on the Mall, the heart of the Nation's Capital. All were virtually within screaming distance of the campus, and all were from savage, sawtoothed throat wounds.

At the microphone, a banjo slapper sang in falsetto (the speakers blaring it out a hundredfold), "Brotherman, brotherman, love is all I unnerstan." His purpose was to soothe the moiling crowd, at least until the speeches began.

First at the podium on the steps of the administration building was a senior in a dashiki. The first two victims were black 16-year-olds, both with substantial juvenile records for robbery. They were found together near the Washington Monument, the guns they had apparently tried to use on what they hoped would be a victim still cooling from the half-dozen shots they had fired in vain. The police, overburdened with gang-related drug murders, had kissed off the teenagers' deaths as just two more ghetto homicides in this crime capital of the United States. Then came the others.

"If the pigs'd gotten off their asses to work on the deaths of these brothers," shrilled the speaker, "our sister"—the third victim was a white coed from the university—"might be alive today. And the guy from Agriculture might be home tonight with his family. The cops say they're trying. I say they got to start *doing.*" The crowd interrupted him with shouts of approval, hand-clapping and whistling.

In the audience, Acting Lieutenant Avery Morgan of the Metropolitan Police grimaced as if he had smelled a dirty sock. He had heard it all before. He resented the hell out of it, this blaming cops for every kind of dissatisfaction. And especially he resented it now. After all, he was here. On his own time.

It burned him even more because it was he who had come up with the only major clue. On hands and knees, under the Mobile Crime Unit's high-wattage floodlight, he had seen crushed grass near the somewhat daffy student who had risked the Mall at night and been killed next to the Reflecting Pool. While an MCU specialist shifted the light back and forth to give shadows to the grass, he had used an oversized magnifying glass to delineate what looked like two huge shoe prints.

And, Morgan thought as he heard the speaker telling the students what they wanted to hear, these guys say we're doing nothing. Why, at seven this morning, at his modest split-level in Wheaton, a close-in Maryland suburb, he had been working on the case—in front of his bathroom mirror. His wife, Felice, had stared quizzically at him as he carefully clipped and combed his short, often unruly beard and smoothed his hair where it had grayed at the sides. Instead of his usual dark off-the-rack suit, he had donned a corduroy jacket and neat khaki pants. He wanted to look the model of a tall and slender 40-year-old mathematics or geology prof.

"Professor Morgan tonight," he had explained.

"Why you? Last night till eleven—" she had begun.

"This guy has hit at three-week intervals. There'll be kids drifting down toward the bus stops along the Mall. They'll be my bait fish."

She had a way of tucking inward her thinnish lips in her pretty round face when she was peeved. "Oh, Ave," she had said, "that's street-cop business. Why not supervise more now that you've got the gold bar?"

Irked, he had replied, "I'll never make a decent supervisor. Every partner I've had I've turned off, except for this present fool. He's so good-humored he makes me want to puke."

She had met the man, Daniel Harvey. She liked him.

Morgan had softened. "He's like you. He thinks I'm . . ."

" . . . brave, honest . . ." she had finished, touching his arm.

"I've got a two-person cheering section."

"That believes at some point you should stop trying to do everything." She was only 29, but in her seven years of marriage to him she had learned that to survive against his unpredictable harshnesses, she had to speak up.

"*There is no such point,*" he had said, annoyed again. "Don't forget that. Undercover is something I can *do*. One way of getting by . . . of achieving something."

She had not been cowed. "This whole cop business, Ave . . ."

He had snapped her off. "This cop business is all I've got." He had seen her face harden, and had taken her in his arms. "I'm sorry," he had said. "Done it again. You know what I mean."

She had hugged him back. But she hadn't retreated. Instead, she had demanded the last word. "And you know what *I* mean. I feel it. This assignment is no good, no good."

Now, at the rally, eleven hours later and still working, Morgan ran the conversation through his mind as he cased the crowd, searching for suspects among the teachers and other adult go-alongs. Most of them were fat with beards or short with beards, but none of them was sinister with beards, and none looked strong enough to kill two hostile gun-carrying youths. And also none, so far, had size-13 feet.

On the platform, beside the university's security chief, sat Morgan's partner, Daniel Harvey, looking in his George Washington sweater and his Bugle Boy slacks like a junior varsity football coach.

He, too, scanned the crowd, but his quick blue eyes came back constantly to Morgan, watching for signals. Harvey's feelings for his partner were complicated. He feared erring and incurring his anger; he resented his rudeness; he admired his integrity, his guts, the monomania with which he pursued cases. He gloried in his few compliments. He wondered how his good-looking wife put up with him.

From the platform, as the first speaker ended, Harvey's busy gaze flicked to Morgan, who cocked his chin at someone to his right. There, leaning against a No Parking sign was a heavy white man in a dark coat, almost as tall as Morgan's six-one. Intervening students blocked his lower body from Harvey's view, but the man's eyes ignored the podium and instead darted here and there among the crowd.

Morgan slowly moved right as if to get a better view of the renowned psychiatrist who had succeeded the youthful demagogue on the platform. "What the police do not seem to know," the elderly Freudian pontificated, "is that this man's unconscious has moved with uncontrollable violence into the realm of his id. If they would only recognize that his psychosis is acting out its childhood fantasies . . ."

Morgan had put himself where he could see the feet of the man by the parking sign. Son of a bitch, he thought excitedly, look at those coal barges. He nervously patted the bulge of the .38 police-issue revolver which he had declined to replace with the 18-shot Glocks used by most of his comrades.

It was almost ten o'clock when the dozen haranguers and explicators had finished speaking, and the banjo man slapped out a last refrain of "Brotherman." The students and faculty sauntered away in twos, threes, and fours.

Morgan, on the edges of a lingering group, tied his shoes beside an illegally parked car, then untied them and tied them again, waiting for the black-clad stranger to move. He saw the man turn his head toward a blond student. She had walked alone from a disbanding group toward one of the well-lit side streets that crisscrossed the university quarter, her short skirts twitching across the heavy columns of her thighs. Morgan, bending down behind the car, saw the man check his watch and amble toward the street she had entered. The detective lounged along 30 yards behind on the opposite side.

Harvey, almost as agile as the 177-pound wrestler he had been in his two years at the University of Maryland, left the platform with a thank-you to the security man. A straggle of other students, then the man in black, then Morgan and Harvey moved in ragtag order behind the girl. Her hair under the street lights was a low-level beacon that disappeared under the trees, then gleamed again as she emerged.

Morgan began to fade into the shadows of the houses. He slunk through the stretches of gloom and flitted quickly across the occasional swathes of light from house windows. One after another the students walked up steps into the old homes along the street that served as college lodgings. The procession was soon down to the blonde, the raven-hued man, and the two detectives.

Morgan was willing to bet that she was headed for Constitution Avenue to catch one of the east- or westbound buses that ran every half hour at this time. She would think she was safe because of the bright lights of the avenue. Bait fish! At the bus stop the man, in an interval between passing cars, could drag her into the bushes that were on both sides of the avenue.

She stopped, waiting to cross. Morgan slipped from the side street and into the bushes across the avenue from the bus stop. Harvey joined him, and the older partner whispered his instructions. There had to be a few seconds to let the man touch her, the element of assault that would let them arrest him and bring him to the Star Chamber of the Homicide interrogation room.

Morgan gave Harvey an encouraging pat on the shoulder and the younger officer moved back onto the sidewalk, turned the corner, and walked down a block with no special haste. There, at a light, he crossed Constitution as if heading onto the Mall. The girl finally found a gap in traffic and jaywalked. The suspect lumbered behind her, looked at a notice on the bus stop pole, and again glanced at his watch. The two stood in the pool of light, surrounded by the night. The girl peered up the street, as if by looking for a bus she could invoke one.

Out of sight of the bus stop, Harvey circled back silently behind the bushes along Constitution to within 20 feet of where the student and the man stood. There he waited, his police torch in his left hand, his Glock in the right. He opened his mouth wide so his heavy breaths would make no noise.

Through the bushes, Harvey saw the man sidle toward the coed, graceful as a lizard. The girl was pudgy, golden, syrupy-looking, like a canned cling peach. She wavered as if, fearful, she wanted to start back across the street. But cars were passing. The young detective tensed to spring as the man's long arm came up toward the coed.

"Miss?" the man's voice said now, almost timid. The girl started and wheeled. "What time is it, please?"

The old gambit—how often had Harvey heard robbery victims describe that question by the men who would rob them, who would strike when they looked at their watches.

"Ten-thirty," she stammered, wide-eyed, paralyzed.

Harvey moved nearer, tense as a jockey at the gate.

But instead, the presumed murderer, still diffident, explained. "My wife is supposed to meet me at the . . ."

Harvey looked out across the street, and there it was, just driving up, the Volvo station wagon with Maryland plates. Through the driver's window, Harvey could see a woman's face. The car made a U-turn, almost in front of Morgan's hiding place. It pulled up at the stop. From its back window came the drowsy voice of one of the two little girls leaning out.

"Hi, Daddy, we came to getcha."

The suspect-no-longer politely asked the girl if she wanted a ride home. She looked up the avenue, saw her bus coming, and thanked him but told him no. The man and his family waited until it came to be sure she got on safely.

"Brotherman," said Harvey disgustedly.

Chapter Two
Swampoodle

The morning after the rally, Morgan sat expression-lessly flipping out cards at a black Humphrey Bogart fedora that lay brim up on Harvey's desk. While some men concentrate best over a toothpick, a cigarette, or Mozart, he did his best thinking while he pitched playing cards into his hat.

When he had run the deck, Harvey counted the cards and said, "Thirty-two. I owe you a dollar sixty." He fished around in the hat like a diviner reading the augury of the current case in the intestines of a fallen crow, and held up the Jack of Spades, Morgan's favorite card. "Good omen. Your card. Add a quarter for the Black Knight. One eighty-five. My turn."

A newcomer to the room might have thought, "Some investigators." Morgan's compeers knew better. Only two days before, it had come through the grapevine that Morgan was going to be named acting lieutenant—without taking an exam. Nosy, quick-witted, and sufficiently upbeat so that even the sarcastic Morgan had not soured him during

18

the six months they had been partners, Harvey had asked an amateur artist in the Robbery Branch to sketch a card.

Harvey had dictated the design: a Homicide detective taking notes over a man with a bullet hole in his head, with the legend: "Welcome To the Homicide Branch. Our Day Begins When Yours Ends." On it Harvey had written "Congratulations," had crossed it out and written "Condolences," and had given it to Morgan.

Morgan had allowed him a rare smile. "They're fattening me up so they can retire me," he had said. "Count on it."

Harvey had pushed back his dark red hair where it had flopped on his forehead. The respect he had for his difficult elder partner had shone on his square, muscular face. "No, c'mon," he had persisted. "This place can't be all bad if they give a gold bar to a wolf-assed bastard like you without even an exam. I mean, even if you have to take it later to keep it, still . . ." He had pumped Morgan's hand.

Morgan had assessed his young partner. Harvey had started to get through Morgan's feelings-proof vest by asking him right after he came to the Homicide Branch if they could partner up. Morgan had sensed tough pride, intelligence, even subtlety, in this open-faced roughneck just up from crime-ridden Anacostia.

"What's the angle?" Morgan had asked.

"No angle. From you I can learn," Harvey had replied.

"Well, learn to call me Sergeant Morgan next time you answer me."

But the brash detective had laughed. "Why? Because you've been one so long you think Sergeant's your first name?"

Taken by surprise, Morgan had prepared a cruel rejoinder. But there was that quality of laughter in Harvey, and Morgan had merely mock-shot him with

a forefinger and said "Wise mother . . ." By now,
his young partner's quickness, loyalty to him, and
general disrespect for everyone else had made them
friends of a sort, at least in Morgan's up moods.

As Morgan mused over their false lead at the rally
of the night before, Harvey took his turn pitching the
cards. A floor below, chiefs and other officials from
nearby jurisdictions, the FBI, the Justice Department, and related agencies were arriving at the ugly
concrete aspirin box of a building to discuss the same
case. They entered hallways catarrhed by decades
of sulphurous downtown air and megavolumes of
criminal breaths, and congregated in the lineup
room of the Criminal Investigation Division. There,
the fifty Pooh-Bahs drank coffee, talked about the
case, gossiped, and waited for the unusual meeting
to begin.

At nine-thirty, Morgan said to his partner, "Communion time." He snapped on his .38 shoulder
holster and pushed a flat little .32 Davis automatic
into his back pocket. Years ago, he had realized it
was better to break regulations and carry a second
pistol than to kill an unarmed man by mistake and
not have a weapon to plant on him. This was a
detective fact of life, and not even idealistic young
sleuths such as Harvey ignored it.

With the special grace that tall men who were
once athletes have, Morgan loped for the door
with Harvey just behind. As they descended the
stairs, Morgan ran the case through his mind for
the hundredth time. He had been lead detective
on it since the two youths were found dead at the
Washington Monument nine weeks ago. When the
girl was fished from her shallow, watery grave at
the edge of the Reflecting Pool three weeks later,
the newspapers and television began calling them
the "Mall Murders." The name was catchy, just
the right size for a headline. The words mooed

out mellifluously from the trombone throats of the TV reporters.

But the same kind of jagged wound on the throat of the fourth victim, found under a magnolia tree near the Agriculture Department, led to a more radical, more inflammatory label. Now the media spoke of "The Vampire of the Mall."

The story made the TV talk shows and the supermarket tabloids. The sensationalist weeklies' reporters vacuumed up old newspaper clips and quack medical stories about Count Dracula and Jack the Ripper. There were ritualistic references to Hannibal the Cannibal. Even respectable papers like *The Washington Post* did features (which offended their most conservative readers).

The city's depleted treasury was called on to fund more overtime duty for the Metropolitan Police. Citizens' patrols were organized by students and professors at George Washington and Georgetown University Law Schools, also close to the scene of the murders. A few publicity-hungry Congressmen suggested hearings on why the police could not solve the cases.

Many frightened residents, unwilling to wait the five days required under the "Brady Bill," bought pistols on the streets. Interestingly, but not surprisingly considering the effects of the worst elements of the media on the superstitious, the sale of crucifixes and garlic increased by multiples.

Nor was it merely the hoi polloi who had such exotic reactions. A letter reached Morgan, bucked down from the chief of police, from one Father Floyd at Catholic University. In it were photocopied articles on the psychology and history of reputed vampires. Morgan leafed through the tales of seventeenth and eighteenth century bloodsuckers, and the modern medical reports about psychotics who behaved as if they were vampires. But he did not need a professor to know their man was nuts. He filed the data away with the newspaper and magazine clips in a background file he and Harvey kept.

The Homicide Branch seemed almost under siege. Every shadowy figure seen by a motorist passing near the Lincoln Memorial or Washington Monument seemed to bring a panicky call. Homicide was flooded with license plate numbers, reports of peculiar neighbors, and descriptions of predatory men in bars.

As he and Harvey entered the lineup room with its multi-uniformed officials now seated in rows, the Homicide captain, Bailey Burstan (called "Belly" by his men for the obvious reason), looked up angrily at them. Likeable otherwise, he had the small man's tendency toward overassertiveness: "Christ, can't you two ever be on time?" he growled.

Morgan tightened the left side of his mouth in a gesture of annoyance. The front row of officials, most jowly, some sprouting inspectors' and deputy chiefs' shields on their uniforms, turned with irritation toward the latecomers. The back few rows of detectives and uniformed sergeants suppressed grins.

"I told him he's about to have history's shortest career as an acting lieutenant," Burstan said, apologizing to his superiors. Morgan scowled again, and he and Harvey folded into seats in the rear.

The Homicide chief first reported frankly that he had no suspects, and then reviewed the cases based on facts, some not yet known to the media. He signaled the projectionist, whose lower face shone by the light of the projector like a witch's above her cauldron fire. "Okay, slide one," he said.

A map of Washington's Mall area flared on, the Lincoln Memorial, the Reflecting Pool, and the Washington Monument at one end, and at the other, the symmetrical Capitol. Three crude red marks, like uneven drops of blood, marked the black and white map where the murders had occurred.

Burstan quickly ran through slides of the corpses

on morgue slabs. "Similarities. First, second, and fourth cases, jagged, deep, fatal lacerations at the throat. GW girl, less jagged, also on the throat." Burstan went on briskly. "All victims showed bruises on the face and/or upper arms. All fought, fabric traces under the nails, in one and two fabric caught in teeth. No flesh tissue found from the assailant.

"FBI lab is working on all the fibers." He nodded thanks at the special agent in charge of the Washington field office. "They say it's from an old, black European-weave greatcoat. Nothing more than that yet. No weapons, no fingerprints. You know about the two consecutive footprints on the Reflecting Pool case. Big-footed bastard with a long stride."

The tubby captain nodded past the officials toward Morgan in the darkness. "We can thank the ten-o'clock scholar there for that clue. Uniformed guy who got there first protected the area. Morgan approached the body area along the concrete stripping around the pool and found the footprints. Take a bow, genius."

Burstan's plug, Harvey knew, was to boast a little about his branch and, more generously, to offset Morgan's general unpopularity with the powerful bureaucratic men who exercised jurisdiction over the area's law enforcement agencies.

"From length of stride and pressure on the grass," Burstan went on, "we figure subject is six, six-two, weight one-eighty, two hundred. Motive for the first murders, looks like the perp was resisting being robbed. From what these two muggers' friends said, they often carried two hundred bucks or so. Their wallets were ripped wide open. So robbing them may have just been a crime of opportunity. The Lola Granola, far as we can tell, only had a few dollars in one of those fanny packs, which was torn off and empty. No rape." He paused. "The Agriculture clerk was robbed of about fifty, his wife says.

"The only other motive was . . . the means of death itself, these throat wounds. It could be he used some jagged metal weapon, or sicced a dog on them, or he could be biting them, a kind of human vampire just like the goddamn media says."

There was a murmur of mirthless laughter. Burstan did not laugh. "There was what looked like dried saliva beside the wounds on the girl, and the Medical Examiner says the first DNA sequences show some freaky female fragments in the male stretches and a total absence of erythropoietin"—Burstan gave up on pronouncing it—"of the gene that tells the cells when to make blood grow in certain ways. They've sent the sample to a genome center for confirmation and further analyses. Keep tuned . . ."

Slides done, Burstan ordered lights on with a peremptory snap of his fingers. While the officials jotted notes, he laid out the strategy under which he was working. He already had an all-points out for information on any similar acts by deranged criminals. He had asked Interpol to check foreign reporting points. The Bureau of Prisons had provided information on released convicts with neck wound-robbery histories, and the state prison systems were helping out with the same data.

Moreover, at his request, the federal and state mental institutions were reporting in on criminally insane men recently freed who had committed similar crimes. Burstan droned on. The Auto Theft Unit was checking for bloodstains in all abandoned cars. The hack inspectors had gotten out a circular to taxis. The First District's uniformed officers had asked laundries on their beats to watch for recent bloodstains on men's clothes.

When he had outlined these tested routines, Burstan said, loud enough to bring Morgan out of his pained slump, "And I am detaching Acting Lieutenant Morgan from *all* his regular duties to work exclusively on this case. If you cannot reach me, please call him with anything that might be of value to us."

Some officials turned again. A few who had passed Morgan by in the 18 years he had been on the force smiled, friendly. Others looked displeased. Burstan then opened the meeting to any suggestions from the brass. There were few takers.

When they were done, Morgan and Harvey walked back to Homicide with their captain. He, like his predecessors, had wisely given the quirky, eclectic members of the branch more or less free reins, and as a result its reputation was formidable. The kidnapper of Senator Louis Patenziol's daughter had been beached by the squad while the FBI churned water. And, on a vague lookout, Washington Homicide had located for New York City the eccentrically disguised "Pier Eleven" Mafia torpedo, strangler of eight men. Morgan had no lack of self-esteem. He had made both cases, and knew that at 40 he would have been a captain if he had not shunned promotion exams with the same sneers that he accorded his bosses and his partners.

As star investigator and special trouble-causer, he had his and Harvey's desks nearest the door to the Homicide captain's fancy corner suite. From the captain's door, the narrow squad room stretched out some 50 yards, a warren of cheap desks, file cabinets, and computer stations ending with the state-of-the-art interrogation room, its video cameras, and two-way glass.

The walls of the squad room were adorned with calendars, a poster for "The Twilight Zone," a balloon with "LOVE" on its side, plaques for "Investigator of the Month," and a dirty Washington Senators baseball hat. Morgan was also aware that he was the arrhythmic heart and symbol of this eccentric branch.

Before Burstan entered his office, his new lieutenant said with amiable disrespect, "Shit, Belly, you might've asked me first if I wanted to put all my eggs into this basket of shit."

Burstan said, "Why bother? Who asked Br'er Rabbit before they threw him in the briar patch?"

"I never read the book," scoffed Morgan. "My mother raised me on Tarzan so I could survive in this fucking jungle." Burstan smiled. Morgan went on. "But now that I *am* Br'er Rabbit, I'd say the best thing is for you and your secretary to field the calls and do the administrative crap. Let me and Harvey and whoever you can spare work the Mall as night maintenance men, clerks, homeless, whatever, asking questions where we can.

"Like Harvey grew up on a farm and can ride a horse. We'll put him in a mountie Park Police uniform. He can make a quicker response than a car or the helicopters around the trees or bushes where this guy may attack or where we're going to find the next body. Okay, Gene Autry?"

Harvey was taken by surprise. "Ave, you're doing me just the way the captain did you!" Morgan eyed him balefully, and Harvey backed down. "Okay, no sweat. It's better than farting up the cruiser all night," he said. Besides, he liked horses.

There was almost a plaintive note in Burstan's voice as he said, "All right, we'll do this. I haven't got any better ideas. But show some responsibility to the branch, to me. I didn't hear from you on the Ferguson case for two weeks."

"Yeah, and Ferguson pleaded guilty to second and is doing twenty-five to fifty in Atlanta," Morgan reminded him.

Above the top of Morgan's front door was a sign on pieces of typing paper scotch-taped together, "WELCOME HOME ACTING LT." He had called his wife as soon as Burstan made it official that afternoon, and Felice Morgan had been watching for him. She felt she had been inconsiderate in reproaching him about police work the day before. As he untaped the sign, she swung the door open and hugged him.

"Mrs. Acting Lieutenant, at last," he said.

"Who loved you when you were poor," she answered.

Not that they still weren't poor. But she had loved him almost from the first encounter. He had answered a dispatcher call about a "man-with-a-gun" at the apartment house where she'd then lived. It was for a First District car and he was already in Homicide, but his cruiser was only a block away.

The man with the gun was a housebreaker, trapped by police in the apartment of a young nursery school teacher who had come home and surprised him there. Morgan persuaded the gunman to let him in by passing his .38 and badge through the gap in the chain-locked door. When he was inside, he saw the man had a choke hold on the teacher. She had the prettiest blue eyes he had ever seen peering out of a stranglehold.

"I wanna get out of here alive," whispered the robber to Morgan. He had put Morgan's revolver on the floor and was pointing his own cheap automatic at him.

He was in his twenties, wild-eyed and unshaven, half high on drugs, or maybe not, Morgan wasn't sure. "I know what you mean, pal," he told the intruder. "Those SWAT team boys draw a bead on you and 'bap,' it's all over, whether you kill this lady or let her go. I'm from Homicide. I assure you *we* are not into killing anybody."

He talked with the man, in whom he had already sensed a sickly-overed resolution and the weariness of excessive strain. After an hour of discussing deals with him, Morgan looked with seeming compassion into the his eyes, and cooed, "Are you beginning to see that we can get out of this just fine?"

Seeing glimmers of hope and indecision in the man, Morgan grabbed the gun barrel with snake-like speed and popped the man's forefinger in the trigger guard. The blast sent a bullet into the bookcase, and Morgan, the hot barrel still in his right hand, knocked the man senseless with a left hook to the temple.

As chief witness in the case, Morgan had gotten to know the girl, Felice Nordlinger. One night, she had invited him to supper and served him chilled white wine and beef Stroganoff (which had left her almost in tears with its toughness), and he had sighed and abandoned his defenses. Having saved her, he treasured her. She saw him unreservedly as good, and he loved her for seeing him so.

At first in their marriage, he had avoided talk of his work except for the essentials. But her point-blank questions soon had him making her his sole confidant. He could not resist calling her, often from a pay phone, every day. He seldom used the office phone lest "Ornery Avery," as one former partner had called him, be seen as a softy at heart.

Felice cooked now like a professional chef. On hearing his news, she had announced a meal of filet mignon, new potatoes, red wine. With her permission, he had invited Harvey to drop by for dessert, a virtuoso lemon meringue pie.

Harvey arrived with a bottle of California champagne, three miniatures of cognac, and a box of chocolates. He considered wearing a rubber Dracula mask, but even given the low levels of police humor, he feared that would be in bad taste.

Felice Morgan, neat in a skirt and blouse, her legs bare, welcomed him at the door. He had been to their house for snacks before with Morgan after particularly arduous days, and liked her. In fact, if she had not been married to Morgan, he would have liked her a lot. She had an eye for colors that showed in the earth tones of the furniture and rugs. The walls matched with subdued Picasso maskers, a busy Brueghel village scene, and a gouache of an Aztec sun design she had done herself. She had a

B. A. from the University of Maryland, majoring in education, minoring in art, gotten about the same time Harvey had been dropping out there. She was quick, and she had a good sense of humor.

After an ecumenical scarfing up of the pie, Harvey opened the three miniatures. All three poured the brandy into their coffee, and as Felice had expected, the two men got rapidly down to talk of the case. "You could be on your horse for a week or more," Morgan told his partner. "I could be undercover for days straight. I don't want Belly to get used to us in the office where he can jerk us around."

Felice interrupted, a bit irked that there had only been perfunctory questions by Harvey about *her* work as director of a neighborhood nursery school. "Well, Belly Burstan is your problem, Ave. But it was three days that *I* didn't hear from you on the Patenziol case and I hope this time . . ."

"Felice, I've heard about those three days ever since," he said. "That was before you got to the branch, Dan. Me in Vegas, nose and jowl with a Mafia guy. No chance to call home. Honey, on this one, I can always get to a pay phone. Not to worry. It'd be a problem only if he leads me out of town, or if I get so close I can't give myself away. If I could ride a horse"—he tried to lighten things—"I could be home every night." It was almost comical for Harvey to hear Morgan solicitous toward anyone, but he made no comment.

She looked unhappy with his answer, and Harvey tried to stand up for Morgan. "C'mon, Felice. Who can think of anything else on a case like this. The pressures . . ."

She rolled up her eyes in mock horror. "Is this a gender thing? Not you too? Not another Morgan?"

"They don't make 'em like *him* any more," Harvey replied, happy to be part of this small family, even in a squabble.

"Right," she said, and put her hand over her

husband's, almost protectively. "Right. They don't."

As they bantered, a telephone call came for Morgan. While he was in the kitchen on the phone, Felice said conversationally to the younger detective, "I like this, eating with friends. I wish sometimes Ave and I would go out to visit other people, if we knew any in common, or to plays, concerts, things like that. Police work: dear God!"

He found himself defending his partner again. "We get on a big case and, especially with him, it's like he's the grand inquisitor purging a heretic. Even on two-bit cases, if he knows the guy is guilty, he'd like to use a rack and an iron maiden for a confession. But we're like that. If we aren't, well . . ."

She shook her head. "Ave won't change, probably not you either."

"He was always this way, right?"

"More on this case than ever."

Even though they could not hear Morgan's words on the telephone in the next room, they heard the intensity of his voice, almost felt his nervous tension.

She hesitated, then said, "Look, Dan, I know he'll call me, he'll do everything he can to, but just *if* . . . if you hear anything at all when he's undercover, could you . . ."

"Let you know? Sure." But in her question and his assent, however pleased he was by it, his cop's nose smelled a honeysuckle whiff of disloyalty. In both of himself and Felice.

When Morgan returned, Harvey looked up, but Morgan shook his head negatively to let him know it was nothing important. They made more jokes about the job Morgan had assigned Harvey, who said, "If I meet this guy, I can assure you I'll be dropping more fertilizer on the Mall than the horse."

He wondered whether he had been too vulgar, but Felice joined in his laughter as Morgan snorted once with appreciation.

Later, when Felice excused herself to do the dishes, Harvey looked up at her, his light blue eyes meeting her dark blue ones. She already had the wrinkles in the corners of her eyes that seven years of being married to a Homicide man had put there. Nevertheless, with the wine and the brandy talking to him, Harvey thought she was beautiful. He hoped his partner was sufficiently ga-ga with love and alcohol not to notice.

When Harvey had gone, Morgan took her in his arms and kissed her, a little guilty about absorbing the evening with cop talk. She hugged him back. "Okay, Mr. Acting Lieutenant," she said. "We've talked undercover all night. I'm ready to go under covers at home."

In a Ninth Street flophouse, Morgan looked down from a bleary window that depended on rain and wind from the right direction for its only cleaning. He turned from the gray day and sailed his cards toward the black slouch hat which he had rolled around in the gutter to make it as dusty as the rest of him. His worn shoes, shiny polyester pants, unmatching jacket, and scruffy shirt had cost him three dollars at a down-and-outers' thrift shop.

What was he looking for down here? The first genome center study on the spit sample had come back. Lots of fancy color blowups of electronic microscope pictures. The missing gene for blood growth was unusual, but not unique. Ditto the odd mix of male and female DNA fragments.

These facts told him nothing. What bothered Morgan was why the guy had committed the fourth murder by the Mall *after* the police presence was augmented? Because his lair was near the Mall? Or hell, maybe he's making some spaced-out political point— kill them on the Mall, the center of the world.

Morgan smiled grimly. The guy would be built like himself, except for those gunboat shoes. He looked

down at his modest nines. First Morgan in generations with small feet and they'd gone flat in the police
business. Picking up his train of thought, Morgan
said to himself that if the killer *did* hide near the Mall,
it would mean a cheap apartment or a room at the
end of a hall or an el cheapo house, someplace where
no clerk or neighbor would see him come and go.

He reviewed again the streets off the Mall that
contained such dwellings. The near Southwest? Not
likely. The houses were too upscale for a man who
couldn't afford a decent coat. Not probable either by
the Kennedy Center. Those ratty houses not far from
headquarters? Maybe. But that close to hundreds of
cops? With nuts, who could say what they would do?

He stopped flipping his cards, and unrolled the
detailed street maps he had brought with him.
Knowing the city well, raised in it, he leaned
toward the sections of the First District abutting
the Mall, just east of where he was now, the area
he called Swampoodle. Few knew it now by its old
name, but it was once even more crime-infested than
Anacostia and parts of the Northeast were now. It ran
from North Capitol and K down on toward 5th and
G. "I'm looking for The Bad Man of Swampoodle,"
he said aloud.

He went back to his cards. The Jack of Spades
turned up and he flipped it out like an odd-shaped
helicopter or boomerang. It settled neatly into the
hat's crown. He counted the cards. An even 40. A
good omen, as Harvey had said. He wished his
partner had been on hand to lose the money. He
picked up the cards. He had missed with the Queen
of Spades. Without articulating it, even consciously
admitting it, Morgan hoped for another murder that
would give him a real clue.

That night, he worked east toward Chinatown on
the cusps of Swampoodle where gaudy fuchsia-
and-lime neon restaurant signs washed the faces

of passersby in psychedelics. Wispy-bearded seniors smoked cigarettes on the steps of the houses,
telling old country tales in their quacking dialects.
On the corners, the inky-haired youngsters, dressed
in leather jackets, more Caucasian than Caucasians,
lounged, kicking at the cement sidewalk cracks with
booted feet. Here, police remained the residents'
friends.

Morgan reasoned that a tall man with big feet in
a European-style wool coat, particularly in the summer, might stand out. He spoke to the people who
sat on their porches and the youths on corners. All
listened. All knew of the murders. None remembered
anyone such as the man Morgan described.

The next day, his whiskers now suitably uneven,
he shifted toward Swampoodle and the city's oldest,
grubbiest streets, a beat he had walked years before
when he was uniformed. A half-block from the Community for Creative Non-Violence, whose founder
had made it famous for housing the homeless before
he killed himself, Morgan sat on the curb.

It was dusk, and soon he would seek refuge
in one of the rooms for the defeated, but now,
alcoholic-wary, he slipped out a bagged bottle of
Wild Irish Rose, and slugged it heavily. He fumbled
the top back on and thrust it with furtive satisfaction
back into his inside coat pocket. Within moments,
two seedy-looking men approached him. One sat
beside him.

"You got a match," the seated stumblebum said,
rheumy-eyed, fingering the cold butt now in his
mouth.

"No," Morgan said, patting himself.

"Just get in?" the older standing man said.

"No, just got out," Morgan told him. The standing
man laughed, then began a phlegmy cough.

"You want to share me a little drink?" Morgan's
curb-mate said ingratiatingly.

"Naw, it's all I got."

The standing man with the liquid cough sat down on Morgan's other side. "Well, goddamn it then," he said reasonably, "we'll just have to drink our own." The man drew out his own bottle, tipped back his head, and drank the cheap wine, then passed the fifth over Morgan to his companion.

"I'm getting inside to bed early," Morgan said, pulling out his own bottle for a draught. "This damn place is too near the Mall for comfort."

"What dya mean?" asked the bottle owner.

"He means the guy that's been killing those people . . ."

"On the Mall, the Mall guy," Morgan finished. "I hear he's a tall son of a bitch with big feet."

"A person hears everything," said No-bottle. "Gimme a pull off of yours."

Morgan gave him the wine. "Yes, a tall son of a bitch. If I thought that guy was around here, I'd leave town."

The other man drank from his own bottle and passed it unconsciously to Morgan, musing, "Is he black or white? If they don't know that they don't know nothing! It could be anybody in town tall with big feet. There's a million of 'em."

"Yeah," sighed Morgan. "I know."

The next night, Morgan worked even further east among scrofulous two-story homes that housed some of the city's poorest blacks. From these slums, down streets where young delinquents had stoned the streetlights, the nighttime vistas opened on the floodlighted Capitol dome. The magnificent home of Congress was as distant from the penniless denizens of this part of Swampoodle as from the cold silver coinage of the moon.

Holding himself straighter than he had with the drunks, posing now as a good man temporarily down, he searched the opaque faces, looking for someone who would chat with him. Most of the residents looked down with apathy or dislike as he passed. From time to time, some old man and woman sitting in their scabby yard under the light from a curtainless front window in paint-chipped, sheet metal chairs might stare at him with curiosity.

With them, he would pause and ask for a match. When he had lit his cigarette, he would say, meek and conversational, "I'm half afraid to walk home anymore."

"Yeah, I know what you mean. These kids . . ." one old man replied, thinking of young hoodlums, the scourge of the aged.

"No, I mean, I was talking about that fellow on the Mall. They say he may live around here."

"Where'd you hear that?" the man asked, a worried rabbit sniffing the air.

"Who said so?" the woman asked more strongly.

"On the radio, a big sucker, not fat but with big feet, they say. You haven't seen anybody like that, have you?"

The answer was always no, followed by a sudden ambience of fear.

He tried Korean mom-and-pop grocers who sold cigarettes through barred windows, a portly African-American gas station owner with a six-shooter in his belt, many others. One night he questioned a wan numbers man crannied in the doorway of a hot dog stand, his lookout a tall shadow across the street. "Man," the gambler said to Morgan with a cackle. "That kind don't bet, thank God!" Morgan returned to the fetid night wondering what odds the numbers man might give on the arrest of the mall killer.

Chapter Three
The Vampire
of the Mall

Between the National Gallery of Art and the gothic spires of the old Smithsonian Castle, two figures, one in moonlight, one in darkness, performed a grotesque ballet on the colossal stage of the Mall.

The lighted figure was on a bicycle, a woman in her early forties, with Katharine Hepburn cheekbones and the lean, linear body of a woman who takes her dieting seriously. Only a woman of great bravery or foolishness would take this risk. In her jumpsuit, she rode as if she might just have been out for exercise. But across her breast ran the strap of a Nikon, and on the back of her bike was an expensive aluminum tripod and a photographer's ditty bag. With the near full moon above, she was an easily guessible charade: "Photographing Washington by Moonlight."

The figure in darkness was undiscernible among the shrubs and shadows. Hunched in the gloom, he was like a deformed animal, a panther with a broken back, or a hump-shouldered wolf. As the woman slowly pedaled, her face tilted at the old building, the creature in the bushes saw her pale beauty in the moonlight and the gazelle lines of her neck. Stirred as if by an irresistible sexual thrill, he grunted softly, deep in his throat.

The woman cycled on a few more yards, then put down her left foot to steady herself. She framed within two thumbs and slender middle fingers a picture of towers silhouetted against the night sky. Unsatisfied, she rode slowly off again, like a single trooper on parade.

The being behind the tall holly tree had been still as the dew-damp earth itself while she composed her photo. But as she moved off, he unfolded like a carpenter's measure. He was of extraordinary height, but muscularly built. Lithe as a tarantula, he glided beside the broad, recessed facade of the Smithsonian Castle. He froze in hideous mime when she looked his way, a tormented smile on his face. Then as she pedaled, he slipped along, attuning himself to her frequent stops and sightings.

At the eastern end of the building, the woman turned her bike to make a final pass and to pick a spot to set up. The towers, pointed, square, tessellated, were at peace there in the moonlight, fairy battlements from an age of flutes and dulcimers, of great logs on hearths and jeweled goblets of wine.

Caught by the night's sorcery, the woman stopped, stretched her model's body in the moon glow, and lowered her long hands to run them tremblingly over her breasts and down to her stomach, a private gesture, as if she recalled other hands on some other enchanted night in early summer.

Clutching the dark, ivied wall, his shadow crooked and complex as a gigantic praying mantis, the predator uttered again his grunt of desire.

Now, the bicyclist began riding, stately as a queen, past the castle. As she came by where her stalker hid within the columned portico, she lifted her head and smiled, eyes open to her dream of towers.

The man in shadows came upright. Like hinged pieces of lumber, his hands sprung from his sides in a debasement of the politicians' victory symbol. Growling, he rushed into the moonlight. He wore a black greatcoat and was hatless. His slack hair flapped onto his forehead and across his cheeks. It gave him the look of an oddly whiskered man, although in fact he was clean shaven. Out of the mass of hair his prodigious white teeth gleamed, a jackstraw field of jagged, miniature tombstones.

The woman saw him. Her mouth ovaled into the choking cry of a person caught in an unwaking nightmare. Then the silent cry refined itself into human tones and shrilled out across the Mall, pure and absolute as an aria about horror.

Her fear did not paralyze her body. She plunged her strong calves down like pistons to drive the bike away from her attacker. The bicycle swerved as he drew near, then she righted herself and sped off, screaming in bursts.

The roc-like bird of prey pounced at her, but stumbled and fell, his limbs asprawl in the street. He rose with the skyscraper grace of a basketball giant and loped after her, metallically sounding his cry like a satanic turkey gobbler.

Standing on her pedals she raced away from him, her body a coiling and extending spring. It appeared she would outdistance him. But she looked back, saw the specter, coattails flapping, arms still up in a V for Violence, fingers topped with the curling talons of an immense condor.

At this sight her foot slipped on the pedal. The bike crashed into the curb; she hurtled over the bars and to the dirt, the bike atop her. As she struggled from beneath it, her hands gripped the tripod and she ripped it from its rack.

The ogre was only a step away when she came to one knee and swung, hitting him on his matted head. With a shout of rage, he fell. She leaped up and plunged the pointed legs of the tripod at his middle. Quick as a mongoose he dodged, and with a backhand cuff, knocked the tripod away and grabbed her wrist. Twisting it behind her with one hand, he dragged her back over the curb, across the narrow street, and into bushes by the castle.

There, as she struggled, he grasped her long dark hair in the other hand and arched up her neck toward his lips. It was only then, through gaps in the bushes that surrounded them, that she saw his full face by the moonlight. The eyes were brown-orange and glaring like those of a rabid tiger. The nose was aquiline. The teeth showed white and broken except for the overdeveloped canines, which were perfect and fang-like.

The texture of his skin was macabre. It had the look of rotting leather, but was liverishly pale. Wrinkles on his chin and beneath his nose focused like ditches running up a mountain and terminated in the volcanic red of his mouth. From that mouth gushed in heavy breaths the very stink of the charnel house. The woman gagged. The atrocious miasma of his putridity and the sight of his ghoulish face vanquished her as much as his titanic strength.

Her courageous heart faltered, even as she lunged this way and that to break away. She fainted, her lips relaxed from her final wail into a simulacrum of lover's abandon. The panting gargoyle touched his hard red lips to hers, even tenderly, briefly, then teeth agape, with a guttural rasp in the larynx, he dropped his maw to the white skin of her throat.

Near Fifteenth Street on the Mall, Daniel Harvey rode his horse in vain for the fourth night. Morgan's inventive idea, his young partner had about decided, was not going to work. Harvey was ready to go back to more conventional pursuits.

Then, abruptly, as he rolled back and forth with the chestnut gelding's relaxed gait, he heard a scream.

He spurred his horse and flicked his belt radio to "send." The radio was connected by a wire to a microphone at his shoulder—equipment that freed up both hands. There was no reassuring crackle in the earplug he had securely taped to his ear. A second scream sounded, this one definitely from the direction of the old Smithsonian Castle. He broke into a canter, shouting futilely into his radio, "One seven one here, screams near the castle, on my way!"

Harvey galloped across empty Fourteenth Street and leaped the curb onto the grass. He knew that compared to the trained "mounties" of the Park Police he lacked class, but he was confident of his farm-boy competence. He tried the radio again, and heard static, but not the dispatcher's voice rallying cars and horses. His call had not gotten through. Meanwhile the gelding, though no Whirlaway, was taking to the turf like a reliable mile-and-a-furlonger. Back on the grass, Harvey spurred the horse into a gallop, the thunk of the hooves and the squeaks of the harness magnified by the Mall's silence.

Then, running from the trees near the castle onto the sward of the Mall, Harvey saw an eerie figure, his moon shadow elongated behind him. "Jesus Christ!" he muttered, flipping the leather snap from his Glock. He felt a thrilling mix of apprehension and anticipation. This was the Mall killer! He swerved the horse toward the runner, but was flabbergasted to see him grab up a bicycle from the gutter. Fast as a Tour de France sprinter, though clumsier, the cyclist headed across the Mall toward the ghettos of the city.

"Halt, halt!" shouted Harvey at the fugitive, who was 50 yards away. He could not relinquish the reins long enough to get off a shot, even if one were warranted—for however valid his instincts, he had no evidence that this fleeing man had committed a crime.

Head down over his steed's neck, the policeman posted determinedly after the two-wheeling Ichabod Crane. Behind them was the Museum of Technology, bulky as a freight car on its side, and further back the Washington Monument, its lighted Cyclops eye seeming to watch the outlandish contest. Ahead was the columned dome of the Capitol, its upper windows peering down like the eyes of an astonished Argus.

"Gyup, Gyup!" bellowed Harvey, and the seven-year-old surged, strong with its second wind, pounding into its best hoofbeat at a hard run. "Oh, you sweet baby," said the uniformed man, adrenaline throbbing, knowing for the first time that there was enough in the horse to overtake the man on the bike. "We're gonna get him. We *got* to get that son of a bitch," he said urgently in the horse's ear.

Man and horse were gaining. The officer could see the stovepipe ells of the man's black-trousered legs pistoning up and down. The pedaler did not look back until he was almost off the Mall. By then the horseman was a mere 30 feet behind.

As the bicycle plunged across Third Street at the foot of the hill where the Capitol stood, a car swerved wildly to miss it. The auto careened to a stop near the curb. Harvey prayed the driver might have a car phone and summon help as his deficient radio had failed to do.

Headed now toward Pennsylvania Avenue, the policeman drew almost up to the coattails of the phantasm, ripped out his pistol, and shouted, "Halt! Halt! I'll shoot!" He could see the man's outsized feet, see they perfectly matched the description of the murderer. Like an owl, the cyclist pivoted his eyes back at the horseman and skidded the bike to a stop so as not to be attacked from the rear. A flash of pallid skin, lank hair, red lips, and snarling white teeth registered on the policeman like a stroboscopic nightscape. Then, in a jumble, all became action.

Harvey pulled up his steed sharply. The chestnut

was well trained for breasting crowds during dem-
onstrations, schooled to flinch neither from guns
nor bricks. He let himself be crashed chest-first
full into the bicyclist. The horse whinnied a war
cry as it made contact, slipped, began to fall, and
righted itself. Harvey kicked the horse again onto
the fallen man.

The struggling cyclist resourcefully grabbed the
gelding's bridle and, with gargantuan strength, toppled horse and rider over the fulcrum of the bicycle.
The policeman hit the street with a thump. But he
had held on to his pistol and fired three shots
wildly before he felt the hard, long form in its
rough greatcoat upon him, and dropped the pistol
to grapple.

The taller man's fingernails grasped Harvey's
throat, his savage voice gurgling incoherently with
rancor from a mouth still bloody from his brief feast
in the bushes. The detective, fighting for his life,
groaned through clinched teeth, "BAS-tid! BAS-tid!"
trying vainly to thrust off the choking claws.

Harvey's muscles had not softened much since
his wrestling days, and here there was no referee
to heed. His knees churned for the tall man's groin,
one hand still ripping at the iron clasp on his throat,
the other digging for the heavier man's nostrils and
eyes, tearing at the ancient crinkly skin.

The teeth lunged here, there, as the policeman
twisted. Harvey freed his fist and hit the gory
mouth. The blubbery lips did not break, but the
maw popped open. The policeman gasped at the
stench. It was like an odor he knew well: the flesh
of a long-dead body.

"You smelly mother," he gasped, as he tried to
break a new stranglehold, lunging his knee upward
with all his might. The man should have folded,
ruptured, but instead he merely broke his neck grip
and involuntarily reached for his genitals.

In this respite, Harvey tried to whisk up the gun

where it had skittered an arm's length away. Failing, he nevertheless spun from under, and as his hip hit the pavement, the radio banged to life in the receive mode. He could hear the dispatcher's voice, all urgency. "What unit's trying to reach me? Come in, please? Are you in trouble?"

"Now you're working! Now!" groaned the beleaguered policeman in disgust. He banged the "send" switch at his shoulder, then swung again at his adversary. "One seven one," he barked. "In trouble, goddamn it! Third and the Mall! Help!"

Once again, the maniac was at Harvey's throat with talons and teeth, but the uniformed man wriggled and broke the vise. The effort, however, left his strength diminished.

"At Third and the Mall," the officer repeatedly howled. He frantically willed the Park Police's "Eagle" helicopter to be up there patrolling. To throw off his assailant, Harvey muscled his back into a bridge. But like a horror-movie leech the creature clung to him. This guy is going to kill me! Harvey's mind shrilled. His back muscles burning, he grabbed the pistol and fired two shots aimlessly to attract attention. Anyone's!

The shots startled the grappler. He drew back enough for Harvey to force the pistol into the shoulder of his heavy greatcoat and fire. The man's body bucked, but immediately his paw closed on the barrel of the gun, and he turned the next shot into Harvey's left arm. The bullet grazed the forearm and Harvey yelped. As the policeman tried to propel the gun around to fire again, his opponent pinned it to the chest of his uniform.

Seemingly undaunted by the gunshot into his shoulder, the heavy man slowly pressed the officer flat on the ground. Just as the photographer had a few minutes before, Harvey saw death in the feral brown-orange eyes of his vanquisher. He grunted as the dreadful stink overwhelmed him, knowing with despair that he would die before fellow police could reach him.

With his right hand, the incredibly strong grappler carefully took Harvey's face and gazed down with psychotic craving at his throat. His lower jaw dropped like the double-jointed mandible of a shark. With a growl, he dashed his great teeth into Harvey's throat. The agony spasmed Harvey, and reflexively he jerked the gun away from his chest.

The ravager reared back and with his left hand sought to snatch away the pistol. But he missed and his nails ripped the Park Police uniform's breast pocket. From it a small metal first-aid kit spilled with a clatter, the Day-Glo red cross on its cover face up. The victorious mauler glanced down to see what had fallen. At the same time, Harvey heard the sound of distant police sirens, his salvation if they were not too late.

In that flash, the ruthless face above him changed to a mask of anguish as if an unseen person had plunged a sword into his back. The lethal eyes bugged and then rolled up in his head, the bloody mouth sprung open across the bestial teeth and emitted a sound like the shriek of a mortally wounded jackal.

The man-beast who seconds ago had been killing him seemed petrified. Harvey scrambled from under him and ran toward the sound of the sirens. Looking back, he saw his would-be slayer grab up the damaged but still-ridable cycle and pedal off across Pennsylvania Avenue. His coat flapping behind him, he plunged into a cross street leading into the dingy slums.

Harvey heard the clack-clack of a helicopter, and saw its 30-million-candlepower eye sweep past him toward the jumble of dwellings where the culprit had fled. Punchy as he was, a peculiar thought burrowed into Harvey's mind. Was it only the sirens that had frightened off his antagonist?

The son of a bitch had been staring at the

phosphorescent cross on the first-aid kit. There *were* those hyped-up tabloid and TV stories. Was it possible the cross was a factor in his deliverance? Implausible. Yet the fiend could have rent his throat with one savage chomp before the police arrived.

Waving his good arm to halt the approaching police cars, Harvey felt a presence behind him, cried out, and wheeled. The patient horse was behind him, pushing out its muzzle for a pat.

The fifth Mall Murder, because of its victim and the horse chase that followed it, elevated the story to world prominence. The victim had been an executive secretary for a lobbyist (published), a judge's lover (unpublished), and a fine amateur photographer who had once done a picture story for the popular *Washingtonian* magazine. The killer's take was bigger, too: almost four hundred dollars.

The wire services carried the story on their "A" menu for two straight days. The peculiarly blood-thirsty nature of it made it a natural for the insider shows and grocery-store weeklies from London to Singapore. Just suppose, read one lurid publication, that the old myth was true, and those who die at the fangs of a vampire become vampires themselves. There were prophecies of a world epidemic of lethal vein-tapping.

A local throwaway paper chillingly fantasized the scene in Washington with five newly created Draculas on the loose. It was enough to send one deranged middle-aged delivery man into the cemetery with an ash stake and a hammer. He was caught there trying to dig up the body of the Agriculture Department clerk.

A pseudo-medical talk show guest said *all* those bitten by vampires would be infected with the bloodsucking virus. That made Harvey decidedly uncomfortable.

On the floors of Congress, the earlier bills to fund more police were expeditiously approved. A few Capitol Hill publicity-seekers called for activating National Guard units. The Mayor went on TV to plead for calm, and the Interior Department put a curfew on the Mall from ten p.m. to six a.m.

In purely police terms, disturbing as it was, the murder was a godsend. At last, they had an accurate description. The suspect was taller than they had thought, maybe six-six or six-seven; of mature years, as attested by Harvey's description of his skin; yet in amazingly good physical shape. He had odd brown-orange eyes, and a terrible stench as if his gums were rotten, for his teeth, as Harvey could attest, were not. And he was probably wearing a Kevlar vest.

The FBI, using its enhancement computer, created pictures of the suspect, based on Harvey's details. They showed the man as he would be with a two-day beard and mustache, with only a mustache, and with a proper haircut, with lighter hair, other variations. These were circulated among the police districts for posting and for showing at roll calls. The chief of police went on television, exhibited the sketches, and announced a hundred-thousand-dollar reward, most of it put up by downtown businessmen, for tips leading to a conviction.

On the morning after the photographer's murder, Morgan picked up Harvey at the hospital where his superficial wound had been treated. The lieutenant smelled a clue in bicycling styles. He had importuned the British, German, and Korean embassies for three of their tallest junior diplomats who were to meet him at the federal court's underground parking lot behind headquarters. There, Morgan pedaled a woman's bicycle past Harvey. Then, in turn, the three bemused second secretaries rode by.

Harvey chose the style of the German—the continental European—as closest to that of the dark cyclist. "Come on, Ave," he said to Morgan as they returned to their office, "was Germany the closest you could get to Transylvania?"

The new description and the conviction that the man was from the Continent were not the only new clues. Harvey had been alert enough to ask the doctors at the George Washington University Hospital emergency room not to dress his throat before checking for dried saliva. They found a specimen, and the Medical Examiner flaked a similar sample from the dead photographer. Conventional tests indicated that the same stalker had also killed the student at the Reflecting Pool. He was not, therefore, a "clone," as secondary killers who surface in high-publicity cases are called.

Three fingerprints that were not Harvey's were lifted by ID from the barrel of his pistol. If the FBI turned up a match in its files, they would have a name, some background, and maybe a mugshot. But by next day, after a half-dozen electronic runs, the FBI had found nothing. They were doing manual checks on older uncomputerized files, but this would take a week or more.

The Medical Examiner assured Harvey that it would have done no good for him to have sought the source of the scream instead of chasing the bicycle rider. The woman had died almost instantly from the first tearing of her jugular. Had the ripper not drawn back, Harvey's own fate would have been as sudden.

This thought led Harvey to ponder the one clue he had not emphasized. He had mentioned the Day-Glo cross in his report but had not theorized on its significance. Now, he leafed through the newspaper clips in his and Morgan's background folder. The colorful ones spun tales of crosses and vampires. The only item with legitimate credentials was the packet sent by Father Floyd of Catholic University, which Morgan had largely ignored when it was sent to him. In it were excerpts from a 1920s author, Montague Summers; a seventeenth century Greek physician; a French priest a hundred years later; and others. These sources were convinced of the truth of vampires, but their "data" was based on conjecture, myth, and hearsay. Yet, thought Harvey, there *was* that cross.

Also in the packet was an article by Father Floyd himself, "The Illusion of Blood: the Psychopathy of Vampirism," from a collection of scholarly works on exorcism. The piece dealt with medical case histories in which patients lusted after blood. One such disease was called haemolagnia, another a rare form of porphyria. But none of the afflicted thought of himself as a vampire. There was only one mention of a crucifix: in a footnote about a German named Haarman with an insatiable blood lust. A priest in 1925 had waved a crucifix before the demented man's face, and he had smiled, crossed himself, and kissed it. So much for the power of religious nostrums against vampires.

Burstan purposely did not release Harvey's mention of the Day-Glo cross. The media didn't need its hysteria stoked with theories that might later prove to be hogwash. Morgan, on the other hand, had succeeded brilliantly as a detective by considering anything possible until it was proven otherwise. Pitching his cards, he said to Harvey, "Maybe our boy *thinks* he's a vampire. I'm not ready yet to make a fool out of myself and suggest every cop have a Day-Glo cross painted on his Glock. But keep at it. If we come up with more evidence, who knows?" Harvey, a fallen-away Catholic for 15 years, dug from a drawer a crucifix on a chain his mother had given him at confirmation, and put it around his neck. What harm would it do?

Chapter Four
Blood Alley

Morgan was exhausted. He had heard about Harvey's injury when he checked in with the dispatcher after midnight. He had gone to the scene of the murder, then the hospital. As soon as the embassies opened, he had set up the bicycle gig. He had then worked a full day. Drained, he went home that afternoon.

He slumbered for 12 hours, waking in his and Felice's sun-bright bedroom with a start of unrecognition. He had dreamed of the madman and murmured in his sleep. In the accommodating way of dreams, he had ingratiated himself with the fiend so as not to be harmed himself. In the dream, the killer had spoken with him of an old cast-iron fire engine that his father had given him. The two of them, Morgan as a child, and the fanged man, had looked fruitlessly for the toy all over Swampoodle. Morgan was still frustrated by the dream when he awoke.

That night he was back in Swampoodle in the flesh, dressed in his sober detective suit, working an area of cheap rooms-for-rent, stepping around clumps of addicts lying around the doorways like drugged flies.

The porno book-and-movie joints were having their usual Saturday night run of perverts and wimps who wished they were studs. Morgan breezed into a shop past three patrons leafing through "beaver books," while a fourth slid back toward the dark aisle where he could drop quarters into a slot for a fading pornographic film and a quick jerk-off.

Logic dictated that a man as tall and odd as the one he was looking for would not show himself in this blue arcade. But Morgan knew that madmen were unpredictable. If this man with his inhuman proclivities had sexual aberrations cranked in, he might have combed his hair, donned normal clothes, and dropped in to look at magazines of S & M, scatology, leather love, and related deviations. Morgan approached the change-maker in his pulpit and pulled out a three-by-five album of the FBI computer sketches.

The young bearded overseer of the pornographorium had seen the pictures on television, as had everyone else in the city. He clearly made Morgan for a cop, but wised off anyway: "I don't look at pictures, I sell 'em."

"Man, I smell dope in here," Morgan said in a low, harsh voice to the man, "and you gotta be wired to talk to me that way." He stepped up to the pulpit and swept a tray of quarters onto the floor. "You want some real trouble? You want me to read you your rights?"

The man blanched, knowing, even if he was as drug-free as Nancy Reagan, how easy it was for a mean cop to make a drug bust in Washington. His hands fluttered toward the album. "Sorry, sorry." He looked at the pictures, then the detective's hard face, and shook his head sheepishly. "None of my clients are into bicycling," he could not resist adding.

*   *   *

For a week, sometimes in street clothes, sometimes as a bum, Morgan prowled the First District near the Mall, inquiring at liquor stores, bars, flophouses, tenements, the houses and haunts of the poor, sometimes encountering the same denizens he had spoken with on his first sweep two weeks before.

One night he ranged as far north as L Street to slums as deep as any in the city. Newspapers and paper bags, caked with mud, served for lawns in front of dilapidated two- and three-story row houses. At the curbs, old cars, cannibalized days or weeks before, stood wheel-less, waiting for police tow trucks.

Slatternly women and toothless old men sat on steps, watching his passage. Existing in fear, hunger, and hopelessness, themselves and their children often involved in criminality, they feared nothing more than the "Man." Besides, even if they were innocent, for one of them to tell a policeman anything might be to bring down the enmity of neighborhood drug dealers.

Morgan had hit every late-night mom-and-pop grocery he came across on the theory that the suspect would buy his food well after dark. These wretched little shops of the area were barred and locked at dusk, their shutters blanking out their small windows. They unlocked after nightfall only for the familiar. Now Morgan went back to them with a new question, one he might well have asked before.

"Where would a person go for food after *you* close?" Morgan began asking. "I mean if they didn't want to go out of their way to an all-night supermarket or Seven-Eleven?"

Some owners mentioned private dwellings where old women on welfare sold from a pitiful stock of coffee, cheap pastries, and canned goods. Tirelessly, Morgan went to them all. He wheedled and he threatened and he got nothing.

Then, a Korean grocer gave him a lead. "People go old black man, two blocks from here when we close. No sign on doh'." Perhaps he merely wanted to put out of business an unlicensed competitor, but he obligingly left his wife in charge, and led Morgan to a half-flight of steps leading downward lighted by a single dim bulb. "He call Blind Billy," said the Korean.

Morgan thanked him, then stopped stock still, his mouth open. Holy shit! Of course. A blind man. The weirdo patronizes a storekeeper who can't see him! The detective, hoping he was not banking too much on instincts, called the dispatcher and told him to find Harvey and have him meet him with a mini-recorder a block from the basement store.

Reached at home, the young detective drove to Swampoodle, a few minutes away. In the old Mustang convertible, Morgan briefed Harvey on his theory. "I want a recording. And I want somebody to testify to what this old guy says." Morgan did not have to add that if Blind Billy gave them a crucial lead, and the murderer somehow suspected, the storekeeper might not be able to testify about anything. Ever.

The basement door was locked, the dirty window covered with a lattice of iron, but through a broken Venetian blind, they saw a bald fat man behind a tiny counter sitting in gloom. Morgan pushed a door buzzer. The blind man murmured into a funnel on the counter, and from a dime-sized hole in the jamb, the terminus of a voice tube, they heard, "Who's there?"

"Police, just want to talk."

"That's all y'all ever want. What yo name and job?"

"Morgan and Harvey, Homicide."

They heard a stopper of some sort pushed into the tube and waited. Presumably the free-lance grocer, unfamiliar with Morgan's voice, was checking them out with a police contact. Then the door buzzed and they walked into the low-ceilinged shop. A small refrigerated display case, half in darkness, held cheese, soft drinks, beer, and cheap meat cuts. Baked beans, cigarettes, detergents, canned peaches, even motor oil were stacked on the counter and a shelf behind it. Also on the shelf was a small radio tuned to a rap station.

The man, his eyes twin pools of watered milk, reached out a small hand with delicate fingers. "Let me feel yo badges."

"You already called."

"I likes to be sure."

The two detectives pulled their badge clips from their belts and watched the store owner touch them. "I knowed fo you say fo words you a cop," the grocer said placatingly to Morgan. "I like to be triple safe. Peoples make a game of robbing me. I lost count how many times. What you want to ask me about?"

"Tall white man, bad smell about him, maybe an accent, like some kind of European, not like a Latino . . ." said Morgan.

A faint ripple passed over the man's face before it returned to impassiveness. Harvey's heart beat faster. "Tall or short, I can't see 'em," said Blind Billy.

"Don't bullshit me, Billy," Morgan said. "Money comes to you high up or low down, and cigarettes or whatever goes out high or low. You know goddamn well how tall your customers are."

The blind man said nothing.

"A man whose breath stinks. Stinks bad," Morgan added, bearing in.

"I don't know nothing at all 'bout that."

Morgan looked at Harvey, who nodded. Both of them were sure there was telltale tension in his voice. Morgan leaned toward the old man, excited, but calm, even soothing. "Billy, we don't want to bother you. Last thing we want to do."

"You bothering me just coming in here."

Morgan took a 50 and three 20s from his wallet, all he had. Harvey pulled out the 60 dollars he had with him. Morgan touched the grocer's hand with the money. "One hundred seventy. A down payment. There's a hundred thousand reward out for this guy. You've heard about him on the radio."

"I know," said the blind man softly, worried.

"Take it," Morgan said firmly.

The old man thought, his face working nervously. Finally he said, "Man, I scared. You don't catch him, he put me where money ain't worth nothing. Now I wish you go, Mr. Detectives."

Morgan shmoozed him some more, and cued Harvey, who did so in kind. But the "Mommy" approach was dead on arrival. Morgan's "Daddy" voice went hard. "I'm sorry, Billy" he said, "I've got to know. I'm telling you now, not asking."

The blind man recognized a statement of power when he heard it, the power to call the city government in to shut him down for doing business without a license, for bootlegging beer, or small quantities of drugs, for maintaining dirty food premises. The power to throw him forever on welfare, or on the grudging charity of others. And these men, unlike more flexible beat cops, would not bend for a few cases of beer or a few bottles of good whiskey.

"Billy," said Harvey, "he's trying to be fair. You don't want to be selling pencils in the snow and rain instead of dope and dog food out of this nice warm little place. Let him have it. He's a lieutenant. He can make sure you're protected."

The old man's blind eyes teared. The two policemen had broken him. "Don't want no police in here for 'tection," he said disconsolately. "Gonna have my own man with me. With a gun. Don't need no cops." Morgan and Harvey waited, and at last Blind Billy turned off the single bulb in the store and also the dim outside light to indicate he was closed for the night.

Then, in darkness relieved only by faint moon-light shining through the scraggly pollution-scarred sycamores outside, Blind Billy told his story. The two officers scrawled in their notebooks, and the mini-recorder spun where Harvey had noiselessly put it on the counter.

Maybe three months ago, a white man's voice . . . yes, with an accent, no, not Spanish, more fancy, no, not British exactly . . . had come though the tube. Only it sounded like it was coming from the bottom of a country well. Billy did not like it, but he had never had any reason to fear a high-class white foreigner.

Yes, his breath smelled bad, worse than bad, like he hadn't brushed his teeth for a year and every one of them with meat caught between them. (Morgan's drawn face grew tighter.) As a matter of fact, the man had bought mouthwash, along with toothbrushes and paste, and a gallon can of Renuzit, must be doing his own dry cleaning, and black shoe polish, detergent flakes. For food he bought meats, any kind of fresh meat, even hog jowl. And when there wasn't fresh meat, frozen meat or fish, or eggs, or even Vienna sausages, but never vegetables. The grocer shuddered, imagining what that meant.

And yes, he was tall. Billy could tell not just from the money and the items changing hands, but from where that strange voice came from. His voice sounded old, but Billy sensed he was quick, like some big animal, from the fast way he came in and out, the efficient way he paid. And no, he was always polite. He came in about once a week, always well after dusk.

"What's he pay with?" asked Harvey.

"Mostly twenties, sometimes a ten."

Surely, thought Morgan, the robberies of the five victims did not provide enough to live on. Had he killed others, their bodies undiscovered, perhaps in other cities? "When's he due?"

"Any time. Tomorrow night. Next night."

Morgan tried to get Billy to slip the tall man a new ten or five in change as if by mistake instead of a one-dollar bill when he came in next time. Morgan was sure this character would be kind in small ways—like Hitler to dachshunds—and would hand back the bigger bill. That would give the FBI another clean print—the three from the gun muzzle still had yielded no leads, but prints on a bill would nail him as Billy's customer.

But Billy wasn't having any. "I ain't playing no games with that bad-assed man. Anyway, he won't come in no more when he see my 'tection in here. Now I done. And I take that one seventy, if you don't mind."

Burstan, when he heard out Morgan and Harvey, was tempted to have Homicide men, backed by other detectives, discreetly try every house in the immediate area to seek information now that they had a "make" on their quarry. But Morgan reasoned that it was wiser to stake out the store in the most secret way, to do nothing that might conceivably spook the culprit into fleeing Washington, assuming he had not already done so.

So each night, the partners sat in the dark in a first-floor slum apartment across the street from Blind Billy's. Six other detectives, three from Homicide, three from the First District, were on backup two houses away, connected by radio with Morgan and Harvey. Everyone was heavily armed, Harvey, generally forgetting it was there, also wearing his silver crucifix.

But there was nothing. The man had vanished. Burstan still sent out weekly all-points asking for reports of new throat slashings. But gradually, he shifted the detectives who had been working the case back to routine assignments. The murderer, he reasoned, had serially killed every three weeks or so, and had not struck for six weeks. In Homicide, all but Morgan and Harvey were convinced the man had decamped to another city or, as likely, to whatever foreign land he had come from.

Morgan, too, was urged by Burstan to give up the vigil, but he snarled, "Leave it? I'll let you know when I'm ready to leave it, Belly." Burstan would have reprimanded a less able man. Instead he bargained Morgan into a compromise: stay on the case yourself, but relinquish Harvey to regular duties. Thereafter, Morgan alone watched, slumped just back from a curtainless window, a shabby monarch in a swaybacked easy chair.

But the grocer's only visitors were late food shoppers or "go-fers," picking up a few granules of crack, a joint, a nickel bag of heroin, not enough to trouble the overworked narcotics cops. Morgan patiently pitched his cards at his hat, now atop an old-fashioned ash stand. And looked out between throws.

At ten p.m. on the fourth night of his solo vigil, in a summer drizzle, Morgan saw a forbidding shape round the corner and stride toward Blind Billy's dimly lit doorway. The wayward locks, the six-and-a-half-foot height, the old-style greatcoat: they all matched Harvey's description.

Morgan slid from his soft chair, patted his shoulder holster and the hip holster, where he now carried a Colt .45 automatic. Both pistols were loaded with armor-piercing bullets. He grabbed up his police belt with its radio, Mace, cuffs, small super-beam flashlight, and two extra magazines for the .45, then threw on his black raincoat and hat and slipped to the dark vestibule. From there, he radioed a terse, "I think I've spotted him across the street," to the dispatcher, and told him to notify Homicide to put the pre-arranged backup team on standby.

Morgan watched the man peer through the crack

in the blind. Apparently he saw Billy's guard-companion, for he turned and slithered back toward the corner. He glided from shadow to shadow, seeming almost to coil and uncoil, without exposing himself to the street's scant light more than an instant.

No mean master of stealth himself, Morgan eased out the door, closed it silently, and moved along the buildings on the opposite side of the tenebrous street. His quarry rounded the corner and the policeman crossed, then watched him proceed until he was a half block away.

The detective concentrated on what the man in black was thinking and feeling. Disappointment and hunger, certainly. Enough to try another store? Or would he return to his lair rather than further brave the drizzle? Or, Morgan thought with a shiver, would he sate himself on some random and hapless passerby, some derelict also out in the rain? No, Morgan thought, criminals such as this, however demented, were often able tacticians. This man would not switch from marketing to murder without planning, would not take major risks on whim.

At an alleyway two blocks away, the man turned. They were now in the heart of the old Second Precinct, once home to the city's most violent felons. Barrels of trash overflowed into muddy tree spaces. Windows were cardboarded over, and where front porch lights should be there were jagged broken bulbs. Morgan sped to the mouth of the alley and saw in the gloom the man enter a backyard gate in a high, decrepit fence.

The detective slunk into the shadows opposite the gate and waited face upward to see whether a light went on in the dark three-story brick building above him. Sure enough, on the second floor, a subdued glow limned a rectangle on the side of the apartment house. Morgan was aware for the first time that the rain was wetting through his light coat at shoulder and thigh.

He's in there, I can get him, his mind said. His heart stepped up its beat. He felt a start of giddiness, but quickly brought it under cold control. There was not a splinter of doubt in his brain that this was the Mall murderer. Morgan turned on his radio, whispered the address, and directed the dispatcher to send the team. "Tell 'em to stay out of the alley," he said.

Two dozen detectives would proceed in total silence to corners within a block from his position. All would be out of sight themselves, but if possible within eye-shot of the front of the house and the two entrances to the alley. So close to victory, he did not want to risk the secret gathering of even a half-dozen trained men in the alley itself. Morgan felt for the L-shaped lock pick that he kept in a canvas key-pocket on the underside of his holster. Nobody, he thought grimly, is going to make any fuss about the Fourth Amendment and illegal entries on *this* case. With the delicacy of a neurosurgeon Morgan manipulated the little instrument along the tumblers of the old back-door lock.

He let himself in and waited until his eyes acclimated to the darkness. Narrow stairs dropped directly down to the drafty foyer where he stood. A hallway led toward the front of the house, where Morgan assumed there was one or more first-floor apartments. A battered door led, he presumed, to the cellar. Above him, he could make out dimly, perhaps from light escaping beneath the suspect's door, a landing at a turning of the stair.

Testing each step for creaks, he ascended, his familiar .38 in one hand, his flashlight in the other. At the top, as he had suspected, there was a slit of light beneath a door halfway down the hall. The other doors on the floor were dark. The night haunter, Morgan was sure, had made certain there were no other inhabited rooms on his floor.

Morgan listened, and in that brief moment lost his prey. The light went out, the door swung open, and a dark shape came out, banged the door shut, and disappeared down the hallway away from Morgan. The man's feet scurried rat-like down the front stairs. Morgan heard with disgust the front door close. There was no way the police team would be already in place.

Morgan radioed the dispatcher to let those on the way to join him know—and other police as well—that the man they sought was on the street. The dispatcher was to stress that the man did not yet know he had been spotted, so there must be no flooding of police to the area, nor any sirens or bubble-tops.

For himself, he would wait for this sinister tenant and if he were not collared on the street, would arrest him when he came back and turned on his light. The bastard may be out digging in a garbage can for food, thought Morgan, or at some other off-the-books store buying nourishment through a crack in a chain-locked door. The apartment door was as easy to pick as the back door. He let himself in and a puff of foulness assailed him, the reek of a long-uncleaned slaughterhouse. He gasped.

The cheap shades were drawn, but in the dim light from spaces on either side of them, he made out a doorway. He edged toward it, one foot probing, then the other following its path. The small room he entered was windowless. He closed the door and, forgoing his police flashlight, pressed on and off the penlight on his key chain. He was in the bathroom.

In the wastebasket were two empty glass mouth-wash bottles, several worn-out toothbrushes. With a paper napkin, he lifted a bottle out and put it in his coat pocket. At worst, he would have a set of prints for the FBI to compare with those on Harvey's gun barrel.

The detective started to open the cabinet above the wash basin. But to his astonishment, he saw that the mirror was covered with black felt with adhesive backing such as that used on the bottom of table lamps. One side had been torn down and bits of broken mirror stuck to the gluey felt. Someone had smashed the mirror. Only the Phantom of the Opera was so ugly he couldn't look at himself, thought Morgan. Or Dracula.

Inside the cabinet was a sprawl of old razor blades. Must be rough shaving without a mirror, Morgan speculated. The blades would be as good as the bottles for prints. He wrapped up one in toilet paper, and gingerly put it in his shirt pocket.

He returned to the living room, not daring to risk using the penlight, but saw indistinctly a clutter of paper on the floor. He felt for it, found a magazine, and held it up to the thin light by the shade. It was a movie-star magazine. He ran his fingers over a small cheap desk for an envelope, credit card slips, a letter, a bill, anything that might contain the man's name, but there were only more magazines and newspapers.

In the kitchen, Morgan plumbed the garbage can. He recalled hearing an adage from long ago: the optimist thinks a man is what he reads, the pragmatist what he eats, the pessimist what he shits. Morgan was a pragmatist. Looking for clues, he pulled from the garbage a Vienna sausage can, a bouillon-cube bottle, bloody meat paper, a styrofoam hamburger dish, but no vegetable ends, alcohol bottles, or soft-drink containers.

The bedroom door was closed, locked. Morgan was ever more nervous about the man's return. Come on, he heard his best instincts calling, get set up by the door so you can nail him. But why was this bedroom locked? Knowing he was a fool, he drew from his key pouch a skeleton key. It worked instantly in the old-fashioned lock. Inside, the room was pitch black.

If there were windows, they were blanketed.

The fetid odor was stronger. With his penlight he lit the floor a second and recoiled. There were towels, pieces of sheeting covered with blood, and on them lay the naked body of a young heavyset black woman. Her eyes were open. Her mouth, gaudily painted, was slack in a ghastly parody of abandon. Her throat was gashed and re-gashed, a terrible butchery, the meat raw and ragged as if it had been chewed into deeply.

He ran the light down her fleshy body to her thigh where the femoral artery runs across the bone. He grunted in dismay. On both legs, there were the same signs of ravenous gnawing. Now at last he knew: the bastard was killing them to drink their blood, eat their flesh. Almost vomiting, he checked the woman's outstretched arms. On them were the same slashes, the same mangling.

His light had thrown back a gleam from the corner of the room. He flicked it there and by the window on the floor, to his amazement, was a long cheap coffin. Had the killer dug up the woman? And her coffin with her? No, the coffin was still shiny, and the haphazard blots of blood on and around her indicated she was alive when her body was mutilated.

Morgan carefully opened the coffin. It was empty, except for a generous sprinkling of dirt. Its cheap imitation silk lining was wrinkled, and slightly spotted with blood at the head. Morgan dared not tarry any longer in this abattoir room.

He sat in a chair in the living room, revolver in hand, listening for even the softest door-slam downstairs or tread on a stair. Five more minutes passed. Maybe the alert he had sounded had led to a arrest. He had heard nothing of value on the earplug and he did not dare switch to "send," not just because of the risks of whisperings, but because the radio might crackle with static.

In any case, the backup team would be on the way, or perhaps elements had already arrived. Could the revenant have sensed or seen the police closing in and fled? Might he have two hideouts? Anything was possible!

Suddenly, a stair riser squeaked. Morgan took the cuffs in the same hand in which he held his flashlight. The knob turned; the low-wattage ceiling bulb went on. The giant form filled the doorway. Morgan sprung up and flashed the light in his astounded face. "Police!" he shouted, "You're under arrest!" The ghoul flitted like a mammoth bat to the corner of the room. The two tall figures were poised for a moment, the detective in a crouch, the apparition glued in the corner.

"Let's just get those hands way up," Morgan ordered with that special anger that threatens a shot. "Way up!" The man's hands went wordlessly to half-mast, the left arm shielding his face from the glare. "Now, on your face, arms behind your back. Do it!" The detective's heart thumped. The man complied, unfolding from the wall and lying face down like a robed penitent before an altar. Jesus, Morgan thought, jittery as he had not been for years during an arrest, what a long mother.

He snapped on his radio at his shoulder, announced the arrest, and called for his backup to converge on the second-floor apartment. The man had still not uttered a word. Gun ready, Morgan approached the figure on the floor. As if reaching out to test a hot iron, Morgan darted his left hand holding both flashlight and cuffs at the man's wrist. The man turned enough to deflect it.

"Lie still, you bastard!" Morgan ordered, and pushed out the cuffs again. This time, the man's left hand swung up violently, striking Morgan's so hard that the cuff flew from it and clanged against the wall. Simultaneously Morgan, though a bit off balance, fired at the man's long back. Seemingly unhit, the man swung his foot, the gunboat shoe catching Morgan on his pistol arm. The revolver went off again, wildly this time.

With another powerful kick, the man sent Morgan caroming against the wall. Before Morgan could aim, his adversary was over him, smacking the pistol to the floor like an angry mother might a dirty lollipop from her baby's hand. Morgan had the Colt out of his hip holster as fast as a gunslinger, and fired as the man plunged through the door.

The detective was sure he had not missed, for his target was jolted sideways by the heavy slug as he disappeared. Morgan charged after him, and caught a glimpse of his coattail as he leaped down the back stairs. On the landing, Morgan fired again, but startlingly the fleeing man smashed through the back door, not even pausing to turn the knob.

The detective leaped down the stoop steps as the man went out the gate. The trash-strewn yard left Morgan's footing too precarious to fire accurately. Still, he entered the alley with the man only 25 yards ahead. If he stopped to aim and missed, the man would be into the street, and perhaps away. Where in the hell is my backup, Morgan thought furiously. As he ran, he heard sirens. Now they send them! he cursed. Losing ground to his contestant, he shucked the heavy belt.

Even as he ran, he was boggled by the failure of the bullets to bring down the towering man. The first .38 slug had probably hit him, the .45 shot certainly had. Even Kevlar could not have blunted the armor-piercers. Did he wear something more bullet-resistent? Yet, the guy had not seemed to exhibit the telltale bulkiness or clumsiness of *any* body armor.

The escapee crossed the street and loped into the opposite alley. The rain made the rough pavement treacherous. The monstrous sprinter ahead of him ran with undiminished energy. Indeed, the strength that Morgan had felt in the man's blow on the revolver was beyond anything the detective had encountered.

The fences, broken-down garages, and weathered houses walled in the pursuer and the pursued like hedgerows. The alley's widely separated streetlights, like those in much of the ghetto, had been broken so many times that the city seldom replaced them. In one such dark stretch, the leaves of a malodorous ailanthus growing over a fence brushed off Morgan's hat, making him feel suddenly undressed, weakened. They ran in utter quiet, save for the thump of their feet on the cracked cement. Morgan's breath began to come hard. The slayer was beginning to outdistance him.

As the taller man began to pull away, Morgan fired once, twice at him. He could not be sure he had hit, but at worst, it might alert his comrades to his location. Pursued and pursuer burst from the alley into another street, plunged through that open space of semi-light, and then ran on to a playground. Its modernistic equipment—swings with giraffe heads, huge turtles for climbing, a monkey bar formed by a horse's back—seemed to stare at them as in some surrealistic sketch.

Then they were back in the alleys, closed in by one more narrow and unused than any of the others. It was only wide enough for a single car. Backyard trees crowded over the fence tops and drooped half over the pavement.

As they ran, the alley became ever more rubbishy, a repository of old car seats, broken stoves, a discarded water heater, decaying crates, and ruined tires. This was the deadly tumor of the city, the core of thick cancers that sent out cells to blight the neighboring streets. The slum houses with their backs to this putrid dumping ground of the poor were deserted or inhabited by squatters nodding on drugs. The windows stared emptily at the racing men.

Morgan slipped on the bloated corpse of a rat, picked himself up, and saw the man ahead come to a halt, searching this way and that for escape. Blocking the end of the alley was a high fence topped with rusty razor wire. Abutting it were the crumbling rears of two deserted tenements, their fallen rain spouts tangled in the muddy alleyway like slumbering pythons.

Seeing no way out, the fugitive waited in the rain. The detective knew that if the man resisted arrest again, he would aim for the head. Only there was Morgan sure he was vulnerable. Breathless, the detective stopped ten yards from him.

"I told you, you're under arrest! I'm Morgan of Homicide!"—words that sounded lost, irrelevant in this forgotten alley of the anthill metropolis. Even the gun seemed to lack authority.

With eerie dignity, the tall man moved away from the wooden wall. He stood straight, his arms at his side, the fingers curved and predatory, yet at rest. Shadows hid all but the outlines of his face, and indeed, Morgan had not seen it except fleetingly when his gun was smashed away. Here, a gleam from one surviving streetlight crossed the man's shoulder like a blazoned sash of honor, leaving the face still a mystery.

From the hidden face, the man's voice issued, sepulchral and immensely cruel. Beneath the cruelty resonated some bass viol chord of profound sadness that transformed the venom, even weirdly ennobled it. "Go away, Morgan," said the voice. "With your kind I have no argument. It is for that reason I flee you."

The detective was shaken by the odd warning. Up to now, he had regarded the man as vicious, whacked out as most homicidal psychotics are. Yet, in the accented tones he had just heard were the relics of Old World gentry, however diabolic he had become. He put the thought aside, and with the man's crimes running on the screen of his brain, he felt again only a will to capture or kill his bloodthirsty foe. His strength and manner had made Morgan fearful, but he had lived with fear and knew that it was bearable, even desirable, so long as it did not paralyze.

"Go away, Morgan," said the voice, as if the sick brain behind it had read the detective's thoughts.

But Morgan had reflected enough. "Slip that coat halfway down your arms, goddamn it, and walk slowly toward the corner," he said forcefully. He wanted the criminal immobilized, his ability to run or fight impaired, wanted to get behind him to march him out of the alley.

The creature stood still. Then his body began to tense and he moved out a step, the streetlight now illuminating his face with cold, pale light. Morgan gasped. There it was, as Harvey had described it, only infinitely more horrible because it faced him in the flesh, and faced him alone, the tiger eyes, the livery red mouth, and the beaklike parody of an aristocratic nose.

Yet Morgan felt much more than fear. His experience, his guile and guts, had broken his most difficult case. Not just his career, but his destiny were tied up in this moment. Did the thing before him sense something of the same, that their lives, their deaths were forever bonded in this extraordinary encounter?

"Morgan," cried the anachronism, as if indeed he too were gripped by the strange fusion. "Fly!" The word rushed out as a captive might from the deepest chamber of a windowless dungeon.

The policeman stood fast, awed but aggressive. A second more, and the fiend stepped out slowly as if to pass. The spell broken, the detective fired and fired again directly into the pallid face. The Colt .45 was designed to stop any human. But although the man's head snapped back twice like a boxer taking a one-two punch, he did not drop. Instead, gory holes appeared on his forehead and cheek. Yet they did not spout blood. As if released from a vow, Morgan's foe laughed gutturally, an animal bark entirely different from the two anomalous warnings.

The sound rose wickedly in volume, finally gushing out in crescendo cackles of cruelty, gales of malevolent hilarity. The arms came up in that reflexive vee. Morgan panicked. The man's magic invulnerability had shaken Morgan's mind into chaos. He thought only of escape. It was hopeless, fatally hopeless, to vie with this superhuman strength. He turned to run but stumbled on the rain spouting. The monster was on him. Morgan wheeled and kicked him over the clutter of pipes.

From his back, the man grabbed Morgan's pants cuff, but with the impotent gun, Morgan beat the man's wrist, freed himself, fired the final two bullets at his face, flung down the weapon, and fled. The phantom snatched up the .45 and thrust it in his greatcoat. He stumbled in the trash, but rose and bounded after Morgan, his throaty cries retching from his throat.

With a whirl, Morgan thrust a garbage can into the demon's path, then plunged again down the alley. The rolling can cut the man's legs from under him like an offensive end's block. But Morgan himself tripped over a tire and sprawled. As he scrambled up, his enemy came at him, swooping down with arms outspread, a black pterodactyl targeting his feed. Morgan kicked at his midsection, folding him as if he were an enormous hinge.

Again, the detective righted himself and ran, bumping a dilapidated wardrobe from which rats scurried helter-skelter. Whimpering aloud, he hurdled an overturned bathtub, and ran on. The monumental figure, clothes and hair flapping, vaulted after him, keening blood-cries. Panting, eyes bulging with weariness and terror, Morgan dumped an old water heater into the path of the pouncing figure, and grabbed up a discarded shovel. The ancient halted, seemingly shocked by the shovel.

But deciding it posed no danger, he rounded the heater and crouched to spring. The detective flailed his head with the shovel, tilting him, but not knocking him down. Instead, the man in black ran by him, blocking his escape. Morgan was at bay. Exhausted, he turned and jogged back through the wash of debris, searching the wooden fencing for some means of escape.

Over his shoulder he saw the stupendous figure striding purposefully after him in the heavy rain. With a frantic flash of hope, Morgan spotted a rotten section of palings. He crashed his shoulder into them, begging them to give. But they did not, and he ran on, followed by the relentless hunter, who moved with the assured lope of a lion certain of his antelope kill. Staggering, Morgan reached the end wall. He leaped to reach its top with his hands, but fell back, muscles depleted. He turned. The criminal's great arms again veed upward, claws pendent.

Morgan saw his archenemy's whole body tense, saw the face with its two polka dots of gore already healing. Caught up by unreason, he cringed as the black figure dropped toward him, teeth agape, talons quivering to pin his arms to the rank weeds growing through the crumbling, garbage-smeared pavement.

"Ah, no," said Morgan, and with a last return of spirit, hit his tormentor in the face, but without effect. The stronger man wrestled him into onto his back. The vampire clutched his wet hair and arched the throat upward. Even in the rain, Morgan could see that parchment skin, the gaping maw, and the fangs. The off-color eyes opened wide, the chin fell like a trapdoor to let the rows of teeth gape.

One last time, Morgan's mind urged him to fight, but there was no fight in him. He heard the glottal clacking of the bloodsucker's hunger, smelled the fetor of foul human matter. The mouth dropped to Morgan's throat, cutting off his scream as the teeth snapped toward the detective's still-vibrating larynx.

Chapter Five
The Welsh Priest

Harvey was part of the backup team and helped supervise the search by a hundred policeman for Morgan that night. The portable floodlights and the helicopters' megawatt beams made the drenched alleys bright as day. The police turned up Morgan's belt with the radio and other gear attached. In the apartment, they found the revolver with two bullets fired and the gnawed and decaying woman, the disturbing coffin.

Shortly before dawn, they came upon the alley with its signs of struggle: the crushed weeds by the end fence, the garbage can and water heater that, despite the rain, still had caked mud on their upturned bottoms. But they could not be sure Morgan was one of the combatants. The casings for the bullets he had fired there were buried under the detritus.

Burstan and Harvey took the fragmented report of Morgan's disappearance to Felice Morgan shortly after dawn. She met them at the door of the house, all prettiness gone from her sleepless and worried face.

"He called every night. I knew there was something wrong when I didn't hear from him," she told them as soon as she opened the door to them.

Burstan felt guilty almost beyond words for letting Morgan stay on the case alone. He was glad enough for Harvey to do the talking. At the same table where Harvey had laughed and drunk cognac and coffee with Felice and Morgan, the young detective told her everything they knew.

What he didn't say was how bitter he was at Burstan for taking him off the case. If he had been with Morgan, his partner would not have had to act alone. Harvey yearned to tell her how badly he felt for failing Morgan, how he longed to make it up to his partner and to her. She was perceptive. Perhaps she understood. She gamely asked what truly were the chances her husband was alive. Harvey looked to Burstan to answer this one.

"It's not impossible that he followed the guy out of town and is still tracking him," the Homicide captain said. "Or he may've got hurt and be unconscious in a hospital out of town."

"Could he be a hostage? Any chance of that?" she asked.

"Anything's possible," said Burstan, wanting to give her any particle of hope.

She looked to Harvey for the truth, unwilling to be deluded, even though clearly she wanted to be. "Felice, we all know this guy's not the kidnapping kind," he said.

She began to weep, and Harvey was rent by her tears. "I'll never give up on this," he blurted, ignoring Burstan. "I'll find out what happened to him."

His resolve heartened her slightly. "Can you call me when you find *anything*," she said, more to him than to Burstan.

Burstan, more burdened than ever by guilt, said firmly to Harvey, "Dan, do that. Make it a point."

Without showering or going to bed, Harvey drove

back into the slums in his convertible. In the Homicide cruiser—its trunk aerial, dark color, and two-way radio a giveaway—he could count on a punctured tire or a cracked window whenever he parked in the ghetto. Street kids learned early to dislike the law, and to do what they could to harass its enforcers.

In Morgan's stakeout room, everything was marked with tape from the Mobile Crime Unit. The crummy easy chair still sat atop its bricks, an empty throne. Half the deck of cards was in the chair, the rest were scattered by the ash stand. He left in a helluva hurry, thought Harvey, just shaking the cards out of his hat and letting them lie. ID wouldn't need them. Harvey picked them up and put them in his pocket.

Late that day, the uniformed men found Morgan's crushed hat by the ailanthus tree. And in the narrow alley, detectives turned up a squatter family who had heard shots. A more thorough search uncovered three .45 casings. And despite the heavy rain, on the weeds they found traces of blood that were rushed to the lab. They were the same type as Morgan's. All this evidence convinced Harvey that Morgan was dead. His heart felt dead too as he called Felice Morgan that evening.

Without speculation, he told her of the scattered cards, the hat, the casings, the blood. Did she want the hat and cards? he asked. They served no police purpose. She paused. Harvey felt her absorbing this terrible news. He imagined her thinking that she would have preferred his badge, his ID. Yes, she said finally in a small voice, and he agreed to bring them by. He brushed off the hat, reshaping it as best he could.

He was so tired he almost fell asleep as he drove toward Wheaton. How many times had he, as new man on the squad, gotten stuck with telling news of death to the next-of-kin, to strangers? How much worse to be telling Felice of his certainty that Morgan was dead? He visualized Morgan's body in a vacant lot or in the river. Or stuffed into a sewer, or in a basement coal bin in a vandalized house, food for rats and maggots.

As he drove, these and other morbid thoughts clouded his usually sunny mind. God, what the sleazy weeklies would do with the dead woman and Morgan's presumed death. More stories about people killed by vampires returning as vampires themselves. Little they cared that they were writing about victims with wives, children, mothers. "Bastards," muttered Harvey, "all bastards." It was an odd, angry mood for him to be in.

Felice worked in the mornings at the nursery school. Today, however, she had been at home with her worries. She had fixed her face, so it looked prettier, less forlorn and worn. But she was controlled, even cold, as she welcomed Harvey into the living room. "I never thought I'd be one of those wives who get a visit from the police with news like this," she said, plucky but weighed down. Then she tried unsuccessfully to sound brighter: "Twice in one day."

Harvey stood before her awkwardly, rubbing his sweating palms on the seat of his pants. He started to do what Burstan had done, feed her hope with a figment. But he could not. Lest she weep again, she asked him to sit while she went to the kitchen to fix coffee and bolster herself.

How brave, he thought of her, hearing the rattle of the saucers and cups. Felice must have built up a layer of self-protective hardness what with seven years of marriage to a Homicide detective.

When she came back, she fixed her dark blue eyes on him. "I'm not a little girl, Dan," she said. "I know you feel awful for me. But you aren't laying it on the line. Saying not much hope isn't enough. Why don't you tell me what you *think*, not just what you know. I get what you *know* on TV. If I cry, I cry. I don't want to torture myself wishing for miracles."

He looked up at her and opened his hands in a helpless gesture. Yet he was glad to be forced away from even the appearance of small hope. "He left the stakeout fast, didn't even pick up his cards," he said, and fished in his pocket for the well-worn deck. He put he cards on the table beside her.

"The hat?" she said.

He gave her the plastic bag in which he had brought it. "I didn't want to give it to you until . . ." He was going to say, "Until I found him." But his sensitivity choked him up. The tears came now to his eyes. To get a purchase on himself, he said, trying to make light of himself with awkward humor, "Until I got one like it to throw my cards in."

Seeing his artlessness, and the love he held for her husband, she smiled in spite of herself. "So the truth is?"

"So the truth is that I believe he's dead. I can't tell you how to handle it. But what I am doing is just making sure I do everything to find . . . the body. And to do everything I can, use every brain cell in my poor stupid head to find this guy."

"And both of those things may be never."

"Yes, both may be never," he regretfully agreed. "We've got an all-points dead-or-alive lookout all along the East Coast. Burstan has personally called every major missing-persons squad. We have special telexes to the hospitals, ditto to pawnshops, gun stores about the automatic, to . . . morgues."

His dismay was again obvious. Miserable as she herself was, she wanted to pat his hand, somehow relieve *his* discomfort. He looked helplessly at her. Christ, he thought, she is so beautiful, so good. Why with a woman like this at home would a guy stay in Homicide? And why would he be so sour? "I feel like such an idiot," was all he could muster. "I'm not saying anything right."

She quickly soothed him. "The kindest thing you

could have done is just what you've done. To tell me everything that you knew or believed and to . . . let me see what's in your heart."

"Is there anything else I can do?" he said, to get the talk back into a mode that he could handle. "Or Burstan, or any of us?"

"No, nothing," she began. Then trying to make it as impersonal as she could, and failing, she said, "If they find him, will he be . . ."

Jesus, she was asking him whether he thought this creep had mutilated Morgan the way he had the first five victims or whether the unspeakable had happened, as with the sixth in the apartment. "This guy is running from us. He wouldn't need the extra . . . baggage. So it wouldn't be like the woman up there. He would do what he did fast, and then get rid of . . . him. I'm surprised we didn't find him in the alley."

She had thought she wanted to hear it all. Now that she had, she wished she hadn't asked. He saw her thinking about the throat wounds on the neck of a man she adored. She wrung her hands, and it was his turn to want to comfort her. When she spoke, it was in a small polite voice. "So you will keep letting me know what's being done? Everything? Even dumb little details?" The words were tumbling out faster than she wanted.

She had tried so hard for bravery, tried to be the policeman's wife, but now she was breaking up and she knew it. "I know you and Homicide will do everything that can be done. But if it doesn't sound too stupid, I'd just like to know everything because it will give me some sense that I'm part of it instead of just waiting for a 'yes,' 'no,' or 'maybe.' Even today, it makes me feel like I'm not just sitting back passively."

"Sure," he said, glad to have something definite to offer. "I'll call and give you a rundown every day." Harvey was smitten, he could not deny it, by this courageous, handsome, honest woman. Felice must have sensed his emotions, for some of the feeling of camaraderie went out of her.

"That would be kind of you," she said formally— and helplessly anxious over how she should feel about Harvey now.

And amid their mutual confusion, Harvey left entangled by tragedy, foolishness, and remorse.

Her husband's partner complied with her wish, and called each day, even when there was nothing to report except "nothing to report." On occasion, he dropped by. The news was negligible: the First District had done house-to-house inquiries on Morgan and the mystery man and had gotten a few hard sightings—who could see this six-foot-six fright without remembering him? None contained a clue as to where he or Morgan was. Missing-person alerts had brought nothing but false leads, evaporating before Harvey found them credible enough to pass them on to Felice Morgan.

A laborious manual and electronic search had turned up one of the steel-jacketed slugs in the apartment and one in the alley. It was possible, therefore, to believe that one or more of the four slugs from the six found casings had hit the suspect and that his armor had retained them, or conceivably that he had been wounded. Or perhaps they were simply missing, gone astray like Felice's husband and his adversary.

Gradually Harvey came to welcome, even depend, on his calls and visits to Felice, and felt in her at least an intimation of the same. Some early evenings, with Washington's muggy summer drawing to a close, she brought him a beer and they sat on the screened porch and talked. It was she, sometimes, who had to keep his spirits up.

"They've kind of given up," he said to her on one visit. "There's not one goddamn thing we haven't tried." He ran his finger thoughtfully around the beaded top of the beer can. "I just feel this guy will kill again, give us another shot at him."

"Well," she said softly, "Ave's not dead. I was willing to accept it when we first talked. But more and more I know he's not. Dan, this sounds like some funny old wives' ghost tale, but if he was dead I'd know it. Now I don't even say things like 'if I only knew,' because I do know. He's not dead."

Harvey could only shrug. As both a street cop and detective, he had seen the odd twists that grief took before it finally dissipated. "I wish your intuitions were a little more specific," he said. "How about your intuitions on us going out for some pasta and Chianti?"

"On that they really *are* specific," she agreed. They had become friends, good friends, glad to share each other's company, sorry when they parted. And as for him, he was in love.

The body of the dead woman in the apartment, now identified as a local prostitute, continued to bedevil Harvey. The wounds were strikingly similar to those in the case histories cited by the Catholic University professor, Father Floyd. Harvey found the folder and reread with an eerie sense of immediacy Floyd's abstract on Vincenzo Verzeni, who had similarly mutilated two women in the late eighteenth century. With no fresh clues, and on an impulse, he called the priest and set up an appointment.

Father Damion Floyd was a dwarfish Welshman in his seventies who rose from behind a cluttered desk to shake Harvey's hand. His jumbled office was full of books and church arcana: old crucifixes, icons of the Virgin, carved ivory saints, holy scrimshaw on a walrus tusk. A miniature refrigerator was within reach of his right hand, and when the detective entered he was just bringing out a small bottle of sweet vermouth.

Father Floyd had the wrinkled, leathery face of a Peruvian Indian taken out of a tannic swamp after two thousand years of natural preservation. His eyes were faded blue behind lashless lids. Wispy hair hung in shreds from the egg of his head. His voice was squeaky and full of Welsh l's.

On his wasted chest hung an ancient Celtic cross the size of a coffee saucer. The wizened man was not lost in the oversized chair or amid the shelves of bric-a-brac, but rather adorned them like a queerly cut baguette in a rococo setting.

"Harvey, a good Welsh name," said the priest in a mousy whisper, "one of us." Harvey hoped the "us" referred only to Welsh ancestry. The professor said he had read everything written in the media about "the subject of your visit. And now I want to hear the true details of these unhappy cases."

Harvey, feeling the role of detective and source had been reversed, nevertheless recounted the history of each case in chronological order. He omitted only those items that Burstan had held back in the interest of public calm—such as the Day-Glo cross. The priest nodded and took notes. When Harvey was done, the cleric said firmly, "Let me say from the outset, whether you believe me or not, you are pursuing a man who genuinely believes he is a vampire."

The authority in his voice irked Harvey. "Wait, Father," he protested. "Have you *ever* come across even one case like this one besides Vincenzo Verzeni?" The detective wanted the professor to see that he had done his homework.

The priest incisively answered. "And he never really *thought* of himself as a vampire. Now listen carefully, Mr. Harvey. I am acquainted with every occurrence of this kind since the seventeenth century. And only last week with the opening of new files in Russia did a fellow arcanist send me copies of a legal history from Novgorod dated in 1939, one that resembles these present cases in Washington.

"This is a man who drank the blood of his own children. His wife was too horrified to stop him. The youngest child died, and only then did she go to the police. The man was convinced he had been killed by a master vampire, had come back to life, and could only die if an ash stake were driven into his heart, or if his head were cut off by a sexton's shovel.

"He was cornered by police, who did not shoot him, but challenged him with a large crucifix. The man surrendered. Before trial he killed himself in his cell with a sexton's shovel smuggled to him by his wife. He had tried to hack his neck with it and bled to death. Admittedly, and you will pardon me the pun, one swallow does not make a spring, but . . ."

Harvey realized that he was in the presence of a legitimate scholar, if a quirky one, who could just possibly help him with the murders. "But where can I apply this?"

"First, note the prominence of the cross in the Novgorod story. Let me ask, are there none in the cases at hand?"

Should he tell Floyd about the cross on the first-aid kit? He fingered the crucifix on his chest, and, swearing the priest to secrecy, told him everything: how the Day-Glo cross—or the sirens—had dissuaded the tall attacker from ripping his throat open with his teeth.

The priest started. "You have told me about a Day-Glo cross. Do you doubt that the mirror first covered, then broken in the apartment bears out what I say? The vampire in all myths cannot abide mirrors. I can give you citations. Sufficient to say, he covers a mirror because he loathes himself so much that he cannot stand to be reminded of what he has become."

The priest poured Harvey and himself a glass of vermouth, dropping in ice from the freezer section. He took a sip, closed his eyes, opened them, and began as if he were lecturing a class.

"Legend has it," he said, "as you know from your reading, that the vampire is the Antichrist. Besides the cross, the sexton's shovel, the ash stake, the weapons against him are such things as paste made from holy wafers to put around his coffin, holy water to burn him with, wild roses—that is, briars such as those forced on our Savior's head—in which to ensnare him. You can dismiss here and now the rubbish about garlic. Nothing in the real literature, medical or otherwise, says anything about it.

"While Christ taught love by day, the vampire kills by night, as we see in the Mall murders. While Christ walked always in daylight, it is daylight that destroys vampires, and I believe you have had no sightings of your quarry by day. Why? Because he slept each day in the coffin you found. Do you doubt it?"

"There was dirt in the bottom of the coffin," observed Harvey, eager to pursue this strange theory of imitation further, for the discovery of the dirt, too, had not been released.

Again, the lashless lids fluttered in surprise. "Even so, even so. Tradition has it that the vampire carries dirt from his birthplace for his coffin. When you find out where this dirt came from, you will know your man's native land. If you catch him, there will be dirt from that land in his pocket, a kind of vampiric port-a-bed." The old cleric's voice had become even squeakier as his excitement grew. "While Christ walked on water, I will warrant that this Mall person avoids crossing it except in a coffin or other box that contains this soil."

Harvey nervously drank off his vermouth, and the priest, his cross bumping the bottle, shakily poured him the rest of the bottle's contents and popped in some fresh ice. "There is more," said the Welshman, then tittered at Harvey's confusion. "Yes, more vermouth, too, but more to my story.

"After certain rare people are victimized by a

vampire, they lie underground forty days and then
emerge as vampires themselves, but the majority, as
we all must, simply rest in Abraham's bosom. Note,
while we are on the subject, that it was forty days
that Our Lord fasted in the wilderness and forty
days between his crucifixion and his ascension to
heaven.

"When the master vampire dies, myth has it,
all whom he created die with him just as these
nauseating tabloids say. What they do not explore
is this: can you imagine the self-protectiveness of a
man who believes a whole tribe of his creations is
riding on his life? The man you seek believes he is
protecting the life, or rather the crypto-life, of his
family, these precious ones he has made in his own
likeness, as God made our Savior in his."

Harvey saw genuine usefulness in Floyd's ideas, if
he could convince himself the suspect had studied
the old myths—as Father Floyd had—and insanely
believed them. The cross, holy water, briars might
be used to bring such a one to bay. But there were
gaping holes in the priest's theory.

"Self-protective is bullshit, Father. This guy *flaunts*
his lack of self-protection. He kills only at the Mall
where we have damned near every square foot covered. If he's out to protect his family, why not move
uptown, or to the Park? Why not confuse us and
protect himself? Even a madman knows that if he
keeps this Mall business up we're eventually going
to nail him."

Harvey saw a glitter in the depths of the eccentric
old man's eyes, and his mousy voice whispered:
"No, you are wrong. *Monstrum horrendum, informe,
ingens*—to defeat this being, you must, as Virgil tells
us, think like him. But you have asked the right
question. He stays to the Mall because believing
he is the Antichrist, he is the embodiment of the
ultimate sin of Satan, fiendish pride, *hubris*.

"As Jesus was the apotheosis of humility, so he

is the apotheosis of *hubris*—that is, arrogance, the deadliest sin in paganism, in Judaism, in Christianity. Believe me, Mr. Harvey, this evil one kills where it is most defiant to do so, at the Mall, the heart of the most powerful nation in the world. He will keep doing so, shaming man and God with his *hubris*. And if he finds a disciple, believe me, that man will be as arrogant as his master. You will find him feasting at the Mall."

Chapter Six
Felice at Risk

For three weeks the Vampire of the Mall was quiet. Perhaps, Harvey thought, he has gone back to wherever the dirt in his coffin came from. Harvey had asked the University of Maryland lab to analyze the soil after his talk with Father Floyd. The agronomists reported it probably came from somewhere in Middle Europe, or the Pacific Northwest. At least, Harvey thought, not a suburb of Washington, D.C.

Then, a Baltimore nurse, returning from a visit to a sick child, was killed, her throat shredded. The shock in Washington was mixed with relief that the sadist's locale had shifted. The frenzied reaction of the media was predictable. "Mall Vampire Moves North! Philly, New York Next?" was a typical headline.

Burstan sent Harvey to Baltimore to work a few days with the police there. The young Washington policeman told the homicide detectives there of his talk with Father Floyd and said he took seriously Floyd's theories of a psychopathic vampire wannabee: the Day-Glo cross, the covered mirror, the bloodsucking nature of the fatal wounds, the dirt in the coffin—none of these could be argued with. He also pointed out where Father Floyd, for all his seeming expertise, had been wrong. The marauder had left the Mall in spite of Floyd's predictions.

Harvey was sure he worked harder on the Baltimore case and the original cases because of guilt over his failure to refuse Burstan's order to abandon the night vigil with Morgan. Yet he could not deny to himself that along with the guilt, he felt a satisfaction in no longer being the brilliant Morgan's sidekick, but his own capable man.

He knew, too, that his acceding to Burstan's order had made possible his increasingly desirable visits to Felice. And further tangling his generally straightforward view of life was the knowledge that he was *good* for Felice. She had let him know, if only by indirection, that she seldom put aside her dark grief except when he was with her. Nor was it any longer just talk over a beer for them. They dined at modest restaurants or at her house, visited a textile show at the Renwick Gallery, shopped and did errands together. Harvey was aware—and was ashamed of it—that Morgan dead had led to a blossoming both of his love for Felice and of his career as a self-sufficient detective.

Morgan awoke in darkness, total darkness. His body felt stiff, yet filled with an electric energy that made him dizzy. His arms were along his sides and the backs of his hands were touching soft cloth behind which there was hardness. He tried to turn, but his arms and hips rubbed against the sides of the form which enclosed him. He was in a box.

He felt upward to the box's top, then gently pushed it. The lid flew up with a bang. Such minute pressure and yet it had slammed upward as if he had exerted all his muscles. This bewildering evidence of unexpected strength frightened him. Outside the box everything was dark. He cramped up, groaning with pain as he bent his knees. The groan had an ugly rasping sound to it that also surprised him.

Must get in touch with Felice, he thought, seeing her in his mind's eye. But the vision of her laughter, her softness, her love and intelligence shattered like a fallen glass. In its place, there came a flood of dark lust, cruel, but ill-defined.

"That's not me," a vestige of clarity observed, but it, too, was buried in a mud slide of craving. The hunger was not sexual, not in that thrilling thought of a mutually devoted coming together. It was, he knew as his thoughts coagulated, a desire for her throat where the blood coursed close to the surface. That image fortified him with guilt, and yet it came back, in stronger and stronger surges, finally overriding the guilt in a tidal wave of voracity.

Soon the want was a constant, at the same time leaving his mind free to remember. What was the last thing he could recall before he . . . went to sleep? Yes, his conqueror's fanged mouth, the stink of decayed flesh and the indescribable pain.

Remembering, he tentatively felt his throat. There were two healed places, small cones of scar tissue. Touching them sent another tide of blood lust over him. He sat up. Dark as it was, his sight was sharp. Son of a bitch! It was a coffin. His mind flashed on the coffin he had seen in the charnel room. This one was much the same, a cheap model of thin steel. Then this hunger, this gnawing hunger drove out all reflection.

If not Felice, then someone. Felice could wait. He would get to her. He climbed from the coffin and went to the bathroom. In his mouth, he tasted rottenness, not strongly, yet somehow his own, different from the sickening odor of the man with whom he had struggled, the vampire, the thing who had . . . changed him. That person was no longer near, not in this city, Morgan knew as surely as he knew his

own name. But Morgan felt a strange bond with
him, a bond of minds, of emotions such as a child
may feel for a father whom he hates, but cannot do
without.

In the bathroom, the mirror was covered with
black cloth, just as he had seen the one in the
apartment of his nemesis. But this one was intact.
Why was the felt cloth over the mirror, he wondered? Something instinctual told him to leave it
there. But he could not, he must see himself, see
his . . . *Morganness*. He loosened the tape and looked
himself full in the face.

He gasped at what he saw. His eyes had become
the eyes of a ravenous wolf. His lips had reddened
and puffed. And when his mouth dropped open in
surprise, he saw that his canines had elongated.
He felt a powerful urge to smash the mirror, as
the mirror had been shattered in his victimizer's
apartment.

Hunching, the thought of reducing his image to
shards still in his heart, he hurried into the living
room. It was small, yet neat, and from its dingy
paper and furniture it was obviously in some poor
section of town.

The keys were on the table. As if from instinct, he
touched his shoulder holster. The .38 was gone, but
at his waist was the .45 and vaguely he remembered
that it should not be. He whisked it free. The clip
and chamber were empty. He wished it were his
old revolver. He grabbed the keys, his hands with
their curling nails clutching spasmodically as he
hastened into the living room. Still crouched, he
left his rundown bungalow through a back door
that opened directly on an alley no wider than the
one in which he had become what he now was.

Morgan foraged Washington's midnight. Adopting
the shadowy techniques he knew from two decades
of police work, he moved through town toward the
Jefferson Memorial. From the darkness near the foot

of its steps, Morgan glanced up at the bland statue
of Jefferson in its rotunda as it seemed to watch the
streams of traffic heading for Virginia.

Behind the Memorial, a favorite haunt of lovers,
a costly four-door Buick was parked, its occupants
panting and grasping at each other in the front seat.
The male was a pampered senior up for the weekend
from the University of Virginia, driving his father's
car. He had picked up a pretty floozy from one
of the city's topless bars who turned quick tricks
after her last dance. Generally, the Park Police told
parked lovers at the Jefferson Memorial to move on.
But tonight they were patrolling the Mall and the
Memorial was, strictly speaking, off the Mall.

Morgan skirted along the side of the Tidal Basin,
passing occasional couples walking hand in hand.
His mind, like a lethal gyroscope, was set on the
parking space behind the Memorial. It was there
he saw the Le Sabre. Semi-supine on the front
seat, the University of Virginia was trying to enter
Miss K Street, but the steering wheel and armrests
alternately thwarted him.

Morgan watched the car like a hungry panther.
He saw two heads come up in silhouette against the
lighted facade of the Memorial, then disappear below
the window level. In his throat was the dreadful
gurgling that he himself had heard just over 40 days
ago. Crouched as low as his long body would permit,
he stole to the rear of the car. Like a hyena sniffing
the air, Morgan ascertained that no other cars or
people were near.

He peered in the back window of the car and
noted the opposite door was unlocked. He circled
the rear, saw an arm go up, and heard indistinctly
the triumphal grunts of the Virginia athlete and the
small, faked rapture of the girl. A leer of hideous
humor stretched Morgan's thickish lips. He slipped
leather gloves on and with a lunge, tore the rear
door open.

The light went on, making him squint and illuminating his bared teeth, then he was inside. He slammed the door, again dousing the compartment and its occupants in darkness. The man and woman's faces popped up from behind the front seat like Punch and Judy puppets. Morgan growled and the woman, stripped from both directions toward her waist, shrieked. The radio still played a jazz rendition of "Heartaches" as Morgan, with a right cross of lethal strength, struck the young man's temple, sending his head smashing against the window.

The renegade policeman's long right hand, sure and sinuous as a serpent, slipped over the seat to the woman's mouth and clamped it shut, aborting her unborn screams. Only her eyes moved, rounded pits of terror bordered by the splotchy black and blue of her makeup and artificial lashes. They stared into the beast eyes of her assailant, almost hypnotized, until at last they seemed to submit drowsily to his silent look.

The attacker slowly took his hand from her mouth, still plump with the kisses of the dead youth. Her lips parted. From them came whimpers but no more screams. Morgan, eyes still fixed on hers, eased himself half over the front seat like a python, gently pushed her long hair from her throat, and dropped his lips to hers. Languidly, he lifted his mouth from her lips. The woman's eyes were closed. The terrible lips of her new and final lover drew away from the ranks of white teeth and, ignoring her naked breasts, he dropped his maw to her wayward throat.

At the Jefferson Memorial nothing was moved until Burstan arrived just before dawn. Harvey was already there. The girl's throat had been ripped, just as in all the earlier murders and the one in Baltimore. The man had been killed with a single skull-crushing blow to the temple. Then his throat had also been torn, but less so than the girl's, almost as if in afterthought.

The Buick was bloody as an old-time butcher wagon. Police in uniform and mufti moved around it under the floodlights. Burstan, smoking a cigar, looked even smaller than usual as he chatted with the sportily dressed Harvey, whose clothes mocked his gloomy face.

"Same guy, hunh?" said Burstan rhetorically.

"You'd think so."

"What dya mean?"

"In the back seat, ID found what looks like fresh dirt off a shoe. Maybe a nine. The dead kid is wearing a twelve."

Burstan craned over to see the white markings around the impression on the back floor carpeting. "It's a nine," he said. "Count on it. I wear a nine."

"Not a thirteen, anyway," said Harvey, "I saw the bastard's feet on those bicycle pedals, Belly. *Big*. Maybe this dirt came off somebody else that was in the car. Somebody they took home."

That seemed reasonable to Burstan. "Does Baltimore have any footprints on theirs?"

"No," said Harvey.

"Any DNA stuff here?"

"Preliminarily, no. There's too much of their blood all over everything to find any spit, if there is any."

"Shit," said Burstan. "Who's the laddie?"

"U of V. Big contractor's son. We got his roommate on the phone. The kid's been whoring, drinking, lousy grades."

"Not enough to deserve this. Anything else?"

"Nothing worthwhile."

Burstan looked at the girl's cheap face. "He had lousy taste, lousy luck, too. Who's she?"

"Dancer at What Sup, that new bar."

They walked around to where an ID man was powdering the rear door handle, careful as a Japanese artist painting with a single-haired brush. "Pulling anything off?" Burstan asked him.

"Nothing green except a smudge."

"Smudged print?" both Burstan and Harvey asked hopefully.

"Nope. Glove. Leather probably. Or plastic."

Burstan saw the elderly fiber-and-dirt technician—the "scruff man"—waiting for the fingerprint specialist to finish. He had driven in from home. "Thanks," said the Homicide chief, thinking he must send the man's boss a commending note.

Burstan and Harvey walked back toward the front of the car. Both were almost sure the new death meant the slayer had killed in Baltimore to lull his hunters. The only other possibility was that some second nut had seen the vampire stories and that they had triggered dormant imitative violence.

"Call Morgan's wife, okay?" Burstan said to Harvey.

"I already did," Harvey said. "Wanted to get her before she heard it on the radio."

Burstan scrutinized him, thinking that a man would have to know a woman pretty well to call her at five a.m. "You little prick," he said without emotion.

Harvey looked down guiltily. But in his heart, he felt a deeply submerged thrill: his love had been recognized.

Two days later, Harvey drove the familiar route to Wheaton. "We've run it all out," he told Felice. "Absolutely nothing new, and you've seen the TV. Same hue and cry. I don't know what the hell else we can do." He was down, and she could find nothing to say to perk him up.

"Boy, I've heard that before," she said, then sighed resignedly. "Can I get you a beer? Do you have time?" She brought out the can and poured it into a frosted glass for him. They walked to the glider on the screened porch.

"I dreamed about him last night," she said.

Harvey didn't reply, but looked up with interest as he did when she said anything. It gave him a chance to gaze at her face without seeming to be mooning over her.

"One of those long involved things," she said. "First he was in the front, looking at the car. It needs a wash." Harvey was going to volunteer, but she hushed him with a touch to his arm. "Then I got afraid of something, I don't know what, and tried to call him in, and he couldn't hear me, so I started out. But I couldn't get any closer than I was. He turned, you know, without being able to walk back toward me either. He kept trying to walk toward the house, but couldn't." Her face clouded. "It was so frustrating. I knew he was trying to come back, but I was afraid he wouldn't be like he was, like he had changed."

"Morgan never changes," Harvey said. He sipped his beer, glad to be with her even though she was upset. They talked of other things—her school, her decision to take some courses in a master of education program, his need to lose some weight. The sun was beginning to set. They both stared at it, the shadows stretching out now to where they sat.

"I've got to get back to work," he said, feeling more distant from her than usual. What a dream, he thought.

Past midnight, Harvey left the office and went to his sixth floor apartment at Seventeenth and P. At the door, he felt a floating uneasiness, but couldn't define it. Once inside, his gun was out as soon as he heard the unaccustomed noise, familiar, yet in these surroundings, shocking, ominous. From the ell of the short hall he could see into the thinly lighted living room. There on his coffee table was a black hat such as one he knew well, and the sound was that of playing cards slapping onto the table or dropping like soft finger taps into the hat.

"Morgan!" shouted Harvey, holstering his pistol and dashing into the living room, prepared to hug the saturnine lieutenant. But he came up with a jolt.

"Hello, Danny boy," his guest said, not rising.

Morgan sat in the easy chair, the deck still in his hand, dark glasses on his eyes. He was wearing a cheap dark suit, black topcoat, and black turtleneck. There was an air about him of sleety reserve. His voice had a new throaty quality.

"What happened to you?" Harvey demanded. "Jesus, you've scared Felice . . . all of us, totally shitless." He stuck out his hand, a gesture Morgan could not refuse. The senior partner's hand was cold, even considering the air-conditioning.

"I couldn't call," Morgan said, and Harvey was again struck by his voice, like a man with a cold, but not exactly. "I was on his trail, sitting on it every day. Literally grabbing food off stands, wherever I could get it. About a month ago I . . ." He looked confused over the time element.

"You've been gone six weeks, man," said Harvey. Even given Morgan's peculiarities, it was unbelievable. What was he concealing? "C'mon, Morgan. What happened? We found the alley. Found three .45 casings, the signs of a fight." He was babbling. "Have you called your wife?" But something cautioned him against intruding into this aspect of the senior detective's affairs.

"One thing at a time," Morgan ordered harshly.

Harvey took a good look at him where he sat sunk in his chair, half in darkness. The turtleneck, he now realized, might mean that he had been bitten by the man with whom he fought. Morgan flipped out one more card. It settled into the hat.

"We got your hat," Harvey said inanely. "We turned it over to your wife." He stopped and collected his wits. "Okay, one question at a time. What about the throat?"

"You guessed right."

"I didn't guess. The turtleneck. And we found blood. He got you?"

"I fought him in the alley. Shot him, but it . . . didn't take. He got away. I followed him, just let's say out of town."

"To Baltimore?"

"No, not to Baltimore. Don't ask me, I said. Anyway, I tracked him four, five days there. Then I was too tired to keep it up. I confronted him again."

"With the automatic. We found the .38. So then . . ."

"We fought again. The goddamn bullets were useless. I don't understand. This time he bit me bad. The throat again. I guess I sort of zonked out. I must have wandered around for weeks while it healed, like a street bum, copping food where I could. I came around about a week ago in a charity ward with the rest of the bums, my wallet, ID, badge, everything gone."

"And you didn't give your real name? You didn't call?"

"Would you if you were in the same town with a guy like that? I didn't know what sources of information he had. All the hospital told me was that the ambulance service had gotten a man-down-in-the-street call and that I was out of my mind three days. So I felt safe lost in that ward. With the beard I had, I must have looked like just one more homeless. When I heard about the business at the Jefferson, I got it together, came here."

Harvey wanted to believe him. But wandering the street for weeks? Another three days incoherent in a hospital, and then a week without calling his wife? It made no sense.

Morgan gathered up his cards. In the motions of his long hands there was a threatening quality that Harvey had never noticed before.

"I don't want anybody but you and my wife to

know," Morgan went on. "For a few days, okay? And don't call her. I'll explain why to her. So keep my confidence, Danny boy. Word gets around. Not even Burstan. I can't afford it with the guy on the loose. That may sound paranoid to you, but . . ."

Harvey sighed. Morgan was off his rocker. Maybe he would be too. Still he hated deceiving Burstan. "Okay, but why'd you tell me? I mean I'm glad you did, but . . ."

"Not out of sweetness, Danny." The unfamiliar rasp in his throat was getting more pronounced. "I need something."

"A gun." That was one thing Harvey would not procure for him. Not even a partner would. And Morgan would know that.

Morgan looked uncomfortable for the first time. "No, I got that. I stashed the .45. That was the only thing I remembered. But I'm going to stay undercover. I need some money. I want you to get me a couple of ready-made suits." The old authority was in his voice now, the lieutenant telling the new man in the branch how to develop the case. "I need some bullets. I need a radio and not one of those worn-out pieces of shit they issue the uniformed men."

"You want me to sign out a chauffeur for you and a limousine too?" Harvey said. Still in the shadows, Morgan made a small laughing sound deep in his throat.

"Why the shades?" Harvey asked.

"The light," said Morgan, "it hurts my eyes ever since . . . that night." At the door, he turned. "Get that stuff by tomorrow night. I'll pick it up here about eleven, midnight. Okay?"

The young detective felt decidedly troubled. Holding the door, wondering as his own heart wrenched whether Morgan really intended to tell Felice, he said, "Well, I know your wife'll be glad you're safe."

"I hope she will," Morgan said expressionlessly.

Harvey, alone, leaned his head against the wall.

Only now did he realize how much he had invested in Morgan being dead. Traitorous it might be, but he knew he had been dreaming of marrying Felice Morgan when she, as he, had given up hope. Now, Morgan had come back and Harvey could not even call to find out how she felt about it. Painfully, he admitted that he half hated the older man for coming back from the dead.

Next night, Morgan buzzed just before midnight. Harvey had quietly and efficiently obtained everything. With hardly a word of thanks, Morgan took the wares in his arms, and started to go. "Remember, nothing about me being back," he said firmly. "I'll announce the . . . resurrection when I'm ready."

For almost a week, Harvey heard nothing from Morgan or Felice. Much of his usual humor gone sour, he trudged through his regular investigations: a woman who had hanged herself in a two-million-dollar house off Foxhall Road; a minor Salvadorean drug dealer pulled from the Anacostia after his bowels had generated so much gas that he popped up despite a bucket of hardened concrete tied to a leg; an undistinguished Saturday night common-law murder.

Harvey had always relived his day as he tried to drop asleep. He heard such crackling echoes of the dispatcher as, "Cruiser Three-one-zero, critical gunshot at Sibley, check it out, please . . ." But nowadays these routine relics of his work were replaced by sleep-impeding ruminations about Felice and Morgan.

Finally, he could bear it no longer. He called Wheaton, and when there was no reply even from the usual answering machine, he drove out. Their car was out in front, unwashed just as in her dream. The house, which to him had been infused with her buoyant spirit during Morgan's absence, seemed begloomed, reclusive, brooding. The blinds were drawn. Her front yard flower garden was sprouting young weeds and stray grass. The lawn had not been cut, contributing to the deserted look.

Harvey felt uneasy. What could have happened? Had they taken an impromptu second honeymoon? If Morgan was well enough for that, he was well enough to notify Burstan that he was back, as Harvey increasingly felt he himself should do. Or at worst, he could tell his partner he was going away.

Harvey rang the bell, and when no one came he rang again. He tapped on the door. He put his ear to the door. At last, he heard footsteps.

The Felice Morgan who came to the door was different from the sunny woman who had brought him beers, who had talked and frequently laughed with him over the last six weeks. The natural rosy highlights of her cheeks seemed to have faded, and he thought perhaps she had lost a little weight. But it was mostly her air of pronounced caution that made him nervous.

"Felice," he said, "What's . . . ?"

"I've been sick," she said quickly.

"What is it?"

"Flu, something," she said, still guarded. "I was in bed. I can't go to work. Dan, I have to—"

He could scarcely believe she was cutting him off this way. "Can I talk with you a minute?"

"About Ave?" She managed to bow her thin lips into a smile. "You see, I was right. He came home." She paused, like an actress trying to recall a badly memorized part. "He said he told you how sick he has been. I'm helping to get him back on the road. He's going to report for duty soon. Above all, he wants you to keep his confidence. For his safety."

Harvey saw they were putting him out in the cold. But he *had* to know more, even though Morgan might be inside, listening. He lowered his voice. "Look, Felice, he was acting strange, damned strange when I saw him. I want to see him. Now. I don't know how long I can keep from telling Burstan he's back."

A fugitive look enveloped her face. "No, if you do that . . . If you do that, he'll take . . . we'll leave, permanently. Dan, you must give us some time. He was sick, very sick. If you tell the branch it could destroy him. Give us some time to get things right again." She was clearly frightened. "Anyway, he's not here now. He stays downtown sometimes, working on the case. He doesn't even tell me where. I pick him up at the Metro stop when he calls me."

"I thought you said he was too sick."

"Not for that. Oh, he's still Ornery Avery when it comes to police work." Her assurances rang false. "It's going to take time for him to . . . become himself again. Please, Dan, if you care about him, us, trust me. Okay? Okay?"

"No, wait," he said, holding the door. Felice had told him she dreamed that Morgan had come back. He was sure she'd *believed* it was a dream. But it had not been. Morgan had been back to her in the flesh even then. That was one of the craziest things about all this. "You told me you'd dreamed he was back. I was sure you thought it *was* a dream, Felice. I mean, I wasn't born yesterday. But he had come back already, right? So did you lie to me, or what?"

She was flustered, again as if she were in a play, and had forgotten her lines. At last she said, "Yes, I lied."

What evil magic was going on here? Had Morgan preempted her mind, fashioned it to say things that she believed to be true but that were not? She was talking to Harvey from a distorted sphere. "I want to get you a doctor, Felice," he said. "For the flu. You don't look right."

Harvey could feel her indecision. "No, if you do that, you'll find me gone. Ave will do whatever needs doing." Hardly breathing the words, she said, "You mustn't meddle."

Harvey stood at the door as she slowly closed it.

After it was shut and he heard the lock turn, he stood staring at it numbly. His first thought as he walked to the car was to call Burstan, to have her forcibly removed from whatever was happening to her. But if he did, Burstan would insist they question Felice about Morgan. And he was absolutely sure that Felice had meant it when she said that she would be gone, perhaps forever.

But every instinct told him not to let it end with their talk at the door. Early the next morning, he called. It was a long time before she answered. Her greeting was as withdrawn and enfeebled as it had been the day before. "Did you tell Morgan I wanted to talk with him?" he asked, trying to sound gentle.

"Yes" she said without emotion. "He said it wasn't time. He said to tell you again if you called that we want to be left alone. I'm sorry. But Ave's . . . I think he's jealous. I told him there was no reason. That my feelings for you . . ." She couldn't finish. "Good-bye, Dan," she choked out.

Morgan lay in the coffin in the downtown apartment where he dwelled when he was not home. Sated and at rest, he felt his mind liberated into a realm of awareness. He was able to imagine he was composing a letter to Felice, whom he had just left. He could think of writing her because he knew he could not say the words to her. When he was with her, she was too much his victim, too enslaved by his power.

"The flame of craving in me is for fresh blood," he would write, "and is parallel to the cravings of an addict for heroin, of a rapist for a woman's body, or of the starving, tortured prisoner for food, any kind of food.

"I have transmigrated from the world of ordinary humanity. But this has not robbed me of all human feelings. I am aware of my gross criminality and yet I still carry some of humanity's baggage. My intelligence, my self-understanding, even faint and fading qualities of decency and humor have made the journey with me. They combine with my complex new makeup, but they are often shoved aside by the most vicious impulses.

"Felice, I am murderous. An ancient vampire has 'fathered' me into his own image. He once was a dreamer and writer who was himself in mid-life created by a still older personage. My creator has moved on, leaving me his domain, as an eagle leaves its wintering grounds to an offspring. Hard as it is to believe, it is true. He is my doom and that doom is yours. I am bound to him, yet abhor him even as I love you."

He thought of how to deliver such a letter to Felice. It would explain, even in a sense justify, what had happened to them. But might she show it to Harvey despite his warnings to her, warnings that he would do to Harvey as he had done to her? The thoughts of the complicated game he was playing shook his equanimity and his mind began to cloud darkly, as it did more and more often these days.

Noxious mists seemed to invade him, confusing him. Oh, yes, he thought one last time with clarity, he knew what he was doing to Felice. But he also knew he was impelled to keep on doing it. In torment, all of a sudden he wanted only to die. And this thought filled him with lust and an overwhelming yet inchoate desire that he not perish.

Chapter Seven
The Broken Mirror

The deaths at the Jefferson Memorial had once more brought the city to the brink of general hysteria. Units of the National Guard were called up to patrol the entire Mall area. Gun stores in Washington and nearby Maryland and Virginia exhibited hand-lettered "Sold Out" signs. On the mean streets, cheap "pieces" that had sold for 50 dollars a few weeks ago now brought four times as much.

A week after the Mall murder and three weeks after the one in Baltimore, there was a similar death in Albany. Police there theorized a "clone," his madness stimulated by the Washington and Baltimore deaths, was at work.

Nationally, the President appealed for calm. All the networks broadcast the Washington sketches. Even David Letterman did not make any jokes about the string of murders. The Larry King callers were consumed with little else. The Balkans, the Middle East, and abortion barely got sound bites on the evening news.

Burstan and Harvey reevaluated their approach. They could no longer count on three-week intervals between attacks. There had been two weeks between Baltimore and the Jefferson Memorial and between the Memorial and Albany. With enlarged grids of the Mall before him, Harvey tried, as Morgan had, to devise a theory of when and where the killer would strike next.

In the whole Mall area, only the few blocks immediately west of Capitol Hill had been spared. They were patrolled by Capitol Police, not as professional, most police felt, as the city and Park Police. And because Congress, not the Interior Department, had jurisdiction, it was not under the Mall curfew.

Harvey argued with Burstan for a week-long stakeout by a picked team of city detectives in that unbloodied area. But Burstan, at wit's end already, snapped, "I can't do it. I got to have everybody I have checking out these goddamn leads. That's including you."

"Jesus, Belly, cut me loose for a few days," Harvey persisted. "It worked when Morgan got me riding the horse."

"And almost got you killed. And Morgan's last great idea," Burstan said, thumping Morgan's empty desk. "What did it do? Got him killed, right?"

Harvey was heavily troubled that he couldn't tell Burstan about Morgan. It was also dangerous for his career. But if he knew anything about his partner, it was that he was as good as his word. He would certainly flee with Felice just as she had said they would. So instead, Harvey challenged his captain. "Yeah, but both times it put us next to the son of a bitch."

Burstan cursed the case, the murderer, the media, Harvey, and Morgan, and finally capitulated.

Harvey, failing to get Burstan to approve a team, had to settle for a single stakeout site. He chose the Botanic Gardens, which once, courtesy of the taxpayer, provided endless free boutonnieres and bouquets for Congressmen. The Gardens are in a low, large French baroque building with a hothouse roof and lie beneath the left foot of the Capitol. Because the west path to its door leads through white pines and magnolias that cast dense shadows at night, Harvey considered it the least risky location for the Mall killer to venture next.

Harvey supplemented his Glock with a sawed-off rapid-fire shotgun hanging at his waist. It was loaded with double-ought buckshot, and there was nothing human that the Street Sweeper would not stop at short range. He chose the shadow of a thickly needled pine as his vantage point, for it gave him a view both of the building itself and its surroundings.

On the first and second nights, the few hurrying pedestrians went unmolested, although vaguely Harvey felt a presence—knowing it could be mere nerves. On the third night, a light burned late in the glass-covered room of the Gardens housing the ficus trees. Harvey could occasionally see a figure in a white lab coat moving inside as he sat, his back against the pine. The woman worker would be his unwitting bait.

Inside the building, the matronly researcher, with bifocals down on her nose, moved among the ficus trees like a fastidious grape picker, plucking the green-colored fruits so she could examine them for diseases the next day. At 11 p.m. she took off the glasses, and rubbed her eyes. She had heard the warnings to Mall workers, but she had been at the Gardens for 12 years, often at night, and was too stubbornly fixed in her habits to change.

As she started to leave, she saw in the dim light a shadow move near a potted jelly palm between her and the outside door. Catching her breath, she recognized it as a tall man, crouched down among the sub-tropical plants. Quickly the apparition emerged from the vegetation and glided toward her. She knew immediately that it was the Vampire of the Mall. The researcher was familiar with every inch of the walkways, the miniature ponds, the dinosaur-era re-creations, the pots of epiphytes, carnivorous plants, and other exotic flora.

Vigorous and cool-headed in her 50s, she knew that her only escape lay in confusing her hunter in the maze of walks and plant settings. She darted down a path past a towering anthurium. The intruder clacked in his throat almost tauntingly as he followed. She could not see his face beneath his black hat. She scooted past a display of herbs used in Chinese medicine, and ran to entryways leading toward giant ferns and cycads. There, vines hung down drinking of the moisture. As she ran she broke into a sweat that beaded on her neck and coursed down her heavy breasts.

As she rounded the corner to the rear door, she saw it blocked by cartons of soil. Thinking fast, she rushed into the nearby work room, locked its door, and snatched up the telephone. She dialed the operator, praying she would come on immediately. Then she froze as the man smashed into the door. From the telephone she heard, "Yes, please," and she shouted "Help!" even as her dread pursuer crashed through the door and fell, knocking over pruning sheers and a pot of poinsettias with a crash.

She fled through the room's second door as he tore the phone loose from its wires. In the cacti room, she bent and ran beneath a giant cactus with limbs like coiled snakes. Her pursuer jumped after her, and snagged himself briefly, howling at the pricks of the spines.

Out from among the cacti, she left the path and ducked under a curtain of Spanish moss. The deter-mined figure behind her lurched into the Spanish moss, fell on uneven soil, and came out with a grotesque wig of moss. Past an ominous Black

Knight plant the researcher fled, then to the long front gallery and along stone-paved passageways. She looked back and saw the raptor shake off the moss hairpiece and pass a 40-foot high eucalyptus tree. He skirted the first of two long pools where good-luck coins dropped in by tourists glistened faintly.

He followed her like a wolf as she wove down one side of the blue-tiled pools, then another. Each time, he put himself between her and the front door, until at last he was on one side of the two-foot deep pool and she was out of breath on the other. He looked like some odd black-barked tree growing from the gentle hyacinths and sweet flag at the pool's border. Her side ached as if she were having an attack of appendicitis.

For several seconds they stared at each other through the Henri Rousseau nightscape as he planned his onslaught. Then, with an animal snort, he started around the pool, a distance of 60 feet. Her breath returning, her side pang lifting, she zipped sure-footedly around to the other side. As he neared, she leaped from the path, circled a sausage tree with its obscene fruits, and again, in unfamiliar terrain, the predator stumbled.

At last, in a bed of dripping ferns, he boxed her in. She felt the water running down her neck, fearing with a great dread that she would die among these plants she had tended so well. Creeping toward her, he raised his talons in their fatal vee. But as he lunged, she brushed past him—so narrowly that he tore her lab coat. With no further place to run, she threw herself into the pool. Her dress and white coat impeded her, but she righted herself and splashed toward the far side. She screamed, straining her legs to traverse the three-foot width.

But even as she imagined his great weight upon her, the man stopped cold at the pool's edge and dropped his arms, glaring disgustedly at the pool with its treasury of abandoned pennies and nickels. Reprieved, she clambered from the water, and again faced him across the pool.

With a yelp, he loped around the circumference of the pond. It registered on her that for whatever reason, he did not want to get wet. So as he whipped around the pool's end, she waded back across, putting the water between them once more.

"You dumb bitch," he growled venomously. He started for the water, thrust out his foot, but then backed away, hissing, timid as a child at a swimming pool who fears it will be too cold for him. Again he sprinted around the perimeter of the pool, and yet another time, she forded it and put it between them. Her ingenuity and his outlandish fear of water was showing her the way. If she could lure him to the south side of the second pool, now that she had the knack of wading speedily, she might just make it out the front door.

This time, as he rounded, she backed up and leaped almost to the other side. Her shoes were sucked off by her urgency as she reached the pool's border. Bedraggled and muddy, she crawled out onto the walkway and ran from the room toward the door. He was close behind. The moonlight shown on them through the arc of the high glass ceilings.

Almost at the door, she stumbled over a tub of briar roses. They had been left by a workman and she had seen and forgotten them during the evening. She sprawled, knocking the roses and their wooden two-by-two climbing rod onto the walk and agonizingly wrenching her ankle. The invader saw her predicament and cried with unrestrained lust. Whimpering, she scrambled on hands and knees toward the doors, a strand of the briar roses at her shoulder like an Ophelia's bouquet.

The exit was only a few yards from where she crawled. Like a crippled doe she tried to struggle to her feet, but the leg gave way. There was nothing now between her and his rapacity but the pole and the roses. His arms went up. But he saw the bridle of white flowers at her shoulder by the lunar light through the hothouse roof. It also fell silvery on the two-by-two with the rest of the flowers, some torn and strewn on the floor. As if these immortal symbols of the crucified Christ's crown had death rays shooting from them, the interloper recoiled. He drew his long arms before his face, and snarled.

His lust vied with his manic fear. He looked again at the woman, straining for breath as she dragged herself toward the door. Then, blood craving overpowered him. Howling frantically at the idea of losing his panting victim, he put his arm over his eyes and ran at her. With her good leg, she kicked the two-by-two with its roses in his path.

He tripped on it, the thorns pricking into his coat, his bare hands, his face. Groaning and growling, as if the briar roses were Medea's raiments of fire, he writhed free.

But she had made the door. She pulled herself up, leaned her weight against it, and fell outward, the corsage of roses tearing from her shoulder. She could see her assailant leaping toward her as she squirmed screaming into the night.

Harvey, lost in murky fancies of Felice Morgan, was jerked to his feet by the screams. He unfastened the shotgun at his waist and ran toward the door of the Botanic Gardens. He saw the woman there with a long form over her. The detective fired a shot into the air to forestall what could well be the instant of murder. To his astonishment, he saw the dark figure rise from where he was kneeling and look toward the shot.

"Who the hell?" came a familiar voice. It was Morgan, his .45 drawn.

The woman was unconscious when Harvey drew up, but he could see her breaths raising the front of her smock. A strand of small roses lay six feet away.

"I damned near had him," Morgan said, breathing hard, his tone acidulous. "He's gone. Call an ambulance."

Morgan? Harvey asked himself as he called the dispatcher for the ambulance and sounded the alarm for the now-familiar Vampire of the Mall. But how had Morgan known to come here? And why hadn't *he* summoned help? The radio's bulge showed on his topcoat. "You almost had him?" Harvey asked, suspicious.

"I figured him to be out here, near the Hill. I saw him pick the back door," Morgan said.

"I figured him here too," said Harvey, still skeptical.

"Well, you learned enough from me to stake him out. But not enough to catch him." Harvey felt the intimidation that had always been part of their relationship. Morgan continued: "If you had, you'd have seen him chasing this little lady out the front door and one of us could've been after him instead of ministering to her."

But, Harvey was about to argue, I *was* watching the door. Or had his surveillance lapsed while he thought of Felice? "You were that close?" Harvey asked.

"Yep, heard her scream and got here just as he let her go. If I hadn't had to stop . . ." Methinks he doth protest too much, Harvey thought, remembering something from some long-ago class. And there was an odd excitement in Morgan's voice, different from the intense zeal he had shown for police work.

"He got away," Harvey said almost to himself. He bent over the woman, picked up her wrist to see how her pulse was running, then, not finding it, tried her throat at the carotid artery. It was strong, a bit fast.

Focused on the woman, he didn't see his partner's lips pull back from savage white teeth or the eyes widen in a paroxysm of hunger. Morgan's hands curved like the claws of a gigantic hawk. Gradually, his arms spread like the slowly opening jaws of a bear trap. His motions became jerky, almost orgasmic as he looked at the middle-aged woman's bare throat. His neck muscles stood out like mole tunnels. Harvey first, then her . . .

But abruptly, like a tiger reading the wind, Morgan heard the blades of the Park Police "Eagle" and saw the beam of its floodlight walking up the Mall like bright silver rain. His coil-spring tension relaxed into a normal crouch. "I'm cutting out," Morgan said, his voice almost a cough.

Harvey looked up.

"Better luck next time," said Morgan.

The helicopter swept the area west of Capitol Hill. The first officers and the ambulance pulled up. Harvey had the police cordon off the area at the building's two entrances. Taking off his shoes, he went into the building to look for clues that might help to locate the elusive man. All he found was the overturned tub of briar roses.

Next morning, he talked with Burstan. Morgan, he said, had reappeared three weeks ago, but his mind had slipped. He wished now he had told Burstan. But, he reported, Morgan had warned it could endanger him, and perhaps prevent him from making the crucial bust. Besides, Felice had told him they would flee if he told Burstan. Harvey explained that he had weighed the consequences, and kept quiet. He would take whatever discipline Burstan handed out.

Burstan thought about what might have happened if Harvey *had* told him. The captain imagined a headline like: "Homicide Detective's Leak Dooms Partner, Probe."

So far, Harvey's silence had cost them nothing. He let Harvey off tersely. "Bad judgment, my boy."

*   *   *

The Botanic Gardens researcher's ankle ligaments were torn badly, but this gutsy woman with her sharp mind was able to talk incisively about the episode to Harvey. First she thanked him—and his partner, whom she had not seen—for saving her, promising to name her next experimental rose after them. Under his questioning, she said, no, her attacker was not six-foot-six, but four or five inches shorter. No, she had not noticed any smell to him, but he had not been as close as Harvey's foe had been to him. No, he did not sound foreign. "He called me a 'dumb bitch.' Does that sound foreign?" she asked.

Yes, she continued in answer to Harvey's questions, he was deterred by something: he had refused to cross either of the ponds, and he had been unwilling to step over the briar roses. This playing with Christian symbols, Harvey thought, it's like being a homicide cop in King Arthur's Court.

An unfathomable gulf now lay between Harvey and his former partner. Of course, Father Floyd's old folk tale about a vampire transmitting that condition to another was too bizarre to consider seriously. The priest had himself said there was no medical evidence of such contagion. Not even the Vampire of Novgorod was accused of that ghastly power. And yet, the ancient fairy story distressed him, not just on Morgan's account, but as to how it touched on Felice. And he himself had been bitten by the Vampire of the Mall. Suppose, just suppose, he carried some dormant strain of this insidious virus?

He called Wheaton in spite of Felice's warning, but there was only the voice on the machine, its peppiness a reminder of the spirited woman who had recorded it so long ago. The hell with it, he thought. He would try her by phone for a day or so more and then, threat or no threat, if he got no answer, he would go to Wheaton to confront her—and Morgan.

That afternoon, Harvey drove to Catholic University to see Father Floyd. He told him of the briar roses and the intruder's fear of water. The tiny professor was kind enough not to say, "I told you so," although his expression said it for him.

"Okay, okay," said Harvey. "I'm convinced this guy reacts the way you said he would. If you thought you might see him, what would you carry with you besides the cross."

"Oh, the cross will work handily," squeaked Father Floyd cheerfully. "I can't expect you to carry a sexton's shovel in a special holster or an ash-stake-and-hammer kit."

He searched his shelves of religious treasures, saw a silver vial the size of a film canister with a cross embossed on its side, and told Harvey to drop by Saint Anthony's three blocks away and pilfer a bit of holy water from the font. The priest smiled widely. "It's in the best of causes, and besides, our Savior was always the first one to forgive repentant thieves."

Floyd asked for more details on the new case, and again took notes. Harvey was sure he had another scholarly article in mind. "Godspeed," the priest told him. "Your cleverness is getting you closer. I wish I could go with you. Be careful."

The papers and television, of course, went berserk over the new attack. Two hundred active-duty MPs were called in to patrol the Mall and the First District. Congressional staffers' clubs and social groups in the federal departments along the Mall got up escort services for female workers going home after dark. And such is the nature of gallant men and lovely ladies during such traumas as wars, floods, and crime waves that the women often wound up spending the night with their brave escorts.

Word went out verbally from the police chief that the citizenry had to be protected even if it meant relaxing strict rules on how and when police used their guns. Inspectors advised captains that too damn many violent criminals were getting away. Captains told lieutenants that there'd be hell to pay if anyone in an assault case outran a man in this district. And the sergeants said bluntly to their men that "if you catch any motherfucker beating on somebody that looks innocent, kill him if he tries to get away."

That very night, police shootings of civilians rose dramatically. Predictably, most of those shot were black, the one thing everyone was sure the culprit was not. The American Civil Liberties Union and black organizations made emergency protests, but the majority of both black and white citizens were pleased, even on the merits, to see the new policy in force.

At headquarters, Harvey, using his old uniformed hat as the target, flipped out cards and pressed his imagination on where the next assault would occur. As he tossed the cards, Burstan, his cigar at the end of his short hand like a fallen torch, came out of his office and watched Harvey for a short time, then said, "Harvey, that gets on my nerves."

The detective landed a few more cards in the hat. "You got a better idea?" he said courteously. "I got a thought."

The captain sat on Morgan's desk and Harvey stopped flipping the cards. "Remember the apartment? Mouthwash bottles, worn-out toothbrushes, movie magazines, bloody butcher paper, Vienna sausage cans, especially the broken mirror. I'm talking long, long odds, but the city could order the garbage men servicing the ghettos near the Mall to look for these things together in a single can. Or just pieces of busted mirrors or worn-out toothbrushes. They're the only real rarities. And offer a couple of hundred bucks to the garbage man whether the clue pans out or not."

"The bastards'll plant the broken mirrors and other stuff and take our money."

"Not if you tell them that to collect they'll have to be interrogated by Homicide, including a lie-detector test."

Burstan thought for a few minutes. "Oh, shit," he said resignedly. "What do we have to lose? We got nothing else. I'll call the mayor's office."

Harvey threw out his last card, the Jack of Hearts. It dropped neatly in the billed police hat. "My card," he said.

"Here," said the captain, "gimme those cards. What would the chief think if he walked in here and saw you? You'd be back on a beat *wearing* that goddamn hat. And I'd be busted to station clerk." Burstan picked up the cards and put them in his pocket. Harvey smiled, both peeved and amused.

A day and a half had passed. Harvey called Felice one more time, but still got only the recorder. He could wait no longer. Without saying where he was going, he put on his jacket and went to tell Burstan he was leaving for the day, but would be reachable by beeper or on his convertible's two-way radio. The chief's secretary waved him through the open door to Burstan's office. Telephone cradled between shoulder and ear, the captain was talking to the mayor's office about the garbage men as he awkwardly pitched Harvey's cards at his in-basket.

The lawn had been cut at the Morgans' house. That was the only change since Harvey's last visit. The blinds were all still drawn. The car was in the driveway, still unwashed. Harvey got down on his knees and inspected the cement behind a rear tire. It had rained two days ago. The tires had left faint marks in the thin skein of dirt washed across the cement by the rain. So it had been used once during the last two days.

He rang the doorbell. There was no answer. He

rang a second and third time. Increasingly troubled, he walked to the rear and knocked on the kitchen door. No answer there either. The house appeared as deserted as an empty tomb. Could he ask the county police to make an entry? On what grounds? There was nothing but his instincts, his fears, to suggest foul play.

On the way home, he allowed his weary mind to think the unthinkable: that Morgan must be regarded as a suspect in the Botanic Gardens attack, and if so, then also in the Jefferson Memorial murders. The thought beat on him in waves, and he pushed them back, looking for other explanations as he listened to the messages going out on the police radio in his car. The dispatcher's voice droned on.

Harvey was almost at his apartment when he heard, "Car Three-nine-nine call the office." It was the number assigned to his radio receiver. He pulled into a gas station and called. The duty sergeant gave him a telephone number in Washington, saying it might be a lead on his garbage search.

The number was that of a garbage man who was obviously eager for the two-hundred-dollar reward, but sounded honest. "I saw it today, maybe six little pieces of broken mirror by the can," he told Harvey. "They was squished in the mud. Looks like I—or somebody—picked up the load one, two weeks ago and these little bits spilled out." Otherwise, there had been nothing today but newspapers and ordinary garbage. The can and mirror shards were behind the house, between a high hedge and the alley.

It was not the lead Harvey had hoped for, but it was something. He turned the car around, drove to the address given him in the far north of the First District, and parked a block from the house and got out. From a side street, he looked at the bungalow, one of the few in this slum. Its blinds were closed. Otherwise it looked fairly neat, even prim.

It was worth a try, thought Harvey, his heart

beating faster. Unlike Morgan, he was going to make the entry by the book, with a backup team. Knowing Burstan would split his ample gut over any new diversion of manpower, Harvey nevertheless got his permission for a half-dozen detectives and a SWAT team to be on hand for the entry.

Burstan himself would immediately swear the warrant, thin as the evidence was. Far better to take the chance of looking like idiots than to do nothing. The detectives and SWAT men would assemble within an hour at the traffic division station at Fifth Street and New York Avenue.

Meanwhile, Harvey was making special preparations of his own. Through the Catholic University switchboard, he reached Father Floyd in his room and asked him to be at the assembly point with two-dozen crosses. The old priest, excited as a young cop on his first bust, said, "Oh, yes. Yes indeed, Mr. Harvey."

As Harvey waited for Father Floyd in the station's squad room, he thought of all the innocent reasons that pieces of a broken mirror might be found in the mud by a garbage can. Nevertheless, he was eager to get on with it. The Welsh priest arrived by taxi, carrying a box of silver-plated crosses.

"From Saint Anthony's Sunday school supplies," he explained to Harvey. On his chest, he wore his oversized Celtic cross. Harvey thanked him, and joined Burstan at the podium for the briefing. The Homicide captain apologized for taking many of the officers from their assignments and calling in others from home. Then he let Harvey fill in the details.

The detectives knew from the internal police reports how their psychotic target reacted to religious objects. The media had made the Vampire of the Mall a fearful celebrity. As Father Flood passed among them, the policeman eagerly accepted the crosses, even the atheists. At worst, they would make authentic souvenirs of the city's most extraordinary homicide case.

When the cleric had rather theatrically blessed the crosses and officers, he turned to Harvey in a firm whisper and asked whether he could come along. Harvey thought of protesting, but the priest, as much as anyone, had contributed to the case. "Why not," Harvey replied, "but in the rear guard, okay?"

Chapter Eight
The Sexton's Shovel

Just after nightfall, the team deployed in alleys around the bungalow to the curiosity of the few people still out on these ghetto streets. Radio contacts were forbidden unless initiated by the entry team made up of Harvey and the six other detectives, all in black. Harvey, after a check with his partners, allowed the diminutive academic to join them in the entry, regarding him as a kind of talisman. His cassock was black, and he had put his white clerical collar in its pocket.

The eight men huddled together by the bungalow's back hedge. Harvey climbed over the sagging gate in the untrimmed foliage, entered the rank yard, and crept to the door in the screen porch. On it was an ancient padlock. Through the torn screen he saw the back door to the house. It had a tumbler lock. He heard a scurrying on the porch and froze. But it was only a rat fleeing from the cushions of an overturned easy chair. Better the front door, he thought. No rats and one less lock.

He posted three detectives in the rear, and the department's best "pick" quickly opened the front door. The remaining five entered, all wearing infrared goggles. Each carried a pistol and a cross, save Father Floyd, who clutched his Celtic cross. Inside, there was silence.

The interior was cool. In it was the faintest stink of death, a phantom of what Harvey had smelled on his assailant in the park four months ago. He turned to his comrades, nodded, and gave them a thumbs-up. The living room was tidy, characterless. The bluish tint from the goggles made everything seem like a faded black-and-white movie. The door to the bedroom was closed. Gently Harvey tried to turn the knob, but it was locked.

He stepped back, heart thumping, listening for sounds, remembering his foe's brawn. Was he inside? Or had he simply locked his bedroom door when he'd gone out, perhaps leaving behind a badly gnawed corpse on the floor?

He signaled the "pick," who withdrew a simple master key. The specialist eased the door open, and Harvey entered, followed by his comrades. The rank smell was stronger. There could be no doubt. This was the lair of the Vampire of the Mall.

The bed was unmade. There on the pillow case was a dark patch. Droolings from the vampire after his feast? The room was simply furnished. Father Floyd touched his arm, and Harvey looked where the priest pointed. Like a window seat, a long object gleamed dully to their right. It was a coffin.

The thought that his quarry was there, waiting for night to deepen, filled him momentarily with terror. Pistol in his right hand, his own crucifix in the left, he inched to the coffin and threw back its lid. The thin metal banged against the wall as Harvey stared into the tawdry silk-lined box.

There lay Avery Morgan in gruesome caricature. Harvey reeled backward. Morgan looked dead. His mouth was caked at the corners with dry gore and saliva. The result of internal bleeding from some abominable death? The thought flashed in his mind that it made sense to believe that the Vampire of the Mall had killed his partner and stashed him in this coffin. Yet even in repose, it was not wholly the face of Morgan. There was an inexpressible cruelty on the fixed features, in the animal teeth.

The team peered in like mourners at a funeral. Harvey, unnerved and trembling, reached out his hand and touched the cheek. It was as cold as every other cadaver Harvey had encountered in his years as a policeman.

And then, as one, the raiders gasped. Morgan, as if responding to the touch of warm flesh, blinked first one eye, then the other. It was unbelievable! The corpse was alive. The eyes, virulent with hate and the only live points in this otherwise inert body, stared out at them.

"Morgan," whispered Harvey as it sank in that his fantastic suspicions were reality. The Vampire of the Mall had infected Morgan, made of him a creature in his own image. And whose blood stained his lips? The blood of Felice? My God, he thought, was she even still alive?

"Morgan. It's you. You did it!" he uttered.

The thing in the coffin made a guttural sound, the clearing of breath or phlegm from his throat. It was then that Father Floyd pushed forward, aged eyes burning. Crossed in his midget hands were two objects he had brought from beneath his cassock: a wooden stake the size of a tent spike and a hammer.

"Are you crazy?" Harvey growled and thrust him back. Pistol aimed at Morgan's malignant eyes, Harvey sidled to the coffin side, watching the face for any change that would indicate the rest of the body was coming alive.

The eyes followed Harvey, unblinking. Morgan

cleared his throat again, opening his mouth, in which Harvey saw the tongue, brown with gore. The nostrils dilated and the head moved slowly from side to side as if it were trying to shake itself out of a coma. Now or never, the detective thought. He slipped his cross in his pocket and snatched his handcuffs from his belt. He had requisitioned a special pair. They were of case-hardened steel, custom-made to hold the most crazed and powerful criminals.

"Morgan," he said, "you're under arrest," the ritual too practiced to forget, even now. He hacked down with the open handcuffs at the wrist in the coffin. But Morgan's hand was too swift. It came up like an iguana's tongue and encircled Harvey's wrist. Harvey tried to move, but Morgan was too powerful. Harvey fired, the noise loud as a dynamite stick in the close room. But he was so off balance that even at this range he was unsure whether he had hit Morgan.

Again, Father Floyd, uttering Latin imprecations, wedged up to the coffin side with his medieval contrivances, but the detectives picked him up and deposited him behind them. The largest of them seized Morgan's arm to wrench his iron vise from Harvey's wrist. He succeeded, but Morgan used the heavyset detective's own grip as leverage, and vaulted from the coffin.

The men bellowed and rushed Morgan, who unfolded like a giant bat and was soon in such close combat with them that they dared not shoot. The rogue policeman lashed Harvey on the temple, knocking him across the coffin. Father Floyd, meanwhile, determinedly butted through the fighters, raised his crossed stake and hammer, and piped in Morgan's face, *"Vrykolakas,"* in what sounded like some Balkan language. The gaunt combatant saw the makeshift cross, shielded his eyes, and uttered a thunderous wail. He broke through his foes, who were swinging on him with experienced police fists, or clouting him with their pistols. One touched him with a cross as he swung, and Morgan screeched.

A quick-witted detective saw the cause of his banshee yell and brandished his own little cross in the livid face. Morgan shook his greasy head from side to side, ducking to avoid sight of the minuscule object. Recognizing Father Floyd as a special architect of his quandary, Morgan gave him a sweeping kick that cut his aging legs out from under him and sent him skidding across the room into a wall. Above the din, one of the detectives shouted into his radio for help.

Another shielded with his own body the stunned Harvey, who was bleeding from where his brow had struck the end of the coffin. Still a third gripped Morgan's waist. But with a dervish whirl, Morgan spun him too into the wall, his pistol firing aimlessly into the ceiling. Like an elongated bear on his hind legs baited by hounds, Morgan looked for a way past the waving crosses. A policeman saw his predicament and, holding a cross at arm's length, resolutely blocked the door.

That denied him, Morgan ran at the window, kicked out its glass like a kung fu fighter, and with a second heel shot, banged out the rusty, poorly anchored security grating. One of the detectives swung upward and gave him a burning goose with a cross. He whooped and dove head-first through the aperture.

Outside, shots sounded and there were shouts and running footsteps as the SWAT team converged. But Morgan eluded the first line of police by high-jumping a fence between two tenements. The police fired volleys as they sprang after him, but he outran them and disappeared into the barrios of the city.

On the floor, Harvey shook his head groggily. He knew the fugitive he had so carefully trapped was again at large. His mind focussed on Felice. He was now convinced that the blood on Morgan's face was hers. Her phantom husband had been with her almost four weeks. Harvey, nearly vomiting, thought of how little blood must remain in her veins, dead or alive. He shook his wrist where his ex-partner's eagle grip had held it, then rose unsteadily and looked for his handcuffs and gun.

The room was empty now except for Harvey, an unconscious detective sergeant, and Father Floyd, who lay on his back. One of the detectives had paused long enough to put a wet towel on his head. A Fire Department rescue squad arrived with a stretcher, but Harvey and the priest, now coming around, both refused.

As Harvey and the Welshman limped toward the door, the priest gave the detective his Celtic cross. "Take it," he said. "Live to bring it back." Harvey put it in his pocket and tucked the little crucifix around his neck inside his shirt. Morgan's reaction to crosses had made Harvey a believer.

Police had the house blocked off. Harvey hobbled to his car as fast as he could. Every instinct told him Morgan was on the way home if Felice were still alive. As Harvey drove feverishly through the still-humid October night he tried to think how he could protect her and capture—or destroy— Morgan. Shots don't kill him. And if five men, six counting the priest, can't hold him, even with crosses, then what?

He raced into the suburbs, pulling around cars to go through red lights, horn braying, pushing his car to its limit. Up ahead, he saw the steeple of a church, thought of the Vampire of Novgorod, and quickly decided to treat the house of God as an armory. He braked at the building's rear, and tried the door of the sexton shed. When it didn't open, he pried it off its hinges with the Celtic cross. Inside was a dirt spade with a long handle. Wedging it into the vee of a tree, he snapped the handle and threw the shovel portion into his car.

In Wheaton, a small light gleamed from a rear room. Morgan could not have beaten him here. Felice! Surely it meant she was inside. Alive! He ran up the walk, spade in one hand, pistol, useless as it might be, in the other, and rapped at the door. When no one answered, he ran to the back.

Through a crack in the shade, he could dimly see Felice lying in the bed. "Felice," he called, tapping at the window. She did not move. He broke the pane with the shovel, cranked the casement open, and knocked out the screen.

"Felice," he said again as he huffed into the room. Her hair, once curled and meticulously combed, was tied back in a short, bedraggled ponytail. The color was gone from her face. She was thin, and not healthily so. She wore a quilted housecoat over a high-necked nightgown.

Harvey slipped to her side and felt her forehead. It was cool, but held behind that coolness the warmth of life. Thank God! The thin face, because it was alive, was beautiful. He gently peeled down the high neck of the gown to feel her pulse. There was a yellowing of the skin, like the bruise tissue on strangled corpses. As he tenderly folded the flannel down further, he saw on her neck two small wounds.

"Christ!" he muttered. They were not flowing, not sawtoothed as the injuries in the other killings had been, but were semi-open, unhealed. The flesh around them puckered them up almost delicately into tiny dead volcanoes. It was there that Morgan had drunk. Lethargically, her hands rose to touch her throat and her eyes fluttered. Once so candid and dark azure, they were bloodshot, suspicious.

Then she realized who he was. "Dan!" Her hand went out feebly as if to touch him, then fell back on the coverlet. She said huskily, "You must go. He . . ."

"Hush, Felice," Harvey said firmly. "I know."

She brushed her hand anxiously across her forehead, shutting her eyes, then opening them with a less fearful look. Her voice had grown throaty. It made him uneasy. It had changed much like Morgan's had. "Where is he?" she said at last.

"I don't know. He tried to kill me."

"He'll come," she said weakly but positively. "Go while you can."

"And leave you?" Harvey blurted. "He's gone crazy. He thinks he's a goddamned vampire."

"Don't say that word," she cried, alarmed.

"What do you mean, don't say it?" he replied more softly than his words implied. "That's what he thinks he is." Harvey thought of the magnitude of Morgan's evil, his strength, his immunity to bullets. "That's what he is," he said soberly. "He's been killing you by degrees. Do you think I'm blind?" He reached out gently toward her throat.

She recoiled, both her hands rising to her neck, yet in her fear there was also protectiveness, as if perversely she treasured the terrible marks on her skin. "Don't you see? I let him do it," she said faintly defiant.

"I know."

She shuddered, edging toward hysteria. "I had to let him. He needed me. *Had* to have me this way. He . . ."

"Bullshit, Felice," he said, still softly, but there was anger in his voice. "He hypnotized you or some goddamn thing. I'm getting you out of here. To the hospital, for those wounds. Right now! And I want cops all over this area waiting for Morgan." He started to pick up the bedside telephone.

"No." She took the telephone in her hands. "I can't go. They won't catch him. He's too . . . strong."

"You're wrong." He brought the silver crucifix from inside his shirt. "Wear this. It scares him. He . . ."

She interrupted him with a cry, looking at the cross with horror, pressing back in the bed from it as if the innocent little object were a scorpion or black widow spider.

He clasped his hand over it. He need not ask why she shrank from it. His fear had come true. Morgan had infected her. Would she, too . . . No, the idea was too awful to contemplate.

"You feel pain when you see it?" he demanded, unable not to plumb her condition. Yet his heart constricted. He loved her, even as he found repugnant what had happened to her.

She began sobbing. "I can't wear it. I can't." She looked up at him helplessly. "Because of this." She pointed to the two wounds on her throat, which had begun to ooze blood. "Even when I see a . . . see one . . . the pain is so much that I . . ."

"The phone. Give me the phone, Felice. Then we're getting out of here." He was getting jittery. It was all so weird. He wanted to summon Father Floyd to meet them at the hospital. Even more than any physician, the priest could counsel him and Felice on what could be done to restore her health. He reached again for the telephone, but as he did, her eyes, looking past him, widened in fright. He spun.

Framed by the window, lighted by the glow from the room, was the terrible countenance of Morgan. The young officer aimed the Glock at Morgan's head and squeezed. The four rapid rounds jerked back his ex-partner's head. He fell from sight and Harvey rushed to the window. But Morgan had disappeared.

Then, Harvey heard the front door bang open and Morgan was in the doorway to the bedroom. His animal eyes drilled into the younger man's. On his forehead were four raw wounds, unbleeding. Harvey fired four more times, sick with fear. He knew the shots were in vain. Morgan waved his hand scornfully as if to dismiss all the weapons of men.

Harvey opened his closed fist where he still held the silver cross and let it dangle from its chain.

With that same hand, he slowly reached down for the spade.

Morgan's bestial voice growled commandingly, "Felice, the light!" If she obeyed her husband, Harvey realized instantly, the cross and spade would be unseen and thus could not deter Morgan. And Harvey—and Felice—were doomed.

"No, Felice," the young detective shouted.

But the light went out. Felice had obeyed. In the gloom Harvey could indistinctly make out the long shape moving serpentinely toward him. Panicking, he threw the useless pistol at the form, and groped in his pocket for his final weapon. His hand closed on the little canister of holy water.

Putting down the shovel, he unscrewed the top and flung its contents at the shadow. Morgan bawled, but briefly, for Harvey had hit him with only a few drops, Still, the holy liquid had given Harvey time to rip his flashlight from his belt, pick up the shovel, and shine the light across both it and the cross.

The prowling figure stopped and grunted like a hyena, fright now in the unnatural sound.

Confident in the authority of cross and sexton's spade, Harvey drove Morgan into a corner. He played the light on the shovel and cross and into Morgan's face, a Greek mask of trepidation, eyes popping, lewd mouth sagging. Morgan clutched his arms to his face to blank out the sight. Harvey was not bloodthirsty, but he knew heart-deep he must cut to death this murderous monstrosity who had once been his partner and friend.

He backed him toward the wall as an animal tamer might a balky lion. There, Morgan ducked to the level of the bed and, averting his eyes, crawled on hands and knees toward the bedroom door. Harvey blocked him, slamming the spade on his shoulder. Morgan shrieked deafeningly and cringed back toward the corner. The shovel must have seared him like a branding iron.

Like a Torquemadan executioner, Harvey slowly approached the hunched man, on whom the flashlight threw shadows of the cross and spade. He cocked the shovel like an ax and started to edge close enough to sever Morgan's neck. The cowering man whined like a gutted dog, and his spider shape folded self-protectively in the corner beside a chair. As Harvey stepped closer, Morgan tried to work his way under his wife's dresser. But there was no room for his rangy frame.

Harvey tensed for the downswing.

And again Felice betrayed him. "No, no," she cried. He looked back at her. Her arms were outstretched, imploring him not to chop. In that moment, Morgan slithered from the corner and grabbed a straight-backed chair. Holding it out to block the sight of Harvey's weapons, he shut his eyes and swung wildly. The blow caught Harvey on the arm, batting him to the floor with such force that the spade skittered across the room and the thin chain broke, sending the cross flying.

Harvey, his flashlight still in his hand, saw the spade and leaped for it, but Morgan hurled the chair at him, catching him in the solar plexus. With a triumphant snarl, the renewed Morgan leaped at his disarmed enemy, who clawed at his pocket for the Celtic cross. Failing to get it free in time, Harvey rolled under the bed and out the other side. Morgan vaulted over his wife, but Harvey rolled back, in a deadly game of tag.

Felice hysterically tried at one point to jump from the bed, and Morgan, lest he hurt her, hesitated, giving time to Harvey to pull out the priest's large cross. Armed again, he flashed the light on the cross. Morgan covered his eyes, and Harvey, equally revived, used the bed as a trampoline to leap onto his back, scraping the cross against his face. Crazed by pain, Morgan launched himself toward the window. But Harvey scooped up the shovel, and blocked him.

With Morgan stymied, Harvey brought the shovel down on his head. The tall man staggered, lolling semi-conscious against the shattered casement panes. Again and again, with short, fierce blows, Harvey beat him. Finally, like a Samson haircut, the shovel did its job and Morgan's amazing strength was sapped.

Harvey raised the shovel blade, certain that this time he could first slash and then behead the vanquished man. Morgan groggily raised his hand to cover his face so he need not see the blow fall, then, in an almost unimaginable gesture, drew down his collar so Harvey could strike clean. All the man's virulence had turned to defeat. Harvey could not strike.

Instead, he dropped the shovel, snatched his handcuffs from his belt and expertly locked the slack wrist to the heavy center bar of the casement frame. Shocked, Morgan drew his hand from his face. He saw his foe had dropped the shovel. Almost instantly, his malice returned.

Roaring outrage, he strained his cuffed wrist against the casement. The upright bent. But it did not pull loose. As Harvey paused in wonder, Morgan kicked. His long leg sent Harvey cartwheeling violently over the chair and into the far corner of the room, where he clutched his right femur in anguish.

"Felice," he called through gritted teeth, "For God's sake, my leg's broken. Get help." The phone lay on the floor within kicking range of Morgan. "Use the kitchen phone. Please!"

The demon stopped straining against the handcuffs, and stared at his wife. "Felice," he commanded, out of breath himself. "The hacksaw, above the workbench. Hurry!"

Shuddering like a wind-blown reed, she looked first at her husband locked to the casement frame, then at the wounded younger man clutching his leg, imploring her with silent eyes to save them. As if shaking off a suffocating nightmare, she modestly pulled her robe around her. She turned on the light, and supporting herself by the bed table, then the side of the bed, she walked like a patient with a wasting disease toward the living room and kitchen. Harvey, suffering as he was, watched her with admiration while Morgan screamed threats and curses at her. She had, Harvey understood, made a decision to live.

But Felice was hardly out of sight before she screamed and retreated slowly into the bedroom. Harvey gasped. What had frightened her? She backed past Morgan, who was also staring at the doorway and whose howls went suddenly silent.

And then Harvey, too, saw. The scene would never leave his mind: he himself braced against the wall to ease his pain; Felice in the classic pose of fearful female defense, one hand over her groin, the other over her breast; Morgan, one handcuffed arm tensed in its effort to break free, the other tipped by talons held out entreatingly toward his wife; and the fourth figure, in malign profile, hands before him formed into dark-nailed claws, mouth open revealing incredibly lengthened canines, his nose a raptorial beak, brown-orange eyes blazing.

Taller even than Morgan, dressed in a worn antique greatcoat despite the autumn heat, limp black hair like Medusa snakes on his shoulders, the master vampire gazed lustfully into the eyes of the frail woman.

Then motion returned to this *tableau vivant*. Felice stepped backward, uncertain as a beginner at a tango lesson. The ancient wraith, emanating the reek of centuries in many tombs, moved toward her in this slow-motion apache dance. Morgan, eyes blazing almost as fierily as his master's with something Harvey could not even imagine, tugged to free himself like a thirst-crazed pit bull on a short chain.

Harvey's leg throbbed. Only shock trauma kept him from fainting. His weapons were gone. He was without means to save his love. The parchment-faced ancient, his fangs drooling sputum, walked in grisly dignity toward her. His arms were half-raised, the claws curved, yet almost relaxed. The eyes of the timeless horror and the young woman did not leave each other as they accomplished their slow ballet. Both dancers ignored the grunts of Morgan, an unearthly mix of ferocity and beseeching, and the dumbstruck presence of Harvey.

The back of Felice's legs touched the bed. She let a hand down, reclined. The repulsive apparition put one hand gently on her shoulder. She made no effort to remove it. He reached out caressingly to touch her chin, and turned it this way and that, surveying the white throat, blemished by its unsightly puckerings. Slowly, his towering shoulders leaned over hers, his crimson lips parting as he moved them to her thin pale ones.

Unbelievingly, Harvey saw her own lips, like iron filings controlled by a sorcerer's magnet, open to the evil old man's, awaiting his foul kiss. "No! No! Felice," he called.

His appeal was drowned by a howl from Morgan. Harvey's jaw dropped. Morgan, ranting incoherently, strained against the cuffs, stooped, and picked up the shovel. He screeched with pain as he touched it, dropped it, then as a man might will himself to pick up a hot poker no matter what the torment, grabbed it up.

Harvey pushed back against the wall in disbelief as he saw Morgan slash at his wrist with the sexton's shovel. As he hacked, Morgan's raves were primordial. "Oh, Jesus," Harvey breathed as the spade guillotined through the wrist, leaving the severed hand curving and twitching within its circlet of steel. The stump flailed uncontrollably, gushing a fountain of deep brown blood, splattering the walls and slicking the floor.

But the grim lover at the bed was unheeding. His

purple lips were glued to Felice's in what he intended to be her final kiss. Morgan, the shovel raised above his head, the handless right arm gyrating and still spewing the air with blood, tensed as if his whole body were a long bow. De profundis, he uttered one last human sound, half love shriek, half prayer. "Felice!" he cried. "My darling! Oh, my God!"

The spade's edge came down on the master vampire's corded neck muscles even as Felice summoned her last strength and pushed the fiendish Dracula free of her lips. Harvey saw the ageless bloodsucker's atrocious face turn back one time, a face blasted with astonishment and resentment at this affront from an adversary whom he had killed and thus created.

Then, the shovel descended again and the long ancient body crumpled beside the bed. Harvey exerted all his strength and crept on his back toward the door, hoping to make it to the kitchen telephone. He well knew that Morgan might turn next on him. As he wormed away, the blade rose and fell in rhythm with the vampire's appalling shrieks. The screams diminished to croaks as Morgan struck and finally sliced through.

Harvey reached the door just as the severed head shot free of the great skinful of infamy in a tangle of bloody hair. It bounced with soft thuds under the bed. At the same time, the body of the felled creature seemed to collapse within its greatcoat and old-fashioned trousers.

Harvey, his eyes popping, saw the head roll from beneath the other side of the bed, no longer a gory mass of veins, long tangled hair, and ragged flesh, but a dry and hairless skull. Inside his garments, too, the monster was becoming a skeleton. The bony matter and the time-worn fabrics rapidly turned to the finest dust, finally disappearing altogether.

Morgan stood like an oak, the bloody shovel raised for a last stroke that was no longer necessary. For seconds, he remained so. Then the shovel dropped from his hand to the floor with a clatter. The lieutenant's contorted face still stared at his wife on the bed. And she, eyes marbled with terror, looked back at him, transfixed.

Morgan's arms faltered. He seemed to relax, to swoon. His tall body stepped backwards one step, then staggered forward, falling across the bed, his left hand reaching one terminal time toward Felice. She touched it, tried to take it in hers, but he slid to the floor, sprawling on his back.

Harvey looked at Morgan. Already the terrible mien of blood gluttony and hatred was evaporating from the features. Before Harvey's eyes, the face progressed from the hideous to the sardonic sneer he had known so well at headquarters, then to a stern manliness, a questioning gaze, and finally to a kind of gentleness, an expression, at last, of peace.

As Morgan fell, a few of his old playing cards had scattered from his breast pocket. Harvey looked at his dead partner, wishing they were in that other world again where he might have offered to pick up the cards and where they could discuss some new intriguing case.

Felice had fainted, and slept like an unbloomed rose. No one but Harvey, marveling, saw how the cratered hills on her throat were healing over to smooth skin. With every inch a torture, he wriggled to the telephone on the floor.

Burstan arrived with the first of the police and the ambulance crew. After he had seen Harvey carried out he looked down at the uncharacteristically serene face of his dead assistant. By his head someone had neatly placed his black hat. But the cards lay scattered. The Homicide captain closed Morgan's dark, quiet eyes and, leaning down with a grunt of discomfort, spread the cards until he found the one he was looking for. Then he picked it up, the Jack of Spades, and dropped it face up in Morgan's fallen hat.

*   *   *

A few days after the deaths of Morgan and the monster, a long line of police cars assembled outside the tranquil little funeral home in Wheaton. The bubble-tops turned, but only slowly, and the sirens were silent. To be sure Morgan—or rather a macabre semblance of him—had murdered, assaulted, and maimed. But that Morgan had been in the spell of a supernatural disease whose origins were still the subject of debate. And for a change the bleeding hearts had applied their sociological goo to rationalize the crimes of a cop instead of those of a criminal.

The freshly polished motorcycles and police cars came from Washington and the neighboring jurisdictions: Metropolitan, Park, Alexandria, Montgomery, Prince Georges, the Maryland and Virginia state police, Baltimore, many others. The cavalcade crept through the city toward Arlington and the National Cemetery—for as a young man Morgan had been a Marine. The motorcycle men, boots shining more resplendently than for any Presidential Inaugural, moved along slowly, their iron steeds coughing, the only sound in the winding parade.

The police were lonely, often hated, more than a little paranoid, and only at a policeman's funeral could they mutely tell the citizenry, "This is what policing is all about. This is the end station of the lousy pay, the wretched hours, the dangerous arrests in back alleys, the vomit of drunks in the cell blocks."

The extended line of patrol cars, sky blue, dark blue, white, spoke as nothing else could of that fraternity who risk death every day in the line of duty, and who bury their own. The social workers, the ACLU lawyers, the teenage cop-hasslers did not take risks in the jungle streets in the name of laws. We may, the threading police cars seemed to say, sometimes be corrupt, cruel, lazy, ignorant, foolish, but we are even more often brave. We are what lies between you and the anarchies of rape, murder, robbery, looting, and indiscriminate assault.

The ceremonial parade was a kind of shriving. The police had lifted the threat of the Vampire of the Mall. And for their part, the media and the citizenry applauded them even as the city rationalized the unsolved mysteries. The talk of a master monster who created other blood drinkers was passed off as the delusion of the ailing Felice and the injured Harvey. The differences in footprints might simply have been a mistake by Morgan in identifying the impressions by the Reflecting Pool, and by Harvey in *thinking* the man on the woman's bike had big feet.

Even Morgan's miraculous escape from bullets was written off as shots fired in haste, or of Morgan being garbed in a Kevlar super-vest that he had discarded before his final stand. Thus did rationalization close around the episodes, for man lives uneasily with the inexplicable except when it is called God.

The burial service by the police chaplain was brief. Morgan had been as skeptical of spiritual powers as he was defiant toward temporal ones. Harvey stood in the bright sunlight of early fall on crutches not far from Felice, who was in black and veiled, her parents in from Ohio on either side.

The service done, she went to the open grave, stooped to pick up a bit of dirt, and dropped it onto the coffin. From her breast, she plucked a white rose she had picked from her garden, and dropped it too. As she passed Harvey, he murmured a greeting, and she looked up at him with a glance of gratefulness and promises before returning to her mother and father.

When the other mourners had also dropped in handfuls of dirt and departed, Bailey Burstan, who had given a strong hand to Harvey as they crossed the grass, helped him move toward the grave. The two detectives, one soon to be an inspector, the other soon to be a sergeant, stared down at the coffin.

"You're sticking to that crazy stuff about the guy

turning to dust?" asked Burstan.

"Yeah," said Harvey testily, "I saw what I saw."

"Well, I think the other guy is still out there. You know the way these serial types flare up and die down, go into remission. Maybe he'll hit again. I'm still carrying the first cases as open. I've been explaining your report to the chief as a delusion brought on by your injuries," Burstan said.

"I know," said Harvey with a chill that reminded Burstan of the way Morgan often made him feel: somehow in the wrong. The captain shook his head and returned his hand to Harvey's arm to help him to their waiting car.

Atop the coffin, Felice's rose still peeked from the handfuls of dirt. The grave digger, patient until now, moved in to close the hole. Harvey lifted from his neck the silver cross which he had retrieved from Felice's floor. He carefully dropped it into the grave. It struck with a minute thud. Shortly, the shovels of dirt would cover it, the white rose, and the coffin.

THE
ALCHEMIST

For Phyllis

The Devil works at me. The Devil does not tire.
He floats about me like the air, impalpable.
I gulp him down. I feel him set my lungs afire
And fill me with desires, endless and culpable....
                    —Baudelaire (L.H.W. *translation)*

CHAPTER

1

Athanor

The figures of Hera, Demeter, Zeus (as bull), Ares, and two later divinities fabricated during the Roosevelt years —National Defense and National Resources—stared stern and self-important from the federal pediment.

Bald and white, they relieved the red tile plateaus of the surrounding governmental roofs. Behind and above was the soft, diluted blue of Washington's spring sky. The red, white and blue!

Before walking into the Labor Department, I looked up again. At head-top, shoulder, breast, and hip the deities sprouted insulators for depigeoning wires. Thus debased, how could such gods be taken seriously?

And yet it *was* serious. The two police guards at the door, tear gas mask cases and canisters at their belts, attested to the new racial uneasiness in the federal city, the unruly times.

I walked into my office and past the elderly secretary whom I shared. In her denim-blue eyes, I saw approval of my fresh seersucker—of me. If only I could see myself as she did—she had once said I looked like a thirtyish Henry Fonda.

My desk was stacked with material from the National Labor Relations Board, the *Wall Street Journal*, the *AFL-CIO News*, the *Washington Law Reporter*, federal and state appellate courts, law journals—the raw effluvia from the fields of labor. I fell to it like a machete man.

7

My job was to make a daily labor legal summary. *Labor Legal Notes*, as it was called, gave the Department, the unions, the U.S. Chamber of Commerce, the National Association of Manufacturers—and numerous others as dull—an accurate thumbnail of labor news to read after lunch.

Without exhilarating me, *Labor Legal Notes* satisfied. Custom had staled its infinite variety, but it did combine the disciplines of law and literature. A news reporter could not grasp legalities fast enough, and most lawyers could not get the thing into two pages or make it comprehensible for busy, dense officials.

I had been at Labor eight years. I knew my place. My job was a comfortable dead end. My salary allowed me a small, unfashionable house in Glover Park, off Georgetown, suits at Swartz's that looked as if they cost more than they did, a new Chevy II, and an occasional dinner at Chez François with a date and a bottle of American wine. It also provided the $2,000 a year support payments for Evie, my daughter. My former wife, Julia, had married the ecologist who had been her lover. The University of California paid him commensurate with his bionomic skills, some of which Julia had attested to when our marriage went brutally into its final nut-cutting stage. Now the two of them were having my daughter's last name changed to theirs.

Although I was a lawyer, my contact with criminal law was limited to illegal parking on the Mall. We government employees gobbled up the spots reserved for tourists, ignoring the two-hour limit, to park all day.

The Park Police, haphazard like everything else in the federal city, caught me with a five-dollar overtime ticket on an average of once in seven times. Thus it cost me seventy cents a day instead of the three dollars charged by the parking lot near the Labor Department. The crime was small, the element of guilty intent total but manageable, the sense of beating the system gratifying. I called my game with the police "parking roulette."

When Bertie Woeckle, the Department Solicitor, called me to his office with a special tone in his voice, I first feared a mild reprimand for getting so many tickets.

Woeckle was a kind old man, efficient and, by turns, decisive and subservient, virtues that had preserved him through party changes. I was fond of him for the freedom he allowed me and the credit he threw my way when he could. He was shaped like a pyramid, small-headed, with a vest that lengthily covered the incline of his great, gradual belly.

"Well, Martin," he said, government-hearty. I knew the nervousness I had heard on the telephone had nothing to do with tickets. "The Secretary wants me to pull you out of the cubbyhole. A new project."

"*Unk,*" I grunted noncommittally.

"For a short time, only."

"There's the *Notes,*" I said.

"It will only be in the afternoon."

"Um," I said, suspicious. If I asked what it was, he had me.

"Martin, I'll have somebody, a lawyer, one of the young ones, work with you tomorrow on *Notes* so he can weed the material for you. The Secretary wants . . ."

"A new man wouldn't know how," I complained.

"I'm sorry, Martin," he said.

"Well," I sighed, trembling even as I surrendered.

"That's the boy," Woeckle said smiling.

He took a Xerox of a White House memo from his desk and explained the project. Some idiot at the White House had conceived it and I was to rework a prospectus on it by tomorrow afternoon so it could be folded into a Presidential announcement. Cutting away Woeckle's counterfeit optimism, it was a sop, one of many, to ease some of this racial steam building up again in Washington's ghetto.

Unlike Labor's own programs, which were practical, underfinanced and unimaginative, this one was imaginative, unsound and probably had about four million dollars behind it. The thing was called "Jobtime Washington." My own piece of this makeshift package was called "Legal Recruit!" The Secretary had balked at the "!" in the title, but had been overruled by the White House.

Woeckle had recruited (!) me with good reason. The present prospectus, peppy and half-truthed, was implausible. The broken-spirited deserters from journalism who wrote for our interdepartmental section could hardly be counted on for accuracy or taste, much less plausibility, when they were rushed.

As Woeckle explained it, Labor, during the next few

weeks, was to find a dozen ghetto youths who had finished at least eleventh grade before dropping out. We would round up scholarships for them in private high schools of the Sterling School caliber. After high school graduation, our recruits were to begin prelaw courses and, sometime in the future, return to the ghetto as defenders of the poor. This fantasy was to be assisted by Health, Education and Welfare, which would provide the sociologists and shrinks first to interview and then to treat the fortunate dozen. The budget for Recruit alone would surely rise to seven hundred and fifty thousand dollars.

"Why me?" I asked.

"I know you can do the prospectus. You're used to deadlines."

Icicles of dread formed in my stomach. I did not want to hoke up a phony paper on a slum deal that could not work. Woeckle saw my anguish.

"I'm really sorry, Martin," he said.

"Can you get me out once I've written the proposal?"

"I believe so," he equivocated. "The proposal's the main thing." He gave me the address near Eighth and H Streets, Northeast, a section I hardly knew, where the HEW people were.

The two- and three-story slums I drove through were their own evidence of the failure of just such schemes as "Legal Recruit!" The Anti-Poverty Corps, the Neighborhood Youth Councils, the Police Boys Club, "Afro-American Uhuru for Youth," and God knows how many others had been rooted in these streets for years. The citizenry was a little more than cynical.

The HEW bunch in the upstairs office, sitting on the random furniture that General Services Administration had just trucked over, looked at me as if they thought I might produce. After all, I came from an agency unaccustomed to chronic failure.

The HEW leader was a black psychologist. With him was an attractive young white woman, her generous bosom modest beneath a neat, but not chic, collared blouse. She glanced up and then away from me with the quick efficient look of a slightly plump minor hawk. A salt-and-pepper-moustached Negro of about sixty-five who was introduced as Sergeant Babcock, was the other "team member." He was an HEW investigator, a retired city detective.

They all worked in the HEW Welfare Division, the girl as secretary-assistant to Mrs. Anita Tockbridge, who ran the division. This in itself was evidence that the White House had the heat on HEW. Anita Tockbridge, at forty-five or so, was an ex-congresswoman on the rise, rumored for an Assistant Secretaryship in the Labor Department. There was even talk that this liberated and reputedly somewhat merry widow would be made Secretary in the Frances Perkins tradition, and thus my boss.

"Well, this is Labor's show," said the psychologist brightly after we had accomplished the dry, ritual introductions of low-level government employees. It was Labor's show. The White House memo said so.

They waited on me. The thing was certain to fail, I faltered:

"How do we get the kids?"

The ex-detective and the psychologist had traveled this road before. We would check dropout lists at the high schools, winnow the possibles. The sergeant would visit the families, the psychologist would give the kids some preliminary "psychologicals." Labor would then talk to them about the law, pay, courses and—the psychologist suggested with a smile—how long they'd have to work in the ghetto before they could toss over indigency law and open up a big office on U Street.

The white girl—her name was Susan Bieber—took notes efficiently. Within two hours, we had enough thoughts together for me to write my prospectus and had roughed out how much permanent staff would be needed.

"Are you typing that up for Mrs. Tockbridge?" I asked the girl diffidently as we broke up. "Could you get a copy to the rest of us?"

"Sure," she said.

"Could I get a copy tomorrow morning?" I ventured.

"Yes," she said, "I'll get it to you. Give me your building."

Drenched in sweat, I ended the meeting.

At home that night, I ate a turkey TV dinner, sorrowful to the mouth of one whose wife cooked as well as Julia when she was still trying. I braced up the meal with a glass of red wine, then took a second.

At least, I mused, there was the luxury of cheap wine and good books. My ordinary life had never met the demands of my inquisitiveness, not now, not when I was a child, and I had turned to reading.

Before I reached kindergarten, I was computing the ages of kings by subtracting birth dates from death dates in our *Compton's Encyclopedia*.

My passion in the second grade was pressing moths. By the sixth grade, I was taken by the night noises of frogs. Using an old wire recorder, I "bugged" their haunts after nightfall. Hushed at the switch, coated with citronella, I was thrilled almost to tears when I caught on my spool the *"err-gut"* of a bullfrog.

In junior high school, I read and practiced chemistry. By the ninth grade, it was photography. My first camera was a restructured Kraft cheese box. My mother called it a Velveetaflex.

Wrestling and good grades got me a partial scholarship at Lehigh, where I studied prelaw. In law school at Georgetown, I read with despair the briefs of Holmes, the closing arguments of Edward Bennett Williams, the opinions of Brandeis. The successful inspired awe and envy in me, and I turned always to books.

Greek temple construction (I modeled them in soap), Baudelaire translations, passé Italian opera, Nostradamus, Tarot: my tastes grew more obscure. Julia, whom I married while I was at Georgetown, did not share my enthusiasms. The only worthwhile moments for her during my Faust-of-the-duplex endeavors were in Nostradamus; my translation of "La Dame seule . . ." put her stage center at a gathering of her old sorority.

"Alone, the Lady remains to reign," I had written.

"Her spouse, unique, first dead on honor's field.

"Seven years she weeps in sorrowed pain,

"Then, by long rule of joy, her woes are healed."

By stretching Jackie Kennedy's sorrow a year or two into her marriage with Onassis, the quatrain fit very nicely. I did not tell Julia that Catherine de Medici fulfilled the prophecy even more neatly.

Julia left me somewhere between Tarot and metoposcopy. Unpremeditatively, I had taken up the occult and now it was in full fad in Washington. College students, the newspapers told me, were holding Black Masses. Hooflike "Devil's Footprints" pendants and goat's-eye rings were sold in drugstores. The staid *Star-News* picked up a column on numerology and a comic strip called "Valley of Evil."

On another level, the occult had become stylish in Washington political society. The present Congress and executive branch were big on astrology, Tarot, and seances. When I thought of it, I supposed that men in power needed escapes from reality. And what was more of an escape than spending leisure time at updated Halloween costume parties and in efforts to communicate with the ghost of Senator Robert A. Taft. There were plenty of antecedents: Vice President Henry Wallace with his soothsayer; Presidents Roosevelt and Kennedy, who had chatted with seers.

The fad produced the predictable jokes at Labor about a supposed coven of homosexuals at the State Department. And Representative Budney Bowers (R-Calif.) the House's only admitted Birch Society member, had taken up three pages of the *Congressional Record* to denounce the "degeneracy" of the occult in Washington.

Bowers' attack, of course, helped to legitimatize the vogue among the more liberal members of Congress and of President Vernon MacGregor's tolerant Republican executive branch.

I, touching neither the mass-produced occult enthusiasms of ordinary Washington, nor the sophisticated black magic high jinks of the mighty, dabbled along.

I had fastened obscure learning to myself as the carrier snail of Borneo uses his body cements to glue on layer after layer of pebbles and rock chips, until even his shell is hidden. At present, my rock chip was alchemy.

Even now, an alchemical furnace was taking form in my basement on the concrete floor. In the furnace, which I had dubbed Athanor, the antique name for such ovens, I planned to putter with formulae of the old *souffleurs* who sought to make the Philosopher's Stone, the substance which, when mixed with base elements, produced gold.

Of course, I did not expect to make gold. My mild compulsions for useless knowledge did not require that. Nevertheless, there was a self-indulgent joy in knowing I was shaping the most definitive alchemical furnace in the United States.

After dinner, third glass of wine in hand, I went to my unfinished cellar to work on Athanor, presently only a circle of Fire-Glaze Outdoor Bar-B-Q Bricks mortared together with No-Crack Fire Cement.

Mixing the mortar, scarring the bricks with my trowel to give the cement bite, I whistled quietly. I set a brick in the cool granular cement. I sensed over the centuries' span how the ancient Alchemists must have loved their furnaces.

Was it so odd? Other men go down to the cellar each night, put on their Southern Railway engineer's cap and work in the miniature yards of HO railroading. My pursuits were more unusual perhaps, but they served a similar purpose. Athanor would pass the time.

But the furnace, my creature, was for me only an imitation of life. Its organic warmths would not soothe the physical ache. I wanted a woman.

I thought of some of the divorced lawyers I knew at Labor. Out on week nights, drinking martinis, feasting at the Jockey Club or Sans Souci with glittery uninhibited women. At work the next day, hungover and self-satisfied.

When my need was too strong (I found masturbation disgusting as only a Lutheran can), I went to a call girl highly touted by one of my Labor colleagues for her loaf-like breasts. She was twenty-three, and wrote rhyming, meterless couplets about "President Jack." She showed me the doggerel, and, maudlin as it was, I was touched by her trust. When I once suggested alternate lines, she was pleased, and refused my money that evening. She gave me the only love I had.

Wed at twenty-six, I had found for a year or two a fine sort of malehood. After that, the very things that led me out of my lonely morass—Julia's strength, her ambition, her passions, her quick temper and sudden recovery into sweetness—became too much for me. She began to use my fears of sexual regression as her weapon. At the last, she mocked me. And what was left of our relations degenerated into loveless consensual rapes or guilty impotency.

Now, except for my patient call girl, I was a sexual unpredictable. When some adventuress tested me, as often as not, my nervousness repelled us both. Gradually, like the snail incrusted with its past, I was receding into a chaste and lonesome shell.

CHAPTER

2

Riot

The alacrity of the young lawyer Woeckle had assigned me made me apprehensive. If my esoterica were so simply mastered, where was my security?

But Woeckle liked my prospectus. The Secretary had it rewritten by his chief PR man into a glowing handout. The local papers gave it three dutiful paragraphs in the body of their overall Jobtime Washington story when it was announced at the White House. All were pleased.

I asked Woeckle if I were finished with Recruit!

"Put this kid on it you sent me for *Notes*," I said.

"Why can't you do Recruit! in the afternoons?" he asked gently. "Could you just get it going?"

"The thing isn't going to get off the ground. It's just public relations," I complained.

I wanted to revert to *Notes*. I wanted a trip to the West Indies, or just my cellar and Athanor's smooth, cool sides. I did not want anxieties from the office following me into my ordered world.

"The planning funds are committed. You know that," said Woeckle.

"My God, Bert."

"Just another week or two, until it's off the ground."

"It isn't going to get off the ground," I sighed again.

Nevertheless, it was easier not to argue. I reported there each afternoon. We had an almost illiterate Negro secretary. The ex-detective had a late-afternoon drinking problem. The days were steaming for April, the motionless air mephitic. Most of the kids who stayed to talk with the psychologist did so, I felt, because of our air-conditioning.

Susan Bieber came in for a short time each day to coach the secretary and retype her letters. To my surprise, we began to recruit some possibles, not among the youths but among the girls.

The idea of an unmarried seventeen-year-old mother being a good prospect for seven more years of study seemed foolish on the face of it. But there was this occasional pattern: a girl making good grades got pregnant and dropped out of school; she turned the baby over to a grandmother or a children's home; she wanted money and respectability. The girls were less hostile than the males, more willing. I saw a minuscule chance of saving the crack-brained scheme.

To make ghetto Portias out of the seventeen-year-olds we needed their commitments to individual therapy and to investing the money we gave them on decent clothes and not on cocky boyfriends. They would also have to leave home for the metaplasia of some snotty private school for girls.

"I'd like to have gone to Madeira myself," Susan said to me one day as I worked on our initial report.

"Where'd you go?" I welcomed any interested word from a woman.

"High school, in Myerstown, Pennsylvania, then Penn State."

"Myerstown, that's in the Pennsylvania Dutch country," I recalled.

"Yes."

"I went to Lehigh."

"That's mainly engineering."

"I took prelaw. I have a knack for the wrong thing at the wrong place." This seemed to edge us toward the personal. I back-pedaled.

"Look. If I rough this memo out, could you type it up now?"

"Yes," she said, glad, I thought, to escape further confidences.

"Of twenty male subjects interviewed," I began to dictate, "antisocial episodes sufficient to warrant one or more police reports or juvenile court allegation sheets occurred among seventeen . . ."

Christ! I thought, how are we going to get twelve possibles, boys or girls?

Susan put her hand in her smooth-brushed brown hair and took down the dictation, moving her lips as the pencil raced and darted. Everything she did, she did well, without fuss.

That evening, for the first time, I watched her as she walked to where her old Dodge was parked. Her shoulders were straight, her hips a little heavy, but there was a tapering at the waist. Despite the flared cotton of her skirt, I could discern the gentle rolling of callipygian flesh beneath. Her legs, rounded at calf, thinned at the ankles. With her birdlike good looks—a pretty, beakish nose—I would have found her attractive, but something about her said: "spoken for." Besides, I consoled myself for my lack of daring, she ought to lose ten pounds, and be a little less matter-of-fact.

For days the unusual heat continued, close and windless, with its odor of strewn garbage and casual plumbing. The windows of two white-owned stores were broken, even though they were latticed with steel bars. Perhaps because we were passing out money rather than collecting it, our building was left alone.

Susan frequently worked late to keep us caught up. There were the forms for children, letters to parents, records to schools, filing of reports, test results. She also conducted some of the preliminary interviews with the girls. The psychologist was a crackerjack tester, but a stickler for the five o'clock deadline. Susan and I worked on.

The oversized air-conditioner was unadjustable, the temperature arctic. I switched it off one evening. Its rumble fell away to a sigh and a drip, and I heard Susan's soft, careful voice from the interview alcove and the quiet answers of a Negro girl.

"Your math grades are just fine except for the eighth grade. Can you remember, Trudence, what happened there? I know it's going back . . ."

"Yes, ma'am. The teacher, she . . ."

I leaned back in the chair. The work exhausted me. When I was in bed, nowadays, my mind nervously fiddled with it, spurning sleep. I closed my eyes now and leaned back. Susan's no-nonsense voice probed on.

"Now you must pardon me for this next question, Trudence . . ."

Wearied, my mind slipped toward dozing . . .

"Mi perdona l'ardimento . . ." I half dreamed of Julia singing along with me to the recording. She had liked the aria.

Susan was purring behind the partition. I could hear her disappointment:

"That gets us to this March. Now, you say your mother needed you around the house. But here, in April, Juvenile Court says . . ."

"Yes, ma'am." A dull voice caught in a lie.

Outside, the barks of dogs, the calls of children, the raucous shouts of older residents were all familiar. Now I noticed a different cadence.

I went to the window. The sun was blocked out by the three-story row houses, but it was still light. Up the street, near the intersection, a noisy group was in front of Luchard's Liquors.

I heard glass shatter. The metal gave with a squeal as the vandals pulled the grate from the store window. This was serious. I stumbled over a wastebasket in my haste to get to Susan's alcove, knocked on the partition wall, and stuck my head in. Her greenish eyes stared up in surprise. The Negro girl's mouth pouted with apprehension.

"I think you'd better put it over for tomorrow," I burst out. "There's trouble outside."

"Trudence, you run home," Susan said. The girl got up. I looked out the window. The youths were still at the store. The Negro girl pattered down the stairs.

"Come on!" I said to Susan, pushing papers into my briefcase. She was putting her ballpoint and note pad in a large handbag.

"What is it?" she asked.

"You'll see!"

She started down the stairs. I clattered behind. The front door had a glass panel, and I restrained her with a hand on her arm so I could peer up the street. Both our cars were parked across the way.

The gang at the corner almost filled the intersection. I started to open the door for her when I heard the siren

and saw some of the teen-agers running down the street
in our direction.

I heard through the crack in the door cries of "Block
'em! Block 'em!" and saw a half-dozen teen-agers rushing
along the parked cars trying doors. The door of a pickup
truck opened and in a moment they had rolled it to the
intersection. My Chevy II was just behind.

Another group swarmed my car. One of them slammed
the front door window with a brick to get at the inside
door lock. My sense of property exploded.

"Goddamn," I screamed. I swung open the street door.

"No," Susan shouted, grabbing my coat. I wheeled on
her to break her grip. "No!" she yelled. "Don't!"

The little bastards were pushing the car. I realized that
if I got to it, I'd never get it away from them. It crept
toward the intersection. More hoodlums were bricking
open the other cars. They shoved out Susan's Dodge.

"Bastards! Bastards!" I screamed from behind the window. Then "Motherfuckers!" I shouted, losing all restraint
as they tipped over my Chevy II. I turned to her for
assent to my wrath. She looked at me with surprise.

"I'm sorry," I said, calmed by her shock. Angry as I
was, it struck me that my insurance would cover it.

The police car was at the intersection. I could see its
rotating red bubbletop beyond the barricade of cars. If
the sons of bitches would just disperse long enough for
us to get to the police. The mob screamed obscenities, all
ending with "Pig."

I saw the red bubbletop backing up. We were being
deserted without so much as a whiff of grapeshot.

I thought with self-pity of my march that long-ago
day down Sixteenth Street with other good, liberal whites
and Negroes to protest the deaths of the little Sunday
school girls in Birmingham. How could other Negroes do
this to *me?* To *my* car?

Susan turned to me, her face flushed.

"How do we get out? My mother expects me."

I wondered if she were worried about being raped.
Until now, it had never struck me that this held-in panic
was one of the big differences between men and women.

"We'll wait here until it blows over. Upstairs."

I turned her, almost decisively. We edged up the stairs
and into the office.

The day was gone over to twilight. I switched out the

light and went to the window. My overturned car was lodged against the pickup. I had loved the damned car, like Athanor, so clean, new, and uncontentious.

The intersection was jammed with automobiles and black people, milling around Luchard's. In front of our building the street light was broken. No one had stoned the lights at the intersection. They shone brightly. It made looting easier.

From the liquor store and the grocery store opposite it, the crowds were pouring out with loot, most of it in bags.

Heads poked from the upper windows in every house on our block, shouting down to the mobs in the street. There was no sign of order, or of police.

"I'd better call my mother," said Susan. We weren't going to get out right away.

"Tell her you're working late."

"It might be better," she said, picking up the telephone. She dialed and got her mother.

"How's Ems?" she asked, as natural as if she were merely rushed a bit at the office. Would that be a daughter? Then where was her husband? She paused, listening.

"I'll call Roger tomorrow," she said somewhat harshly. Would they be separated? Or was she divorced and this "Roger" some unsatisfactory boyfriend?

"Everything okay?" I asked as if I had not heard.

"Yes," she said. Knowing that she had been married, was a mother, knowing that domesticity had rubbed away the sharp, little neurotic edges that attach to sex in unwed women, I felt considerably more relaxed with her.

Outside the window, the mob had grown to hundreds. They pushed more cars out to block broad H Street. The barricade of automobiles stretched onto the sidewalk. A little ball of dread began to form in my stomach.

I picked up the telephone and called the police. I wanted a rescue party. The emergency line was busy. Finally, the police operator came on.

"There's a riot going on out here at Eighth and H!" I shouted.

"Action is being taken. Is this a serious-injury call?"

"No," I began, "but . . ." She hung up. I looked with trepidation at Susan.

"Don't worry," she stuttered. Her brow was scrunched

up with fear. What would she think if she knew her faith was in a man building an alchemical furnace?

"Don't *you* worry!" I countered.

Through the closed window, we could hear loud voices just below. A half-dozen men were passing two bottles around. Across the street a woman leaned from her second-story window and railed at the looters. Their faces turned up to her.

I saw one of the boy's companions wind up. The bottle shattered against her wall. The frightened woman slammed down the window. Another bottle smashed into a pane, splintering it. A crowd had rushed down to see the action. They started throwing beer cans and a few food cans up at the woman's window.

Beneath us, I saw an arm suddenly point upward. I pushed Susan from the window, tumbling us both to the floor as a bottle burst glass into the room.

"You all right? You all right?" I demanded. A can hurtled through the shards still in the frame and struck our wall inside.

The can rolled on the floor. I snatched it up, feeling it round, not serrated like a grenade would be. In the semidark I could see it was Campbell's Cream of Tomato.

"Provisions," I said. The little joke made me feel rather dauntless for a moment.

"They won't set this place àfire?" she said, halfway between question and assertion. I saw she was really frightened.

"Susan, I truly think we're better off here," I said. "They're drunk and wild and I just don't want to take a chance on our white faces."

"The police?" she said, still with an edge of hysteria in her voice. We were lying chest down on the floor near, but not touching, each other. I took her arm and gave it a shake.

"Now, come on. My guess is they're getting together enough police, or calling National Guardsmen to move in here and clear out everybody with one push. Show of force. They wouldn't make a two-bit effort that would just encourage this mess if it failed." I paused. She said nothing.

I crept up to the window, Stone Age man looking out the cave entrance to assure his mate that the mammoths and sabertooths couldn't get in. The group below us was running to the corner. I saw why. Near the store were men with jerry cans.

"They're going to burn the store," I told Susan.

I could hear her rustling in the darkened room behind me as she crept to join me at the window.

"Wait." I crawled toward her, using my forearm, with its shirt and coat protection, to brush the glass from her path. I reached out to her and touched her hand by mistake. It felt warm and tidy.

"Now crawl over here." At the window she knelt beside me to peer out, making a little "oh" noise of consternation as she saw the mob. I, too, was afraid now.

We heard the shrill shout of a rioter.

"Anybody in there? Hey?" he called into the liquor store. The whole boisterous gathering—hundreds of them —went silent for a moment awaiting an answer. There was none.

The two men with jerry cans went to the door and sloshed in gasoline, then one splashed it into the empty sockets of the store window. The match was applied on the side of the store away from us. In a great whooshing gulp the flames swallowed up the show windows and door and turned the whole street into a scene of Boschian shadow and fire. They made of Susan's pleasant features a Satanic mask. Her imagination had already hooked into the same horrible thoughts as mine. If they did that to our building, it would only take seconds . . .

"Should we call the police again?" she asked. I scuttled to the desk and picked up the receiver. Dead. No dial tone. The lines had been destroyed at the corner, no doubt.

"I can't even get a telephone repairman," I said, crawling back.

"Thank God I got my mother," she said.

"Ems is your daughter?" I asked. "I couldn't help hearing."

"Yes, Mary Martha. We call her Ems, for the two M's." She paused. "My husband is dead."

"I'm sorry," I said. I had no time to announce my own status.

On the carbonic night air, I heard the sound of sirens. No fire engines would be up here without a police escort. But how would they breach the barricade? In a moment, the fire trucks' lights swept at the buildings. The rioters on our side of the barricade crouched in close to the shadows. I could hear the police bullhorns clearly.

"Get back into your home! Get back into your home!"

Men clambered over the barricade of cars. Apparently what police were present had guns, and no one wanted to be on their side of the ramparts.

The liquor store flames were lower, flickering orange on the finishes of the cars. The bullhorn roared on ". . . to your home!" I heard what, for one moment, I thought was merely static or, the second moment, firecrackers. There, crouching behind the cars, I saw a man with his hand pointed out. The sound was a small-caliber pistol.

Snap! Snap! Snap!

"He's shooting at the firemen," I whispered. Susan had not even noticed the reports.

"Where?" she cried. I pointed. The single gunman bent over, reloading perhaps. Where the hell were the police?

The bullhorn was ominously silent, but not the sirens. Impotently they wailed, separated from the fire by the barricades and now by the lone defender of the destructive status quo. I was sure then that only a token police contingent had come with the firemen. Suddenly, the sirens went quiet too, a silence broken shortly by the huge coughing of the firetruck engines. They turned and withdrew. I looked in the darkness at Susan.

"They're giving up, too."

I was both heartsick and afraid now. The first police cars had failed. The firemen with a light escort had been fired on. An army of police or the National Guard would be next. The youngsters screamed congratulations to themselves.

"We beat the pigs! . . . We beat them motherfuckers!"

The riot, itself, was, for all purposes, over. The looters had withdrawn to the stoops of their houses, satisfied with the grocery and liquor stores. The bigger stores around the corner, outside the barricade, had been spared. We could see the dwellers, close together by their wretched tenements, ready to flee inside like rats in holes as soon as the police arrived. They knew the gunfire would bring police. I felt an uncharacteristic strength in having a woman so near, so dependent on me.

"Two of them down there now, crazies thinking they're going to shoot it out with the cops," I whispered. "My God, there's a third one!" We watched a half-dozen more join the men behind the barricade. These weren't going to run. Far away, there was the call of the sirens again.

"Get away from the window. Lie on the floor in the back of the room," I ordered her soberly. I gave her a soft shove. She took my hand from her shoulder. "Go on, Susan," I repeated.

She pondered her responsibility.

"I think I'll scrunch down here a little more and watch," she said.

The streets were empty now except for the crouching men with guns. The sirens were louder. Suddenly, I saw one of the men with a long weapon wheel and point it, I thought, toward us. I pushed Susan to the floor. She grunted sharply in surprise. There was an explosion. I threw my arm over her and we clung together on the cool linoleum.

"You all right?" I asked.

"Yes," she said, freeing herself.

I crept to the window and stole a quick glance at the street. The only light now was from the dying flames of the liquor store.

"He was only shooting out the last streetlamp," I assured her.

The street's residents had tumbled into their houses. My fear now was that some of them would break into our offices looking for a haven.

"Stay low," I said. She inched toward me, brushing the glass out of the way as she came. We peeked out the window, a comfortable couple settling down to a good TV thriller: except our actions were threaded with hysteria. The police were now just on the other side of the barricade.

The humid night air was motionless. Then a bullhorn cut through:

"This area is a curfew area. This area is a curfew area. All persons found on the street will be subject to arrest."

The magnified electronic sound kept coming.

". . . curfew area . . . subject to arrest."

They had been so long coming and now it seemed as if they were moving according to some formal program:

9 P.M.—Bullhorn announcement of curfew. Captain Mouth.

9:15—Loading of shotguns. Inspector Blast and the
Cordites.

9:20—The Intersecction March. The Gun Ensemble
accompanied by Bullhorn (Mouth).

Nevertheless, my sympathies were with the police. I
heard again the *snap! snap!* of the little pistol.

In answer, the whole night erupted in sound and gun-
flashes, the whumping bangs of shotguns and sharper
cracks of police revolvers. It was unbelievable, the thunder
that greeted the small rapping of the pistol.

Susan and I cowered below the window, fearing rico-
chets. After that first enormous outpouring of fire there
was a hiatus. I bobbed up to get a look at the defenders.
They were pressed in close, beside the wheels.

In the pause, I heard scattered police fire from across
the intersection. The sides of the three-story buildings
were floodlighted. Methodically, the police were blasting
out the upstairs windows with shotguns. Snipers were
there, I assumed. From one of the windows an astonishing
gush of orange flame spilled out, splashing a bandanna of
brilliant light across the face of the building before the
fiery stream hit the street and blazed up like a bonfire. A
Molotov cocktail! The police blasted at the brick building
from which the Molotov cocktail had dribbled.

The gunmen below me waited behind their metal bul-
wark—General Motors' finest hour. They had survived the
first wave of police fighting and hoped, I assumed, for a
clean shot when the officers breached the barricade. The
idea of bushwhacking shocked me. But I did not dare
shout a warning to the police.

Suddenly one of the men behind the barricade fired his
shotgun. The flash of his weapon flared on the smoky
night as we fell to the floor.

The police responded again with a tidal wave of gunfire. Another of our windows shattered. A piece of the
glass hit my back but did not cut me. Finally, it ceased.
New *snaps*, like those of the pistol, sounded, but less se-
quentially and with no response. As still as the night air
was, I smelled it, a chlorinous smell like a public swimming pool. The tear gas sliced the funky oil and gunsmoke
air like a knife through soft Limburger. Behind the barricade, a man lay sprawled spread-eagled on his back. Over
him a second man squatted, one knee down, working at
the wounded man's leg.

"They got one," I hissed. Susan scrambled over the broken glass to the window. The intersection on our side was empty except for the motionless gunman and the improvising medic. Then the squatting man sprang semierect and ran toward us, not looking back.

"He's gone, he's . . ." I interrupted my words. "Oh, shit!" The man, now joined by another was crouching in our entranceway. I could see the arm of one of them cocked with a pistol in the fist.

They were crazy! Deserted by their riotous constituency, rejected by the residents, these two still planned a last-ditch attack. It was unbearable, the fanatical, stiff-necked-ness of the early Christian martyrs: uncivilized, despicable to rational men, and fit only for lion food.

I was furious. They were endangering *my* life. I looked around the office for something to hurl at them. I was panicked by the thought of indiscriminate police bullets and perhaps even grenades bursting through our windows should the two men fire from their hiding place. The two snipers were as still as the door's woodwork. Only we could see them.

"Susan," I said, my heart beating with apprehension. "Get in the closet. Scrunch down! Get!"

"What? . . ." she started. I pushed her roughly, almost making her fall from her knees.

"Do as I say," I snapped angrily. "Move!" I gave her a hard shove. She scrambled to her feet and ran to the closet in the back of the room. I shouted out the window with all my voice:

"SNIPERS!" Then I threw myself to the floor, not knowing whether the *snap!* I heard was directed at me—the tocsin—or the police. The police gunfire erupted again. The crashing and smashing had me whimpering with fear. I pressed against the wall of the room and prayed.

Plaster popped from the laths as ricocheting pellets entered the window. I coughed and gasped. Was Susan safe? I did not budge. The intensity of the firing dropped, then sprang up again. The room was raining plaster now. Obviously the police were shooting out every second- and third-story window on the block. I prayed on to the old-time Lutheran God whom I had ignored so long. "Lord, let me out of this mess and I'll never be bad again." But all I could think to promise was not to screw the call girl again.

At last the shooting stopped. I rushed to the closet and found Susan against the wall, crying with terror, but safe. I ran back to the window to see what was going on. The police were crouched in doorways, looking apprehensively at the windows.

In that silence, I heard it. Downstairs, someone was trying our door. If I shouted, they might break in, rush up the stairs and kill us both. I had to act, fearful as I was. My right hand was shaking with fright.

"Stay here. Stay here no matter what!" I hissed at Susan.

Bent over, I rushed to the stairway. From the top I heard a crash as a heavy body sprung the door's lock. The door smashed inward against the hallway wall. Without thinking, I rattled down the stairs, my eyes tearing from the heavy gas.

A shot sounded, but it was too late for me to stop. I could see the black face in the near-dark looking up from where he hugged the wall. At his feet, across the door's threshold, was the crumpled figure of his companion.

He had shot at me! This was my office. He was shooting at me in my office after ruining my car! Almost on him, I stumbled and fell down the last four steps. *Bam!* The smell, like caps, only stronger, sharper, assailed me. My fall had saved me. I pushed off from a step like a sprinter from his toehold in the rack and bulled into the man.

He was lighter than my 170 pounds, lighter than I thought. He fell backward, cursing me with a sob.

The man hit me a glancing blow on the head with the pistol. I grabbed the gun with both hands, burning them. His finger gave under my wrench, and popped free from its tendons and musculature. He shrieked.

With his other hand he raked my face, seeking my eyes. I ducked them to safety and reared up to butt his face with my aching head. We were gasping for breath, wheezing curses. I knew now he was no more than a boy, but I had no pity, only hate. Even then I may have thought, "Not because he is a black, but because he is poor," but what I said was, "Dirty nigger!"

We were close, caroming off walls of the narrow building, grabbing for eyes, knees working wildly to find the other's testicles. He got my lower arm in his teeth through the thin jacket and I howled in pain feeling my flesh crushed to the bone, then I blindly dashed his head backward into the hall radiator, stunning him.

I broke clear as he fell and kicked with all my force at his side when he tried to roll away. With my whole weight behind the kick, my foot caught the floor and my ankle electrified with agony. Even as I tumbled down in anguish, I struck him with my other heel in the flat of his temple.

Sick from the pain that throbbed up the bones of my leg, I rolled weeping to the floor. Beside me, groggy, my opponent flopped like a fish out of water. I saw his hand thrust awkwardly toward the gun on the floor.

I came to my good knee, grabbed his head and bashed it once on the floor. It thudded him into unconsciousness, leaving me remorseful with guilt and nauseated with pain.

"Help!" I screamed. "Police!" The youth's companion lay face up near the door. He was older, an outthrust beard bristling from his chin. In the silence, I heard Susan's footsteps on the floor above and then heard her shouting my name.

"Get back!" I growled up at her. I crawled to the doorway. "Help! Police!" I called. My eyes wept from the gas. My ears were droning with high-pitched buzzing. I knew I was going to faint.

"Come out! Hands up!" I heard the bullhorn. I wanted to vomit, I was so afraid they would shoot.

"Don't shoot me. I'm white!" I cried shamelessly.

"Come out! Hands up!"

I went up on one foot, unable to put even a touch of weight on the other. Hands high, I hopped over the sill and onto the stoop. A stream of light hit my face and I leaned faintly against the wall. I could hear the harsh voices. "He's white. He's hurt."

"Any coons back there?" someone shouted at me.

"Only wounded," I said loudly as I could. I felt the rough hands of a cop grab my arms while another one patted me down for weapons. I recoiled. The light was even stronger in my face now.

"Nothing on him," said the policeman.

"That damned light," I panted. "My ankle's broken. There's a white woman up there." Things had gotten to basics, them and us.

Still semiblinded, I saw two helmeted men stride purposefully from the shadows. Rescuing a white woman was a policeman's cup of Sunday tea. My ankle throbbed with the torture of standing and I toppled myself to the stoop even as the two big policemen stepped into the doorway.

Simultaneously, I saw the first cop pitch backward and heard the sound of the pistol shot. The other cop fired, and the stench of powder flooded me again. I flopped from the stoop onto the sidewalk, face down in the dirt as the shotguns roared over my head.

This is it, this is it, I sobbed.

The volleys stopped and my ears rang. I looked up and saw a policeman over his fallen colleague and two others kicking a sagging form off the stoop. Through my fogginess I heard Susan's voice, raised an octave in pain, screaming for help.

But death had missed the police too narrowly for them to venture again into that house. Except for the policeman tending his wounded buddy on the sidewalk beside me, the others were in doorways or by the house walls. I crawled up the stoop and into the entranceway. Susan was sobbing.

"Lights! Lights!" I called. In a moment, one of the officers shot his flashlight around the doorjamb. Susan was half fallen upon the stairs, her hands clutching her leg. Dark blood ran between her fingers.

I scrambled up the stairs but my ankle gave way with a spasm of pain. The policeman fixed the light on her now. She had been my charge and I had let her get wounded.

There was blood all over her lower leg, coagulating already in the poor, torn stockings. She was crying silently now.

"Get her down," a young voice said behind me. It was the policeman with a flashlight. He shone it on her leg. "It's not bad, lady, you'll be okay."

He and another policeman carried Susan to the street. "I'm all right," she sniffled now. "I'm all right." But a line of blood followed the path where her feet had dragged. "Could you call my mother?" she said to me as I hopped up to her.

"Yes," I said, wondering how. Guilt flooded me as a policeman peeled off her stocking. There in the white flesh were the two wounds. The upper one was hardly bleeding. The other shot must have caught a small artery and the blood was flowing.

The *whoo-hah* of an ambulance siren sounded.

"Can she go to the hospital with your buddy?" I asked a young cop.

"Yeah," he said. My ankle, where I sat on the curb, began to throb with great beats of pain. Nobody cared about me.

"Can you call one for me?" I said to a sergeant who was overseeing the gentle handling of Susan by other uniformed men. He stared.

"What's the matter with your face?"

I reached up and brought back my hand wet with blood from the fingernail wound. The sight of my own blood weakened what was left of my resolve. I must call Susan's mother, I thought, feeling dizzy.

"Nothing," I said. "It's really my ankle." I lay down on my back.

"How'd you get in there?" demanded the sergeant. How persistent his voice was. It came from a distance now.

I wanted to go on, to explain it all, to exonerate myself from all blame. But my thoughts were no longer forming words.

"I must lie down," I murmured.

CHAPTER

3

Buffi's Party

Athanor. Peace. The rain splashed down heavily from the clogged gutters. It splattered mud up onto the lower part of the panes. I was in a glass-and-mortar tank gradually submerged into a rising brown sea.

My injured head was healing itself, as was the deep rake the Negro boy had given me. The scar would, no doubt, give my average features a somewhat saturnine cast. My ankle might better have been broken. The musculature was wrung and twisted, a swollen violet-and-yellow-ochre heap at my instep. It was picketed by an Erector Set girderage called a Merritt brace.

The papers had mentioned my vanquishing of the gunmen, although far down in just one of the riot stories. Woeckle had told me to take all the time I needed. Susan was recovering. What with the riot and Susan's and my injuries, the project was being put aside for the time being, meaning canceled, I hoped.

My wounding the gunman, who was now something of a folk hero among those whom we had hoped to lure into our program, had made me an ally of the police and thus no longer a useful social worker in the vineyards of Eighth and H Streets, Northeast.

Now sitting before Athanor on a three-legged stool, a cold mint julep, extract type, in my hand, I was content. My venture into action, while evidencing some presence of mind, even courage, had ended in injury. I would soon be back in my Labor Department nook, safe from further sallies into the great world.

True, I had found a certain mild stirring of old lusts with Susan, but the complications of pursuing a widow with a child, a woman living with her mother, did not invite me to leave my accustomed cubbyholes.

Susan, in any case, struck me as the kind who would not dabble and—based on her phone call to her mother—she was already bespoken. Besides, I knew almost nothing about her. Nonetheless, she lingered as an ambiguously romantic aftertaste of the riot.

On my first day out of the hospital, metal brace on ankle, newspaper clip of my heroism in pocket, I journeyed by taxi to Southwest Washington where I spent forty dollars and the afternoon on my call girl. Relieved and guilty, I turned back to tinkering with Athanor.

The circle of bricks was growing. I chipped, slowly but exactly, the three bricks which would surmount the stoking door.

My plans looked like this:

A. was a hearth of firebrick; B. the cylindrical furnace base made of curved Fire Glaze Specials; C. the large inverted iron pot, its bottom laboriously drilled out; D. an aluminum bowl whose rim I curled inward; E. a glass alembic fitted to a hole in the aluminum bowl; F. the isinglass window from an old oven; G. a small furnace door; and H. a stovepipe feeding into my oil furnace chimney pipe to take off the smoke.

To summarize how it functioned, the wood charcoal fire at the bottom heated an open bowl on a rack just inside the isinglass window. The contents of the bowl evaporated, went up through the iron pot, condensed on the aluminum bowl, ran into the curled-up sides of the bowl, and dripped into the glass alembic.

That liquid, refined and mixed, would finally be put into the philosopher's egg—the "aludel"—and I would bake it on the rack behind the isinglass until it was ready to fall apart and there . . . And there would be the saffron granulations, the Philosopher's Stone, the "pelican," in mystical old alchemical codes. It would, in theory, make me a wiser, better man as well as a rich one.

The whole apparatus was inefficient; I could do better with a double boiler and the kitchen oven. Just so, a model clipper ship with its spars and halyards all in place can be bought at Woodward and Lothrop in spiffier shape than it can be made from the keel up. But where would be the challenge?

The adulation of ancient alchemists was warming, but what I longed for, after enjoying my tranquil communion with Athanor down-cellar, was to go upstairs to a cold fried chicken leg or a Swiss cheese and Polish ham sandwich and a wife who would say, "How's it going? When will you be able to fire it up?"

The telephone rang upstairs. I stumped up and answered.

"Mrs. Tockbridge is calling, just a moment please."

That was Susan's boss. The secretary announcing her message to me was not Susan. She would still be in the hospital. I had seen a newspaper photo of Mrs. Tockbridge—a dark-haired, attractive woman. Did she smoke a cigarette in a long holder like Copper Calhoun? Professional women, especially political ones in high places, frightened me.

Click. The phone comes up in the ringed fingers.

"Hello, this is Mrs. Tockbridge. I hope I didn't bother you, making you come to the telephone."

"N . . . no," I stammered.

"I wanted to thank you for protecting Susan."

Her saying it made it seem true. I glowed. France was proud of me. I felt a de Gaulle kiss on each cheek.

"It was Susan who was brave. I'm sorry the project fell through," I lied.

"We'll be back with it." Her voice was deep for a woman's, but there was little warmth. She was making a speech. "I didn't put you together with the editor of *Labor Notes* until today. I read it, well, scan it, daily."

My God. There was that rumor she was coming to Labor. As in many civil servants, panic toward superiors ran just below my skin. What was wrong with *Labor Notes?* She quickly pacified me.

"It's the one thing there that's broad enough to tell a person what's going on in *all* of Labor."

"Notes is maybe a bit too general," I said. "But thank you."

That might have ended our conversation. To my surprise and even a nervous pleasure, it did not.

"We need more generalists. It's an age of specialists. We ought to call it that instead of the Age of Aquarius." She laughed at her little joke. But she had broken one of my ampules of knowledge.

"Actually it's more the Age of Pisces, Mrs. Tockbridge," I said gently.

"Ah? I thought Aquarius." She dropped the speech-making tone and said sharply, but with an edge of humor, "Dammit, there's that old song. I'm sure it's Aquarius. Are you an astrologer?"

"No, no," I assured her.

"Then how do you . . ." She stopped and said with good-humored determination, "Mr. Dobecker. Explain yourself."

Mrs. Tockbridge was obviously a woman of enthusiasms and the current occult fad was apparently very much one of them.

"Well, I dabble . . . ," I mumbled.

"In astrology?"

"Not really."

"Oh, Mr. Dobecker, stop being coy. I don't bite."

I didn't believe that. But I was intimidated.

"Alchemy," I surrendered.

"Alchemy?" she laughed. "You make *gold?*"

"No, no. It's a hobby, like model railroading, or golf. A sort of science project." I wanted to assure her I was one of the herd. "And you get a little of the zodiac, astrology, along with it."

"And this isn't Aquarius?"

Even as anxious as I was by this sudden turn of the talk, I recognized in her that combination of nervousness and assertive drive I had observed in officials on the governmental make.

"Well, people like to think it's Aquarius, that the Christian Age, the Age of Pisces, is over. But I could show you old books that give Pisces at least until two thousand, maybe longer."

"I'd like to see them," she said. "I got more than I bargained for in this thank-you call." She was conversational now, friendly, but there was an alloy of motive in her voice. I wondered if she wanted to pick my brain about Labor. This one was easy to analyze. My work made me a good contact for general information about the Department. The idea of her using me as an informer depressed me.

"How did you come to study alchemy?" she asked.

"Oh, reading up on it, and . . ."

"And?"

Lonely crank that I was, I was won over by her zest.

"And I'm making an alchemical furnace in my basement."

"Ah," she exhaled. "That is the little secret you've been holding out on. I'm glad it's no worse," she said with mock severity. Even I laughed at her tone now. "Can you make some gold for my next year's budget?" We both laughed.

The idea of her possibly pumping me on Labor no longer upset me now that she seemed also interested in my small curiosity shop of a mind.

"It's a slow thing, building an alchemical furnace," I ventured a joke. "Can you hold out until the next fiscal year?" By then she might be in the Department, even its Secretary.

"Where else has your alchemy taken you?"

I saw that it was not just my knowledge of Labor. There was something else she was probing me for. I was wary again.

"Look, I do work hard at the office, you know. I mean, these are just my off work . . . just killing time," I stammered.

"Well," she sighed. "Most of us are a helluva lot more interesting away from work. I don't mean me," she hastily added. "Do you do magic tricks, too?" she asked with light sarcasm as if to callus over her moment of vulnerability.

"No," I said. Her inadvertent confidence had warmed me toward her, despite my caution.

"Aren't you interested in fortune-telling and sorcery and vampires, things in that vein?"

"Not really. I did have a Tarot phase, like the furnace, reading about it at lunch." What was she leading up to?

"There aren't many alchemists who are heroes too," she said with the same bright mockery. "One of my good friends is having a party April thirtieth. Would you like to come? It's Walpurgis Night, you know, the European Halloween. It's a costume thing. You wear a costume, an alchemist's in your case." Now she was all enthusiasm again.

So, my hunch had been right. She was one of those clever, younger officials playing the trends, looking for something new to say about seeresses, Tarot decks, Black Masses.

I was taken aback.

"I'm out of action. My ankle's sprained."

"You don't have to dance. You can bring a date or come alone." She was not, at any rate, proposing the unthinkable . . . that I go with her. So the host, whoever he might be, needed a magical expert or two to ornament his party, to spice his guest list. And my recent brush with the riot made me an acceptable temporary notable, a wounded hero.

"I'd like to meet you anyway," she added. To interrogate me about Labor? Well, why not, if I were careful?

"Well," I said. "It might be fun. You're sure I wouldn't intrude?" It was only a week away.

"No, no. It's a very big thing. You'll feel just like one of the crunch."

The possibility of losing myself among the partygoers gave me a little pluck. I could wear a mask and look at the important people, lions in their habitat.

Mrs. Tockbridge told me she would have the invitation sent out to me. The break in formality was sealing up.

"Thank you, thank you for helping Susan. I'd be lost

without her," she said. We were firmly back on safe ground.

I ended on a note of unabashed diffidence:

"It was awfully nice of you to call me. I hope Susan is better."

"She'll be at work on Friday." She ended amicably. "I'll brush up on my astrology."

The invitation came, a five-by-three piece of bristol board with a colorless embossed crest. I ran my finger over the engraved black script.

"M. Le Baron Bernhard de Plaevilliers At Home . . ."

The Green Book showed he was the First Secretary of the Austrian Embassy. As I polished off *Notes* for the day, I mused about my alchemist's costume.

For the first time, one of my hobbies had gotten me recognition from the mighty. Up to now, the soap temple, the Tarot cards, even the long-ago moths had been individual satisfactions. Necessary, unobsessive, they were the moorings that stabilized me. And they had helped the time go by. Now, I studied my old books for a different reason.

From the engravings and writings, I found I should go in rags and smell of rotten eggs and boiled urine, two sometime ingredients of the Philosopher's Stone. Instead, I rented a costume that looked as though it were once worn by a courtier in some road show *Rigoletto*. The green velvet hat was shaped like a beanbag; a dark green plush cape with a dull orange lining came a bit below the knees. The black boater shirt was also of plush.

My big problem was how to get the black hose past the ankle bracing. By slipping them through the girderwork, it proved possible, but I had to settle for one fur slipper.

Once in the spirit, getting ready was fun—it would, after all, be a once in a lifetime thing. I went through my books on alchemy and then bought one of those linked wooden snakes that wobble to give them the appearance of life. This I sprayed with silver aerosol paint. I hooked its tail to its mouth—Ouroboros, symbol of the first Gnostic alchemists, signifying wisdom. That would be the necklace.

At the trick shop across from the Post Office Building, I bought a plastic lizard and silvered it too. Equipped with two eyescrews and a safety pin, it made me a hat emblem—salamander, alchemical fire.

The night of the ball had none of the Mussorgskiesque lowering skies that should accompany Walpurgis Night. Instead, the softest kind of mid-spring breeze blew in through my windows, carrying the smell of young mown grass and a hint of car exhaust.

Ankle erector set or no, I was a dashing, anachronistic bastard with my cape and silver salamander. I looked in the mirror and wished I weren't so waistless, but blessed my potless gut and my acceptable chest: Clark Kent coming out of the phone booth.

From the road a tall hedge hid de Plaevilliers' house, but once on the driveway I could see golden light along its two floors. The glow splashed out onto the trunks of ancient trees which grew haphazardly in front of the Georgian building.

A man in a tuxedo took my car. At the doorway, I caught my breath. A second man, pitchy torch in hand, wore the head of a large black goat with curved horns. It sat atop his head; there were partially obscured eyeholes in the wooly neck of the goatskin, which fell over his shoulders. The rest of him was in tails.

My own mask gave me a feeling of secure anonymity.

De Plaevilliers stood in the biggest foyer I had ever seen in a private house. His pale face and that of an old woman, his mother by the resemblance, were profiled before the immense living room. It was draped in black velours and lighted by bare papier-mâché arms bent at the elbow, each holding a rosy light. I was impressed as hell.

The host was opulent: black cape with blood-red lining, black shirt, red leather laced at the throat, black knee breeches with patent-leather puritan-buckle shoes. Above his right calf he wore a red garter with a medallion on it. A second monkish figure gave him my name.

De Plaevilliers saw the snake at my neck before my name registered on him. Then his eyes, dark brown, flicked up to the salamander and were suddenly wary.

"We are glad Mrs. Tockbridge could convince you to come," he said, smiling, his lips prim. His hand was clammy and I dropped it, I hoped not noticeably fast.

"I shall call you Monsieur Ouroboros," he said with a slight accent. As he spoke, lisping slightly, I saw his teeth were bad, darkened at their sides as one is told in childhood that teeth become from too much candy. His face was as flinty-looking as an old Indian arrowhead. His hair was black. Dyed, I wondered? His recognition of the snake shook me.

"I . . ." I stuttered.

"Our good snake of knowledge crucified for giving man the forbidden fruit, yes?" he said, self-satisfied with his bit of arcanum. He passed me to his mother, a woman about seventy-five, her face the powdered and frail simulacrum of de Plaevilliers, her voice charming and flirtatious by rote, her manner quick and birdlike.

Relieved to be past the host, who had intimidated me, I looked at the guests. At the infrequent office parties, the highest-ranking guest would be a junior congressman or some writer of mysteries. Here was big money, powerful people who reputedly were intelligent and talented.

Some were famous enough to be recognizable despite their masks. Senator Kirsted's aging movie-star jaw was unmistakable. Dressed as a witch doctor with a leopard shawl around his shoulders and a crown of small bones, he tapped his palm with a feathered fly whisk. Mrs. Kirsted had the wasted outgrown look of many famous men's wives. She stood with, or rather under, him, elfinly dressed in forest green, a Peter Pan grown old.

The band was playing a rock 'n' roll number. "Rockin' in the Brocken," I said to myself. I was excited and nervous.

Around the Senator were a Frankenstein monster in a finger-waved sheepskin coat and two Draculas, a personage abundantly represented. It took only tails and a vampire mask to accomplish the trifling transmogrification from lobbyist to hemothyme.

There were over a hundred people at the party already, some spectacular. One man carried on his back a glistening black coffin from which arms and legs protruded, wrapped, like his body, in mummy bindings. A woman in sequined green body hose draped with netting wore a tight mask that distorted her features into those of a fish. There were several Satans, none so deftly dressed as de Plaevilliers, many and varied witches, one nearly naked with a beautifully made hag's mask, wizards with conical hats, an Egyptian high priest in funnel-shaped skirt who waved his uraeus as he danced.

I lifted a glass of champagne from a tray carried by another monk, safe in my role of invisible man.

The Attorney General, a corpulent former industry lawyer, was dressed as a headsman, his black mask pushed up on his forehead. He carried a huge bloody-looking ax of composition board. I admired his felicitous sense of humor.

Looking at them, I wondered momentarily why de Plaevilliers had brought them together. Not for romance or gain. Washington was not a city of love or money. Power made it tick. Those of us who grew up in it ingested the truth of this as if it were dirty air. De Plaevilliers' summoning of the powerful was a symbol of his power, the currency of his chic.

I had read up on him as best I could in the Labor library. There had been an *Evening Star* feature on him two years ago: now forty-seven, nicknamed "Buffi," second son of a man who owned the holding company for most of Austria's grain import firms. His family was Huguenot. All those generations of French shrewdness had finally won out for this family over Austro-Hungarian indolence.

As to the society represented at his party, even I from my closet was aware, if only by osmosis, that things had changed since the Kennedy days. The general tone had gone up in efficiency since the early sixties, but down in morals, hard as that is to believe. A few years earlier, under the Democrats, it had been Negro poets. Before that, it was psychotherapy. Now there was this shifty interest in the occult, and, all unwitting, I found myself the professional, in a manner of speaking, among the tyros.

The party was leavened with writers and artists, enough to give it some dash. The diminutive homosexual writer, Crzestewski, was there dressed as a bridge troll. He, and a prima ballerina who had danced under Balanchine, and the Kennedys' creaky painter-in-residence were weighted by senators, diplomats, assistant Cabinet secretaries. Near me I heard a woman whisper, "Look, the wölfin," and I followed her eyes to the doorway.

Slim as a girl, with small, widely separated breasts delineated through the fur of her costume, was a woman dressed as a wolf. What looked like a real animal's head was on her straight shoulders. There was a quality both respectful and knowing in de Plaevilliers' bow as he leaned to kiss her taloned hand.

The woman was tall, perhaps five eight in the gray ballet slippers that were the only human clothing showing. She left the host and his mother and walked toward the bar, stared at by men and women alike. Hidden behind my mask, I admired her walk: sure, animal-like, yet womanly. Beneath the fur I could see the undulative bulge of her buttocks. I thought: she smells like a wolf, too.

Still invisible, I worked my way toward her. I saw the barman mix her a vodka and bitter lemon. She glanced around, saw across the room Senator Kirsted's leonine head above his group, and moved slowly toward him. I watched her cross the polished oak parquet until first her calves, then her back and her head were lost to me among the strangely dressed people.

De Plaevilliers, walking lithely, not mincing at all as I had thought he might, came toward the guests in my sector. He saw me, lifted his head slightly, and strolled over, champagne in hand, cigarette in mouth.

"Where did you get the idea for the snake, my friend?" he said lightly. "I think most of my guests have been reading comic books for their costumes, not books on the hermetics."

He made me uneasy.

"I'm reading up on alchemy," I said.

"Ah, in the midst of a gold crisis. . . . Tell me about your eft, your salamander." He pointed to my beanbag hat with a finger extended from the stem of his champagne glass.

"It stands for fire."

"Oh, yes, yes. That old language of the alchemists. I have forgotten more than I remember in that field. They used animals as rebuses to disguise their formulas, yes?"

"That's right," I said, pleased to find anyone interested in alchemy. Now, I was almost proud of my specialty.

"Such pursuits are endless and useless." He sighed. "Where else has your interest in the old arts taken you?"

For the first time in my life I felt that I did not have to explain my dipping into the obscure. If only "Buffi" were less repugnant.

"I'm building an alchemical furnace," I ventured. "Mrs. Tockbridge may have told you."

"Yes, yes, Mrs. Tockbridge did so," he said quickly. "I

am genuinely interested. In a century of Dachaus and hydrogen bombs, the old arts seem irrelevant to most. Yet for those of us (I was a seminarian) brought up in theology or history, the things of the past, the heresies, the great blasphemers have a romantic . . ."

I saw, past him, the wolf lady approaching. My heart thumped. Her thighs, clad as they were in fur, rubbed together as she walked. My glass was dry. I longed nervously for more drink. I fixed on her eyes, hoping they would hint of her age, or ways.

"Buffi, when are we taking off our masks?" she asked, glancing at me for only an instant, "I'm steamed." It was the voice of Anita Tockbridge. She sensed my surprise and turned to me.

"What's that on your hat?"

"It's a salamander . . . You're . . ."

Her wolf face stared at it. Her eyes were a pale, very intense blue, like ice in a technicolor movie.

"For fire," said de Plaevilliers. "Salamander is for fire. This is your friend," Buffi went on. "You do not recognize him? He is your guest, the hero of the riot who saved your Miss Bieber." He was laughing at her.

The blue eyes were suddenly less haughty.

"Ah," she said. "I thought alchemists wore sheets and hats with stars on them. I'm sorry. I *did* mean to find you."

"It's all right," I said, blinking at her gaze. My foot was hurting. I wanted to say so, elicit some sympathetic word or look.

"You can take your mask off at midnight," said de Plaevilliers to her. "We will have an important guest," he added to me, with some solemnity. He turned again to her and said, with a little bow, "I thank you for that, Anita."

The Austrian must have mistaken my uneasiness over Mrs. Tockbridge for anxiety over who the guest would be.

"The Vice President," said Buffi conspiratorially, "that is why the Secret Service man has been here all night, by the door, dressed in a tuxedo that does not fit him. That is his horror costume."

Mrs. Tockbridge laughed, a contralto chuckle. I echoed her faintly. I wondered how she had gotten the Vice President, Harold Frieden, the "Golden Jew," to Buffi's party. Her eyes, they looked younger than forty-five, were staring at me above the lacquered snout and the yellowing ivory teeth of the animal.

"I wish I could take this damned mask off," she said. "I'd like to chat with you a bit." I was thoroughly disarmed.

"She wants to chat with you about Tarot. She told me you know Tarot and she wants to know . . ."

"Oh, shut up, Buffi," she said through the mouth vent, but not angrily. He laughed, his thin lips parting only slightly.

". . . whether she will be your boss, the Secretary of Labor."

I lurched on to my good leg in surprise. This combining of party gab and talk about a Cabinet post was heady. "Oh, I'm no expert in Tarot fortunes, more the history of the cards . . ."

She interrupted, briskly now. "I am not sure I would like to know my fortune right now." She fanned a breath of air with her clawed hand into the maw of the mask.

"Don't run," she said to me agreeably. She touched my arm with her paw. "I have to take off this damned mask for a minute," and she was gone, her back straight, graceful as a wolf, leaving me with a sharp, sudden feeling of loss.

Shortly before midnight the band struck up "I Left My Heart in San Francisco," and I looked toward the foyer. We had heard the song ad nauseam during the campaign. Sure enough, there was the college athlete figure, in a tuxedo with a simple eye mask: the Vice President, Harry Frieden. Damnit, I thought, it *is* exciting.

All-star fullback, war hero, Republican reform governor of California, father of four, wedded to old, gentile philanthropic money from Massachusetts, and buoyantly proud of his Jewishness, he had captured the kids' idealism as Eugene McCarthy had in 1968. The high school youngsters canvassed for him, wearing yellow and black "Harry the Golden Jew" buttons put out by an enterprising novelty company as "in" badges. Their parents saw in him some last national hope of vigor and health. He was the perfect match for Vernon MacGregor, Presidential nominee, honest conservative from Ohio, closest thing to a universal father since Eisenhower, and a better administrator. Frieden seemed a sure bet in three and a half years.

I found myself edging toward him with the rest of the

guests. He magnetized: the word used to be "charisma."
De Plaevilliers, all dignity and grace, guided him toward
the Attorney General who moved forward, the bloody ax
trailing in his left hand. The Vice President was con-
voyed by a trio of Secret Service men who fanned through
the guests with ferrety, self-important looks. The clean-cut-
looking one from the front door whispered in Frieden's
ear, and he removed his mask, the signal for the others to
do the same. I looked for Anita Tockbridge.

She was with Senator Kirsted and his wife. Her dark
hair was drawn back, fastened with a silver clip. I moved
closer in the press of people. She had made up her face
after taking off her mask, but in the strange rose light, I
could see above her lips the tiny glistening globes of
sweat, like diluted blood. Her brows were full and arched
well, only slightly plucked. Her mouth was generous without obtruding on the spareness of her cheeks. She lacked
softness, but she was a handsome woman, a Loretta
Young without the purr.

Dizzyingly, it struck me: She was what I wanted!—as
distant as the idea was from possibility.

Buffi's guests drew toward Frieden, the beautiful woman in bird feathers, little Crzestewski, even the wrinkled
ivory husk of de Plaevilliers' mother. Anita Tockbridge
had not moved. She remained that exotic metal among
the iron filings which the electric magnet will not pull.

Frieden's eyes, large, frank and intelligent beneath the
shaggy brown brows, moved easily across the crowd. They
passed by the many apish costumes and to the face of the
erect woman in the wolf masquerade. He took in her upper body and raised a boyish hand to her, twenty feet away.
I darted my eyes to her, saw her incline her head slightly.

Years ago, the private detective recommended by my
lawyer had looked, before he took the case, at the photo-
graphs in Julia's scrapbook. In one, my wife's eyes had
pointed toward a group of four or five men at a New
Year's party.

"That," said the private eye, putting his pencil point on
the ecologist, "is the man who is screwing your wife." I
was just that sure that Anita Tockbridge and Frieden had
been lovers.

Where did a Vice President meet his mistress? At the
empty suburban home of a friend who could be told the
Vice President needed it as a haven for thought away

from downtown Washington? And he would use a gray, humdrum car. What did he tell the Secret Service as he went to meet the woman inside the house?

When the Vice President left, about one, Senator Kirsted, the Attorney General, and those others who had come mainly to see Frieden departed, too. Tirelessly the band maintained the diastole of "Blue Moon," almost unrecognizable in rock 'n' roll. The dancers seemed even more strangely dressed now—their costumes were surmounted by human heads. I munched lobster tidbits from a plate at a sidetable, resting my ankle.

De Plaevilliers was at the main food table. With him was a man in a werewolf costume and a woman dressed half as a nun, half as a sorceress. The two men were laying out crackers from a small box, an odd role for a man with a half-dozen waiters. I limped to the table.

De Plaevilliers looked up.

"I am glad to see you are staying, Monsieur Ouroboros," he said agreeably. The couple with him ogled me, rudely, I thought. The man was in his early fifties. His Germanic face bulged above the luxurious wolf hair collar of his costume. The woman was dumpy and plain with small quick eyes. They were out-of-place at the party, but seemed relaxed, even co-conspiratorial, with de Plaevilliers.

"These are my friends the Krals," he said to me. "Mr. Dobecker." They nodded, almost bowing their heads to me. "Herbert," the diplomat said to the wolfman, "can you get the air-conditioning to go a little cooler? Lisel, I beg you to press Marie to put out one more tin of caviar."

Krals, a bit mad of eye, I thought, disappeared with his wife.

"I have . . ." the diplomat said, snapping his finger on his small hands to recall the word he sought. "Dabbled! I have dabbled with some of these things," he said pointing to my snake and then the lizard.

"But"—he shrugged as if to dismiss the symbolism of the animals—"other fields are more interesting." The mocking tone came and went in his speech as if he wondered whether to dare to be candid. "Alchemy, well, you know, the alchemist's work on the homunculus . . ."

"That was getting on into the degenerate stages," I protested weakly, not really sure of my ground. I did not

want to break whatever bond my mutual interest with
Buffi gave me with Anita Tockbridge.

He nodded aside my objections, looking at me oblique-
ly and darkly, and a bit distractedly.

"A rabbi in Prague . . . part of the Empire," he added
with a smile. The smile quickly dissipated and he went on,
"Rabbi Lwov, made a homunculus, a Golem, he called it,
but it wouldn't come alive." He was no longer looking
into me, but was caught up in some remembered and,
to him, apparently exciting bit of exotica. "It would not
come alive like Frankenstein's monster." He poked his
finger at a monster in a curly wool jacket dancing jerkily
with a thickly mascaraed witch. "The rabbi tried to bring
it to life, but it would not work. So he wrote the name of
God, the Tetragrammaton, on parchment and forced it
into the dead little thing's mouth. It came alive!"

He shaped his hands a foot apart, emphatically.

"The good rabbi snatched out the parchment and it was
dead again, collapsed . . ." He opened his palms, face up.
Now de Plaevilliers' eyes were hot. He looked into mine
inquiringly. I pulled back, thinking suddenly that he must
be some kind of homosexual. But even as I recoiled at
this thought, I realized that wasn't quite it.

Surely he had caught my gesture of distaste, but he went
on, his eyes now intent on mine. I was trapped in that
dark brown iris and black cornea. "The echt"—a separate part of my mind noticed that he language-dropped
in German when excited and at other times in French
—"way for the homunculus is out of Paracelsus, *De na-
tura*, oh, yes," his voice lowered.

"One puts sperm in the alembic and there it must
putrefy forty days, you note, the term of Christ's return,
and gradually it takes the shape of a man, but you see
through him, like a film."

I tried to interrupt him. To me, a prude, this seemed
as obscene as any dirty book. What was, to me, a passing,
if absorbing, interest, was to him obviously much more.

"Well, I just . . ." I started. But he threw back his head
slightly in annoyance and went on.

"You feed him with blood for forty weeks, keeping him
all the while exactly at human temperature, and you will
have your Golem, your homunculus."

The man was both frightening and repulsive.

"Well, I just puddle around with alchemy for the hell

of it," I said, scrambling to safety. I saw Anita Tockbridge drawing up to us and I dismissed all considerations
of Buffi. Casually she asked de Plaevilliers for a cigarette
and I scratched in my cloak pocket, finding one of the
folders of matches I had picked up, black with the embassy seal on them in gold.

By the yellow match light I saw her age, even though
the powder smoothed her coarsening skin and softened the
faint beginnings of pouch beneath her pale eyes. Anita
Tockbridge caught my scrutiny and she flinched. She had
perceived my recognition of her age which first her enthusiasm on the telephone and then her mask had disguised.

"You look as if you thought I should have left my mask
on," she said, turning a corner of her full mouth down.

"Oh, no, you . . ."

She covered up my gaucherie with a laugh.

"*You* look like a government lawyer in an alchemist's
costume."

"I *am* a government lawyer in an alchemist's costume."
In her eyes I saw a momentary assessing glint and my
heart thumped.

"Well, Mr. Dobecker," she said, a wide smile breaking
over her white teeth, "we administrators are always in
need of a good lawyer." Was she confirming my suspicion that she wanted to pump me about Labor? Buffi's
hint was strong that she was getting the job.

That could wait. Now, despite my apprehensiveness, I
was aroused by the thought of her softly sweated breasts,
there beneath the wolf fur, and the almost arcless line of
her stomach.

This thought, and her civility, even respect, for that
small courage I had shown in the riot and, apparently for
my odd lore about a current fad, made me feel more
manly than I had for years. Awash in her look, I was
taken aback when Buffi intervened.

"You must let me invest in your alchemical furnace. I
will bankroll it," he said, pleased with his slang.

I replied, trying to keep up some pretense of urbanity:
"I am afraid President MacGregor would have first patent
rights on it for the national debt."

My ankle had begun to throb so that I could hardly
stand on it. I would have suffered its pain gladly if Anita
Tockbridge had continued to stay beside me. But the two

of them, heeding the waves of friends, nodded and began to drift toward a group at the bar.

Before she was swallowed up, she turned and said simply, "I would like to talk with you. About Labor." At last, there it was, in the open.

"Fine," I said, as she turned with a smile toward her friends.

I had a last glass of champagne, limped to where Buffi was saying good night to a half dozen others and made my good-byes.

In the morning, I bought the *Star-News'* first edition and looked for the society page:

"Vice President Harry Frieden a-masking went at the witching hour last night," it gushed.

"The pre-Halloween (by almost six months) party was at the Fairfax County residence of Austrian First Secretary Bernhard 'Buffi' de Plaevilliers. And if the black velours décor and rose lights were 'way out,' the guest list was 'way in.'

"Baron de Plaevilliers billed it as a Walpurgis Night party when the witches, so it is said, take to the mountains for their annual broomsticking. At Buffi's, it was strictly non-protocol, the handsome Austrian bachelor's unusual way of saying, 'I want who I want and never mind the diplomatic list.'

"The Vice President—he explained his wife, Sandy, has the sniffles and wanted to stay home—came in tuxedo with light mask and his arrival was the signal for general unmasking.

"That Lord High Executioner with the terrifying-looking ax was Attorney General . . ." and so on. I skipped down to the end of the list. After the senators and congressmen and the arty bunch was "and as svelte as a teen-ager in an authentic wolf's head was former Congresswoman Anita Tockbridge, now an HEW official. Another striking costume was that of . . ."

It was Saturday. After I ate my lunch my hangover began to fade. I dug in my sparse front yard at some early weeds. First the riot and now this party had pulled me out of my shell, my cellar, my cubbyhole. As I rooted in the moist earth with an old table knife, the faint breeze blew in a smell—lilac, I thought. I wanted Anita Tockbridge, with her powder off, bare.

And was it so impossible? The politically prominent in

Washington had traditionally indulged the vices that could destroy them. Growing up in a government family, it seemed to me sometimes that politicians needed that flirtation with scandal to heighten the headiness of their power. They were as heedless about it as, when children, we hopped up our already caffeined colas with No-Doz tablets.

In my mind I had catalogued them from the newspapers and from the gossip one heard from other departmental lawyers. Senator Thruston Morton had his whiskey. John and Robert Kennedy had bedded down blondes—a columnist and a celebrity, precisely the liaisons that could have finished them most spectacularly.

The pious Senator Boume had been caught by a private detective in the arms of one of his clerk-typists and Senator Fjordvaar was taped telling Mrs. Habib Browne, the Washington hostess, how grateful he was their alliance had only been sexual—and thus noninvolving.

Even more darkly, President Johnson's most trusted aide, Walter Jenkins, instead of finding some patrician and discreet fairy, had been arrested in a YMCA toilet with an Old Soldier's Home pensioner. The FBI had squelched a blackmailer (one of my Justice colleagues had told our assistant general counsel) who had the goods on Congressman Zindler. Senator Mead Preayes reportedly had a statement in his safe all ready to explain his affair with one of his masculine financial backers—in case they were ever caught.

Now, the craze in Washington was the supernatural. And who knew how many on Capitol Hill or in this medium cool administration were fooling with seances or playing at Black Mass during recess in some Bahaman or Majorcan retreat?

In such an atmosphere of risk, did I not have reason to hope that Anita Tockbridge might find my niggling knowledge of the occult and my considerable knowledge of Labor enough for her to award me a moment of wayward love?

Clearly she was already tied to an odd enough individual in Buffi, in whose circle she apparently indulged her flirtation with the occult. I thought of her in the wolf costume, moving toward me through the motley of guests.

Recluse and coward, I wanted her. What high dance would I have to do to make her say, "I must have you"?

CHAPTER

4

Confirmation

It was just over a week later that the *Star* carried a one-column cut of Anita Tockbridge, slightly younger than she remained in my mind. The caption said that the President had nominated her as Assistant Secretary of Labor for Planning. I gave an involuntary "Ummf."

Her hearings would be perfunctory; she was a former member of Congress, if a somewhat rambunctious one. A liberal freshman Republican, she had noisily favored stronger regulation of the drug industry, even when her party's leadership and the Southern Democrats had destroyed the bill. Only when Cardylzide killed nearly a hundred heart patients did she win honor in her party; then, of course, she was a prophet. But, like the Dirksens and Kerrs of an earlier era, the McFaddens and Chidgers did not forget. Her second-term victory was assured, her third-term defeat just as certain.

The new administration needed women in high offices despite the appeal of the fatherly President and the swinging Golden Jew. Anita Tockbridge, courageous widow, mother of a Navy ensign and a West Point cadet, humanitarian, youngest woman ever to serve on the Hershey, Pennsylvania, city council, was a perfect embellishment.

On the day of her Senate confirmation hearings, I came into the office early so I could get *Labor Notes* out of the way. I had lolled in a dream of her and needed to know whether the evening at de Plaevilliers had or had not also seeded me into her thoughts.

The Senate Labor Committee room swallowed up the small crowd. The TV lights were on, and the front row, with its dignitaries in dark glasses against the glare, looked like a high Mafia conclave. Anita—Mrs. Tockbridge—sat beside the Secretary, a former professor of government, wearing a vest and Phi Beta Kappa key. On the other side was the Health, Education and Welfare Secretary, a distinguished and compromised Negro who had gone to Harvard and thereafter yas-suhed with alacrity.

From my seat, I could see Anita Tockbridge in quarter profile. She wore a black raw-silk suit. When she turned I saw a man's pocket watch, an old octagonal one, perhaps her father's, suspended from near her lapel by a gold fleur-de-lis pin. Her face, softened by the distance between us, had not yet been turned on. It was serene, confident, the lips as if slightly swollen; the chin was level, hiding the creases on her throat that otherwise would have been harshened by the TV lights; her shoulders were straight. I felt hopeless and lonely and tormented. To lust for her? Why, I was like an old man in an upstairs fleabag yearning over photomag pictures of movie queens.

Senator August Chidger, Democrat of Nevada, "the desert louse" to his enemies, was presiding, appropriately in view of his old opposition to Mrs. Tockbridge. He could be counted on to carry out the ceremonial duties as oilily as anyone. Kirsted, a committee member, was there to lend his classic jaw to the television cameras and the nominee. The senators looked down from the dais above the witness table.

The hearing had about as much relation to the Senate's constitutional duty to "advise and consent" on Presidential appointments as the Roman Catholic ritual has to the simplicity of Jesus. Chidger called the session to order and looked down at Mrs. Tockbridge, then my boss, the Secretary of Labor, made one of those ritualistic interventions.

"Mr. Chairman, if I may just for this moment say a word . . ."

"Why, yes, Mr. Harvey. We are glad to see you, sir, glad. Come right up to the witness table, sir."

"Mr. Chairman, I would just like to say that we are grateful to the President for nominating this fine lady to one of our assistant secretaryships. I have known her for

fifteen years, and her splendid husband, the late Paul
Tockbridge, and would like simply to add my endorsement
to that of the President, who has recommended this outstanding American."

That was the way it went.

Temple, the Health, Education and Welfare Secretary,
made his humble-pie endorsement, too.

"May I add, Mr. Chairman, that Secretary Harvey had
no mean job in getting the President to talk us into relin-
quishing Mrs. Tockbridge. Her work, as this committee
knows, was outstanding as head of our Welfare Division."

Chidger called her to the stand with a silly little joke
about capsuling her testimony if she did not think this
would compromise her position on the drugs. The old bastard had clearly not forgotten or forgiven her.

Her testimony was a neat set piece which gave me a
view on her past life and on her ability to play the pusil-
lanimous role of nominee-on-the-Hill.

"Since my graduation from the University of Pennsylvania, I will confess more than twenty years ago, I have
been in public service except for the years when I was at
home getting the boys, my two boys, ready to go off to
school.

"As a district leader, first in Hershey, I worked with
many fine Democratic people in joint projects, and I then
began part-time work as a state committeewoman in our
party. For six years I was a councilwoman in Hershey
before Governor Chasbue appointed me chairman of the
State Advisory Committee on Labor and Social Welfare
and later Director of Public Health for my state of Pennsylvania. I served in two congresses, working on much
labor legislation and I am at present director of the Welfare Division at Health, Education and Welfare. I think
you have other material, Mr. Chairman, on advisory posts
and on committees, including the President's Commission
on Labor and Business Cooperation.

"If I am confirmed, Mr. Chairman, I will do all in my
power to efficiently implement the Plans and Program-
ming requirements of the Department. I would hope to
use whatever sense of fair play and morality and common
sense that a mother and government official can develop
in forty-five years of life. I will be pleased to answer any
questions."

There was some sparring with her by Senator William

Yardee, the liberal New Yorker, over whether she favored a stronger investigatory staff for industry violations of the Labor–Management Act. She came back nicely noncommittal with a statement about "that tiny handful of businessmen who might have fallen by the wayside" needing to be prosecuted.

Yardee seemed ready to pursue the question for a moment. He repeated her phrase back to her and I saw to my surprise that she dropped her hand down to her skirt, wiped its palm on the haunch, then dipped into a handbag for a handkerchief. It was all done in a moment.

Yardee, however, skimmed on. I wondered: had the question stimulated anxieties in her over some scandal involving her and a business firm that had "fallen by the wayside"? I had not heard of it.

She gripped the handkerchief again when Chidger recognized her congressman—a Democrat—and called him to the table. He was a swarthy man with gray hair combed back long behind his ears, Emanuel Plulazzo. He bowed and wove up to the table, nodded with diffidence and made his speech.

"I came only to add my endorsement on behalf of this great Pennsylvania lady from my district. She has served our state well, although of the other party"—chuckles from the audience—"but I might say she has voted so much with our party that I feel she is very much at home there." More chuckles.

And so it droned on. I listened to her sidestepping, she who as wolf-woman had been so frank. What a cast of characters: Chidger, with two district court and one federal appellate court judgeships open or opening. He did not want to endanger his personal choices for these patronage plums by bucking the President on Anita Tockbridge, despite all the cake he had gotten from the pharmaceutical firms she had fought. And Plulazzo, wretched creature of the "syndicate" in Reading. His own brother, a priest, had campaigned for his reform opponent.

The hearing broke up. Anita Tockbridge and her convoys ceremoniously left, shaking hands with senators, with each other, with Congressman Plulazzo, who was basking in the phosphorescent light of the grander chamber. The TV technicians began pulling out lights and equipment. They had filmed what cheesecake the Senate affords, the nomination of an attractive woman.

Mrs. Tockbridge wore a pleased, deeply-humble-at-this-honor expression. Behind her I saw Susan, with stacks of folders hugged to her breasts. She wore a blue linen suit. A friendly face on my level. I edged up to her.

"How are the battle wounds?" I asked.

"Fine. We'll be coming over your way, I guess," she smiled.

Susan and I had been tossed into the same stew pot as haphazardly as a turnip and a carrot, but we had not complemented each other particularly well. I turned to the star.

"Hi," I said, wanting to add something clever about lupine guile or fortunes of the cards.

She darted her face away from Secretary Temple for a moment. "Thank you," she said with the gracious smile she was giving everyone. The group was moving on through the massive doors. She didn't even recognize me.

I must have shown my disappointment, almost outrage. She glanced back at me, looking first irritated, then flustered.

"Yes," she said quietly, "My friend, the alchemist. You don't look the same in a suit. I'm sorry. Thanks for coming. I guess I'll be seeing you in Labor." She was pleasant, but that was all.

"I hope so," I said. Cold indeed compared with the exchange of intimate, fugitive looks I had dreamed of. Susan hurried after the entourage as they went into the hall. There would be the big, black limousines waiting outside for them in the No Parking Except for Members of Congress zones. I watched Anita Tockbridge's athletic stride, the enthralling rhythms of her calves in sheer hose, among the departing pants legs of the mighties. Behind them all was Susan. She still hugged the folders that vouched her boss's essentiality to party and to country.

CHAPTER

5

Tapir

Back at my desk, I put my head in my hands. I tried to buck up by thinking of Athanor, of my front lawn, of the call girl. I even tried to gold-plate Susan sufficiently to build fantasies about her. Nothing would work, short of poison.

Always, I had hidden, run, fortified, done all I could to prevent confrontations. What was happening to me now?

Late that afternoon, while I numbly finished up the day, Anita Tockbridge called me. There was a telephone ritual in Washington in which, as Emily Post might have said it, Mr. Important's secretary first gets Mr. Middle Level's secretary on the line and then has Mr. Middle Level himself put on so that she can say, "Just a moment please for Mr. Important." In this case, Mr. Important—Anita Tockbridge—called me direct.

"Sorry not to have been more polite this morning." Her voice, always low, sounded mellow, an unaccompanied viola note. I wanted to yip for joy into the mouthpiece.

"Not at all . . ."

She went on without waiting for a real answer. "The hearing's out of the way and all of a sudden I realized how woefully uneducated I am about Labor."

"Now, I'm sure . . ." I began.

"No, really. I mean historically and all that. I wonder if we couldn't meet"—I inhaled sharply—"and maybe you could give me . . . with your newsletter and everything, you must know the books to read and the congressional hearings that are really vital."

This was too good, too simple to be true.

"I'd like to get the general grasp of things, how things are, I don't mean any disloyalties . . ."

"I'd be glad to," I said, knowing then, from that word on, that what she wanted precisely was "disloyalty." She would ask me to give her a fill-in on the Department's weaknesses. She would want rumors, feelings, facts on its personalities, information that eight years in Labor's legal division had forced on me. All that, assuredly, she would want, bit by bit.

"No personalities, or anything . . ." she assured me, thus confirming my apprehensions. I was being used. But, joy! It was me she had singled out. We settled on five thirty at the Washington Hotel bar.

At the Washington Hotel, the powerful could drink in privacy. It was a dimly lit non-hail-fellow-well-met lounge. I got there early, to preempt her arriving first and attracting to her table some official acquaintance who might be hard to ditch. I ordered a vodka gimlet on the rocks, uncommonly potent drugging for me. I wished to hell I had not given up smoking.

I saw her before she saw me, and rose. Her questing look turned to a smile of recognition. She walked toward me, striding in her alligator pumps as in ballet slippers. That face, with prominent lips and cheekbones and pale eyes, was already for me a shape of love.

She held out her hand. When my fingers met it, the static electricity from her walk across the carpeted floor discharged with a tiny shock, a distinct *click*. It startled us both.

"What does that mean?" she laughed.

"I only read about magic; I don't believe in it," I said, feeling the wetness in my armpit.

Once she was directly across from me I could study her face, meeting her eyes as I did, and glancing at her as she took the first big sip from a vodka Gibson.

"I'm a vodka and bitter lemon person," she said, sensing a question in me. "But the hearing's over. Besides," she added, "you don't look like you bite. Can I relax?"

"Yes," I said. How few seemed the twelve years that separated her forty-five years from my thirty-three. "Certainly."

"I read the official history of Labor," she began.

"By Bulic? It's . . ."

"Too dull."

"Well, the government departments . . ."

"Oh, I know that. But there is a certain amount of horse racing in all of them. You get some spirited people in Labor and Justice and at State."

"Yes," I said. "They don't stay very long."

"Perhaps I won't either," she laughed. "When Ronquette"—the previous Assistant Secretary of Planning—"tried to put more domestic help under the new minimum wage why didn't the Secretary at least make some noises in support?" she asked.

I was taken aback by the abruptness of her sortie into this prickly thicket. If I were going to be with her, if she were to like me, then she must see that I was not cautious with her. I plunged.

"No, no. Ronquette's speech to the Trades Council—that's what you're talking about isn't it—wasn't even his idea. The Secretary had him do it. Neither of them ever wanted it really, but there were the elections . . ."

"Ah," she said, nodding. As we talked about decisions and policies I felt her total grasp of the uses of power and the subterfuges it required. It was only the channels of power at the Labor Department she did not know. And under her questioning I soon initiated her.

We had second drinks. With a sharp rap of guilt, I took one of her unfiltered Chesterfields.

"First one in two years," I said, holding it up.

"Now, I am supposed to say that I have led you astray." She looked up at me with a smile. "But that wouldn't be fair, would it? You led yourself astray."

After an hour, I was feeling a little tipsy. And I had begun to feel comfortable with her. Perhaps it was that I had put myself snugly in her hands with my revelations of the Department's inner workings, of the scandals handled by the legal office that never made the newspapers. I did not care.

I felt her, too, losing the patina of politician, administrator, feminist, the accretions of the years that both protected her and gave her the small fame she had. I was satisfied that her comfortableness came from her instinct that I was no threat to her ambitions, yet would prove a loyal subaltern in furthering them. How quickly she had plumbed my fidelity and put her trust in it.

We were talking about Woeckle, the Department solicitor, my boss:

"You don't seem to have a desire in the world for his job," she said.

"No, why should I?" I came back. "There's some talk he will go to the White House. So everyone could move up. But I don't think of myself as a government worker, you know."

"That's funny for a man who's spent . . ."

"Eight years at Labor and two at Commerce."

"Ten years in government." She fixed her light-blue eyes on mine with some interest. "I'll give you this satisfaction: if you aren't a government employee, what are you?"

"I'm a scholar."

"Like Secretary Harvey?"

"No, not like the Secretary." My guard was down totally with her. "He isn't a scholar. He's a former professor who's now a politician-administrator. Besides, all his knowledge is useful. None of mine is." I was feeling even complacent. "I am unsuccessful. You and the Secretary are successful . . ."

"Poor scholar," she laughed. A quick light came into her eyes. "Why didn't you bring your Tarot cards?"

"I thought you were scared of them. Besides," I added with unpremeditated spite, "when you asked me out, I understood it was to get me to spill the beans on the Department."

"It's childish of you to put it that way," she said. Her sudden asperity snapped me from the alcohol. My God, things had been going so well. Was I going to ruin it by asserting a disagreeable truth?

She started to say something else. Instead she tightened her lips and stared angrily at me. Shaken, but emboldened by the gimlet, I stared back. Her eyes lowered to her drink.

"It is true," she said mildly, the anger quenched as quickly as it flared. "Yes, it's true enough. Thank God I'm through with the committee. It's done." She picked up her previous thought. "I wouldn't have pumped just anyone." I took a tiny sip. "How did you get this way, I mean, unambitious?" She still was drinking quickly, almost recklessly. The committee must have been a huge obstacle in her mind.

"I don't know. I guess something to do with my family. Maybe watching my mother try to push my father. How did you get ambitious?" She ignored my question.

"Everybody blames everything on their family," she said. "Was your father a scholar, too?"

"No, he was at Agriculture. He was a sort of Eskimo about emotion. I mean, somebody, Toynbee maybe, said that the Eskimos were so oppressed by environment that they never got beyond making primitive feldspar seals. My mother . . ."

"Why blame them? My sons blame me. They think I was too manipulative, that's the word Wesley, the older, used once. I hardly see them anymore. Why should they complain? My God, they turned out well enough." She looked at me, and tamped a cigarette a little tipsily. "And I did it, really. I don't mean to make this a confessional, but Paul, my husband, drank himself to death. I suppose if a person wanted to they could say Paul's drinking . . ." She shrugged.

So there were her two sons, the one saying, in hot anger no doubt, that she was manipulative, maybe shouting at her that she was trying to ally him against the drunken Paul Tockbridge.

"Look, I must meet someone." She had turned off the personal talk and was looking at her watch.

My face fell. I had begun to feel nothing would ever intrude on this cosy vodka world in which we had so rapidly become confidants, perhaps even friends. She saw my disappointment and she assessed me for a moment.

"I'm meeting a friend at the Mayflower. A campaign fundraiser, an old, old friend. Come and sit with me until he comes."

So, a reprieve. I summoned the waiter. I was pleased beyond words that she made no effort to pay. In the cab, she moved over to make room; it disarrayed her hair and twisted her skirt. I copped a covert glance at her knees, the Roman dome of patellas and the lines of age at their base. The wrinkles gave me a twinge of pity. She seemed entirely feminine, vulnerable.

Anita was looking out the window in the near dusk toward the statue of Jackson in Lafayette Park. She, a woman of some importance, had let me talk of myself. It did not occur to me then that this genuine interest in people is what makes some politicians successful. Others, totally egocentric, remain groundlings.

"You are like Buffi in a way," she remarked. "Both of you funny about odd knowledge."

"He takes his much more seriously," I said.

"Yes. That's why you're easier to be with."

At the Mayflower, I helped her from the cab and felt how unsteady the drinks—she had had four, or was it five—had made her.

I didn't let go of her hand immediately, and she looked at me curiously. Even through the mists of drink, her eyes now seemed more wary.

Yet inside the Mayflower, there was again a juvenile, wanton quality in the way she—and I—drank. We knew there is a point where highballs or even beer should be substituted for undiluted drinks. But we stuck with the gimlets and Gibsons.

When Mr. Fred Pauhafen arrived, Anita introduced me as an attorney at the Labor Department and that pacified his old man's look of hurt. He had a long, soft nose, permanent scowl and receding, baggy chin. His complexion combined the paleness of heart cases with the floridness of hard afternoon drinking. I recognized his name. He was chairman of the board of Dyestone Wood and Paper—a pulp giant. I was suitably awed.

"Sit down, sweetie," Anita said to him as a nurse would to an aging patient. "How was your day? Oh, Fred, I'm finished with the committee."

His tapir-like features smiled, the sly old eyes sparkling.

"Anita, Anita," he said, shaking his head indulgently. "We'll have a lady in the White House yet. When's the confirmation?" He must have been between sixty-five and seventy, but seemed older. Dealing with exact procedures, however, he was less the befuddled old man. "Any problems on the committee?"

"No, I'm certain not," she said.

"Don't need any letters or calls? Sure now?"

"No, Fred darling, it looks lovely.

Feeling ignored and even put out by her change from honest companion to fawning starlet, I rose.

"Listen, I've got to be going," I said politely. I saw him look quickly, inquisitively at her. She stared back at him with a strange look of uneasiness. The drink had surfaced something odd here. That much I knew; what it was was beyond me.

"He may have some appoint . . ." she began.

"Stay, stay," he interrupted her.

"I should . . ." I started. Yet I did not want to leave her.

The next hour was a fuzzy time. Tapir servilely flattered her. She should write a newspaper column. She should run for the Senate with his backing. He told of his plans to finance a labor-management conference at which she could speak.

Anita was drinking foolishly now. So was the old man. Only I was slowing down and that was because my thoughts of her had degenerated now pretty much to lust: seemingly so inaccessible a few hours ago, she appeared now very possibly a drunken lay.

At one point Anita shook off the vodka and turned to me. She looked upset. "I never do this," she said. I believed her. Tapir's eyes, fired up by his martinis, glittered excitedly. He was slurring:

"She's the most beautiful little lady we've ever had in the legislature, here or anyplace. They don't grow them as pretty in Maine as they do in Pennsylvania." He turned to me, an old man's nasty lewdness in his look, "You know what I mean?"

Anita's face was flushed. Her mouth was relaxed, giving her a bawdy look. I thought if the Chidger Committee could see her now, she wouldn't get confirmed as Senate janitress.

Tapir's voice was getting louder. I knew we had to leave the bar. He was beginning to pat Anita's leg.

"We've got to go change, I mean, I got to, for dinner," he said. He looked at me with what I took for anger, but what he said was, "You come upstairs and have a drink with us." He was imperative. I disliked this wicked old man, but I was like a mongrel dog with a hunger for a bitch. The party had become shabby. There was an overtone of indecency in Pauháfen that Anita seemed to share. At one point she tried to pull out of her wooziness.

"I don't think he'd better," she said. "We don't even know him." She was distressed with me for not siding with her, but we had drunk away all the niceties of intellect and manners.

We crowded into an elevator with a group of convention-aires, all in their fifties, wearing badges, rich, loud, and frowsy.

Tapir's suite was quiet. His big voice seemed lost in the large rooms.

"How 'bout fixing one for us all?" he said to me with a sweep of his hand at the icebucket and tray. A bottle of Johnnie Walker Black and an opened bottle of Beefeater's gin were on the tray. What had she done with this old bastard to become his financial rathole? I suddenly loathed him. Plenty, I thought bitterly. Plenty in her younger days, I bet, and her husband alive, too. No wonder Paul Tock-bridge had been a drunk.

"Sweetie," he said to Anita, "I'll be changing in here for a minute." Bulgy in his fine worsteds, he lumbered into the bedroom and slammed the door. I looked at her in the cool, quiet room. She sat on the sofa sedately, except that her crossed legs had hiked her skirt up. Her fingers worked back and forth nervously on the petit point of the chair. I switched on the TV and took a quick sip of my Scotch and water.

"You really are going to have to go," she said to me quietly as I walked over to her. Lucidity broke through the alcohol.

"Why?" I asked, all my deviousness dissolved in drink. "Can't you leave him and go with me somewhere, to sup-per . . . ?"

"No," she interrupted sharply. I had made sure the TV was mouthing with some volume. "You don't understand a damned thing."

I took her drink out of her hand. One arm on the sofa arm, the other on her shoulder, I kissed her. She let me, but did not respond, then broke.

"That's stupid," she hissed. Above the TV, I heard the shower, as did she. I kissed her again.

This time she pressed back; her lips began to work gently on mine. I slipped down on one knee so I could hold her. When we broke, both of us were breathing fast. I knew it was mere drunken passion. But even that was something.

"This is damned awkward," I said, lifting her to her feet and into my arms so I could pull her body against the length of mine.

The scene was so seedy: the old man in the next room,

her breath full of smoke and liquor and vermouth. I had wanted it to happen in some sunlit room on a wide, sheeted bed.

I drew her buttocks to me, despairing at the feel of her girdle. It demanded not just acquiescence, but active cooperation. My hand inside her jacket, I felt her nipple rise into a firm bump under the brassiere. I wondered how the hell I could unlatch it.

"Look," I said, breaking the kiss. "Let's just get out of here." I was breathless and my heart hurt with desire.

"No," she said. She paused without moving her body from mine. "The shower's stopped."

"I don't care," I said, drawing her to the sofa. Tapir out of the shower: that gave me no more than five minutes. She was pushing me away but without conviction. At least, I thought, I've stirred her, even though I despaired of vanquishing the girdle.

"Can't we take it off?" I gasped.

"No," she said, but she let me amateurishly climb half on to her.

"I love you," I said in my excitement, brushing my lips back and forth on hers.

"That's a lot of crap," she said surprisingly. I moved over on top of her and she grunted with my roughness. The door opened, shocking me rational. I rolled away.

Through the door's narrow opening I saw the tapir face, eyes red, a face surprised and thrilled in an ugly old man's way, alight with lechery. Then he closed the door.

She turned to me on the couch now, and took my head in her hands. Her eyes were intense, drunken, even a bit manic.

"Stay," she ordered. She reached up and unbuttoned the top of her jacket.

"Let's go. He'll see us," I groaned.

"That's what he wants."

"You're crazy," I said. She had thrown off the jacket and pulled the slip straps from her shoulders. Her breasts were thrust out as she worked with both hands at the brassiere clasp. Her face was ruddy and twisted with haste.

It struck me: I was being used as the substitute pawn. Presumably, Tapir and Anita had already lined up some regular to play stud for the impotent old voyeur, and I

was now, by chance, cutting the gigolo out of his job. It
was revolting! Or should have been.

"Come over here," she said. I glanced at her bare chest
for an instant, then to the bedroom door, still closed, and
back at her. Her breasts were small, separate, puckered
slightly at the nipples. I reached out to feel them, touching
the smooth skin. She put her arms carefully around my
neck and kissed me. But the thought of the old man was
too much for me. Slowly now, I moved my lips from hers.

Suddenly I heard a hideous aspirant gasp in the next
room. Something terrible was happening to Tapir!

I scrambled away from Anita and flung open the door
even as Pauhafen uttered those horrible *KKKKKK's*
again.

The old man's naked pouched body was making an
ungainly pirouette toward the bed with tiny, jerky steps.
I ran to catch him. From the midst of a forest of black-
gray hair on his buttocks I saw a hypodermic syringe
bobble like a tail as he stumbled.

Anita, her slip across her breasts by one strap like
Jane in a Tarzan movie, brushed past me toward the
flabby, falling figure. As we grabbed his arms, he collapsed
beside the bed, his face a bewilderment of hurt.

"God, God, God," I could hear her choking out.

Tapir flopped heavily out of our grasp and onto his
stomach. I rolled him over with horror, knowing in that
instant the derivation of "dead weight." I was sick at my
stomach, almost vomiting. I thought of the needle and
tried to turn him over to remove it.

"What are you doing?" she hissed.

I ignored her. The syringe had fallen out. I let him
slump onto his back again. The horror had almost sobered
us.

"He's dead," I said, at the same time contradictorily
laying my ear on his hairy ribcase. As I did, my eye fell
mercilessly on her breasts. The incredible idea came to
me of taking her to bed, now that the—to me—impedi-
ment had removed himself. She looked up at me, completely innocent terror and paralysis in her pale eyes.

"He had a needle in him," I hissed. "What was it?"

My words snapped her into thought.

"B-12," she said, looking wildly around for the needle.
"It pepped him up so he could . . ." She did not finish,

spotting the syringe beneath the bed. It was still almost full.

"I want to call the doctor," I said. The needle was scary.

"No," she said, almost desperately. "They mustn't know I . . ."

I looked at her angrily.

"Listen," I said, "there are a helluva lot worse things than a scandal."

The terror was still in her eyes, but now she was thinking of her own sweet ass.

"He had heart trouble," she said. "You're a law er. You can handle the police. Say you were talking labor law with him." She had taken my hand in hers and was staring at me. "Just say he had an attack."

"I want you here to back it up!" I demanded.

She screwed up her face.

"I can't," she said. "Because . . ." She looked sickly pale.

"Because it's a well-known fact that he's queer this way?"

I saw assent defeat the last vestige of her pretense.

"There's already enough of a suspicion about you and him, isn't there? So his family or somebody . . ." She put her hand to her throat. Her face was suddenly haggard.

All the courage from the alcohol suddenly deserted me. I felt my thousand failures and knew I could not do it.

"I can't," I whimpered. She looked at me wearily, then I saw the spirit building up in her eyes. "Well, I can! Call the doctor," she snapped.

She stood there tall, youth flushed back into her face with the anger, the slip fallen down now from the cups of her breasts. I thought about those nipples. Goddamnit, I'd try.

"Wash the glasses," I said. "Take this damned thing with you." I gave her the syringe. She studied my eyes now, I knew to see whether I *could* carry it off.

For a hard moment, we stared at each other, compacting.

I looked around and found the deep-red B-12 vials on the dresser. I gave them to her, feeling the nervous moisture on her fingers.

Turning her back, Anita put on her brassiere. As she finished making up her face, the full force of the chance we were taking seemed to strike her. She leaned against the wall, and put her hand to her forehead. The criminal consequences of a false report to the police were bad enough for me. For her, getting caught would finish her —at her apogee.

"God," she said. "The undertaker, the hotel people, the police too."

"I wish I were back with my furnace," I said, glumly trying to be cavalier. She did not understand for a moment, then remembered, and smiled weakly, beginning to recover her courage again.

"Monsieur Ouroboros," she imitated de Plaevilliers' accent, taking my arm for a moment. Then she left the suite, and me to my dirty work.

My head throbbed with worry. I flushed her cigarette butts, leaving only mine in the ashtray, then her drink, and washed her glass with soap and water. Holding it in a towel, I touched it a half-dozen times to Tapir's dead right hand, and put its rim to his lips. Averting my eyes from his, I returned it to the coffee table and poured half my diluted drink into it.

I touched a piece of toilet paper to the tiny trace of blood at the needle mark, rolled him over, gave his corpse vigorous Boy Scout-style artificial respiration for a full nauseating minute to make sure that if such efforts at salvation left subcutaneous evidence, it would be there, and picked up the telephone to have the hotel summon a doctor.

I checked among the hairs to make sure the needle mark was not bleeding again, and flopped Tapir over on his back, covering him with a sheet. Thank God for legal training.

The doctor, balding, in his fifties and a drinking man himself from the looks of those cheek veins, mechanically felt for his heartbeat and found none. I jabbered away of what I had done: artificial respiration, in the old-time way, and pressing his heart up and down.

"Nothing worked," I said woefully.

"No," he said. "Nothing like that would."

Mr. Pauhafen had said something about a heart condition, I explained. He was chairman of Dyestone—the doctor perked up at this—and we were conferring about labor law. Yes, I was a Labor Department lawyer. Cloaked in this respectability, one professional man to another, the lies came easier. We'd had a drink or two before he'd come up to get dressed for dinner. Yes, he'd seemed a bit pale, you know, Hell, I didn't think he should be drinking—that florid look on the old gentleman's face . . .

The doctor sighed, took notes in his grainless leather notebook.

He glanced around the room and I froze as he walked to the dresser, but it was only to pick up an engraved gold pill box. All the B-12 vials were safely with Anita.

The doctor looked at me as if for permission and I nodded, "of course." Inside the box were the distinctive tiny white pills I had seen on my father's night table—nitroglycerine, the mark of the tightrope heart patient. I sighed inwardly with relief.

A minute later the hotel's chief security officer arrived and shortly two homicide detectives who swapped gruff greetings with the security man and looked at me and the doctor with suspicion.

The doctor uttered a few brusque, almost defensive words about the nitro pills. People, after all, simply did not get murdered at the Mayflower.

The two homicide men strolled around the room, a pair of hoary hound dogs with no reason to think they'd bumble on a scent. Alternately I was sick with fear and impressed with the job of befogging I was doing. Still, the question of an autopsy lay ahead. Would they need one if the doctor said he died attended?

Desperately, I dissembled.

"Do you want me to talk to his family," I offered to the senior homicide man when he found a card in Tapir's wallet giving the telephone number of a son in Philadelphia. The detectives found the idea of being spared this onerous duty appealing.

"Maybe you and the Doc could call . . ." he allowed.

As the doctor contacted the son, a hotel official arrived and somberly advised me—I assumed he designated me as friend and chief mourner—that a great American and Mayflower client for thirty years had passed on. The managerial type was a classy fellow whose solace gave me obvious cachet with the two police.

The doctor was murmuring professionally into the telephone to the son.

"Yes, an attorney with the Labor Department . . . We did what could be done, of course." Oh, glorious "We"! He was building toward an attended death. The doctor turned the telephone over to me. The death of the chairman of Dyestone had become an occasion.

"It was very rapid," I said. "A brilliant man, in the midst of a conference on a labor matter when . . . Yes, he was totally comfortable. The doctor was here only moments after he lost consciousness." I felt sorry for Tapir. There was no feeling in the son's voice.

"I assume he will be taken to a funeral home," I said in answer to the son's question. Then I turned to the doctor and detectives. "Will Mr. Pauhafen be taken to a funeral home?" I was all innocence, feeling the panicky dishonesty eating at my grit. If only I could get him directly to an undertaker, could avoid the autopsy that might reveal the needle prick and loose the Furies.

The doctor looked at the security man. I palmed the mouthpiece.

"The son said there was a history of heart trouble," the doctor murmured, shrugging. The security man looked at the homicide detectives.

"Will the Doc certify to the coroner he was in attendance at the time the gentleman died?" said the senior detective.

The hotel official looked at the physician.

"I don't see why not," sighed the doctor and all relaxed.

"What funeral home do you prefer?" I asked the son. When he did not know, I recommended Gawler's. The words "Chairman of the Board" worked wonders with Gawler's. In less than an hour, Tapir's remains had passed into the hands of those more experienced in handling the mighty. Without autopsy.

The detective made his pro forma farewell, advising me I might be called. Then I was free. Shaky, as if I had killed the man myself and lied my way out of it, I nevertheless felt the rhythm of pleasure. I had brought it all off and I was ready to report to Anita Tockbridge.

The Marlborough Apartments were old and expensive. The elevator, a relic cage with a frieze of gilded bas-relief sphinxes and Pans below the mansard curve of its roof, trundled me to the seventh floor. My heart beat fast. Its echo in my ears was almost painful.

Anita—I could no longer think of her as Mrs. Tockbridge—wore a white cotton blouse and black slacks.

"Whew, some night," she said, an apologetic, even embarrassed, note in her voice. She led me into the rich apartment and we sat facing each other across a coffee table.

"They don't suspect?" she asked with concern, as she had on the telephone.

"I think we're okay. Unless somebody at the funeral home sees that puncture in his tail."

"Good God," she said wearily. "When will we know?" Her "we" both alarmed and thrilled me.

"In a day or two," I said, trying to hide my agitation. She rose, fretted the corner of a picture frame for a moment, then sat and hunched her shoulders, waiting for her anxiety to lift. "Well," she said, finally, "we'll just have to see. Thank God for a lawyer, I mean you . . . to handle the police." Her calm and her compliment softened some of my own tension. "So tell me," she said.

"After you left, I flushed the cigarettes," I began, and accurately detailed what happened. She interrupted for questions—the doctor's name, how the son took it, had he mentioned her name? The recital of events protected her from my real questions: how did she manage her two lives, not just physically, but psychologically? How did she integrate the mother of soldiers and high government official with voyeur's "mistress" and intimate of weirdoes like Buffi?

"I'm bewildered by today," I said at one point. "I don't know what to make of you." She passed it by.

"You'll just have to stay bewildered," she said with a shrug, but her tone was friendly, even respectful. I smiled. By two quirks, I was to Anita Tockbridge much the opposite of what I had been to other women. I was "brave" because, in a manner of speaking, I had rescued Susan. I was "resourceful under extreme stress" because I had saved us both from a seedy hotel scandal, a potential front-page death. Even my portfolio at Labor was an asset to her, with its fortuitous blue-chip investment in her current job.

I had a Scotch and water to keep up my attitude of self-worth. As we talked, sometimes earnestly, sometimes with laughter, of the tragicomic events of the night, the ease slipped back into our relationship.

As I went back over my talks with the police, the doctor, filling in the gaps I had forgotten on the first telling, she listened, nodding, her eyes thoughtful. I could see the politician and administrator at work, could understand why she was effective, as she weighed what she had participated in and computed her possible losses.

When I had finished, she put out her cigarette and looked appraisingly at me.

"When I was on the city council," she said quietly, "there was a phrase the police used: 'to get someone in your pocket.' A used car dealer would give the beat policeman five dollars a day for not ticketing customers' cars parked in front of his place—he had the policeman in his pocket. And now you have me in your pocket, don't you?"

Surprised, I said, "Do you mean am I going to blackmail you?"

She didn't answer, but merely looked curiously into my eyes.

I went on: "No. I'm in on it, too."

Then, from the weariness, or drink, or despair of ever having her, or perhaps because I appreciated that she saw me as one who had played the man instead of the craven, I risked, "Besides, I have a yearning for you, if that's not too old-fashioned a word. I've had it ever since that night at your friend's party."

She dodged a direct response.

"Well," she said with a sigh, putting her feet on the coffee table in front of her. "I don't have the option of not trusting you. I have to like you, don't I? And that's not so hard. You're such a nice, healthy young man."

There was a slight pejorative in her "nice, healthy . . ." I deserved better of her than scorn.

"If you mean I prefer something normal to that queer business up there . . ." I decided to name it. "Voyeurism . . ."

"Oh, come on," she said with exasperation. "I made the mistake of letting my guard down, out of sheer relief that the hearing was over"—she looked at me wryly now rather than with irritation—"and also because I trusted you more than I should have. You must have guessed that I have my hang-ups with sex, my little neuroses, just as I expect you do. I won't ask you yours. Now leave mine be."

I started to question her. She had asked me to lie to the police and now, implicitly, she was asking me to silence my curiosity. But I was almost as close to her as in my basement fantasies and I did not want to risk alienating her. I said, in a weak attempt to be both funny and truthful:

"I don't mean that what happened up there wouldn't have been better than nothing at all." I rose from the chair and started toward the couch where she sat. I was convinced she would go to bed with me simply because it was less complicated than making a fuss.

I started to speak some word of love, but she cut me off.

"Look, Mr. Dobecker . . ." I smiled. "Martin," she corrected herself. "Right now you have the alternative, not I. You can choose whether each of us ignores the other. You can choose to go on with your decent corner of Labor and your furnace-building. Or you can try to involve yourself in my life."

On my lips were the words on involvement, but she went on.

"If you press me, I'm hardly likely to stand on virtue," she said. "I know a debt. You saw some of that upstairs there, debts."

"Then . . ." I started. She still held me off with her look.

"Then why don't you think about things a little? We're locked into each other with our secret anyway. I can't run away."

Should I let her put me out this night, when I had most call on her?

Yes, I thought. Probably. If I wanted the relationship to bond. Okay, I thought. I'd take a raincheck.

"Then, we *can* talk again?"

"Yes." The smile made her seem my age. "Sure."

"That's very affirming," I said, warmed and awkward. "You are saying that you will see me again in a non-office circumstance?" I wanted to be certain I had not misunderstood.

"Yes," she touched my shoulder. "Monsieur Ouroboros."

Flustered, I blurted out:

"Why are you doing this?"

"What?"

"Well, the trust. Being open."

Now she seemed taken aback. Part of it, of course, was

the Labor Department business—my specialized knowledge. But I felt now there really was something, a little something more.

"Ah, you want to be patted. Then: you are a brave man and, I suspect, a loyal one, and those are uncommon types of people in Washington." She laughed. "Now, will that flattery hold you?"

"Yes," I smiled. "I'm not brave," I added.

"You'll have to do," she said, rising.

When I left, I kissed her lightly, but at some length, to remember her lips and to recall me to them, if possible. The kiss, after so much had happened, seemed paradoxically as friendly, unextorted, and simple as a bluebell admired but unplucked.

I searched the Philadelphia papers. Pauhafen's obituary appeared on the second day and was fulsome and innocuous. The article overlooked his most interesting trait. I imagined what the headline might have been:

RICH VOYEUR DIES
"EN VOYANT" WITH
FEMALE BIGWIG

Instead, the headline said:

DYESTONE CHAIRMAN
SUCCUMBS IN D.C.

Anita, confirmed unanimously, was sworn in by Vice President Frieden in the Indian Treaty Room of the Executive Office Building. About sixty of us from Labor were there. My presence did not seem unnatural: even lower-echelon functionaries than I were there from her own section. I assumed it was she who had sent me the invitation.

The ceremony was meticulously dignified. The Vice President's distant formality with her before the still cameras re-confirmed to me that he had slept with her. I was jealous, grindingly. But I did believe now that someday I, too, would have her.

On the next Sunday, Meters and Zagstein, those breathless columnists, included the following as one of three short items:

The GOP tacticians in their colonial-style head-quarters building here are studying the vote-pulling potentials of a fine crop of newly hatched chicks in the Vice-Presidential brooder.

The cock of the walk, Harry Frieden, as heir presumptive to the Presidential nomination, will do the picking of a Vice President some three years hence. And for the first time since 1968, the Republicans have some semi-newcomers along with the older, still-hardy quadrennials.

Gov. Virgil Pyrmides of Connecticut and his New England confrere, Maine Gov. Bernard V. Leason, both would, being tried, prove most likely. From the Midwest, note Senator and former Gov. Permit O'Shaugh of Illinois or Justice Martinez Jorge-Rios of Chicago, the first Spanish-American on the High Court (for those with a penchant for a pure non-WASP ticket).

On the dark mare side is Anita Tockbridge, newly named Assistant Secretary of Labor. Another long-shot is HEW Secretary Hughlett Temple. Mrs. Tock-bridge could break the gender line on the Vice Presidency, Secretary Temple the color line . . .

CHAPTER

6

Madam Secretary

I did not hear from Anita for a week after her swearing in, although I went out of my way several times to pass by her office on the third floor. Once I saw Susan.

"How do you like it here?" I asked, pleased by her smile.

"Too much work," she said.

"How's the boss adjusting?"

"Great, about like I suspected."

"Want to grab lunch?" I could at least hear of my love secondhand.

"Glad to when it quiets down a little. I'm swamped."

"How is your daughter?" She paused briefly in her rapid answers, perhaps remembering more vividly our ordeal in the riot.

"Fine. You've still got a little limp. Will it heal?"

"Oh, I guess so."

It was more than a week later, May's heavy rains on the city, when Susan called. After a moment's chit-chat, she said, "Mrs. Tockbridge would like to speak with you."

"Help!" Anita said humorously when she came on.

"What's the matter?" I bit.

"I have to make a speech in Wilmington on youth programs. The Secretary was to do it but he's gone home with a cold."

"When?" Part of me was suddenly eager to help. The

rest of me wanted out—I had begun to adjust to her absence, to relax in my shell.

"Today, in about four hours. Can you help with it?"

"Hmmm," I said. My heart began to thud. To be with her, if only for a little while. But, but . . . "Why can't you use the Secretary's speech?"

"He'd planned to announce a preliminary cost-of-living survey showing us Republicans have stopped inflation for the first time since the Eisenhower days, or something. He wants to do that himself, maybe Monday. So I've got to fend for myself."

"Well, I can get some stuff together for you." Breathless, I plunged. "You're flying up?"

"Haven't you been out?" Yes, I had. The rain. "The Secretary is letting me have his car and driver. Can you work on it on the way up? Do I have to call Woeckle?"

"No," I said. "I'll tell him."

I pulled my clip and data file on youth programs. Incomplete as it was, there were enough statistics and anecdotes to put together a speech. I hoped the Secretary was giving her some morsel to announce. After all, even in Wilmington the wire services and Philadelphia papers would be covering, particularly since they thought the Secretary would be the speaker.

Susan was slipping typing paper and carbons into an attaché case when I came in. On her desk was a portable with a light blue case.

"Cleaning out your desk already?" I said to her with a smile. I felt very much the stitch in time. "Can't stand the place after all those Tuscany days at HEW?"

She laughed at me.

"You should be so funny in *Labor Notes*," she said.

Susan's hazel eyes remained reserved behind the surface good humor. I noted her full breasts. My God, I thought, my lust is impartial.

Susan pointed me into Anita's office. She, too, was busily grabbing up papers. How much taller she seemed than Susan. She turned. The pouty lips and the blue-ice eyes held me. The old octagonal watch stood out on the soft brown linen of her dress front.

"Madam Vice President," I said, unable to resist.

She looked up smartly, irritated at the liberty, and said:

"I don't know a damned thing about Labor's youth

programs. He's having me announce a four-state project and I have to work it into a thirty-minute speech. That's a lot of words."

"No big problem," I said almost jauntily. I swooned inside at her look of deliverance.

Fifteen pages double-spaced, I thought.

"I've made a million of these things," she went on, "but I'm always in a horror if it has to go down on paper. That formalizes it so the press can nit-pick it." She handed her documents to Susan. "We'd better get going. I have to drop by the house and get something to wear."

We picked up Anita's dress and headed east, Anita in back with me. Susan, portable in her lap, sat in front with the Secretary's stern, grayed chauffeur.

The big car sped through the rain down Massachusetts Avenue, past the fine new and old embassies, then on through downtown. It smelled snugly of light perfume, cigarette smoke and new-carness.

Anita was fidgety as we pulled onto Interstate 95. I was starring and underlining my data. It was her first speech on the sub-Cabinet level.

"Why can't you just begin writing it?" she asked nervously.

"We alchemists mix our ingredients before we cook up a nice mess of Philosopher's Stone," I said. I glanced at her rather slyly and was taken aback to see her eyes, telling me peremptorily to shut up. Obviously she did not want me to tread publicly into that other life, even by the most obscure indirection.

Taken aback, I went back to work, blocking out how the sections of the speech should fall. That done, I turned to her, and saw with a pang of rapture her look of apology for her anger.

"I need the first little joke now," I soothed. "Pull one from another speech, maybe," I suggested. She thought for a moment.

"Susan, what was that thing about a woman preaching you found in T. S. Eliot or somebody?"

"It was Samuel Johnson, Mrs. T.," said Susan pleasantly, but with diffidence. I was delighted to see Anita so far off the mark. Susan continued, "I think it goes, 'A woman preaching is like a dog on its hind legs . . .'"

It was an old saw, but would do.

"Got it!" I began writing:

"Now it may seem strange to this fine audience of Republicans, and Democrats, too, that I should come all this way to quote from the persuasive ·Mr. Johnson. Particularly when I tell you it is with the blessing of my boss, Secretary Harvey.

"But let me explain, before you reporters here start speculating about traitors within the administration, that I mean Samuel Johnson, not Lyndon B.

" 'A woman preaching,' he said, " 'is like a dog walking on its hind legs. The wonder is not that she doesn't ·do it well, but that she can do it at all.'

"Now I don't expect to speak well, but I do expect to say a few things about youth, both as a concerned mother and ..."

I finished the first page and turned it over to Anita, who pored over the long-hand scrawl. She shortened a sentence here, changed "fine audience" to "wonderful turnout," grunted with satisfaction at my occasional felicitous phrase.

Anita's yellow dress hung from the hook by the window; I could see its flattering, concealing roll-collar. I glanced at her, rereading my first page. It was she who smelled lightly of perfume. Crossed as they were, her legs were lovely, the left calf bulged out provocatively where it pressed the right shin.

I looked out the window, trying to focus on how to get the important news of the project into my frivolous vessel of words. The rain streaked down the pane. We were in Baltimore and I could see the ships outlined drear in the harbor. A romantic shipboard fantasy washed tidally into my brain. I imagined sailing away from it all on a tramp steamer with Anita.

The fantasy aroused me uncomfortably. I absented Anita for a moment from the fantasy and tried Susan in the role. It had a possibility, but not that tumbling surf-slip into eroticism that I could imagine with Anita. With Susan, it was easier to dream of lying abed in a ship cabin of mornings, thinking on what we would order at breakfast.

The car swished on the concrete through the flat, rainy countryside. I did not want us to get there; I was, from my Baudelaire period, the "roi d'un pays pluvieux, riche, mais impuissant, jeune et pourtant très-vieux . . ." Ah, my cubbyhole: There I could hug my futile arcana! Where was I venturing now?

Back at the writing, I finished another three sheets and my tail almost wagged with a dog's appreciation when she murmured, "Fine, just fine." We crossed the Susquehanna Bridge. Anita, her own window partially blocked by the dress, leaned toward mine and I turned, catching her eyes. Her shoulder unavoidably touched mine. I wanted to hold her, the rain outside, the soft, wide backseat housing our love. She watched the river go by us.

"Upriver is Harrisburg," she said. The nostalgia in her tone, so uncommon, made me curious for a moment until I remembered that her years in the State Capitol were the political roots of what she had become.

While Anita dressed at the Hotel DuPont, Susan and I ran off copies of the speech on a mimeograph machine. Susan's round arms moved quickly, adjusting this screw, tightening the bail. Efficiently, she tested the machine on a sample stencil, found the ink too low and replenished it without getting inky herself.

"You look as though you'd be pretty good in the kitchen," I said admiringly. Then I wished I hadn't, assuming that I meant and that she recognized I intended "bed" for "kitchen," once-marrieds sensibilities being what they are. She looked up and smiled, as if to say it didn't matter. She knew I was a paper tiger.

We stacked the speech copies, then stapled them. Susan's body jerked with the speed of her work. I had forgotten how unobtrusively good she was at everything I had seen her do—stenography, typing, interviewing the Negro girls.

Yet, it was of Anita I wanted to hear.

"How long have you been with Mrs. T?" I asked.

"This will be my fourth year."

"Hard taskmaster?"

"No," said Susan with some thought. "Not really."

"How'd you happen to come to work for her?"

Susan paused for a moment in her stapling, then picked it up again.

"My husband died—was killed—in a car accident. Mrs. Tockbridge needed help. She got me going again." I wondered about her boyfriend, now that she was confiding, but could think of no delicate way to ask.

The union, business, and state government fat cats who made up the Penn-Jersey-Delmar Development Council (PJDDC) were noisily filing into the banquet room.

"You want to sit back here with me and eat after I get this stuff up to the press table?" I asked. Short of Anita, Susan seemed the best company I was likely to find.

"Thanks. I think Mrs. Tockbridge would rather you sat with the press. In case they have any questions." I cringed at the idea.

My exhaustive daily exposure—from compiling *Labor Notes*—to the lassitude, ignorance, and pomposity of the "national press" in Washington had made me doubly wary of the idiot scribblers of the marches.

"What the hell do I tell them if they ask?"

"Just explain it very slowly and simply," she said. I was pleased at this mutuality of distaste for the press.

"Come on and sit up there with me then," I said.

"I'm watching calories anyway," she demurred.

"Nonsense! You're perfect as you are."

Susan laughed. Flattery, I thought: that golden key that never grows rusty.

Anita sat at the head table between the governor of Delaware and the lieutenant governor of Pennsylvania, an old friend, I gathered; they laughed together to my jealous annoyance. She had on that public face, a constant semi-leer, Greek mask of half-laughter, framed so that no matter when a photographer pressed his shutter button, the result would be a picture of healthy exuberance.

But I was proud of her when she spoke. She delivered the yak about Johnson with neat timing, culling her laughs for a moment, then, as if unable to resist the good humor of the audience, joining in. The model major politician, she was by turns modest, assertive, pleading, and reflective.

Anita had come by the technique on a thousand stumps. It de-sexed her. I could not frame fantasies of her, breast and body, while she mouthed the political claptrap I had written. The blue eyes registered sincerity. Or was that really she: a marionette with a brain; an actress; a title, Mrs. Assistant Secretary-on-the-Make?

They applauded. The wire service men followed the speech scrupulously, underlining and scribbling on the text.

"What's new in this?" one of them asked me when she ended.

"The four-state deal," I said.

"How much federal money in it?"

"Twelve point two million in round figures spread out over three years."

"What's your name? Can I quote you on the money?"

"Just say," I enunciated with a certain vainglorious pride, "a spokesman for the Assistant Secretary." His mongrel-terrier eyes flicked to the attractive woman who smiled at her applauders. Then he glanced back at me. Like that long-ago private eye, he knew.

On the road back, all of us relaxed. Susan and I told Anita how well she had done; she praised my speech; I lauded Susan's efficiency. Anita, her voice a little strained from the projecting, remembered a detail:

"Susan, can you find out who in the Department is supposed to get copies of these things and get them around first interoffice mail Monday and also into the press room just in case?"

"Yes," said Susan, instant aide.

"And arrange to get the local papers, maybe you'd better call an out-of-town newsstand tomorrow"—it would be Saturday—"and have them hold them, Wilmington and Philadelphia anyway."

The car, with its blessedly silent and capable chauffeur, hummed on across the wet pavements. At the highway, the marginal business establishments gave way and we saw only the rain. Anita worked her feet out of her shoes. She had changed back into her brown suit. All of us stared wearily out into the drenched night. I pushed off my shoes.

Susan, in front, said, "Is there anything else, Mrs. T?" in a drowsy voice. "If not, I'm going to doze." There wasn't. Susan laid her head on the back of the seat.

I slipped into sleep, but awoke as we came to a toll stop. In the light from the booth canopy I saw Anita was awake. She stared out the window, thoughtful, or simply tired, but as we pulled on out into the night and fog, she caught my stare. I could not bridge the darkness and plumb her expression. The car purred on and as she shifted to slump in her corner, her foot touched mine, perhaps accidentally. She did not remove it, and I pressed back. There, circumscribed by the night, my foot, cal-loused, bent-toed and a long day unwashed, was the focus of my erogeny. Was she signaling me what I had feared and wanted these weeks? Even in the dark, I did not dare take her hand. Susan, or even the chauffeur might turn under a sign light. I made small overhearable talk as if to confirm the touch of her foot.

"Is the job about what you thought it would be?"

"Yes, much confusion. Much reading. You have to find out pretty well what the whole Department is doing before you can begin to plan ..."

"More demanding than HEW?"

"Yes, I suppose." She thought for a moment, then said, "More dangerous in a way."

"Oh?" I said, alerted. There was something she wanted to tell me.

"The more visible you get, the better target you make. There was that Meters-Zagstein column. The old-timers in the party will be sharpening up the spears." She sighed again, but still did not take her foot away. "They'll be digging up what they can."

"There's not much to find, or they'd have found it before," I sought to assure her.

"Yes," she said, but there was a worrisome lack of conviction in it and I wondered what old skeletons rattled in her closet. I felt sure now there were some.

Our feet still touched. I played with fantasies of her. Again, I imagined the two of us in an affair, inexplicable to others. Oddly, I mused on a witch trial at Sainte-Claude in 1596, a trifle of knowledge I had squirreled away. A young woman was accused of committing the most hideous acts with a middle-aged tanner, the local wizard. When the president of the tribunal, surely inured to almost every act of witches, asked her why a girl of good family had performed the multiple perversions, she replied, as if it were obvious:

"Mais, il estay mon amy et mon frère."

Then the first twitchings of sleep caught me. When I awoke we were sliding into Washington, a town of sleep at two o'clock on a Saturday morning.

Susan, her cheek puffed from pressing against the car seat, volunteered to take the extra copies of the speech to their office. I offered to carry the typewriter, but she was already out even as the chauffeur rounded the front of the car. Before the uniformed man returned, Anita said with admirable aplomb considering how little time she had to say it:

"Why don't you come by for brunch, if that doesn't ruin your Saturday?" She must have seen my surprise. She smiled. "I want to talk to you about your future." It was deftly done. "Call me about ten thirty."

The chauffeur stepped back in.

"Sure," I said nervously.

"I want to get some advice and help," she said pacifically.

In bed I dreamed I was at my grandfather's. We were cleaning out his barn, near Gaithersburg, with fire. I was burning cobwebs that hung thick as ivy vines, trashy hay in corners, and old sacking. All the time we tended the fires with long poles, like those which were once used to open school windows. My only fear was that my father would come and make me stop or that the barn would catch fire.

When I awoke about eight o'clock, the dream disturbed me until I saw its simple, vivid, and reassuringly masculine symbols. Mental hygiene, as the ancients recognized, depended largely on beginning the day with the proper explanation of dreams.

CHAPTER

7

The Compact

As I drove along Wisconsin Avenue, I saw the teeny-boppers already beginning to straggle in twos and threes toward Georgetown. The boys' Jesus hairdos still made me ponder, but the barefooted young girls in their outlandish Mother Hubbards were attractive, their hair long, tied back from their fresh, natural faces.

The sun was hot, the air humid after yesterday's rain. I was apprehensive despite my casual slacks and Madras jacket. Waiting for Anita to come to the door, I both lusted for her and feared the encounter. The most delicious erotic daydreams alternated with the calming thought that perhaps my visit would be only business.

Anita was gracious, ushering me into the sunny room. She wore a friar's gray shirt, cowled modestly at the neck, and subdued plaid slacks that fit her closely. The breakfast makings were on a low table. Washed by sunlight, the orange juice was poster-bright in the crystal pitcher. And the stubby, colored glasses, pottery mugs, sugar and cream bowls and two-compartment marmalade and preserves server glistened on the checkered cloth.

My heart, for all its fear, sang out—"Freude! Freude!" —at the smell of fresh coffee. How long had it been since someone else fixed the coffee in a room I was entering for breakfast? What little things distinguished the complete man, his wife up those few minutes early to fill the kitchen with coffee aroma, from that other man manqué who fixes his own instant coffee with freeze-dried grains?

When she spoke, it had the warmth of woman in it that I had gone so long without hearing.

"I can't remember whether you ate anything last night," she said. "You must be starved."

So simple. It was a lovely big breakfast: scrambled eggs, link sausage and hot warm-and-serve rolls.

Susan called to report Anita's speech had made the front page, though modestly and well below the fold, of the *Philadelphia Inquirer,* and had a two-column head on the city page of the *Baltimore Sun.* Anita was delighted, and cooed at Susan. She did not mention my presence, an omission into which I read meaning.

I sat in the warm kitchen while she washed and dried the dishes.

"Well," she said with pleasure, no doubt from the good press play, "it was a fine speech and you got it done so fast."

"It was good because the Secretary gave you something good to announce," I said. "If it had been only my statistics, you wouldn't have made the Wilmington *Building Trades Council Gazette.*"

"You're right." She took off the apron and went back to the table, the coffee pot, reheated now, in her hand. I sat across from her, watching those long fingers on the bakelite of the coffee pot, as she poured. "Look," she said, glancing up at me. "You really should be more ambitious."

I savored the foreknowledge of an offer.

"If I were ambitious, I'd be in private practice."

"Yes, but even so." She had not touched her coffee. I nervously poured too much cream in mine again. "You have a first-class way of doing things. Really. You must know that."

I smiled. Heavenly! But she had caught me out.

"Christ, look at you." She laughed. "You'd sit back and let me tell you you're a lovely duck for hours. You know what I'm asking. I need some experience in my shop."

"Yes," I said, "but I'm not sure I should shuck off my shell. I've found a home in it." Then a chill of truth hit me and I said incautiously: "I *was* more or less happy in it until I saw you in your wolf costume."

She thought about that for a moment.

"That's sweet."

"Besides, I don't think I want to work for a woman."

"*That's* ridiculous. I'm not hard to work for. Ask Susan." She had not said it querulously, but as a statement of fact. "My God, you'd be somebody instead of a nothing writing that little *Notes* sheet. You *know* you can do better than that."

"You assume I'm interested in advancement." I was getting a little panicky now that we were at the stage of a compact. As things stood, my road up, assuming that I wanted to go up, would be shifting around in the legal department for fifteen or twenty years until I got a crack at the job of Deputy Solicitor. She started to speak again, but I said defensively:

"We went through the ambition thing that night. I'm not. Really. I know that it's power that makes this town go round. Hell, I was raised here. But I don't care about it. I don't want to. My wants are simpler and cleaner."

I'd said the wrong thing. Her eyes narrowed.

"And chickenhearteder," she snapped. I took it like a coward, and she went on. "But I *am* interested in power. And you are competent and unclaimed and uncommitted."

"How do I know it would be any better than what I have?"

She took a sip of her black coffee, baiting me with the pause.

"It would be Deputy Assistant Secretary of Labor," she said. "You would be my Deputy."

The impact shocked me. My God! It was a jump from a lawyer, one who doubled as a sort of rewrite man, to the footstool of power—to a policy position. The salary increase would be enormous. My first thought was of a red Morgan, my second of a bottle of Chambertin with Liederkranz, saltines and sweet butter.

"Jesus," I said, genuinely awed. "You're crazy. You couldn't get me that if you wanted to."

"I can name my own Deputy," she said coldly, then burst out angrily at me:

"It's sickening to have to beg you to do something for your own good."

I caught her change of humor, but wasn't man enough either to rebuke her or to cast aside my reservations and simply say, Yes, okay, I'll do it.

"I'll think about it," I said. "I'd be giving up my Civil

Service protection. I want some time." I could hear the whine in my voice.

"You'll think about it," she parroted me.

"I'm not sure I'd want to work for a woman," I repeated, taking a second cheap shot at her. I was too craven to meet her head on.

The sleazy bolt hit her in the heart. Before my eyes, the face of the woman changed from anger to rage. I could hardly believe what I saw. At the edges of her lips, the muscles bulged into tenseness as she tried to hold her temper. Her lids dropped over her eyes until they seemed no longer light, but dark. She bit off her next words as she spoke them, mean, her voice rising:

"You save Susan in a riot and you lie to police like a trouper and then you sit there like a goddamned dog of some kind and whine . . ."

I was horrified at her loss of control and her criticism.

". . . I mean, you act like some kind of faggot, some kind of weakling . . ."

I interrupted:

"Faggot?" That was too much.

". . . you might as well be. Just look at you, cowering to get back to your damned furnace and your stupid little cards. Oh, you sit off in a corner and pretend you're smarter than everybody because you know something about whether it's the Age of Aquarius or Kiss My Ass."

"Anita!" I broke in.

"Don't you Anita me. You Mrs. Tockbridge me!"

She sputtered on. I took it, an open-mouthed ninny. Mutely, I felt tears of humiliation coming.

I got up to go, my head bursting with anger and hurt.

This was what I had taken from Julia, her ranting at me for not being the man her ecologist was.

"Period or no period, he wants me," she had berated me.

This was the way my mother, her thin arms tattooing the table, had talked to my father: "You'd bite your tongue before you'd ask for a raise!" And some gutless mousetrapped grandfather must have heard it from his wife, the generational curse of castigations unreplied to.

"Shut up!" I yelled at her suddenly and saw her face freeze in the middle of some outrage, the big mouth already curled around some unsaid insult. "Shut up!" I rose and flung the chair backward.

"You aren't even a lady. Listen to *you*. A whore! Fucking a rotten old animal like Fred Pauhafen for money! A whore! No wonder your husband was a goddamned drunk." She had gone red beneath the light powder, her eyes shocked, but I spewed it all out. I wasn't taking her shit anymore. "No wonder your kids hate you. A whore." That was too much for her, but not enough for me.

Choked up in fury and frustration, I struck the table with my fist, turning over the cream. She made an instinctive grab for it.

"Your kids hate you," I shouted at her again, knowing that was where to hit. "And we laugh at you. The whole lot of you. Me, Woeckle, all of us. You come into our town, from nowhere, from some lousy little hick town in Pennsylvania. Society whores! Playing black magic games because you think it's 'in.' Hicks! And you think you're big time . . ."

"Get out!" she screamed at me. "Get out!"

But I was rolling. I was getting rid of it, of Julia, of my mother. Of the whole lot of them, the women I had hated and had let squeeze the manjuices out of me, the politicians I had worked for at Labor, that my poor, goddamned potato-grader of a father had worked for.

"You come into the big city. Oh, I've seen you and the rest of you come and go ever since I was a kid. And you. You're the worst of the lot. Why you'll be the first American woman President if you have your way and the first American President of any kind to crawl into the White House on your back. Look at you! Sitting there with your face falling apart. *Me* a dog? *Me* a fairy? Look at yourself!"

I had shattered her. I had beaten her down with my words and my rancor and its truth. I stopped, panting.

"Get out!" She bit it off. "Out!"

My fury was done. I felt sick. I had never broken out at anyone, not in my whole life, in that way before. And yet, I was relieved. I could indulge my emotions no more than that. That was the bottom. She had bullied me and I had had my say.

"You're right, I'm going," I said.

I looked over at her, not even angry anymore. She had beaten the horse and the horse had kicked her in the tits, where it hurt. She had shut up. Her face was damning a breakup inside her head. Then it came; she flopped down in her chair and plunked her head onto the table, upsetting her coffee forward. I could hear the animal snorts of her sobs. It didn't sound the least bit romantic, but I did begin to feel sorry for her.

"Anita," I said. "Stop crying."

She cried on, although the snorting stopped. I sat across from her, blotting up the coffee with my napkin.

"Please go," she said at last, without raising her head.

"No, listen."

She brought her head up, wiped her eyes and her nose with her napkin and looked at me. Her face, even with the little makeup she had on, was streaked, a smear of eye black running a quarter of an inch from the corner of her eye, giving her a slight pirate squint.

"Look," I said, "there's a precept in law, a right of response. If one man socks another, even lightly, the other man can ram his teeth down his throat on the theory that there is a right not just to respond but to stave off any further attacks." I raised my palms, not apologetically, but as a gesture asking understanding.

"Such awful things," she said, "and not true."

"I'm sorry if they weren't true," I said.

"He drank too much before I married him." She began to tear up again. "You're thinking I married him because he was a drinker, because he was weak."

"I wasn't thinking anything." That was more or less true. I was thinking, if anything, that crying made her look old. She went to the kitchen and got a Kleenex and blew her nose.

"My boys don't hate me. I didn't give them enough time . . . if anything, they feel sorry for me. They just ignore me."

She kept wiping her eyes.

"I'm not a weeper," she said.

"It's all right."

"It's not all right. And I'm not a whore."

"Well, I'm no faggot," I said.

"I know," she said. "I'm sorry." I was touched. "I've been pushing too hard and this was bound to happen," she said, reasonably now.

I could hardly believe that I had won, that I had for once stood up and won. Even so, the fissures of instability I had seen in her unnerved me.

"Why did you lose your temper at me?" I asked, trying to lift the seriousness. "I was about to say 'yes.'"

She smiled ruefully.

"You sit back and sneer at those of us"—she paused—
"at those of us who are ambitious, because . . . it's true, we
do things that you who sit back don't do." She had herself
fully under control now.

"We could manage," I said to her. Did I want to work
for her? My God, did I? Now that I had seen a hint of the
cracked china she carried around inside.

"Christ, you do have a temper," she reflected.

"You're the first person to see it," I said.

"Do you want to give the job a try?"

"If it doesn't work out, can I go back to *Labor Notes?*"

"If Woeckle will take you," she laughed slightly.

Anita looked at the coffee, then got some paper towels
and went to work, spreading back the cloth and wiping the
table. I took off my jacket and carried the cups to the
kitchen. As she worked, she talked.

"You have all the right tickets: respectable schools; you
certainly have done a good job in your pigeonhole. Besides, Woeckle doesn't want to give you up. I've made
some inquiries. Anytime you've got somebody you want to
keep, it's a sure bet that he can do more than he's doing.
The Secretary has raided too many not to know that."

She smiled openly at last. Her full lips, without lipstick
now, were paler, but all the more attractive. "E. G.," she
said, putting her thumbs in her armpits and waggling her
fingers in the child's timeless expression of self-pride.

I laughed with her. It gave me an excuse for audacity:

"I don't think *he* raided you. I think *somebody* did so
that when the Secretary resigns they can put a lady in as
Secretary and win the hearts and votes of fifty million
ladies."

"Don't I wish," she said.

She walked over to the window and I followed. The
sun came hotly into the air-conditioned room. To the
left the National Cathedral squatted, unfinished and huge.
Across the summits of the trees in Rock Creek Park I
could see the Capitol atop its hill, steaming off-white in
the noon sun. I could almost feel the soft heat of her
body beneath the gray cloth and the plaid. From behind
her, I took her upper arms in my hands. She did not
flinch or turn away.

"I would be nuts to work for you," I said, knowing at
last that I might do it. Power she wanted, and that, truly,

I did not crave. But I wanted love, yearned for it more, perhaps, than she for power. And that in some form she could afford me.

I dropped my left hand and turned her to me, easing down my mouth to kiss her as she stood in the sunlight. Her breath smelled heavily of the sausage, coffee, and cigarettes. Where face joined neck her skin was roughened. But what was that to me?

Her lips, sophisticated by loves I could not contemplate, first gave gently then withdrew to brush mine lightly, not missing the corners of my mouth. I was breathing so hard I was dizzy.

Under her friar's shirt, her ribs were covered with good, taut flesh. As I broke from her for a moment, I saw the white teeth within her wet parted lips. Her eyes were smoky with concern. I figured after a morning like ours, she probably needed a little reassurance too. Now, if only I didn't do something stupid to mess it up.

She was pressing into me hard at the hips and I moved back enough to unsnap the brassiere and caress her left breast, around, but not on, the nipple. That much I remembered. The nipple sprang up like an enormous goose pimple.

"Look, let's get off our feet somewhere," I panted. She took my hand and led me into the bedroom. On the bed, I undressed her, since that was what she wanted. I rolled her slacks off, and panties, and turned her, kissing her belly, the old borning scars white there. From then on, it was swift and passionate. Too early, with a groan of pleasure and regret I pressed up against her haired mount until the spasms ended.

I could have cried, but was not, of course, really surprised. As the tension released between our two bodies, I said as lightly as my embarrassment permitted:

"So, is the job still open? I almost flunked the entrance exam."

"Poor baby," she said.

But I was not going to apologize. If she could survive my anger and I hers, then we could survive my precipitancy.

"Was it so bad?" she said.

"No, it was lovely while it lasted," I said honestly. She rolled out from under me to get some Kleenex, the universal blotter—for tears, for noses, for semen. When she came back, we lay on our backs holding hands. The shades were drawn, but I could see the outlines of pictures, the dim reflections of our bodies in a wall mirror hung aslant. It caused me a ripple in my post-coital calm. I wondered for whom the mirror had been hung.

"Then, I'll come to work for you," I said.

"That's nice," she said softly. She added more sharply, "If I had pushed you off when you kissed me out there, would you have said you'd take the job?" The question was apt.

"Probably not," I answered.

"Then I seduced you into it," she persisted.

"No," I turned on my side. Her breasts had flattened out, but the mount of hair stood out in the half-dark below her bulgeless belly. "It's more complicated than that. You accepted my advances and I accepted your job. It's a matter of acceptance rather than seduction."

She rose up on her elbows. Her breasts delineated themselves as she did, separate, the nipples in relaxation as big around as quarters that had been like cherries to my lips. She dragged on the cigarette, lighting us slightly like lazy Satans with the red flow. With her free hand she touched my chest and traced down with a finger to my navel.

"It's nice you're youngish," she said reflectively. Then she came back to what I had said. "Acceptance is nicer. People who are seduced wind up rebelling. Acceptance makes for binding compacts."

She rolled to her bedtable and got me a cigarette. Then she lit it for me, kissing me on my lips before she put it between them.

"Acceptance, that's what corrupts us. People give us things without our asking and we accept, we don't protest and . . ."

I tried ineptly to quote the quatrain about vice from Pope, but she thought I was just trying to say something about sex, so I dropped it. I had taken a step, avoided for ten years, toward chasms of power. I had tied my fortunes to a woman who, while capable, was also dangerously drawn to things that could bring her to disaster and who, to judge by her blow-up this morning, was somewhat unstable.

"Anita," I said at last, "I am formally pulled from my cranny of the coral reef. I am. But please, just this once:

I don't know what other things may be part of your life. I see the politician, the civil servant and I am impressed. But Buffi, Tapir? What else am I wedded to?"

I made my speech on my elbow, turned to her. She lay flat, a long, slender form, dragging from a fresh cigarette. She answered, looking not at me, but at the dim ceiling.

"You *are* getting into some strange waters, Monsieur Ouroboros. I am not very good at self-analysis, but what you saw of me this morning was probably a surprise for you, yes?"

I took her cigarette from her and tapped its ash off in a tray on her bedtable, then I put it back in her fingers.

"I don't really know enough about women to know what is ordinary," I said truthfully. "I mean . . ."

She stopped my own gambit at confession.

"Let me see if I can tell you what you are 'wedded to,' " she said. "Then there won't be any 'if I'd only known.' " She went on deliberately, "I am forty-five and I am an ambitious woman and I have my quirks as you've found out—found out more rapidly than either of us expected," she added.

"I compete with men, and it's a cliché, probably some man thought it up, but it's true, I guess, that women who compete with men become a little odd, like women who don't compete with men," she added.

"I *am* ambitious," she went on, gathering up her thoughts again, and talking almost as if to herself. "I *do* like this exhilaration of moving up. It gets obsessive, in a way. When they made me Assistant Secretary, I could feel my stomach, like it was drifting loose from me with the excitement, because I was so thrilled, well, something almost sexual. And then there was the swooping thought that maybe the next step . . ."

"Would be Secretary," I finished for her.

"Yes. So that's part of it. The drive to get up there."

"But . . ." I started to ask her why, if she were so ambitious, she took such risks. She was already thinking ahead of me.

"Yes, I know. You think I carry my own built-in disasters, and I *know* it. You've seen some of that. Why should I hide it from you? When I was with Fred Pauhafen, for example. You pretend that disgusts you. Doesn't it occur to you that some people like to watch? Well, he did. Fifteen years ago he became my lover. A decent man. And if later, when he got older, he couldn't function anymore—missionary-style like you good boys were taught was the only decent thing—well, what of it? Maybe I got some sort of thrill in it, too."

Jealousy and the beginnings of shock struck me and she saw it.

"Ah, look at you. You ask and I try to search myself and give you an answer and you look sulky and put upon."

She smiled and then took my palm and kissed it: this same woman who had called me unthinkable things only an hour earlier.

"Well, is that enough?" she asked. I shook my head "no," but it was likely she would have gone on anyway, to bale it up completely, this once.

"So I liked him. And other men. Ah, now you're thinking, 'nympho.' I see it. But that's too easy. I enjoy men and I enjoyed you and I have been discreet. Grant that the times have at least liberated us enough to be ourselves *that* much. And if the men I liked gave me money for my political campaigns when I needed it . . ." She grew more acerbic. "If Fred Pauhafen helped me out in ways that might grind a little on the goody-goodies"—there it was again, that hint of unknown scandal—"then so what? If they wrote letters I needed or made telephone calls, why shouldn't they? I accepted." She smiled with gentle mockery again. "Like you have accepted me with all my sins on me, sweet Jesus, and I you with your peculiarities."

I imagined armies marching through her bed. Me! One of the multitudes. The thought was damnable, and she was trying to make it sound so rational.

"But the whole thing," I said. "The ambition and then these crazy risks of scandal. It's flaky! Buffi: does he give you money, too? I mean *us* money." It was the closest I could come to humor.

"Flaky? Well, maybe it is flaky, if that's the word. My parents, my mother especially, always thought I was such a priss, but, well, I'm not going to give you a family history·. . ."

"Why not?" I said.

"Because it's dull," she said in good humor. "The weak fawning father conspiring with the only-child daughter against the strong mother. You don't have to know anything about psychiatry, and I don't, to . . . Anyway, by

the time I was fifteen, I was editor of the high school
paper and vice president of the class, and, on the other
hand, that summer I was with a man, a young lawyer, in
his wife's bed almost every afternoon."

"Well," I said weakly, "you've been consistent with your
past."

"And I guess that's the way it's always been. Besides,"
she said, brushing back her hair abruptly, "I'd go crazy if
my whole life was being Madam Assistant Secretary to
these Midwestern horrors at the office, in Congress, loyal
to their wives, disloyal to everything else, like Temple and
Harvey and McFadden."

"Okay," I said. "But one last question. Buffi . . ."

"All right, Buffi," she said, obviously eager now to wind
it up. "*His* father started *him* off in a seminary, over his
mother's objections, of course. She knew what he was
like from the beginning. And he *is* crazy. Well, that's too
strong. But you see how he is, or maybe you don't. He is
still at war with the Catholic church."

"Because his father is dead and he can't fight a dead
man?"

"Oh, maybe something like that, if you want to be a
shrink about it."

I remembered Buffi as he began to speak of the Rabbi
Lwov, his voice pitching higher, running faster. I could
believe that he was one of those who could be sane in
every way but one, and that his bane: As some anti-
Semites are so normal until one says the word "Jew," or
the way some people hated the Kennedys. Or, my father,
Roosevelt, for all that Roosevelt's agriculture programs
got him his start, and my father otherwise so contained,
so reticent about his feelings.

"So," and she paused a few seconds, as if to sum up, to
give me a fair answer this once. "So, it's this: I'm ambitious, yes, dreaming of the Presidency like everyone in
government does at a certain level. We see mistakes and
we think we can do better."

"That's not the problem," I said, "it's . . ."

"That I've used people to get there. Well, I *have* used
men. Liking them . . . you . . . I have let them give me
money and do favors to help me move up."

"And the rest?" I asked softly. "The kookiness?"

"In D. H. Lawrence . . ." she looked up at me now in
sly self-deprecation. "I do read books when people tell

me I must . . the hero, to get a thrill, lay with his girlfriend just off the road so there was that danger of getting caught. A sort of stealing watermelons." She sighed, then went on more harshly. "Maybe that's making it too literary, or too rational. Because, at the bottom of it, I have a perverse streak, a sexual feeling about being watched and about flouting the establishment, the Church even, just like Buffi has, only not quite as strong." She stopped now.

"That's a lot for me to buy," I said.

Now she was assessing me.

"Well, that's the way it is and you'll never get it that straight from me again."

She turned to me, exhaling the last of her cigarette, and kissed me even as she put her thigh partly on mine. I felt the pull of my plastered and entangled pubic hairs as my passion returned. There were more questions to ask, but they would wait. Stealing watermelons. There was a line in Baudelaire, kisses, "frais comme les pastèques . . ." For a man starved for love, for respect and consideration from women for so long, and such a bungler when I found the shadow of companionship, Anita was on that day a kind goddess.

Only the sexually fearful can imagine my gratitude for her passion and her patience. The kissing went on. Shortly, with a bliss of thrilling, I slipped into her. Blessed second time around! There was almost ample time for experimentation before, at length, I felt the trembling in my middle spine. She sensed it and, with a succession of "oh's" against my mouth, locked my pumping into her until I pumped no more. Oh, baby, I thought, before I drifted into semi-swoon, I am a man again.

My mind lolled off to boyhood: I saw the tires of my father's car as they vee-ed water up from the ford in Rock Creek Park. I smiled at the fountainhead of this recall: the odd zoo smells, so like the animal perspiration and connubial odors that had made their way through the canned fortifications of her deodorant. I felt marvelously human. With tenderness, I pushed the sweated hair up from her forehead.

"You is my woman now," I said tritely.

"Whew," she replied.

So we lay, until the anxious haunts of the day intruded and she murmured:

"I have to scurry. I have things to do this afternoon."

I watched while she bathed, her breasts buoyed by the water, rimmed with a thin line of lather. They began to excite me, but she saw it and laughed.

"Think work. I need some help from you next week while I'm working on getting you," she said. She ticked off what she wanted from me: a breakout of planning funds from the total projected budget for the next two fiscal years, where the soft spots were—programs run by second-rate people, ones faltering on their own, and those which Congress had simply become bored with and would appropriate less and less money for; who ran the programs that were really working, not just the ones we ballyhooed; who in our Investigations branch could be counted on to do a thorough job on union and business violations of Taft-Hartley; field offices that were worth a damn and would give an honest report on local programs; where the "non-Negro/non-white minority" money was going.

When she said "non-Negro/non-white minority," I laughed and she joined in. Negroes were no longer fashionable, it was true. But if the Labor Department moved faster for the Eskimos, the Indians, the few slum Chinese, some Mexican-Americans—ah, that was a sure way to publicity and to the great white masses' hearts.

I told her to wait, went to the living room and came back with a ballpoint to jot down her ideas. They continued to pour out of the tub. Susan had been getting her some information, but she was new, too. And most of her staff were cagey timeservers.

"Can you get started on that? And get your own work done, too?" She asked it almost rhetorically.

"Are you sure you can cut me loose from Woeckle?" I wanted everything done according to Department protocol. "You must get Woeckle to come tell me it's okay for me to work on your stuff." She did not chide me for my caution, and I could see her recall our fight. She nodded and I went on: "It'll take me at least two weeks to train my replacement."

"That's too long," she said, taking the sole of her foot in her hand to scrub it with a little brush. It was disconcerting to watch her in the bath. I wanted to jump in. But I could feel her anxiety now to get on with the afternoon and whatever it was she planned to do.

I glanced around the room as she concentrated on her

toenails. On the shelf was a liquid douche in a bottle shaped like a pepper mill. Either no man or only one man regularly shared her bathroom or it would be in a cabinet, I speculated. On the walls were two framed copies of mosaics, woman with vase and youth with donkey, their rusts and whites matching the bathroom. Nice, normal bathroom. No hint of her penchant for the bizarre. I wondered where she kept the wolf costume.

She stood up in the tub and wrapped a towel around her.

"I'll call Woeckle and tell him I'm going to the Secretary," she said. "You know, the necessity for moving good personnel up, the fine career opportunity and the need to get policy and planning back on the ball."

It would work. That I knew. It had the Ad Majorem Secretary Gloriam quality to it.

"When will I see you again?" I asked.

"Monday, at the office."

"No, I don't mean that."

She gave me a peck of a kiss and reached to open the door.

"Don't think that way. I'm glad you're going to work for me. And you're young and I like you and I trust you. You hurt me with the things you said. Some were unfair. That's done. I gave in. But don't think of me as some kind of wife. You've been married and you're not a fool. You know the difference."

She said it seriously, even with kindness. Yet it was an unsettling way to end my job interview.

That weekend, I was in an agony of jealousy over her. I traced on my mind every movement and each kiss. I suffered the hatred of our argument, my initial failure. Then I imagined variations on our lovemaking, visualizing the elaborations that I might have attempted on each touch and each thrust.

Sunday morning I was groaning with lust for her and thought of calling, telling her I had to have her again or I would not work for her. I fretted jealously in fury over other men who had touched her, self-tortured, seeing her lying beneath de Plaevilliers or the Vice President, while Pauhafen leered—and she winked back—at his animal snoot in a doorway crack.

At another time I might have disgustedly eased myself with masturbation. Instead I went to the call girl Sunday evening. She read me her doggerel for the last time, "The Ballad of the Golden Jew." Whether it was my self-confidence with her, or something else, she sensed, I think, that I had found someone who would keep me from coming back. For she said those same revealing words I had uttered to Anita:

"When will I see you again?"

CHAPTER

8

Deputy
Assistant Secretary

Monday, I felt by turns anxious, guilty, and elated. God-damnit, I thought, a Deputy Assistant Secretary, the sort of appointive job I was so accustomed to see going to the administrative assistants of senators or their favorite committee aides. I would never have schemed for the job. But being given it was something else, like a compact-car owner winning a Lincoln Continental in a soap contest.

All day Monday I sweated out a call from Anita or from Woeckle. None came. Susan did telephone and said, with what I felt were some reservations, "Mrs. T. told me you were coming with us and I just wanted to tell you I'm glad."

"Anybody who can keep a good assistant like you for all these years has got to be a good boss," I replied, I hoped graciously.

Woeckle did drop by on Tuesday. He sat in my small office and said with a nervous hale-fellow kindness:

"Well, they're moving you up, it looks like." I could see through the layers of government wariness that he was proud of me and I was touched. Yet I sensed he had something more to say than that.

"I hope to hell they know what they're doing," I answered—the bureaucratic "they" covering all sinners, all sins. "I'm not sure I do." Woeckle, I knew, wanted to hear just exactly how I had swung it, but I gave him no clue. He got down to his real purpose:

"I don't want you to take this in rancor or ill-will," he began.

Astonished, I could see he was letting himself talk to me from his heart. The words were old-fashioned, as if he had learned governmentese long ago and these real feelings had atrophied until now.

"Martin, aside from my wanting you to stay, there's something to be said for the slow way up. That planning and policy deputyship is not the best one in the department, but it's certainly not the worst."

He blinked his guarded old eyes. "Martin, you get up there, high in the tree where the limbs are thin, no Civil Service protection, and it's rather shaky when the wind starts blowing."

"I *do* like working here for you," I said doubtfully.

"And if you didn't like it, I would find you something else," he said firmly. He wasn't the sort who wanted yes or no answers right away. God knows he never gave them himself, to the Secretary or anyone else, which probably accounted for his longevity.

"I never thought of you as ambitious, though maybe you should have been more so, but if *Labor Notes* isn't enough of a challenge . . .

"Mrs. Tockbridge is a very talented woman and would have moved up very fast on pure ability, and with the President eager to get the ladies into the responsible positions that have been denied them for so long, it's no wonder she's doing well, but administrations change, Martin."

"I do wonder . . ." I started, but he lifted his hand, its back so wrinkled, spotted and veined, and went on:

"You think about it. If I put up enough of a squawk and give you a little promotion, they won't buck me. You'll stay. But I want what you think is best for you. You've given me good service, made the solicitor's office better known around town with *Labor Notes*. I'll be the last one to hold you back, if you really want to go." He emphasized the last phrase. Then, easing the seriousness he added, "If the President asked me, why I might answer the old fire bell myself." I laughed politely.

What this old veteran said chilled me, for I knew he was thinking of me, offering me, in his way, a promotion. He was saying as clearly as he dared that Anita's advancement might be too tainted with politics to last, even in Washington, and that my star might go down with hers.

"Thanks," I said. I was feeling almost tearful. "I will never have a better boss, that is, if I do decide to go." Woeckle got up fatly and slipped back into the relationship we had established through the years. He told me only a native Washingtonian could stand this heat. I asked after his grandchildren.

The new job gave me a 40 percent raise. I sold the secondhand Chevy II that had replaced my riot casualty and bought a slightly used maroon Morgan, a car which, like corduroy suits, I had always admired, but never owned.

My new office was 11 by 15 feet, plus a room equally large for my secretary, who was middle-aged, unobtrusive, adequate—and my files.

I worked like hell, first getting up the summaries and the fact-supported opinions to educate Anita, then establishing links with the field offices. I gathered up their reports and collated the material from university and foundation projects, from city and state annual reports, into manageable noncontradictory chunks of data.

Thus, on youth in Cincinnati or Tucson or Fairbanks, for example we had a précis on standard of living, unemployment, youth migration from the community, racial percentage, education level at each age group, dependability of municipal, state, federal and voluntary organizations, and total expenditures on youth projects by each. We were working up similar stuff on the aged, handicapped, and on employable women.

Anita was right about being easy to work with, even fun. She recognized how much it takes to get a city thumbnailed on a single page, with a workable manpower training proposal summarized in the last three paragraphs. I didn't have to show her the three-foot-high stack of data I'd plowed through to make sure the one page was correct.

And it was "socially useful." I was proud of what I was doing to help America, maudlin as that may sound. My research and summarizing helped get programs going where chances of graft and failure were lowest. They put some sense into the chaos of budget projections, to the delight, Anita told me, of the Secretary and the Office of Management and Budget. And if my proposals were overruled for political reasons and funds went to the corrupted and the venal, my hardy figures at other times won out over dreamier plans that would have cost more and failed.

Susan, more and more, worked with me on the projects. Anita wanted the initial work out of the way quickly. Susan farmed out the typing, goosed our researchers for more rapid statistics and cajoled the field offices into taking up our requests before those of other bureaus in the Department.

If we worked late, which was often, Anita sent out to Bassin's for roast beef sandwiches, a carton of soup and a couple of bottles of wine or beer. Susan worked indefatigably and cheerfully. I made no subjective inquiries of her and she reciprocated. With Anita she was loyal, grateful, but curiously uninvolved, a relationship both women ratified.

Sometimes I drove Susan home. She never asked me in. I gathered that her mother came frequently from Myerstown to stay with her.

Occasionally, I scooted away from the Labor Department lot with a roar toward Anita's. Lovemaking with her always had at least the illusion of being unhurried. With practice, it grew more sophisticated, even exotic. Once, in the darkness she concluded a fellatio so vigorous that I felt turned inside out. Pained and giddy, I saw a trail of light sweep past my eyes and thought, My God, I'm hallucinating, seeing stars, until I recognized that it was only her wristwatch with its luminescent dial as she moved up to lie beside me.

I remained enraptured.

In her bed, Anita restored precisely that masculinity my wife had aborted and then battered into a frail scarecrow, in which form it had remained during the impoverished years that followed our divorce.

If, in some sense, I was Anita's Galatea, I knew I also brought her satisfactions deeper than the pride of amatory creation. She was moving in her job on the wavecrest of my work. Grateful as she was for that, she also trusted me personally, and at times some flagrant innocence burst out of her from her long ago.

"Oh," she sighed once after conventional Christian intercourse had climaxed us at the same time. "Ah, Martin, you *are* a nice man. You *are* good for me."

One Saturday, she called me early and asked whether I wanted to go swimming at Buffi de Plaevilliers' that afternoon. I heard some nervousness in her voice and asked what was the matter. She skipped past my question. But there remained a timorous tremolo in my strings.

Going to Buffi's home with her was indiscreet, I knew. She must not be whispered about over a man much younger— and her employee as well. But I dared not suggest this for fear she would not take me.

"De Plaevilliers is a little nutty for my tastes," I said as we drove toward Virginia.

"Nutty? You're a fine one," she said, with a laugh. "You with your alchemical furnace. By the way, how's it coming along?"

"Fine," I lied. I had neglected Athanor since I went to work for Anita. Mention of the furnace gave me a brief burst of nostalgia for that less anxious life.

"Buffi gives me the creeps," I persisted.

"Ah," she said. "You're playing Mrs. Grundy again."

The enormous old oaks and sycamores of Buffi's estate looked formidable, their leaves motionless in the July heat. We drove past the front door and onto a leg of the driveway that led to the rear. The swimming pool seemed anomalous in the backyard. A huge fish pond further on at the edge of thick woods glistened. Flagstone paths led to it past pedestaled statues of white stone.

Buffi was not alone at poolside. Two others were with him, but only he rose, pulling his black, red, and white swimming robe around him and coming to meet Anita's car.

Out of his devil suit, he was not impressive. His legs were spindly and he was tanned the way old, tired flesh tans. His face, where I could see it below the sunglasses, looked wasted.

"Hello," he called with his faint timbre of theater.

He kissed Anita's palm and turned with a smile to me, his lips compressed over bad teeth.

"Monsieur Ouroboros. How good of you to come."

We shook hands.

"You have a new job," he said pleasantly. "You are going to make our Anita into a big cheese with your hard work."

So they had discussed me.

The other couple rose from their deck chairs as we approached. Herbert and Lisel Krals, whom I had met at

the party. Both were fleshy in their unattractive bathing
suits.

I finished changing before Anita and when she came
out in her black one-piece suit, I was enraptured all over
again by that tall startling loveliness I had seen in the
wolf costume.

She dove in, as graceful as she walked. I swam two
laps and climbed out, sitting with Buffi and his guests, all
of us watching Anita, first in the crawl, with her energetic
racing turns, then slowing to a side stroke.

"You're in the diplomatic corps, too?" I said to Krals.
He laughed wetly as if he were gargling beer.

"No, a stonecutter."

He held up square hands, as calloused as the pads of a
big dog's feet. His voice was heavily accented, but he
nevertheless spoke rapidly. His wife seemed constantly to
fear some foolishness from him, or worse.

Krals tended to roll his eyes like a panicky horse.

"Herr de Plaevilliers helped us to get to America, in
the Nazizeit, the German time," he said. "We are Austrians."

Frau Krals smiled with wan patriotism.

"They worked for our family," said Buffi agreeably.
"Now they are more than friends." De Plaevilliers encircled Krals' thick wrist with his thinnish hand and gave it a
shake. "He worked on the East Front sculpture at the
Capitol here when they remodeled," he added, proud of
his former servant. Then he dropped Krals' wrist and
turned to me.

"How are your investigations in alchemy going?"

"I haven't had much time to work on it," I said.

Buffi was all good humor.

"A delightful hobby! You will find us the Philosopher's
Stone, dear Ouroboros. You must chase your formulas.
After a while, they become as important as reality. Our
hobbies, yours and mine, are"—he sought the exact word
—"particularized. We plant gardens of nightshade and others plant zinnias in straight rows."

Buffi's bad teeth seemed to stain every word that passed
through them, even when what he said was true. I did not
want to know about his hobbies. I assumed they would be
nastily related to the occult—and that he chased them as
if they were reality.

"I seem to go at my hobbies in stretches," I said, thinking of the fickle sequence of my pursuits.

"Well," said Buffi, turning to Anita, who still swam: "Come out, Anita, your athleticism is embarrassing us."

She side stroked one more lap and came to us, her lips blue, her chest heaving. The sun, glaring full on her, blurred her into an overexposed picture in which she appeared so young that I longed to cradle this Anita while the illusion lasted. But she was upon us; in the shadow of the umbrella, age came once again upon her beauty.

"What are you doing with my Monsieur Ouroboros," she asked, towelling herself, dashing our sunhot skins with drops of cold water. Buffi laughed and moved to the small gazebo to fetch drinks.

"We spoke of the importance and complexity of hobbies," he said. I thought I saw a hint of apprehension on Anita's face. "Mine and his have their overlaps."

The diplomat brought Lisel Krals a ginger ale and Anita a vodka and bitter lemon. It struck me that he had not asked her, so familiar was he with her, and I felt a wrench of jealousy. We sat and talked, of Tarot, of politics, of Washington gossip.

The Kralses listened, nodded as Buffi spoke, obsequious and loyal, the perfect retainers. I looked at Anita, as hungry for her as if she wore nothing instead of the trim suit.

The day settled on toward late afternoon.

Buffi rose to fix more drinks. Returning he said:

"Come in, I will show you some of the house. I want you to see—" he paused, "—*my* alchemical furnace."

"Why don't we eat out here," said Anita with some firmness. "I like the fresh air."

"Lisel is setting up inside," Buffi said more peevishly than Anita's statement, on its face, warranted. What was happening between them? "The bugs will begin to eat us," he added.

I stole a glance at her. Her face disclosed nothing.

At Buffi's bidding we changed from our suits. He led us through the ground-level door. Inside, down a hall, Buffi unlocked a room and let us in before him.

For an instant I was frightened in the chill darkness; then he flicked a switch that lighted—how could I not have expected it?—a Roman Catholic chapel. It was small, no more than thirty by twenty feet, but sumptuous. The light came from two electric candles on the altar. There were no windows, only a pattern of pentagons and triangles of rose and black opaque glass making up a much larger pentagon on the far wall. Behind the altar, where Christ might have been, was a smoky old painting of a black hen, on a heraldic shield.

Well, goddamnit! I thought. Buffi has got a coven, right here in Fairfax County. I was shaken, amused slightly, then angry at Anita, both for luring me in and for being a part of any such craziness. I flashed my eyes at her. She stared back evenly, then dropped her gaze.

"How do you like my bar-restaurant?" Buffi joked, nodding at the bucket of iced wine and the big tray of sandwiches on the long table. An ovoid, the table dominated the room where the pews would have been. A half-dozen cushioned chairs were around it.

"Quite a bistro," I said, genuinely surprised.

The others laughed. Buffi began to open a bottle of wine. Not exactly bat's or baby's blood, I thought.

There was something pathetic in all this witchery. Buffi, who was, in fact, sinister, even dangerous, mad at least on this one subject, was also childlike in this playroom. He was, I realized, as Anita said, still at war with a church, a church no longer gripped, however, by witchcraft and sacrilege, but instead by birth control, environmental pollution, racial equality, even automation. Crazy Buffi still believed. He fought the church of the cinquecento.

I sighed. I had not bargained for Black Masses when I signed on with Anita. I saw her glance at me, and now there was no fondness in it. Only apprehension. What the hell, I thought, as long as I don't have to bugger somebody at some screwy Sabbat, or be buggered, or eat human flesh or excrement. I wondered how far Buffi carried it.

There were bookshelves around three walls of the room.

"Sort of hard to read titles," I said, as Buffi handed me a glass of the icy Austrian white wine. He switched on shielded light tubes that shined down across the books.

"You will find some here about alchemy," he said. "I haven't read them all myself," It was a superb collection. I recognized one here and there, Don Calmet, Malleus Maleficarum, books on nats, on Shamanism, and there, the most familiar of all, Montague Summers.

Buffi joined me before the books.

"Summers. I knew him when he was living in France," he said with pride. I wanted to ask him about that curious man, but did not. Buffi's words had the namedrop quality he used in telling of the Vice President coming to his party.

I sat down across from Anita to the caviar and cream cheese and the sliced turkey sandwiches. How serene it was in this coolness, washing down the food with the fragrant wine.

I think we were all a trifle high, even Lisel, who drank nothing stronger than wine. And why was this not a pleasant way to spend a Saturday afternoon in July, now that the booklight gave the place an atmosphere no worse than a poorly lighted bar?

Before I knew it, it was seven thirty, and Buffi said:

"I must go into town and pick up some papers to work on tomorrow; yes, I work, Anita." I rose, to make my departure with Anita. I was hopeful, even though it was a bit early, that we would return to her home to make love. The Krals made murmurings of going, too.

Buffi demurred easily:

"No, no. Stay. Stay. I will be back in a little over an hour. I have something to show, really, particularly you, Monsieur Ouroboros. And to speak with you about, and with you, Anita."

"We have to go," said Krals. Buffi patted him and took Lisel's hand. "Why not stay?"

His tone to them said, "Yes, *you* will be excused." For me the thought of staying, while annoying, was not altogether unpleasant. I would be here with Anita, and jawing with the Austrian diplomat was something that might be enjoyable every year or so, like Indonesian Rijsttafel. Moreover, the longer we stayed, the later we got home and the more chance I had of spending the entire night with Anita. So I rationalized.

I looked at her to see whether I should persist with good-byes.

"Let's stay," she said without enthusiasm. "I want to take a last dip."

I wondered at her tone. While she went to change I glanced restlessly at the books. She had been a little subdued, distant all afternoon, and I felt uneasy now.

It was eerie in the chapel. I poured some more wine and scanned the book titles, wishing for a moment I had gone back out into the evening to swim. The volumes that always turned up in footnotes were there, mostly first editions: Berthelot, Jung, Waite, Figuier.

Down the shelves, I pulled out a book newly bound in leather. Inside, the paper was ancient. Delicately I turned to the title page—my God! It was the original of *Speculum Alchimiae*. I ciphered out the Roman numerals: 1602. There were other equally ancient leather-bound books. I opened them carefully.

Despite all the expense of Buffi's party, it was only then that his wealth came home to me, that I saw, as Fitzgerald, that the rich are different. These books were valuable beyond guessing. I leafed through some more.

There was a soft rap on the door. Taken back, I opened it. Anita stood in the darkness of the hall, in her bathing suit.

"I only wanted to swim the two laps," she said. Then she slipped inside. I eased the door shut, my heart beginning to bump. The latch clicked.

"Have they gone?" I asked.

"Yes."

"Was there something the matter this afternoon?"

"No," she said. "Nothing." She touched my arm and I pulled her to me. Her bathing suit's wetness did not matter. How cool her moist back felt to my hands.

For four hours I had been wanting her, as she swam, as she walked with us on the flagstones, the back of her legs rippling slightly with age, and the blue veins behind her knees. Perhaps I had wanted her particularly because of the quality of her hours running more quickly than mine.

We kissed, standing there at the door, touching and caressing until I felt weak. Sex here meant the table or the floor or some wild, unsatisfactory acrobatics on a chair. But I could feel her desire coming on, too, in her quicker breaths. Then, she broke.

She went to the altar, slipped her hand behind it and pulled out a small key.

"What are you doing?" I asked, suddenly nervous.

"Hush."

She unlocked a wall cabinet. I walked over behind her and watched her draw out a ciborium and from that a vial. She shook out a minute number of tiny clear platelets into her palm.

"What the hell is that?" I said. She did not answer but put back the vial and ciborium and locked up. Whatever it was, her procedure showed an intimacy, a familiarity with Buffi that I had not wanted to believe.

She dropped the platelets into a goblet, poured in a half glass of wine and took a dainty sip. Then she came to me, the wine glass in her hand, kissed me firmly, loosened her lips and slipped her tongue, still moist from the wine, between my teeth. But my passions had died in anxiety.

"What is it?" I asked.

"Just to make us last longer." I drew back.

She put the wine glass to my lips and I tasted gingerly. The wine had, if anything, a touch of bitterness. She placed the glass on the table and unbuttoned my shirt with one hand, running the other across my chest, knowing this excited me. She pushed the shirt back from me and pressed her wet bathing suit in to kiss me.

The idea of the drug was unpleasant. Still, she was in my arms now. I reached for the zipper of her bathing suit just above her waist in back. She unzipped it herself, pulling the garment down to her navel. She hugged me again, her breasts cool and pronounced now against my hot chest. Her lower stomach pressed into my groin, I could scarcely control myself. The damned potion wasn't working. She ran her hand to my trousers front and I thought, goddamit, it's going to be all over. But she pulled away and picked up the wine glass.

"Drink it all, it won't hurt you," she said.

"What is it?" I asked again, breathing hard, glad of the respite that saved me from precocity.

"It will make you feel better to me."

"And last." I said dubiously.

"Yes," she said. She took another sip herself and handed me the glass. I wanted none of it. But I was too hot for her now to last, I knew. I drank it down and put the glass on the table. Again, there was the aftertaste of bitterness, stronger now, a little like quinine water. I shuddered from the draught.

She slipped back into my arms and I dropped down to kiss her puckered nipples.

"How much longer will he be gone?" I gasped.

"Long enough," she whispered. I worked at my belt buckle, stepped on the heels of my tennis shoes to get out of them so I could drop my pants.

Once I was stripped, I worked her suit over her hips, kissing her wet belly as she kneaded my hair. The laced wine had given me a premonition of ill-ease.

But I was too lustful to worry. I bent again to mouth the buds on her breasts. She pulled my head up slowly and kissed me softly, not pressing.

"Take it easy," she said quietly.

"I'll try," was all I could say.

She turned, her buttocks moving whitely as she pushed the food and wine bucket down to the far end of the table. I threw two of the big chair cushions on the table, and then embraced her from behind. I knew that what she had given me was more than a delaying drug. I felt slightly nauseated and was uncomfortable in my kidneys. At the same time, I was feeling excited, helplessly tumid.

She had given me something weird, I knew now. The thought angered me. Nevertheless the stimulant made me crave relief. I tried to take her there, thrust up against the table. But she broke away and rolled onto it.

"The pillows. Be careful," she hissed.

She had not pushed the food down far enough. Crazy for her now, all of a sudden, hating her for drugging me —I swept the food from the table with a pillow, wine bottles and all.

She rolled across the table. Naked, we stared at each other, she appraising me. Yet, there was a hotness in her, too.

I walked around the table. "I won't hurt you," I said. She let me kiss her, slipping her lips back and forth across mine, to my ear and then to my chest and back again. Then, slowly, caressing my back, she eased me onto the table. I was panting. I had to pull in my abdomen against a growing pain in my kidneys. At the same time I felt full of exploding foam.

With a quick motion she put the cushion under her buttocks. I placed the other under her head, some residual love there amongst my anger and lust.

I settled my lips and then my body on hers, my heart seeming to rattle against my ribs, and entered her.

Her long legs around me, she pumped her body upward with mine for the few brief seconds before my orgasm. I felt the familiar swooning spasm of relief, but the relief only lasted a few moments, like a blank space on a tape of frenzied music. Like Priapus, I was not delivered by the orgasm. The crystalline irritant kept me erect. I knew now it was something like Spanish fly.

It was on these terms, me sick to my stomach now, dizzy, priapismic, yet still stimulated, that she manipulated my movements until she came, uttering a harsh hum. She clutched me for a few moments, then stared into my eyes.

"You gave me too much," I said. "I'm sick."

As with Kafka's sinners in the Penal Colony, my Deadly Sin was proving my agony. Queasiness mixed with lust. My kidneys ached and I wanted to urinate.

I, who had so long been precipitate, could now not end my erection.

I went back at her, believing that if I could only find a small spasm of remission, I could detumesce. Anita, mechanically now, assumed positions and roles that had thrilled and sometimes embarrassed me in calmer times.

Sweating and groaning, I followed her, still enjoying, though in pain, the friction on my irritated muscles and the concomitant tingling along my nerves. But it was a thrill on the subbase of illness and alarm. I knew she was trying to give me some surcease.

Now coition no longer stimulated, it only hurt. I remained erect, wrapped in pain and nausea. I was on my back. She crept up to where my head lay on the cushion. Her breasts hung down to me, but I took no pleasure in seeing them.

"That was a shitty thing to do," I groaned. Her face was flushed.

Her hair had fallen, stuck by sweat to her cheeks. The protrusive lips were puffy. I could not see her iris, only the slits of her eyes, in the indirect light. Still, I could not hate her—that emotion had gone as fast as it had come. I only wanted help.

"How long will it last?" I pleaded.

"Not much longer," she said, her voice pained. "I'm sorry, Martin. I gave you too much."

"Spanish fly?"

She grimaced an assent.

That goddamned Buffi! *He* had used it with her. Maybe that was the only way he could screw. But I hurt too much, I was too upset to be jealous.

A stab of pain hit me in the kidneys, terrifying me. Anita winced.

"I've got to get a doctor," I said. Her eyes popped open with alarm. "I've got to throw up."

I rolled off the table and ran outside to the bathhouse by the pool. When I switched on the light, the glare lanced into my head. I vomited and vomited, my back aching with each heave. I tried to urinate, horrified at my irritated and erect member, but only a small trickle came out, with tiny threads of blood in it.

My kidney pain dulled for moments at a time. I left the toilet. She was outside, dressed, her face worried.

"Is it better?"

"No," I said. Would a doctor have to turn me in, I wondered.

"I'm sorry," she said.

"God damn you and Buffi!" I burst out. "You're a pair of pigs."

She blinked at the slap of my remarks, but was clearly worried.

"Why did you do it?" I demanded, angry again as my kidneys began to ache. "My God, you might have killed me with that stuff."

She didn't answer.

"I want to get you home," she said.

"I want to *go* home," I answered, mollified that she was thinking of my welfare. God, how ludicrous it had all been.

She paused, then hugged me quickly.

"I have to stay until he comes back," she said hesitantly. "Can you take the car?"

"No," I shouted, seething now. She had poisoned me and now she was kicking me out. She was going to stay with the monster who stocked the stuff. "Drive me to a taxi," I ordered.

"I brought your clothes out." I dressed in the darkness.

On the way to Falls Church, I began to feel like vomiting again. She stopped and I heaved, shooting pain into my back. The priapism had waned, but my penis burned.

"Why do you fool with these crazy people?"

"Do we have to start that again?" she asked.

"Yes, we do," I growled each word.

She considered. I did not look at her.

"I'm sorry," she said at last, wearily.

"You may have messed me up for good with that stuff."

"I didn't think it would make you so sick."

"Because that much didn't hurt Buffi?" I yelled. "You fucked him when he was full of it. Shit, he can't do it without it, can he? You prime him up with it, like Pauhafen and his B-12."

In the instrument lights, I could see her lips tightening.

"That's my business." She was intimidated. Knowing she was defensive, I allowed myself to be furious.

We were coming into Falls Church.

I could see filling-station lights ahead.

"Stop the car," I said. "Shit, you're nothing but a crazy, rotten whore."

She jammed on the brakes, her face wrinkled up with loathing. But she said nothing. I got out and slammed the door without looking back. At the filling station, I called a cab.

That night, I thought I would surely die. I heaved and heaved and when I was not heaving, my bowels ran bloody stools. By morning, the worst was over, but I was exhausted and depressed. I had resolved I was done with Anita. I would return to my cranny. I longed for some decent, warm, efficient soul like the Julia of our early days, or what Susan might be, to fix me a little tea and bring me some water. But I tended myself. Water would wash the stuff out of my kidneys, I reasoned, and drank all of it I could hold. I vomited up the first glass, but did not dare take anything that might settle my stomach for fear of what chemicals would do mixed with the cantharides.

Urination was still painful and blood-streaked. I wished I had been well enough to go to the library of the National Institutes of Health and read up on treatment. During my Baudelaire period I had researched aphasia and tertiary syphilis there. In our new world of pharmaceuticals, being a doctor was the easiest thing in the world, once you got the ailment diagnosed, as long as you didn't have to practice surgery. The NIH library gave you everything you wanted.

But the jarring of my kidneys from the stops and starts of driving out Wisconsin Avenue would have been more than I could stand.

Still weak, I lay in bed. Why had she done it? Surely not for the reason she gave, although the Spanish fly had worked on me with a vengeance. More likely, for the kicky reason: to try on me what Buffi had tried on him-

self and then on her. In her master's steps. The idea of
her, of sex with her, was nauseating. My kidneys gave an
exclamation point of pain to my thoughts. I had to be
quit of these crazies.

Good Athanor. I would finish him up and run through
my formula. Possibly *Speculum* would take a brief article
on my experiments, if my tone were light, and my procedures and footnotes thorough. Bored and uncomfortable,
I put *Nerone* on my phonograph—who knows that noble
failure now?—and desultorily worked on the formula for
the Philosopher's Stone.

It was honest diversion, reducing the peculiar directions
of Ramon Lull—even his name brought a painful thought
of Spanish fly—to a serviceable chemical equation of
gold, silver, sulphur, and various acids. My chemistry was
shaky, but I was sure I could find someone to correct it.

The result, when I ran it through Athanor, would be, in
Lull's hopeful old formula, the Philosopher's Stone. A slow
stirring of a nip of this into mercury would, in theory, turn
the mercury to gold.

I sighed. If it had worked for Lull he would not have
had to trot all over Europe begging funds for his university. And people who could produce gold on demand
probably were not often stoned to death—even in the
fourteenth century—as Lull was, in some lousy Algerian
port.

Through it all, I was hurt that Anita had not telephoned
to see how I was.

On Monday, most of the pain had left. I called to tell
my secretary I would not be in. Goddamnit, I thought as
I dialed, I am a fool, a goddamn fool. Now was the time
to go back to Woeckle, to quit Anita. The nasty business
in the chapel had given me the excuse. Now was the time
to go. I should get Anita on the phone and resign.

But when Susan answered, there was no resolve in me.

Patty—my secretary—was getting coffee, Susan explained.

"What's the matter with you?" she asked.

"It's no worse than a bad cold," I said, trying to be
funny.

Her voice was crisp, detached, not unfriendly:

"You sound sick. Do you need anything?"

"Yes," I said, feeling both forlorn and humorous, "I
want you to come mother me. I feel awful."

"Don't be funny. If you want mothering you had better call your mother."

"She's dead," I said, feeling guilty for my cheap draft on her sympathy.

"Oh, I'm sorry, I didn't know," she said, suitably contrite.

"I'll try to be in late Tuesday. Anything cooking with the boss?" My voice trembled slightly.

"No. Do you want to talk to her?"

"No," I murmured.

"Sure you don't need anything?" She was winding up.

"No," I said gloomily. "Just give Mrs. T. the stuff on Duluth. Get it off my desk. Tell her I still plan to go out there on Thursday."

I had been sapped by Anita in a cuckoo chapel with Spanish fly, but the wheels of government went on turning. Anita would be dealing efficiently with several million dollars in Labor Department projects today, she who had squirmed like a Corybant on Saturday, and did so still in my memory.

And so I stayed.

With an irresolute moan, I shuffled to the kitchen to make milk toast, the only solid food I dared risk.

CHAPTER

9

Columbia

I went in Tuesday afternoon, wan, but in my new seer-sucker suit. By the time I reached the office, my armpits had sweated through the coat from anxiety about how Anita would greet me. I was sure she had sugared her shame with self-righteous anger at my calling her a whore. But when I went into her office, she was pleasant and brisk.

"Well, I'm glad you're all right. I needed you."

"You sure did."

She paused only a moment, then went on quietly:

"Well, I do need you in the office. Are you going to Duluth?"

What she was asking me was whether I would stay with her. This was the time to say, "I'm going back to Woeckle." But it wasn't only Anita. There was something about the job, some salt taste of accomplishment.

"Yes, Duluth," I said, and it was sealed. A trace, only a trace of tension had been in her face and my answer relaxed even the trace away.

"That's fine," she said. "Can we talk about it just before you go?"

In the outer office, Susan said:

"You look pale. What's the matter?"

Susan *was* motherly.

"A virus. I'll shake it in that fresh air from the steel mills."

116

She smiled, her upper lip dipped ever so slightly in the center. When I first met her, she had compressed her lips to cover the minor malformation, giving her smiles a simpering look. Was it ease with me that made the persiflage no longer necessary? Or had she come to love the man she spoke of on the telephone—or someone else— and in that secure soil found a blossoming of self-esteem?

Duluth was my first trip of many on behalf of Anita and of the Department. For while there was no doubt that Anita harvested the first grain of my trips, in the long run the country was the beneficiary. And in the annals of junketeering, any benefit was exceptional.

My purpose in Duluth was to make sure our youth grant, the first under Anita's manpower training planning program, would be spent in employment projects, real ones, not boondoggles. Of the dozen cities we had studied, Duluth appeared to offer the best chance of speedy results. For one thing, the city's temporary unemployment problem might solve itself even as we put the program into action, thus cloaking our effort with the ambiance of success.

The liberal Republican mayor gave me a glad hand. He introduced a brainy social scientist deputy from his office, plus a slick young city lawyer as my guide.

On the ground floor of a lawless "garden" complex, we listened to the local Welfare Recipients Association talk about their jobless, dropout sons. We got similar grievances throughout the day—the terrible clichés of the poor —from the local NAACP chapter, the Union of Black Frontists, the GOP precinct captain, also black, and the Negro lawyer-insurance man who was the political boss of the area.

I was host that evening to my two companions and their wives.

Driving along a bluff and looking down at the crescented lights of Duluth, I could imagine Genoa or Cannes and for an instant felt the impulse to flee—to Europe, to anywhere.

But the meal had compensations, attractions I had not tasted or imagined during my cranny days. Over cocktails, talking of politics, I could see the guarded envy of the two men and in their wives' eyes a reflection of something hungry I had perceived before in women looking at men in power.

Had I changed? Inside I still feared my shadow. I still drew my security from the introvert pursuits. But there was something new. Here, in two handsome midwestern women's eyes, was evidence that to the world I was now something that heretofore I had not been.

Next day I made the rounds of the city officials individually: Welfare, Health, Employment, Education. Implicit in everything I said was that Anita and the Secretary, in that order, were looking to Duluth as the focus of the new planning grant programs.

"You're very big in Duluth," I told Anita. We were alone in her office on the Monday after my trip. She had moved in Hepplewhite reproductions. A table dominated the room. She used it as a desk. My discomfort had disappeared to the point where I could view the table with wryness, if not humor.

"I got a letter this morning from Mayor Boas, telling me what a good boy you were," she replied.

"We ought to start there," I said. I had typed up that morning a dozen pros and cons. I started through them, but she took them from my hand.

"Let me see." She pushed the spectacles she wore while working a fraction closer to her eyes and looked down at the paper. The wrinkles in her brow were accentuated by her foreshortened posture, giving her a quizzical look. I felt a bite of my former passion. I alone saw that touching quality in her, the honest child in the neurotic woman, I thought. "But she poisoned me," I mused and the dilemma gave me a feeling close to tears. It passed quickly as she questioned me about the city and its politics.

Concisely I outlined, while she listened, her eyes on mine, but her thoughts on Duluth and what its programs could mean to her.

"That's good. That's good," she said, when I was finished. Puckishly, she slipped the glasses to the end of her nose, and looked over them with those ineffable blue eyes.

"You're not mad anymore?" she asked simply, parting her pouty lips. It was the Moment of Invitation. I could say, "When can I see you again?" and our affair would go on. But I did not.

Instead, I murmured:

"No, I should be, but I'm not."

This said, we were at armistice, but no more than that. I left her office, my heart thumping, palms sweating. My want for her would return. I had, nevertheless, bought myself a little safe time, and a little honor.

Staying away from Anita had uncomplicated my existence. The fact remained that it had been her attentions that had restored me to sexual health. Once I was fully recovered from the cantharides, I began to think of women again. There was the call girl, of course. But there was also the reflection of my worth in the eyes of those two women in Duluth. I thought more highly of myself now. I didn't want to pay for it anymore.

And Susan: I began to dwell on her softness. It was like thinking of the creamy centers of Fanny Farmer in those early days when a box of Fanny Farmers was the pinnacle of desire. Susan and I were together more often now.

Anita was defending her budget against the annual Departmental chopping that preceded the real bloodletting by the Office of Management and Budget. Duluth was already approved, and Susan and I were getting up data on Columbia, South Carolina, a vastly more complex and extensive program—our second city.

Many nights, Susan and I worked until seven or later, my secretary staying on from time to time. Sometimes I dropped them both off, but more often Susan had a ride. When I suggested to her once that we have supper together after work, she turned me down politely. After that she was even more wary. I knew now that she had a boyfriend, "Roger," and that he was jealous and thus serious. It was inevitable I should find out whom she was seeing.

One night, I walked with her to the front entrance. The rain poured onto the thirty yards of steps and pavement leading to Constitution Avenue, sliding like shiny treacle from the streetlighted magnolias in front of the building. At the curb, parking lights shining dimly through the wash, her ride waited. I had my umbrella.

"Come on," I said, raising it. I took her arm, feeling its firmness—and an instant's resistance. I held the umbrella over her as she got into the car, then I stooped as she introduced me to her beau. At last, the mysterious "Roger."

"Roger Conyers," she said. A young balding head

bobbed at me. In the dim light, I saw a perfunctory smile.

"Hi," he grunted. There was enough in the word for me to hear the Boston Irish in it, and to feel his terrible and oppressive possessiveness toward her.

Startled, I said officiously, "Take good care of our Susan." Then they were off.

Standing on the Constitution Avenue curb, I knew the stiff-necked nature of Conyers. The poor son of Irish Catholics. The uprightness of the totally self-made man. The Saint Pauls, the Philip Henry Sheridans, the Conyers of this world: righteous, paranoid, and incorruptible. Instinctively, I disliked him.

Worse, Susan informed me when I asked next day that he was a Justice Department lawyer, more than my guilt-prone faculties could smoothly abide.

Conyers, too, apparently had been unsettled by our brief meeting. Divining that I was not a Catholic and assuming that I was a liberal, and therefore liable to fatuousness, or worse, he became even more protective toward Susan. If she were not out front, he came to the office to pick her up. When she was not looking at him, his eyes rested on her with almost obscene passion, a mix of raw lust and possessive hunger, as if he feared that his food would be snatched away from him before he could wolf it. If lust were still a sin in the Catholic church, he must have plenty to confess each week.

Susan and I were concluding the Columbia proposals. One Thursday night we resolved to finish in time for a morning conference which we had ripped from Anita's hustling schedule. Conyers came up at seven thirty. There was still a good half-hour's work and I sent out for coffee. I was damned if I'd order a bottle of wine and lumpfish on pumpernickel for a beer-drinking Justice Department cop. But I tried to be polite.

"Ever been to Columbia?"

"No," he said. "South Carolina's an honest state."

"You only go to dishonest states?"

He was ruffled.

"No. By that I meant that most of my work is on white-collar crime and you get more of that in urban states."

"Like corporation presidents conspiring to destroy competition?" I could have bitten my tongue for my nastiness.

"That would be the antitrust division," he said.

I could sense Susan, as she worked away on our summary of businesses grossing under $100,000 a year in Columbia, listening and assessing our dialogue.

Even as Conyers intimidated me, laden as I was with the new guilts I had accumulated through Anita, he was easy to sneer at. But at the same time as I despised him, I knew I was making a mistake that bordered on the foolhardy.

"And you are in the criminal division?" I asked, moth at the flame.

"Yes," he said. "Mostly on the east coast."

"I should think you'd get your share of white-collar crime right here in Washington."

He glanced at me curiously. There was intelligence in his eyes, angry as they were.

"Political cases are hard to make," he said, "if that's what you mean." The thought froze me. I thought of Anita. God protect us from ever becoming the quarry of such a man as this.

"No," I said weakly, "I was just speaking generally."

Conyers had cowed me. Could he see through my veneer of officialdom and into my heart where lay that ugly secret of lying to the police about Tapir? Did he sense my fears of unknown horribles in Anita's past?

No, of course not.

But, bully that he was, he could not let me rest.

"If we had the manpower we could indict half the unions in the country. You talk about corruption in business . . ."

He shook his head as if he'd like to tell me some more about the perfidy of unions and the sanctity of business, but feared I would streak to inform some liberal politician.

"I suppose you find crooks wherever you go," I muttered evasively.

I was coming out poorly in all this.

Conyers shifted his big body in the chair. He was younger than I, but surer. He looked down at the leather-banded watch on his hairy wrist, making certain Susan saw this indication that he wanted her done and away.

"How much longer, Susan?" he said redundantly, making an effort not to seem patronizing toward her. How could she love him, I thought angrily. I watched her eyes to see how she would take his boorishness. They had the loveless but tolerant look of an old woman being given her stomach tonic.

Turning back to my coffee, to the neat tabbed folders that told us more than a person could want to know about Columbia, South Carolina, I had a sudden insight, a hearthfire of vengeful delight. Unless I guessed wrong, he was not sleeping with her and it was like hot acid eating a hole in his pious black heart. Thus he was silently, gnawingly envious of every man who came near her. Lust, anger, and envy, that's three out of the seven deadly sins, I mused with bitter pleasure. If it ever did come to the two of us confessing, we were numerically, if not qualitatively, equal sinners.

I called Anita that night to make sure we had enough time for talk on Columbia. I was excited about the project, both idealistically and politically. The mills in the Piedmont part of the state were opening up to Negroes. There were two colleges in Columbia and we were shooting to get some fairly high-level Southern black technicians into the big textile plants after graduation instead of letting them bleed away to the North. On the low education levels, Negro manual workers were needed for the construction boom around the city. A little training could boost them into carpenters, masons, even electricians. The unions were weak, depressing wages. But this weakness made them more susceptible. We could force them to give a fairer shake to young, eager blacks.

The city had a progressive government and the state government, while conservative Republican, was new in office, and willing to experiment to stay in power. They wanted all the ties they could get with Washington and the national party, short of losing the redneck, woolhat white vote—the inevitable result if they did altogether right by the Negroes.

There was movement.

"You sound like a missionary," Anita said. "It looks fine. When do you need to go? How long?"

"Next week. Four days."

"Too long," she said. "You have to shake out the budget by Friday a week."

"I could put it off until the week after, but it ought to be in the works now, well, should have been by now."

"I know," she said.

I thought of Susan. She could cut the time down to

two days, doing some of the survey work on retraining while I talked with the city officials. My throat constricted. Since what I drolly called the "Spanish connection," I had pushed back thoughts of Anita. But I had begun to fantasize about Susan, about taking her away from that bastard Conyers.

I had imagined seducing her at some beach hideaway far from Conyers and Anita and Washington. Taking her to Columbia had occurred to me, but suggesting it to her would have been disastrously direct. Yet, I suspected she —who had worked so long on the Columbia plan—secretly wanted to go. I could not invite her. But Anita could.

"I can cut it to two days if Susan goes," I said bluntly.

Anita paused.

"Ah," she interjected, comprehending. She paused. "I've created a Frankenstein monster."

"That's silly, Anita," I said. "Susan's practically engaged." Then, with a hint of spite, I went on. "Why don't you go with me?"

"I don't detect any great warmth in the invitation," she said.

I felt myself smiling. Goddamnit, I thought, tickled, my not seeing her has cut into her after all.

"Seriously, send her," I insisted. "She deserves it. She's worked like hell on the project." I stopped, thinking if Anita were jealous, even a trace, logic was not the way. "Look, Anita, she's got this guy in the Justice Department that picks her up every night and looks like he would kill the first guy that looked at her. My God, she's been working for you for four years. You know she isn't going to play around."

"You're making too big a thing of it," she sighed. "Ah, Martin, you're as bad as I. Take her along. You want me to tell her, don't you? All right."

Thus, Susan was delivered into my hands by Anita.

When Susan met me at National Airport she had on a new semi-fitted coat dress. Her hair was freshly tapered, short and stylish. She had put on her makeup with unusual precision. It was touching that she would make such an effort at chic and almost succeed. She had not, however, done it for me.

"They'll mistake you for Madam Secretary," I said as I took her luggage, also new.

On the trip down, we reviewed our "must-sees"—Pursell and Benedict Colleges, both Negro schools; a new community center; the slums that festered in rings around the white areas. There was also a "work clinic" near the colleges for training secretarial help and, at Cayce, on the other side of the river, a makeshift office in a factory wing for teaching data processing to the black college kids.

The data processing had been paid for by Danielson-Tyree Mills, one of the most conservative industries in the South, run by right-wing Baptists, Communist-baiters, and segregationists. Old man Tyree donated twice as much to help Columbia's Negroes as all three of the major Northern-owned mills.

He had integrated his clerical help, even his own office staff, "goddamning" as he did that no Northern "chicken crud was going to say a nigger in South Carolina ain't got a chance."

"Did it ever strike you that liberals as a group are the most hypocritical people in the world?" I mused to Susan.

"Not you, too," she said. I bridled. Conyers' antiliberal refrain was in a different key. Her comment reminded me of how I resented having that relentless ironass coming into the office.

"I don't mean it quite the way he does," I said.

"Oh," she said blandly. "Anyway, I don't always agree with him."

A cup of bouillon and we were in Columbia.

On the way to town in the limousine, I read *The State* newspaper. To my surprise there was an item on our arriving. Susan, as we represented to the mayor's office, was identified as a "Labor Department Project Officer."

"Susan"—she turned away from the landscape of scraggly palmettos and underbrush—"we're celebrities."

She leaned slightly against me to read the article and I smelled perfume.

As in Duluth, the mayor here gave us bright young people to work with. Susan, who was beginning with the data-processing survey, drew a lanky sociologist with a long tanned horse face whose accent made him almost unintelligible. He yes ma'amed Susan in one of the softest voices I ever heard. As they left, I could see his covert speculative look as his eyes went across her bosom, and I was seized with jealousy. It was just such a damned intellectual, hiding behind a cornball South Carolina Geechie accent, that would attract her, particularly if I had correctly sensed a last gush of premarital rebellion building up in her toward Conyers.

Pursell College had the antiquity of all the places that house people no one cares about: county poor homes, asylums, nursing homes for the poor, Negro hospitals, rural jails.

The college president chatted with us for a moment, telling us that some of the buildings had been built about 1890. He talked with some dignity of the school's needs. But the truth was without dignity: Its Negro alumni had no political power, therefore no budgetary breaks from the legislature, therefore low faculty salaries, inferior faculty, low morale and only a trickle to pay for maintenance.

In the early Fifties the legislators had kept up an appearance of repair at Pursell as an earnest of their separate-but-equal mouthings. But now they were letting it run down, saying cynically, "If a nigger student is good enough, the University of South Carolina'll let him in."

Pursell had given me their faculty pride and joy as an escort, Dan Mints, a feldspar black agronomist whose courage and brains had got him through Clemson and who was staying in his state.

I wondered how I could get the Labor program away from the decrepit Uncle Tom who ran placements and into Mints' hands. After all, I thought, we're going to lay out money for a new placement center for the two colleges, and for the transportation to get the kids up to Greenville for job interviews, and for expenses while they're there, and maybe even some kind of salary subsidization for the mills.

The mayor's man and Dan Mints went through the grades and records of the seniors as they were handed to us.

"So how good is an 'A' here in Business Administration compared with the university?" I asked. The old Negro started to beg the question. The mayor's man, a white man, deferred to Mints.

"About thirty percent as good," said Mints. "And the university ain't all that good either."

I groaned. How much better the picture had appeared from Washington. Looking at the dull, or foolish, or optimistic or bright black faces staring up at me from the photos in the folders, I thought that, no matter what, the Federal money would help. It would make sure some of these kids get into office work instead of a city sanitation truck.

My God! I thought. All three of these men are leaning on me: the old-style Darkie, the white city-manager-to-be, the black leader whose counsel the white man will someday have to seek at voting time to learn what the South Carolina black will settle for.

"Don't worry about losing the program," I said, sensing their fear that their raw material was too coarse to be worked. "Tell me the worst of it, then there's no disappointments."

The white man alone smiled with relief.

"My boss is a woman," I said jokingly, still trying to bolster them. "Her intuition tells her Columbia is a great place to do something even if it did go Democratic the last couple hundred times." All three laughed politely.

Before we left for Benedict, the agronomist asked me a bit defensively, I thought. "Where're you staying?"

"The Wade Hampton." So there would be more complications. Mints wanted to tell me some even uglier facts away from the mayor's man and the Uncle Tom. "Call me if you think of anything we forgot," I obliged him.

Duluth had been so easy. Columbia was tough and unpredictable. But here was this black man who had taken a job in South Carolina when token black faces with B.S. degrees were drawing fortunes in the rest of the country. If he could stand it in South Carolina, I thought, so could the Labor Department.

The overestimations we had drawn together so carefully in Washington gradually were whittled away one by one during the day. Still, at the core there was sound wood. At day's end, I met Susan in the hotel lobby. She was discouraged that our data had not hit closer to reality.

"We can do something, can't we?" she said.

"Yes, if we rejuggle."

For the first time since that night in the riot, I saw something like interest for me in her eyes.

"Besides," I went on, "think what a bad show it would be for Mrs. T. if we flopped."

Susan napped briefly while I put together the papers for the next day. That night we were going to a barbecue on the lieutenant governor's farm twenty miles from Columbia, an annual event we had lucked—or unlucked— into.

Susan looked marvelously fresh when she came down in the elevator. Dressed in a rich blue smock, costly, I was sure, and blue pumps whose heels would not be quite right for a barbecue lawn, she was feeling, I sensed, the stylish Washington lady. It was charming, this little self-conceit: Susan as female executive.

I drove our rented car out along the main street of town, a diverse clash of tawdry modern, pseudo-southern classical, and jerry-built nondescript. The street was garishly bright and full of soldiers from Fort Jackson.

"It's not just finding the people to run it," Susan said, her mind still on her day. "It's like Eighth and H. I mean who do we select? Everybody, really everybody, the whites too, are willing, maybe eager to do something, but there are so few competent enough . . ."

"Gutsy enough, smart enough . . ." I completed for her.

She smelled of perfume, faintly. I was tired of talk of grants, the city's pro-rata share, joint hiring of personnel, all the details the mayor's man and I were slowly compromising out.

"You've got a Tockbridge chin on tonight," I said. "Relax. Smell sweet."

"It's hard to forget the day. It's so different from the office. Better in a way."

"Columbia would be flattered to know that a sophisticated Washington Project Officer is excited over it," I said, glancing over to catch her smile.

We were a pair of strangers in a foreign land here in South Carolina, away from everything familiar. I longed to confide in Susan, thus to shrive myself of Anita, of lying to the police, of the grotesqueries in the chapel.

"It's good being away from Washington," I said.

"Washington's been good to you lately," she observed, meaning the promotion.

"And to you."

"I know." There was a hint of rebelliousness in her voice.

"You're not thinking of leaving?"

So that was it. Conyers was going to make her quit

working if he married her. I decided to risk the pass gentle.

"Even if you marry this guy, you shouldn't quit. Who
else has my tastes in wine?" I joshed, but I was nervous
at playing even a tame wolf with her.

"I'd miss work," she conceded.

"Are you going to marry him?"

"I don't know." How naturally we had fallen into these
personal things, now that we were away. She brushed
back a hair with her hand. "Maybe."

"He's the sort who would give you and your little girl
security."

"Ow."

I laughed and turned again to catch her smile. My
palms began to sweat on the wheel.

"It was more fun for me when you were the wild, convention-be-damned Susan Bieber," I said.

She laughed with mild rue.

"I'm convention-be-damned enough for Roger," then
she added to my surprise: "You have quite enough to
occupy you, I'm sure."

She meant Anita, I was certain. And she was jealous.
However foetal, it was the Green Monster.

"Hard work in the service of the Lord," I said with an
equivocal smirk. Her nearness, now I had this hint of
jealousy in her, discomposed me. I had been chaste for
some time. I imagined Susan kneeling on a bed, her large
breasts aswing. The car seemed hot.

I opened the vent, and the auto filled with the acrid,
weedy smell of goldenrod and milkweed and the heavier,
stagnant odors of the swamps. Now, though, the air was
beginning to cool.

"It's another country," she said, looking out.

"And besides, the wench is dead."

She looked at me inquiringly.

"It's a steal from a poet who stole it from a play-
wright." I was ashamed. My pendantry, once so vital to
my self-image, increasingly now seemed pompous to me.

"If you weren't such a snob you'd be easier to live
with," she said, adding with mock primness, *"Work* with,
I mean."

Taking her hand as if companionably, on the car seat, I
laughed:

"If you weren't such a prude, you'd be easier to travel with."

After a moment, she withdrew her hand. I glanced away from the road and found her looking at me cautiously.

"I hope I've got better sense than that," she said.

"I would be the last man in the world to make a pass at an attractive and desirable young lady on a business trip," I intoned. "Especially one who is already spoken for."

"You're a very sneaky man," she said pleasantly. I was sorry we had reached the turnoff to the lieutenant governor's.

The gravel road was under live oaks, pines, and wild pecans bearded with Spanish moss, made gray-ghostly by the headlights. We approached the white-painted rail fences surrounding the grounds. At the plank gate, a middle-aged Negro in a black suit nodded and smiled and pointed to the cars pulled up on the lawn across the road from the house.

I walked around the car to help Susan out. When I took her hand I looked at her conspiratorially: we were the *auslaenders* come to palmetto land and we must do our own country proud.

"I would rather be with Madam Project Officer than any belle in the South." She smiled as she let go of my hand—did I dream that it was with a faint reluctance?

"You are being most attentive, Mr. Deputy Assistant Secretary," she mocked back. "We of the hired help hardly know how to respond."

The lieutenant governor had seen us. From the veranda of the rambling old one-story frame house, he moved through the crowd to greet us.

Silver-haired and tall in his Sidney Greenstreet linen suit, he was a cliché of the Southern gentleman. We suspected from our research that he was an exception to the general rule of South Carolina's honest administrators, as Conyers had superciliously laid it down to me.

The guests were a mixture of politicians, fat-cat neighbors and industrialists, some state and downcountry officials, a handful of clergymen and a writer on entomology representing The Arts. They milled on the lawn which stretched for a hundred yards to cultivated land. The rich, level flow of the fields went on for miles, cotton and watermelon.

We strolled toward the two barbecue pits. Susan and I watched overalled Negroes by one fire pit, roasting a spitted shoat, the smell luscious from the seared pork. A third man basted the pig with sauce, which sizzled as it dripped into the coals.

"Martin, I can't afford another ounce," Susan sighed in a low voice. The familiarity of the remark touched me. She was not a person one should play games with. I looked at her gratefully for relaxing her guard this way with me.

On a trestle table nearer the porch, another Negro, apron over his black suit, carved the first shoat, hauled from a now-darkened pit on a huge bar spit.

"My God, this is good," I grinned at her, oily to my chin. The pig skin, burnt almost black in parts, crinkled greasily as I bit through to the soft fatty meat beneath. I washed it down with Seven-Up from the bar.

When we had eaten all we dared, we strolled among the guests. The mayor's man and Susan's Geechie sociologist had been invited—Mints had not. They sought us out and soon Susan and I became separated, the centers of two small groups. I hated now to drift back into shop talk with strangers, my sojourn with Susan had been so warm and exclusive.

As our group separated, Susan's lips broke slightly across her teeth, her eyes reflected pleasure and, perhaps, mild regret. Then she disappeared in the crowd.

With my soft-voiced interlocutors, I turned to bourbon and water and the inevitable talk of Washington, civil rights, South Carolina's senators (one Republican and one Democratic) and, of course, the Columbia project.

The overalled servants, their hands in work gloves, strained and staggered past us toward the trestle table with the freshly cooked pig.

Even as I listened to the persuasive white voices, I thought of those motionless photos of students. The young black faces were not my kind, less so even than these white Southerners, but I had felt, while Mints and I had looked at those young people's records, a power in me to help. Not that I could make life "better" for them. That word would not do. But less marginal, with some future prospect of dignity.

Now, with these Southern whites, I felt no desire to help. I knew these men and women fawned over me because I came down from Washington with a pocketful of cash and the authority to say yes or no.

Yet they were addictive.

The women's eyes told me all I needed to know about Southern women: their greed for strong men was like a smell. I was strong, not by any trait of mine, quite the contrary, but by the power of my job. The women in Duluth had been flatteringly interested in *me*—but in these Southern women there was something Gothic. Their voices, sweet as Loreleis or vampires, excited. Their tissues of cold steel, these were women whose vulvas could fell a bur oak without changing the blade.

It was another country, as Susan said.

At the barbecue, all was convivial. I came to see that these Southern people had merely succeeded in parking their perversions, hostilities, longings. It was a question of discipline, really, not basic difference. Buffi's guests were not more reprehensible, simply more vulgar.

The entomologist author was introduced to me and after wangling from me that I read books, he made his ex voto to South Carolina. I listened, wishing Susan would save me.

"Stendhal could just as well have been talking about South Carolina, I mean the way we let things go, when he said, 'une mouche éphémère . . . comment comprendrait-elle le mot *nuit?*'" He glanced at me, his drink-fleshed face subtle, and began to translate, "A mayfly . . ."

I interrupted him with a quick nod.

"*We* just never did conceive of night," he went on, unperturbed. "And here it is. Riots and Negroes in the schools. South Carolina needing federal money, even looking for it. The night is here and we're as uncomprehending, really, as naïve, about it as mayflies."

I was more interested in gnats than mayflies. The former were delivering their nasty little stings to my ankles and wrists. The entomologist saw and gently shifted metaphor.

"These midges, they know very well when old autumn's coming. They know they are going to die. Everything they do speeds up eight times—by my rough laboratory calculations, I ought to say—even making love."

He laughed and I saw his bad teeth. He and Buffi were

brothers under the gums. Both had some airless, rotten cavity in their spirits. The pudgy middle-aged man—I saw now he was homosexual—dropped his voice still softer, the lovely accents, silken, honeysuckle, fluid.

"It's like the gypsies. While the Jews were dying nobly in many cases, if passively, the gypsies in vans on the way out of town for asphyxiation just had a big old sexual time all the way. Just like the midges, sensing death."

"Yes," I said, noncommittally. He was a reminder of what I had left behind in Washington. Covertly, I peered over his head and found Susan, talking with her sociologist escort. Now, truly, I yearned for her, to gossip with her over the strangeness of this place and its denizens.

I began to feel the strain on my bad ankle. I worked my way to Susan. We could go now. Her face was flushed by the talk, by the heat and liquor, by the excitement of being sought after, wooed in the continuous, indiscriminate, impersonal way of Southern men.

"They don't seem to drive themselves as we do," I said finally in the car. "Why do we . . . I? I'm not really ambitious, I don't think, yet I don't know how not to work. Won't you be glad to get out of the rat race?" I asked. "Down to keeping house for a sound young government lawyer and raising more kids?" My tone had an edge of sarcasm in it.

She thought silently, the slight warm wind tatting at her hair.

"It's what you want, too, isn't it?"

"What?"

"A home, a wife. Children."

She had never spoken so with me before.

"An end to loneliness," I added, then, feeling mawkish, I rallied to jest:

"Every time I see the sort of hausfrau I could be happy with, she turns out to be a good Catholic lady who doesn't want to fool around with a WASP divorcé."

"Well," she observed shrewdly. "I know I'm a hausfrau at heart. But I've found most men are husbands at heart."

I considered this truth for a while. Was she saying she had chosen Conyers over others, perhaps even over me? There was some sort of challenge buried in her remark.

"And from the innumerable lists you have selected Roger Conyers, attorney at law?" I asked.

"You keep coming back to that, don't you?" she said, still pleasantly.

"I'm jealous." It was true at the moment.

"Ah, not of him as my potential husband."

"I wish we were more companionable," I parried.

"Well, it's silly with both of us in the same office to begin with. And besides, you are thinking of me in terms of one among many companions."

"Not many others." None at the moment, I thought.

"I think women prefer their boyfriends or husbands to have *no* other companions."

I thought of Julia and her ecologist.

"Yeah," I agreed glumly. "It cuts both ways."

Yet, how relaxed I was with Susan. I was tired and sleep was not far off. My lust was only a flicker.

"What was your husband like?" I asked quietly.

"Oh," she breathed out. "A good man. Like Roger, only not so . . . ordered." I looked at her. The weight of thought made her lower her chin. "We were a good match, really. He had this lightness." She thought some more. "You have some of it."

She said it as a fact, not a compliment. In her, there was no subterfuge.

"You mustn't say dumb things like that. It's that sort of honesty that incites. A man with a stronger ego would take that as an invitation to make a pass."

She laughed.

"I thought you were too tired for that sort of thing."

I took her hand on the seat again, lightly.

"That's clearly flirtatious," I said.

She left her hand in mine until I finished the sentence, then withdrew it. I brushed her cheek and touched her hair at the ear.

"Yes," she said quietly, "I guess it was."

My heart had begun to thump. She was not unassailable.

"You're very hard not to touch, you know," I said, aware that it sounded rehearsed, pat. But I *did* like her, did want her.

"Well, resist the temptation."

We were coming into town. Soon we were back on Main Street. Only a few GI's still prowled the sidewalk hungering for companionship.

Gratitude for her suddenly gushed over me.

"Those guys are alone," I said. "And we aren't. We are dancing little defensive pavans with each other. But we aren't lonely. We have been talking to each other and we aren't all by ourselves, wondering when the last bus leaves for the barracks. That's something, huh?" I was full of the naturalness of the day with her.

"Yes," she said. "It's a lot."

"And however obvious my motives, and unhelpful for you, you know that I like being with you—that I'm not just a somebody preying on you, I mean, I don't think I am."

She acknowledged the truth silently, awaiting the rest.

"And part of it is what happened today. That we care a bit about doing something for somebody and that we work, well, hard at it."

Surely she knew that while I was sincere, I was also putting forward my noblest traits to trap her. I almost warned her. But then, she knew anyway.

"Yes," she said. "We work hard. That's part of it."

I parked the car in the lot and flicked off the lights. Had Susan wanted to, she could have reached immediately for the door handle. I took her left arm in my hand, feeling the full softness of it, and turned her toward me.

But when I reached for her chin, she bowed her head and I could only kiss her on the cheek. Without more ado, I walked around the car, feeling like a bastard. I could tell she was distressed.

When I handed her out, she looked solemnly in my eyes.

"I'm afraid you'll think I've said all these things just to draw you to me," I said, feeling a whimper in my heart. "I am a fool and not very good at seduction." The rejection had all but destroyed my laboriously built up self-confidence.

We were walking to the hotel. She reached out and took my hand, squeezed it and released it.

"I don't mean to wound your pride," she said. "It's just . . . that it would cause trouble all around." Her few words had kindly let me off the hook of my failure.

We rode up together on the elevator, but I made no effort to get off on her floor.

"So, sleep tight. Tomorrow it's the officials," I said.

"It was a fine evening, Martin," she replied: the safety of conventions.

When I called the desk to have them wake me at the hellish hour of six thirty, the clerk checked my box and said a Mr. Mints had telephoned. He wanted me to call back before seven in the morning. It gave me something to think about besides Susan's pretty knees in her new dress and the roundness of her arms.

Dan Mints was cold water in my face the next morning.

"Sorry I missed you at the lieutenant governor's last night," he began with a sardonic laugh. I was taken aback by his brashness, then recovered:

"You should have crashed. There were plenty of blacks there—opening doors, cooking pigs, serving drinks. The lieutenant governor said some of his best friends were Negro voters."

Mints laughed again, a harsh bark.

"Listen, I wanted to talk to you before you went in with the big shots. You got a minute on the phone?"

"Sure," I said.

Mints laid it out for me. That the mayor had to get the program to keep the conservative wing of the party from putting a do-nothing label on him. The mayor would compromise like hell to get it. That the Health Department would show some guts, but that I should forget the Welfare Department if I wanted the money to go anyplace except into doles and ancient Uncle Tom elevator operators. I took notes as he talked explicitly and with superb organization. I was sure he had outlined it on paper before he called me. At the end I questioned him, getting the same lucid conciseness.

"I thought you ought to know who's on first," said Mints.

"Yeah," I said. I thought a moment. "Can we really show any results down here? I mean it's so much more screwed up than I thought."

"You mean if I can be objective about it?"

"Right."

"Compared to where?"

"Well, Wichita," I named another city we had under study.

"I don't know Wichita. I know Columbia. Yeah, it'll get us a few jobs if you can get some promises out of the Chamber of Commerce. They're racist bastards, but they'll stick to their promises. The mayor looks like a flaming liberal. He'll buckle and suck."

The agronomist sounded depressed.

"You want to come up to Washington?" I ventured. He was an impressive catch for any bureaucrat. Not just because he was black.

"Nope. I'll let you know if I do, okay?"

The meeting went well for me as a result of Mints' call. There is nothing like a fifth column within to make a city fall. The mayor wanted to run the construction training program through the Welfare Department on grounds that the State Labor Commission was already overloaded. I balked and got it under Education, which Mints said was next best to Health. We forced the mayor into matching us dollar for dollar on the city kids at the expanded data education center. The Chamber of Commerce executive secretary left the room to call his board director and said tight-lipped that the businessmen would underwrite up to 25 percent of the city's share, if the City Council backed off. I pressed him and he called and came back again with a promise of 35 percent.

For my benefit, even the state police director tried to say Negroes instead of Nigras when he talked of hiring some more black trainee highway patrolmen and a black investigator or two.

We would foot the bill for six men, at least two blacks, at Northwestern's or California's or anybody's criminology courses if the city would come up with the money to carry two more. It was odd, we spoke of "youths," but we meant only "Negro youths."

During the late afternoon, while Susan and the city department heads sifted the candidates from Benedict, Pursell, and the other youth reservoirs, I met with the politicians.

The state Republican leader, the assembly speaker, a well-to-do Negro insurance man from Orangeburg, and three county leaders gossiped with me, speculated and joshed me, a bit crudely I thought, about working for "the first woman Vice President." We drank bourbon in a meeting room at the Wade Hampton where a few years before the only Negroes would have been the waiters. The vote had integrated where all else had faltered.

"Well, honestly, now," said the assembly speaker, the most powerful man in the state, primed on Old Fitzgerald, "who does wear the pants in your office?" The other men laughed.

"I wear the ones that *show*," I said. "She wears the ones that count."

"Now, there's no serious talk about her being Vice President," the assembly speaker went on, "is there?"

"No, sir," I said. "Just speculation. The idea rubs against the grain with me, too, but I think it'll happen one day and we could surely do worse." That brought a general hum of dissent. "I know she'd like to argue with you over dinner on women's place in government," I said. "She asked me to say that, and invite you."

Predictably, that hit home. Dinner in a big Washington restaurant with an attractive woman on her way to a Cabinet office. They shifted their sagging guts from above to below their belts and we got back to the real talk about how well structured the party would be in two and four and six years.

I called Susan after the meeting. We had no time for supper before our plane left. I was totally weary, and felt soiled from playing a role as traveling salesman for both a program and a politician. I wanted a shower. My ankle ached.

Susan was also punchy. I put our bags in the rented car and headed toward the airport. We passed a belt of Negro dwellings, packed earth yards and weather-gray wood shacks on cinder blocks. Then a belt of white-owned ramblers. For every white ring, a black ring to serve them.

I was depressed with the complexities.

"I wish I'd stayed in my cubbyhole," I told Susan.

"I wish I'd stayed in mine."

I took her hand from her lap and held it on the seat. She did not try to remove it.

"What we're doing is just a drop in the bucket."

"Maybe not," she said, but there was no life in her dissent.

"So, let's run away from it all to Myrtle Beach."

"My Lord," she said with a tired laugh. "You never give up."

At the airport, I parked the car and tried to kiss her again. This time she relented. I kissed her firmly but chastely. When she broke it, she looked at my eyes. I

could see she did not trust me, but the dam of her virtue was cracking. She liked me. And I liked her.

On the flight back we talked quietly. I sensed the soft,
tired conversation and the casual touches excited her as
they did me. We had become friends.

Our plane canted. The lighted cube of the Lincoln
Memorial was below us and beyond the shaft of the
Washington Monument. On farther was the Capitol, its
dome afloat in the dark. I thought of those it had har-
bored, the Chidgers and the McFaddens and the Plulaz-
zos—and yes, Anita.

"Listen, Susan," I said, putting my hand over hers
where it lay on the arm rest. "You are going to see me,
aren't you?"

"Yes," she said. "I suppose so." Then she tried to make
a little joke. "In the office, anyway." But the joke swiftly
faded and she said, "It makes things so much more complicated."

I carried her bags down the ramp. She wore the coat
dress she had come in. Its back was wrinkled now. I
noted the swing of her body inside it as she walked, her
legs picking their way down the steps.

Susan turned to wait for me and I tripped on the last
step of the ramp. Bags in both hands, I had no way of
keeping the wrenching weight from my bad leg. I yelled
with pain as I fell to the cement, my ankle aflame with
agony.

Frightened, Susan helped me up and I limped to the
terminal, embarrassed by the two airline agents who
cooed and helped us first to the baggage pickup and then
to a cab. I was afraid someone would think I was drunk.

I worked the next few days on Anita's budget, staying
off my feet, crutching to and from the street for cabs.
Susan was solicitous, although I felt clownish, a victim of
bathos. By Friday afternoon the ankle hurt so much I
knew I would have to see the doctor. Within an hour after
I was in his office, he had me back in the Merritt brace.

My dealings with Anita and Susan were rapidly turning
me into a permanent invalid. The more contradictory
then, that when Susan called me on Saturday morning, I
felt as sunny as a bridegroom.

"I think I'll drop by and bring you something to eat,"
she said. The false courage in her voice turned my sunni-
ness to anxiety.

Her visit, whatever the outcome, forced on me a responsibility I had courted but was not altogether prepared to accept.

"Great," I said. "As soon as you can."

"About noon. I can only stay a minute."

We were both frightened, I thought.

CHAPTER

10

Susan and Athanor

I stumped upstairs, straightened my room, and put clean sheets on the bed. In the refrigerator I iced two bottles of good Moselle. Then I limped all the way downstairs to work on Athanor, the closest thing in the house to a tranquilizer.

The day outside threatened rain. My mood was buoyant, if nervous. The furnace needed dusting. It was all but finished. Since my continence with Anita began, I had worked on it on weekends.

Sitting on a cushion, my braced leg outthrust like a fallen skyscraper model, I refitted the stoking door and tried to do a cosmetic job on the rough spots around the isinglass viewing hole.

When Susan rang, I yelled for her to come in. Holding my breath, I heard the door slam.

"Martin?"

"Down here. Through the kitchen."

At the top of the stairs, she stopped.

"What are you doing down there?"

"I have a surprise to show you. Come down. I'm harmless."

"Where shall I put the food?"

I limped to the bottom of the stairs.

"Bring it down. Susan, in the refrigerator is a bottle of wine—I've got the corkscrew."

"My God," she said. "Listen, I can't stay."

"Then bring the wine for me," I said. "I won't bite."

"What's the surprise?"

"Come down."

She got the wine. As she descended, I saw first her sandals and the strong, well-shaped legs. She wore a neat brown cotton dress, snug at the waist, full bloused and modest as a Puritan.

How clean and pretty she looked. Like Little Red Riding Hood, except for the clear green bottle of wine she held by its long neck.

She smiled, although with apprehension.

"You look like a construction project. What's the surprise?"

"It'll take some explaining."

I exaggerated my awkward movements as I walked with her from the el at the bottom of the stairs to the wider basement.

"My Lord! An indoor barbecue?" she asked. She began to laugh. "Good grief, Martin, what is it? That pot on top!"

"It's Athanor. An alchemical furnace."

"An Athanor what?"

I took the wine from her hand.

"If you'll have just one glass with me, I'll explain." My heart beat fast. Now, more than anything, I wanted her to stay.

"Pity the poor war-wounded," I said.

"Ah, in the battle of the Budget," she added.

"Yes. We gave up our limbs for our womenfolk."

"And," she laughed, "I suppose you brought the glasses down?"

"Yes."

"My God, you're obvious," she said. "Well, what is it?" She sat down in the reject, overstuffed chair I had painfully dragged up near the furnace. I sat in a folding chair near her and began to open the wine.

"An alchemical furnace is what you make the Philosopher's Stone in."

"Alchemists?" she said. "The stone that makes gold?"

"Right."

"Am I supposed to believe that? I've always thought there was a nutty streak in you." She laughed. "A Deputy Assistant Secretary making gold out of lead?"

"Silver, mercury, a pinch of sulphur," I corrected. I was pleased with her reaction.

"It's a hobby?"

"That's right," I said. I poured her a glass of wine.

"That's too much."

"I'm trying to make up with alcohol what I lack in maneuverability."

"You never give up, do you?" she said pleasantly. "Do you think it will work?"

"You mean will it make gold? No."

She laughed at me again.

"No, I mean can you build a fire in it?"

"Yes. I mean, I think so." I paused, heart in throat again. "Can you stay and give me a hand? It's the first test run. No gold this time."

She grinned at me.

"That's a new approach . . ."

Hooray, I thought. She'll stay. I wanted to hug her.

". . . What would I have to do?" She looked at her watch.

"Oh, Susan, don't be so wary."

Glass in hand, I eased myself out of the chair and sat heavily on the floor. My ankle twinged and I took a good jolt of the freezer-cooled wine.

"If you can hand me the charcoal. There, in the corner."

She dragged over the twenty-five-pound bag of wood charcoal.

I began placing chunks carefully on the little raised grate inside the stoking door. She watched me a moment then sat down in the overstuffed chair and sipped the wine.

"Are you going to use an old recipe, or just make one up?"

"Old recipe. I got it at the Library of Congress."

"It's no worse than golf," she said. "My husband . . ." she backed away from the personal. "You ought to get some charcoal lighter fluid."

"Too modern. I'm going to do it the old way. I should have charred the charcoal myself."

"Ah," she said. "Listen, I have to call my neighbor about Ems. I'm going to tell her I've been delayed." It was blissful having her here, the gray day outside, even if nothing came of it.

"Tell her to expect you when she sees you," I said. "It's a complicated procedure. Needs four hands."

She came down and I poured her another glass of wine.

"Okay?" I asked.

"Yes," she said. "I'm stupid to be here."

I looked into her serious eyes. Wasn't I making some sort of commitment, too? I started to say so.

"How's Conyers?" I said, instead, rearranging the charcoal so I could get some kindling underneath.

"Why do you ask?"

"I think you're too good for him," I ventured.

She expelled her breath, startled. Then she said after a moment:

"He doesn't."

"He thinks he's doing you a big favor?"

"Something like that," she said.

I asked her to get me some splintered kindling in a coal bucket by the staircase. We had broken down the protecting conventions on our trip to South Carolina. Now, it was almost with relief, I sensed, that she talked of her problem with Conyers.

"I don't feel that way about you at all," I said when she set the bucket of wood splinters beside me. She stepped back to the chair, away from me, knowing I wanted to take her hand.

"How do you feel?" she asked, suddenly very serious. "You've said all these things." She saved me the discomfort of answering by replying to her own question. "You may not feel *that* way, that you're superior, even if you are, about books and, well, your Athanor and things. But you aren't exactly the marrying kind either." She was a bit sharp.

"*You* aren't the marrying kind," I countered.

I felt her thinking about the injustice of her religion denying a woman the freedom to marry a divorced man, particularly a divorced Protestant.

"Well," she said with some irritation, but not at me. "I know what you mean." With that she turned off her talk of her church and marriage.

"Maybe if the damned thing works, you'll come back and give me a hand when I run it recipe and all," I ventured.

"Maybe," she said.

I could feel beginnings of a dry-throated sexual tension

between us. In me, I could tell it by the beat of my pulse, the tingling in my groin. And I could not be wrong about her. She might marry Conyers. But she did not want him. I almost laughed nervously. She actually liked me for my goddamned furnace. She wanted a fling with an alchemist. Maybe more than a fling.

"Susan," I said. "Could you fetch me a kitchen match? On the stove." She got up from the chair. "And bring me down the other bottle." I looked at her with a smile. There was both confusion and liking for me in her eyes. "You've got to help me split that lunch basket. We *can't* eat it dry."

She went upstairs without saying anything. When she came down again, I knew she bore a load of guilt. It was like making an assignation. Should I be doing this, I thought? But why not? My God! We were grown people. We were not evil people out to hurt. We were lonely. And we were single. Who would it hurt? Why guilt?

When she gave me the matches, I touched her hand. She said nothing, but put the wine at the bottom of the chair, by the basket of food and picked up her tumbler.

"Here it goes," I said, striking the match. The anticipation of whether Athanor would pass its sea trials returned us to our earlier easiness with each other. The smoke was pouring out the stoking door.

"Is it drawing through the back pipe?" she asked. She followed the pipe to the oil furnace chimney pipe.

"I don't know."

She hopped up and opened the oil furnace draft.

"That's the kind we have in Myerstown," she said.

After a few moments, the heavy smoke stopped. The flame pushed bright now past the isinglass. Threads of smoke still curled out from leaks between the pot and the bricks. I marked the leaks lightly on the brick with a piece of charcoal.

"That was predictable," I explained.

"Why don't you cement it on?" She took the charcoal out of my hand—"Here, let me." She marked the leaks on the other side.

"It's the reverberating dome," I said. There were more gaps than I thought there would be. "You've got to be able to take off the dome to get the Aludel—that's where the stuff to make the Philosopher's Stone is cooked—to get it set up on a little triangular rack I've got inside.

Here, look through the isinglass. There's just a pan of water on the rack now."

She knelt to peer in. Her body was so near me, it was difficult not to touch her bare arm, or her breast which would be heavy now against her confining clothes. I felt a little dizzy. She stepped back to her chair agilely.

The charcoal was giving off a low heat with almost no smoke. The first fumes had cleared some and the smell of the burning wood was not unpleasant. The rain had begun and with our hearth glow, the cellar was cosy and yet not hot.

"Not bad, not bad," I said rather proudly. I lurched into my folding chair and began to open the second bottle of wine. Susan pulled her skirt down over her knees. When I looked over at her, she smiled, relaxed now with the wine and the fire.

My plans called for the water to evaporate from the pan, condense on the inside of the aluminum bowl atop the pot and drip into the alembic. I reached over and took Susan's hand and she, safely in her chair, let me hold it, albeit a bit stiffly, on the chair arm.

"The theory of this thing is really pretty sexy," I said. "The alchemists believed that making the Philosopher's Stone was like making a baby. You need male and female symbols. They took gold, which was the sun, that is man, and mixed it with silver, the moon. Athanor is the same kind of thinking. The coals represent the male. The liquid is evaporated by the coals and the condensations— the seeds of water—form in the alembic, the womb of the thing. That's part of the process, anyway."

Susan rose and picked up the piece of curtain rod I'd been using as a poker. She rearranged the coals, her face placid and intent.

"You do everything just the same way," she said, interrupting my lecture gently. ". . . everything all planned out, all perfect like we tried to do in Columbia. I'll bet you've got the recipe all figured down to how much gold you'll need, how much you'll have to pay for it, a teaspoon of this, a dash of that . . ."

"Yes," I said.

"You're like my husband was"—I started to ask her about his death. We were in that easy stage where such interruptions flow naturally. But she stopped me, her dark hazel eyes intent in her desire to finish her thought—

"and like Roger, oh, I know you don't like him, but all of you, you want things so packaged. Then your plans, or his, don't work out, and we, I, get the kick in the pants. Why am I here, Martin? Don't I have enough problems with Roger? Why don't I just make my life with Ems and stay away from you both?"

"I'm glad you don't, I mean, stay away from me."

"Oh, I know. I know."

Her speech said, she rose to look at the alembic.

"Shouldn't it be starting to drip?" She grinned at what she was about to say, "Shouldn't our child be forming in there now?"

I pushed myself up from the chair, and stood beside her. She was right. The distillate should be draining into the alembic from the aluminum bowl.

"I don't know what's the matter," I said.

Susan flicked a drop of her wine onto the iron pot, then one on the aluminum bowl. Both sizzled.

"Shouldn't the thing on top be colder? Like a kitchen window? In the winter it's the coldest part of the kitchen and that's where the condensation is."

"Ice," I marveled. "There's a pitcher in the cupboard."

She fetched the pitcher and ice and put it on top of the aluminum bowl. We sat, her hand in mine again, and waited, sipping new glasses of wine. How different Susan was from Julia. A quick little dribble of water ran into the alembic from the bowl, and settled into a sporadic drip.

"Well," said Susan proudly, "look at that."

"There's our child." I picked up her earlier joke.

"I wish it was that easy to have a real one . . . I mean, just putting a pitcher of ice on your head." She picked up the pitcher and put it on her head, looking up to see me laugh.

"The Philosophers are stoned," she said. Our inertial laughter ran on with her terrible pun. In the vacuum silence that followed, we could hear the rain itself, not just the dripping from the eaves. It beat flatly on the wet ground outside. The wind had shifted.

"Success makes me hungry," I said. "Shall we stump upstairs?"

"Your leg?"

I shrugged.

"We can eat down here if you like," I said. The coals still red made it cosy. Upstairs would seem foreign, formal. "You can wash up in there." A half-bath was in the laundry room. There was no talk now of her going home.

Her "picnic" was as carefully prepared as her reports, as neat as she.

Susan, digging into the basket, brought out individually wrapped deviled eggs, smelling of mayonnaise and oregano, fried chicken, even spring onions. I watched her capable hands opening this, setting aside that.

God, it was good to be eating a home-fixed meal, so unlike the food I served myself, the endless TV dinners, omelettes and French toast. As I "ohhed" and "ahhed," I thought of all the meals she had cooked for her husband: getting him off to work after breakfasts, and at supper, while the plates were still on the table, she would have brought him coffee. Julia had done that for me. Such absences made our meal now warm, familiar, and sad.

"Does your mother live with you?" I asked.

"A lot of the time. She'd like to make it permanent."

"Oh?"

"It makes her feel useful, with Ems. She's already planning how she'll babysit Ems when I marry Roger. I feel like everyone is trying to push me into marrying him."

"Not I . . ."

"No, not you," she conceded with a smile.

"How long has your husband been dead?"

Four years, she told me. We had finished eating. I sat there with her, holding hands, slightly uncomfortable in my folding chair. She began to talk of his death, of the young intern telling her of it at the hospital. I said nothing as she reeled it out. Death is worse than divorce. In divorce there is at least the consolation of reciprocal hate.

"So," she was saying. "Thank goodness for Mrs. Tockbridge. I had worked for her for a few months when she was in Congress, then quit when Ems was born. Anyway, she heard about it and called me."

Susan smiled.

"She said it just right, something like, 'I feel dreadful taking advantage of this disaster, but I have to beg you to come back, even this soon afterwards. I'm afraid you'll go back to Myerstown and I'll lose you.'

"And, of course, that made me feel needed, which was

just what my mother has tried to prevent—by moving in with me. So, really, Mrs. T. was a salvation."

As she was for me, I wanted to add. I had enough wine to want to purge myself with Susan, who was so clean, already such a familiar, decent person. I wanted my past relationship with Anita to be understood and my present one approved, as I approved Susan's with Anita.

I compromised my confession.

"She did something for me, too," I said. "When my wife left me, nobody stepped forward to save me and so I went underground. At home, I piddled with alchemy, Tarot, curious things like I've done all my life, soap temples and forgotten operas. At work, it was my cubbyhole at Labor, writing my *Labor Notes.*"

"From which Mrs. T. pulled you," she concluded my thought.

By the cock, I almost said. Would Susan have accepted me as I was before Anita gave me back my manhood? Would she have accepted her companion of the riots?

Wasn't she, too, magnetized by power? And Conyers: was she attracted in part by the power he represented, endlessly, vengefully drawing up his draft prosecutions, sharpening his indictments against the Mafia for income tax evasion, perjury, forgery. Did Susan abide my eccentricities with Athanor because she could reason, "How could they be wrong. After all, he is a Deputy Assistant Secretary."

Or was that unfair? This speculation, which should have been so distressing, did not break the cosiness. We sat, side by side, sipping the wine, watching the glowing coals.

"Susan, suppose I weren't divorced"—I felt her stirring, sensing where we were drifting back to—"and suppose I were back in my cubbyhole, do you think you would marry me instead of Roger?"

She sipped at the tumbler of wine. The bottle was almost gone.

"Well, just for the sake of supposing . . ." she stopped. "I suppose it's possible if the religious thing could be worked out."

"But if I were back in my cranny, it wouldn't be so exciting for you, would it? In a way, you like excitement, being close to power, to Mrs. Tockbridge. It would be hard for you to give it up, right?"

"Yes, hard to." She sighed. "But with children, and all

the housekeeping again. Oh, I don't know. Why think about it?"

It was a half-a-loaf concession to a half-a-proposal. I was aware of the tenebrous day sifting into the cellar. I rose, even as she put out a hand to stop me so she could do it herself, and I knelt awkwardly in front of the hearth. Into Athanor, I offered more of the wood charcoal, then wiped my hands on my khakis.

Painfully, I walked to her chair and knelt again. She moved her legs aside so I could come closer and I reached to her in the old deep chair and took her forearms in my hands.

Her eyes, darker in the thinning light than I had ever seen them, were settled as if her mind were made up. It was I who was fearful and excited, almost breathless.

Gently I moved my hands to her elbows, momentarily aware of the roughness there and of the pain to my knees as I leaned toward her and she bent to my lips.

Feeling her warm mouth, the fear ran out of me. This first coming together—me with a crate of metal around my leg—on cushions from the old chair thrown on the floor, was a mixture of trepidation and, at its climax, avidity. But the tumbling, gasping lovemaking might still have left us both embarrassed were it not that we found in each other some comfort beyond sex.

Susan stirred beneath me.

"You're heavy," she said softly, pushing me on the shoulder. I started to ease from her. "Be careful of your leg." I lay on my side and brushed the sweated hair back from her forehead.

Her face was flushed, healthy and attractive. Yet, I did not think I loved this face. The thought gave me a start of guilt.

"I didn't have anything on," I said.

"That's all right. It was a safe time."

"Do you have to tell the priest about this?" It was something I had always been curious about.

"I don't know. I guess so."

"So you like me?" I asked. The guilt had given way to friendliness toward her, gratitude that she had given in to me.

"Yes. I wish it didn't complicate things."

"With Conyers?"

"And at the office. Well, I don't want to marry Roger.

I'll have to tell him that much." I despised myself for not liking her as much as I did before she succumbed.

"You must do what you want," I said.

"You might be a little more concerned than *that*," she said. "God, why do I do things like this." She sat up. Feeling her sudden alienation, I tried to humor her back into friendliness.

"I hope you *don't* do things like this."

"No. And I shouldn't have with you."

My fondness returned with a rush. I reached and touched her breast. So, she had been chaste since her husband died. I felt a boyish pride in myself.

"Why not? I worked at it so long. I even think I love you."

"Thanks a lot," she said with resignation. Then she smiled, cutting whatever losses women cut at such a time. She pulled my head to her and gave me a brief kiss. In a warm, mocking voice she said:

"Yes. You worked so hard for it and you deserved it, didn't little boykins?"

I kissed her. She responded, but only for a moment.

"I have to go," she said.

Athanor's coals were graying. The rain had stopped, but the day was still overcast. She put on her clothes, quickly, without prudishly taking them somewhere out of my sight.

"Will you help me with the formula after I do the patching?"

"If I haven't got better sense," she said, with a smile. "I never had an affair, never," she said with some wonder. "And, my God, here I am."

"I hope you don't think I'm any great Lothario," I protested.

"I hope not," she said dubiously. Did she mean Anita?

"If there was anyone, then I am all done with her if you will see me again."

She looked at me with annoyance.

"You don't want to cancel your old airline ticket until you're confirmed on the earlier flight," she complained. "No. I won't go along with that."

"But you *like* me?" God, why did I beg this assurance?

"Yes. Oh, Lord," she sighed, putting her hand to her temple. "Ems and Mother . . . and Roger. Oh, Lord."

We put the trash from lunch and the wine bottles into

the picnic basket. Athanor's condensation had stopped—
the alembic held the water. I detached it and poured it
on the remaining coals carefully so as not to crack the
hearth.

I called her the next day. Her mother answered and
sounded frightened and cold. But Susan and I chattered,
missing each other already. On Monday, when I limped
in on the brace, I saw Susan had done her hair and wore
a new blue dress with a mock turtle neck and a loop of
white beads.

Now, in the office, I sensed that Susan and I were
somehow allied, not against, but to the exclusion of Anita.
We continued to work hard for her, harder perhaps than
before as evidence to ourselves that our affair did not
affect our allegiances.

The recent riot in Washington had started a new gush
of money for both police and for poverty. It was all very
well to have rioters burning Detroit, or Harlem or Rox-
bury, or even Washington one time, as in 1968. But it
was quite another thing for it to happen so near the
White House and the Capitol a second time. On the Hill,
it was "Bread, bullets and birth control," although not
even such troglodytes as McFadden or Chidger ever put it
in the "Congressional Record" quite that way.

So the office had funds to plan with, if not to spread
around. Anita was busy making the dollars count for
next year's elections—and for elections to come. We
drafted programs for Los Angeles, San Francisco and San
Diego. They were needed and there were enough sophisticated colleges nearby to staff them with their graduates.
The other consideration was that these cities were the
power base of Vice President Frieden.

Less explicable in social terms, though equally so politically, was the Wichita project, the home burrow of Representative Joe McFadden, ranking minority member on
the House Appropriations Committee.

McFadden, Kirsted, Chidger, they swayed the legislation that a President and Vice President and a party had
to run on.

Anita's prominence and the potential scandal of discovery of our liaison had both spiced our meetings and made
them circumspect. With Susan, I was freed of such fears.
Anita, to be sure, knew or suspected we were lovers,

but she was occupied with her projects. And now she was frantically lobbying for her budget. Besides, had she not herself deposited Susan in my keeping with the Columbia trip?

Susan continued to hurry home as soon as she could on week nights to see Ems to bed. On Saturdays, we often took the little girl with us on walks, or to the zoo or else-where. Susan's mother, told by Susan in effect to shut up about Roger and about me or go back to Myerstown, babysat on Saturday nights.

Surely it was the happiest fall and winter of my life, for all my anxieties. We both knew at some point Susan must choose between me and her Church. We talked of it for a while, then let it drag along until she should want to make up her mind. For my part, in my rickety way, I was ready for marriage.

Susan cooked well, had a warm, sometimes tart wit, was dainty, a good housekeeper and a sane mother. She made me feel at ease and manly, was pleased with my looks (as I was with hers), and even took some pride in my eccentric pursuits of knowledge.

Her faults were tolerable. She was no intellectual, nor pretended to be, and was certain to try some way to re-turn to her religion even if she did marry me. In bed, we were, at worst compatible, often far more than that, al-though the soaring fireworks I had with Anita were be-yond Susan and me.

Ems loved my Morgan. Her blond hair blew in the late Indian summer wind as we zipped down into Rock Creek Park and along the Parkway. Ems pointed at the precious old maples and oaks and called out their colors—"Bwowhn," "Yellow," "Wed"—as she spotted especially bright splotches of trembling leaves. Susan corrected her, "Brown," "Red," and Ems went on blissfully, reluctant to give up her lisp, "Nother Wed."

Susan, in her kerchief, was more young matron than mistress, and I wore a big offwhite Irish handmade sweater I had splurged forty-five dollars on at a Lewis and Thos. Saltz sale.

We were, on that day, on the road to Great Falls, the long way, past the magnificently muscled, sexless Italo-Amazons and their steeds who guarded Memorial Bridge, then across the unruffled brown Potomac and on into Virginia.

The sports car roared evenly. I thought ahead to the evening, a meal at Pouget's and a bottle of white Bordeaux, then the warm enmeshings in my bed. Susan, while not very experimental, was showing an optimistic randiness.

"Look, Ems," Susan said pointing to the river below us.

There were three river rocks, leaving long weed-laced wakes in the old Potomac, like Columbus' ships. Susan squeezed my hand.

"Now, you look back, just for a second."

I craned back over my shoulder and saw the towers of Georgetown, and the city beyond, stretched distinctly back, all the way to the bland, evanescent blue of the horizon.

"I love your mummy," I said to Ems, and Susan put my hand to her lips and kissed it, while on her lap, the child babbled of browns and yellows and reds.

Roger Conyers had behaved like a shit when Susan gave him the heave-ho. Prosecutor to the end, he had demanded answers instead of simply accepting Susan's, "I don't think it would work out."

To my delight, Susan had answered him directly that she was in love with me, was thinking of marrying me despite the Church, and had never been sure she wanted to marry Roger or even liked him very much. He had asked for it.

I cannot deny a sort of savage joy in coercing Susan to describe the talk.

"So, did he find out we were sleeping together?" I had asked her.

"I think so."

"My God," I said in feigned outrage. "How?"

"Oh, I don't know, he just seemed to know. I don't know how."

"How, Susan? You must have said something. What did *he* say and what did *you* say?"

"Good grief, you're as bad as he is."

"Come on, tell. I'm not mad. Just genuinely interested."

"He asked me how I knew we would get on."

"And what did you say?"

"I said I was pretty sure we would."

"Then?"

"He said people like you had no more moral conviction than to take advantage of people like me. And that was too much for me, so I must have smiled, or looked funny, because he lost his temper and said, 'You let him go too far, didn't you?' "

"Did you say 'yes'?" I asked, beginning to laugh.

"No, I wish I had. No, I didn't. I didn't answer him and he pushed me with his big Irish voice so I said, 'None of your business!' "

"And what did he do then?"

"He blew up again, only this time it was almost scary. He wanted me to go with him to confession, right then. I guess he felt he still had a grip on me and that if I'd confess I'd be getting right with both the Church and him at the same time. Well, that's getting crazy, so I said then, I thought he was going a little too far, and that was that."

"It serves the bastard right," I said, immensely pleased with her, and with myself. Conyers' instinct for bringing out the facts had cost his vanity dearly. But I also knew he would actively hurt either of us if he could. I had seen enough of him to know the virulence of that maniac possessive strain. It would fester in him.

The thought distressed me. I harked back to my concealment from the police at the time Tapir died, and the crime, if there were one, of Buffi's Spanish fly cache, not to mention the possibilities of scandal surrounding Anita. There was her affair with Buffi, her hints of adultery with others and veiled suggestions that campaign contributions may not have been always according to law—a common enough failing in Congress.

Conyers would as soon strike us by striking at Anita. All the more. That would let him cloak his revenge in sanctimoniousness.

There were also other problems for Susan and me. For one, Susan's mother was convinced of her daughter's perdition. She regarded her going with a divorced Protestant as so hellfiresome that sleeping with one was just adding on one more lump of coal. But such irritations I could abide.

Susan and I talked of honeymoons even before she had made up her mind to flout the Church. We had tentatively agreed that Mother Prune would depart the instant we got back from a honeymoon in Barbados, or perhaps Grenada. There, I could question Quashees firsthand about "Jumbie trees," "Duppies," "Obeah," and the "loogaroos." Even more invitingly, I thought of Susan's warm, familiar skin beside me on the white-sand beach.

Winter passed. Our affair was taking on the give-and-take qualities of a durable marriage. We spatted, working all day in anticipation of the evening, when we could argue out our differences. I usually won. She pouted awhile and forgave.

I dreamed of having my daughter visit us and of rearing a couple of sturdy sons. Susan, caught in a trap of logic on birth control (why was it sinful to practice it when she worked daily on population control projects) agreed she would soon find a priest who approved contraception.

At the office there were the tables and statistics, the demographic studies of Detroit, of Columbia—where our project was about to start—of Seattle, and Erie. I was writing more speeches for Anita, often on nonlabor subjects like women-in-government and even on Latin American economic alliances.

Anita was friendly, the good boss she had said she would be. Talking with her in her office, I visualized the agile loins and tensing belly that I knew hid beneath her suit. Silently I hated whatever present lovers she had. I could not eradicate my lust for her. So when such days ended, Susan, without suspecting, I hoped, dissolved the residuum of my passions for Anita.

CHAPTER

11

Contracts

In early April on a night when I was working late, Susan unexpectedly asked me to leave and take her home. My first thought was one of foreboding. We were using condoms sometimes and nothing when Susan thought it was safe, but several times we had played it pretty close to egg-drop time.

I brought the car around to the Constitution Avenue entrance. I had the top down. The air was choked with exhaust fumes and the sun was bronze and hazy in the city dusk.

"Mrs. Tockbridge wants me to get rid of some files," she said when she got in.

"Files?"

"Some of her personal ones." Susan hesitated. I had seldom seen her so nervous.

"What files?"

"She got a call from one of her friends at HEW today, one of the people in Public Health Service. Then she came out and asked me to clear out all her old Congressional files, just to keep the most important letters."

"So?"

"So most of the files are just old inquiry letters from constituents. But there is one case . . ."

"What case?"

I thought of those tremulous hints I had inferred from

Anita's nomination hearing and that she herself had dropped. I was shaken.

"Public Health was soliciting bids on a clinic or something in her district, a seven-hundred-and-fifty-thousand-dollar building at Benn City. She wrote Public Health, you know, pushing a local contractor, one who'd helped her with contributions."

"Everybody does that," I said, relieved but curious.

"Well, General Services checked out his construction record after he got low bid and turned him down. He was that bad—on previous jobs he'd been using bad materials *and* had safety violations, lots of them. So they gave it to second high bidder."

"So she pressured them to reverse?"

"No, she tried. But they just cut the thing out of the budget. Anyway, two years later, she went to Public Health and had the whole file referred to her. She took out the letters she'd written them in support of his contract and sent the rest back."

"So she wanted to get rid of it. I mean it made her look like she wasn't checking out the people she was recommending for contracts."

"Yes. That's what I thought."

"So? Is that so bad? She's not exactly Saint Clara, you know."

"No. But today, before I cleared the Congressional file, I remembered and I looked to see if she'd kept *her* copies of the Public Health letters. They were already gone. She must have thrown that out, too, without my knowing."

"Ah," I gasped.

There must be some kind of heat on right now for those letters about the contract. Anita had to be able to contend she didn't even remember writing a letter for the contractor. And she had to be able to honestly say that since all her old files had been thrown out, *if* there ever were such a letter, it was thrown out too. But why all this trouble over a simple favor for a constituent, even a contributor?

"Anything else?" I asked.

"No. Public Health finally built the clinic, but I don't know who did it for them."

I told Susan not to destroy the files until I could talk to Anita.

Without doubt, Susan had accurately sensed a problem

way beyond the fragmentary facts she knew. I did not want her touched by any of Anita's old dirtiness.

When I came in next day, Susan and I looked soberly at each other. Before I confronted Anita, I wanted to take at least a cursory reading on what was going on. First, I had Susan unobtrusively dig up the name of the Benn City Public Health project from our library. Then, I got its contract file number from the General Services public file room. Without identifying myself, I called the file clerk and asked if the old file were available. The clerk said it was out on a routine duplication order and would be back the next day. I gasped.

"Who signed it out?" I asked, panic everywhere in me but my voice.

"Justice."

"Who over there?"

"Looks like somebody named A. D. Langley," said the clerk.

One quick call to Justice's information switchboard confirmed the worst. A. D. Langley was a clerk-messenger in Roger Conyers' division. Shit! I thought desperately, what's Anita done besides helping a contributor?

I walked into Susan's office.

"Conyers has the file from General Services," I said. "He's after Anita."

"Oh, Lordie," she said, hand to her mouth. "I got her into this."

"You?"

"By getting Roger so mad."

"Oh, God," I said disgustedly.

Anita did not get back from the Hill that day during work hours. I sent Susan home, and waited in the office for Anita to show up.

Finally, at 7:00 P.M., she came in. I saw from her face she knew why I was waiting. I followed her into her office. How frivolous the Hepplewhite furniture seemed now.

"Where were you?" I asked.

"Out. What does it matter?" She hesitated, then asked cautiously:

"What do you know?"

"What do *you* know?" I replied.

"Only that somebody at Justice talked to Public Service two days ago. What did Susan tell you?"

"Oh, come on!" I said. Anita nervously evaded my gaze.

"How do I know it isn't just a security clearance?" she asked. "I mean something routine, or maybe about the Secretary stepping down and . . ." She was growing even more upset.

"Don't worry about that," I said grimly. "Justice has pulled the GSA file on Benn City . . . not Security, the Criminal Division."

She dropped her head into her hands. Even now, her face blasted with worry, I thought of those lean, soft shoulders and noticed her blouse fluffed at the neck.

"Jesus," she said quietly. "Is it Susan's boyfriend?"

"Yes, her ex-boyfriend."

"My God, Martin. If you had let her alone he would never have done this. He's getting back at you two by cutting my throat." I had already considered that chain of events.

"If you had never brought me here," I replied harshly, "I would have let her alone." And one could go farther. If Anita and I had both not flirted with the occult, we would never have met at Buffi's party. And . . . but what point that? "Look, let's just talk about whatever it is you did."

"Did Susan get rid of those files?"

"I told her not to."

She exploded.

"*You* told her!" I saw how much on edge she was and tried not to answer her in kind. After all, it was her ass in the crack. But I was worried sick, too, about Susan and me.

"It's silly to start doing panicky things like that until you see if there isn't a way out," I said. "I don't even know what you've done. If it's just getting rid of a couple of letters . . ."

Her eyes were constricted with pain. She shook her head that this wasn't all. I could see she was about to cry.

"I've been scared sick," she said all in a rush.

I pulled up a chair and put my hand on hers.

"Just loosen up, Anita. Why don't you tell me about it?"

She wiped her eyes on a Kleenex. In a low, controlled voice she began. A contractor, Brendan Doolittle, who had given her a campaign contribution and promised more, had pressed her to get him the Benn City PHS contract.

"How big a contribution?" I asked.

"Five thousand," she said and I whistled. There had to be a quo for that quid.

As Susan said, the contract was turned down. After Anita was in HEW, the Doolittle contract was reinstated.

"With your help?"

She nodded.

"You called in the big guns on it?"

"Yes," she said.

"Pauhafen?"

"Yes, he called McFadden. McFadden was chairman of HEW appropriations."

"And Pauhafen?"

"Built some damned paper mill in Wichita."

Honest Joe McFadden, I thought. Never touches the hootch or the ladies, or the public till. He only steals for his district.

"So," I said, "these things happen."

"Doolittle never finished the Benn City building."

"What?" I asked, incredulous.

"He borrowed money using the contract to secure the loan, but he didn't put the money into the building."

"And you split that money with him, the money that didn't go into the building." I spat it out harshly. She was not just a crook, but a common, clumsy crook. She had robbed the Treasury as surely as if she had done it with a gun in her hand.

"I don't like your accusative tone," she said defensively, and I saw then that she was barely hanging on to her self-control. She began to blink back tears again, and said in a small tense voice, "Can I go on?"

I nodded, feeling contrite.

She stammered out that he had given her this second "contribution," $10,000 from the stolen funds.

"Contribution!" I gasped. "My Jesus! You weren't even in Congress for that one; you were in government! It was a goddamned bribe! Robbery!"

"Oh, God," she whimpered. "Call it what you want. I considered it money to cover previous campaign costs." I tried to hold my temper, but couldn't.

"Bullshit, Anita! You stole ten thousand dollars in federal cash! You split fraudulently obtained cash with a goddamned thief."

She was thoroughly intimidated; I was angry.

"Was it in bills?"

"Yes."

"Thank God for that. Will Doolittle talk?" I was still astonished.

"I don't think so. He's guiltier than I am."

I was suddenly furious. By getting Susan to destroy those files, Anita would be roping *my fiancée* in as a conspirator in a federal felony case!

"Guiltier than you?" I sneered. "Why hell! Don't you know Conyers will give Doolittle immunity from here to the grave to nail you up, or me, or Susan—particularly you because we depend on you? Do you know the leverage Conyers can put on Doolittle? Conversion of federal funds, grand larceny, false bankruptcy count, bribery, my God, even the Corrupt Practices Act. We're talking about fifty or sixty years in potential time over his head and you don't think that guy will talk!" I was almost screaming.

"Conyers wouldn't!" She looked frantic, but full of anger for me now.

"Wouldn't? He hates crooks, particularly ones *I* work for."

"Well, what are we going to do?" she demanded.

"*We* going to do?"

"Yes," she said. She had risen from her desk. Tall, her eyes half shut in fury, she looked like a Kali. "You're going to be in this. You're a lawyer. You can get me out."

A year before I would have cowered. But she had abetted a genie in escaping his bottle. The genie turned on her.

"Sweetie," I snarled. "It's one goddamn thing to cover up for you and Pauhafen with a little lying to police or to get named in the paper as the guy who's your stud when you want a normal kick, but it's another thing to get my pecker hammered to the wall with a half-dozen federal conspiracy charges. You get your own lawyer."

She staggered back from the table desk. I thought for a moment she would collapse. I ran around to get her. She rubbed at her forehead.

"All right," she said. "You're right. I'll burn the file myself." There was a reed note of hysteria in her voice. "I won't involve you. I'll get you and Susan out of here before all this breaks." Instead of fighting me, she was collapsing.

My resentment evaporated.

I poured her a glass of water from the pitcher on the table. She drank it, her eyes downcast. When she put the glass on the table, her nervous fingers tipped it over and it spilled on the thick carpet she had pressured the GSA into getting her.

"I'm sorry," she said. The hysteria was back in her voice. "I'm sorry. I'm sorry," she repeated.

"My God, that's all right," I said, helping her into the chair, sure now what was coming. She began weeping, first, then her shoulders shook violently and she moved into barking uncontrollable gasps.

"Anita!" I said, taking her shoulders. The barking slowly turned into regular sobs. I thought of getting her a doctor. The sobs began to accelerate again into those dreadful barks. I shook her shoulders, made her look up. Her face had fallen apart. The eyes were pinched with pain, the black pupils tiny in the too-light eyes. Her eye makeup was streaking gray-black, her lips almost as pale as her face.

"Come on! Pull out!" I begged her.

We stared helplessly at each other. Then the acceleration began again. I dashed the water into her face, hoping to shock her out of it, almost panicked myself by seeing her so.

The water jolted her. With deep breaths she fought for control. The water dripped down the rich silk of her blouse. Like a hurt child, she sniffed back her running nose. I gave her a handful of Kleenex and she daubed at her face, then her shirt.

"I'm all right now," she said. "I've got to be at Nancy Fisher-Smith's. The Vice President . . ."

"Bullshit," I said.

"No, I have to." The tears flowed into her eye corners as if she were a little girl crossed.

"Anita," I said calmly, fearful of upsetting her again. "I'll call your sorries to Mrs. Fisher-Smith. I'll tell her we're going to be all night on the Los Angeles project. That will take care of her and the Vice President. Huh?"

She looked up, her face, crinkling with silent tears, devoid of any glamour or liveliness now, miserable and naked. How sorry I felt for her who, incredibly, had thought she would never be caught, nor ever hurt if she were.

"Make up your face a little," I said to her softly. "I'll get the calls out of the way."

I called Mrs. Fisher-Smith, carrying it off nervously. Then I called Susan. I said Mrs. Tockbridge wasn't mad at her, then lied and said the case wasn't nearly as bad as it had seemed. I could tell her what else needed to be told in the morning. Meanwhile, one upset woman was enough.

The night guard nodded like a courtier as Anita and I passed. She had parked her car in front and I had to restrain the guard from walking out to hand us in. There was agony among the mighty tonight, I thought; how lucky that guard in his mindless job.

As we drove up Massachusetts, past the lighted embassies, the crouching mass of the mosque and its sudden moonstruck minaret, she turned to me and said in a tiny held-in voice:

"I never broke up like this before."

I took her into her apartment. She walked unsteadily to her bedroom, sat on the bed, and took off her pumps.

"You've got to learn your limits, Anita," I said, standing in the doorway. For weeks, she had been going all day, and then to parties every night. She was becoming a big name in the society pages, but she was worn thin. She was in no shape to be hit with a bomb.

"I pushed too hard," she said, the resonance gone from her voice. It sounded gravelly.

"Ah, maybe there's a way out." I stopped. I must not get into this thing voluntarily just when I had escaped by facing down her threat. But could I resist playing this new role of man and master?

"Stay just a little," she said. "Fix a drink."

She went into the bathroom in her stocking feet. I mixed a light brandy and water. She came back in her robe, her face washed, old-looking now from the strain, without pretension, open, totally without guile.

"That was a bad time," she said.

"Better?"

"Yes. Thank you." Her voice was grateful, I was touched. Disloyalty to Susan welled up in me. I thought of Anita's small perfect breasts and the warm, slick trap of her thighs. She lay on the bed, her head propped up by a reading pillow. I sat in a straight chair.

"What am I going to do?" she asked calmly.

Well, the first thing, I thought, is to try to figure out what Conyers knows. Maybe he doesn't even have ground to indict Doolittle. But no, I was enough of a government lawyer to know that if he were working on Anita, he already had Doolittle.

That meant he knew the damned building never got built by Doolittle and that Doolittle had borrowed a large amount of money at about the time the building project failed. That was the money which was secured with the government building contract. Thus Conyers would be able to prove that Doolittle defaulted on the loan and that the lender collected government funds to make it good.

There was the point of robbery. In a nutshell, Conyers would be able to prove that Doolittle got a lovely chunk of money through a phony bankruptcy, a federal felony, and the only thing he would not know was that $10,000 of that government loan money went to Anita—*after* she left Congress and came to government.

In addition, Conyers would probably know that Doolittle got the contract through Congressional pull, McFadden's. Maybe he had even figured out that the leverage on McFadden was Pauhafen's paper mill in Wichita, and that Pauhafen was Anita's fiduciary patron.

While he might also suspect Anita had a role in all this, might even have some old memo from McFadden, or Pauhafen's files, or from within Public Health Service, still only Doolittle would know positively of the cold, hard cash going to Anita.

And that would be where that remorseless bloodhound would now be sniffing. I turned back to Anita.

"Well, I won't help you," I said. "I can't, Anita. But I can give you some advice." I was trying to have it both ways, man and mouse. "The key to this thing is to get this Doolittle to keep quiet, for him to cop a plea and do six months, say." I hesitated, then, heart beating, added:

"You've got to get him enough money to make it worth his while to do six months in jail, and a good enough lawyer to make sure that's all he gets."

Fatuously, I considered whether I could palm off this advice to bribe a witness as a legitimate part of our dubious client-lawyer relationship. But no law association ethics committee, sleazy as they were, would buy that.

"I think that if I could talk to Brendan," she said. "I think he would see that to testify against me would ruin him forever, worse than jail. How much money do *you* think he would want? That building cost him his reputation. He must be just about broke now."

"For six months?" I thought a moment. Doolittle was a hungry bastard. Maybe $100,000 clear. Plus the lawyer. Once more, I drew back from the brink. Then, I plunged.

"A hundred and fifty thousand," I said, "counting the lawyer."

I saw her hope fade.

"That would clean me out," she said. Well, I thought, with Tapir dead, who then?

"Buffi?" He was wealthy. And discretion would be no problem, not with the kind of eccentricities he must be hiding.

"Maybe," she sighed.

I felt the dull ache of treason in my head. I was talking now without veneer about a bribe, an illegal act. I was myself committing a crime by advising her to commit one. I was throwing away all the honest time I had built up with Susan to help a woman who did not deserve my help. My palms ran sweat.

"A good lawyer, one tough enough to put the Justice case in doubt, might get them to accept a cheap plea to stealing a few thousand. How much did he steal?"

"Maybe a hundred thousand."

"You got fifteen thousand altogether. He's spent all the rest since then?"

"Easy come, easy go." She was rallying. "He used his share as a down payment and got a private loan to build a shopping center. He bankrupted that one honestly."

"He should have tried honesty the first time." I drew a smile from her.

"Buffi might give me seventy-five thousand," she said, returning to the major problem. "But he's getting crazier and crazier. I asked him today about money. All he wants to do is talk about Black Masses. My God. In the midst of this." Then she paused. "How can we even talk to Doolittle? If I call him, won't Conyers be tapping my phone? I'm afraid to write. That's even more of a record."

"I won't contact him."

"I wouldn't ask you."

"Buffi?"

"No," she said. "Krals might. If Buffi tells him to, he can be trusted. He could tell Doolittle to call us—me—at a bar someplace at a certain time from a pay station. We could work it out."

In my heart I cursed her. She had ruined her chances for the Vice Presidency by her cheap thievery. I wondered whether anything could be salvaged. Did I want to help salvage a Cabinet post or the Vice Presidency for a federal bank robber?

She had shut her eyes now. Her long, perfect legs were bare from just above the knee in her robe. She blinked and caught my stare at her legs.

I thought with a pang of Susan. I should be calling her again to reassure her in some way. For the moment, I pushed her and Anita's predicament aside and considered Buffi's money. Then I imagined what Anita would have to do to get $75,000 from him.

"You're all crazy," I said. "Somebody like Buffi . . . I wouldn't get tangled in his sickness the way you have." I thought of the chapel. "Willingly," I added. "And Pauhafen. And this Doolittle . . ." I went on.

"Doolittle was just money," she corrected me.

"Well, whoever . . ."

Anita smiled. The near breakdown had passed. The persistent optimism that had carried her so far was beginning to come back.

"Martin," she butted in, "please don't pick on me. I don't reproach you. I don't say sex for you must be this or that . . ."

"Yes," I sighed resignedly, "I know." I began to want her, glad enough to feel something besides anxiety over her monstrous predicament.

She smiled wryly, seeing my incipient desire.

"Stay tonight," she said.

"No," I said. "You'd better take a sleeping pill and sleep for about twelve hours."

"I never use them," she said. "I don't believe in drugs."

"Very funny," I said.

Anita reached out, the loose robe falling away from her arms now, baring them.

"Martin, stay. You don't have to do anything. Just stay with me. Just *be* here."

Her face seemed so susceptible in the weariness that had taken it, the lids lowered now and the lips without their lipstick. Ah, I detested myself.

I was gritty from the waves of sweat that had poured

from me during the day. "I need a shower," I said, my heart beating with want for Anita's familiar body, my mind, my loyalties wanting to postpone my treason.

Anita climbed out of her bed long enough to pull down the covers and to throw her robe from her night gown. I saw as I walked past her into the bathroom the bulge of her breast through the armhole of the gown. The nylon clung to and delineated her hips.

When I came back from the shower, the bed lamp still burned. Anita was asleep. I meditated lying chaste beside her. I had thought much of her in the months and minutes I had been away.

She lay with her back to me, her knees bent fetally, her nightgown up, exposing her to above the hips. The lamp washed her rumpled bed and long body. Slowly my anxieties lifted and I studied her.

From the crevice made by the confluence of her thighs and lower buttocks fluffed out tufts of pubic hair, sparse promises of the luxuriance on the other side of her body. The configuration of the tufts, so random, was insistently human, innocent contradictions of her worldliness, her power, her ambitions, her beauty, even her age. They spoke of simple animality, the human flesh, its juices and excretions that insure us against worshiping familiar humans as gods.

Did I want to go back to Anita? To renew the itch for this lovely crook, who chiggered in my skin?

If sex were only all—and God knows it was a substantial part—I could desert her. But there was in her that quality of helplessness which made a man of me when I was with her. That, as much as sex, was what had finally pushed me to think of betraying Susan. The thought loosened an avalanche of anxiety. Oh, there was real enough reason for some of it, but why was it so intense?

Whatever else it did that night, it kept me from Anita's bed. After an hour of sweating, of kicking at my anxiety seizure, I fell asleep on her sofa.

I awoke at six and thought for an hour uneasily of whether my panicky torment of the night before would have been any worse if I had crawled into bed with Anita.

I got up to put on the coffee and when I came back, Anita was drowsily coming awake. I scrambled some eggs, fried some sausage, and she ate hungrily, sitting now in a blouse and slacks.

"You were very good to me about this thing," she said, lighting a cigarette, drawing on it gratefully. Even in the small measure, her dependence flattered me.

"We'll try," I said. "I wish I weren't involved." But I was, and my mind worried pickily over the case. "You'll want some close pal to get a look at Conyer's file at Justice," I said. "Can you get Frieden to have it pulled?" But I rejected that the moment I said it. The last thing she wanted was for Frieden to know she was the quarry of Justice.

"I'll get Kinsante," she said. "He can make it look like he's thinking of the son of a bitch for a judgeship." Kinsante: that would be the sharp dresser whose wife stayed in Delaware, ranking minority member on Senate Judiciary.

"Can you trust him?"

"Yes," she said simply, and to my jealous mind, suspiciously.

"Conyers' file will read like the Missal," I grunted. Now, scheming as I was for a look at another civil servant's personnel file, my safe and moral days with Woeckle seemed in the lifetime of some other man.

When I walked into the office, Susan looked up at me with her worried, trusting face.

"I think it's going to work out," I lied. "Leave the files alone. If anyone comes in about anything, refer them to Anita."

"Are you messed up in this now?" she said. Her hazel eyes were so sad that I wanted to take her in my arms and cry, for both of us.

"God, I hope not," I said despairingly.

"How mad is she at me for telling you?"

"Don't worry about that. She's not mad at all."

"I feel like it's my fault," she said gloomily.

I was angry every time I thought of Susan taking on a guilt load for angering Conyers.

"Poor Mrs. Tockbridge," said Susan.

"Poor Mrs. Tockbridge damned near got you snagged into a conspiracy case," I said.

She looked dispirited.

"We'll go out for supper," I said, trying to brighten.

The thought brought a quick smile to her face. But by the afternoon, she was depressed again. I thought it was despair over Anita, to whom she owed so much. I did not think she suspected that disaster had nearly drawn me back into our patron's bed.

At about four, Susan came to my office, trying to mask her depression with a brisk, upbeat tone.

"I think I'd better get on home to Ems tonight."

"Why?"

Her face creased with the effort of a plucky smile. "Oh, Martin. I'd just make you feel bad too. I know it's not going to be as easy as you say."

I smiled consolingly and sympathetically, but crawled with apprehension that she might sense I had leagued myself to Anita's cause.

"Well, Saturday, a real night out," I said, bringing a small smile back to her.

Already my thoughts were on Anita. My return to her had been nerve-racking and sexually unsatisfactory. But that very unsatisfactoriness whetted my lusts. I played the consoling fiancé with Susan. Secretly, I basted in desire for Anita.

Looking at Susan's face, the dark eyes a troubled reflection of unselfish concern for me and for Anita, I felt for the first time in my life truly damned.

That night, Anita called me at home.

"How'd it go?" I asked her, meaning the talk with Buffi.

"I'm getting leary of the telephone," she said.

"I'll come over," I volunteered.

At Anita's that night, I drank an unaccustomed two martinis with her as she efficiently fixed the meal, a can of clam bisque, two filet mignons, and sliced tomatoes topped with oil and onions. I sat on the tall three-legged kitchen stool as she worked.

"Buffi's getting weird," she said, smiling ruefully, "even for me."

"What about the money?"

"Martin, he keeps talking about a Black Mass, a real one."

Oh, Jesus, I thought, what a condition for a loan.

"And if you take part in it, he'll come across?" I asked.

"Something like that."

"Well, what's the rest?" I added with light sarcasm,

"I'm your lawyer." She smiled; it was a mode between us that both of us liked.

"He's looking forward to a rather exalted guest list." She took the plates to the table. "He wants the Vice President there."

It was so absurd I laughed.

"You're kidding." She began to laugh. "No, I'm serious. I mean, he's serious."

"And no Harry, no seventy-five thousand?"

"Well, that's the way he's talking now. We can try to bargain him down."

"You can bargain me right out of it too," I said. The crazy bastard would want it authentic. "You use baby fat in Black Masses."

"Buffi said he knew you would bring that up. He said the form of the Mass was negotiable—that the Austrians never got quite so—he said 'basic'—as the French."

I snickered uncomfortably.

"It's nuts. We won't do it," I said.

"He wants us to have lunch with him," she countered.

I ate without real appetite, washing down her expensive food with her expensive wine. Now that I could afford good wines, my stomach and palate were upset too much of the time to honor them.

I sensed her concealing something from me. It made me doubly nervous.

She poured coffee and lit her cigarette.

"Up until this thing at Benn City, I never really felt threatened," she said.

"Why not? All this stuff with Buffi was like carrying a time bomb around in your . . ." I skipped the vulgarity. "Indirectly, fooling with people like Buffi is what set the bomb ticking, got Conyers going."

She thought a minute. I could almost see that sequence which I had considered so many times go through her head. Her interest in Buffi led to her interest in the occult, led to me, led to my affair with Susan, led to Conyers.

She looked up, half stricken, half searching my eyes as if to risk a final damning confidence. I felt even more uneasy.

"Martin, I don't want to go to jail."

"Maybe you won't even get caught." My mind again rolled with the legal possibilities. "We don't know exactly how much Conyers knows. Maybe not even enough to indict Doolittle. Even if that happens, Doolittle will plead guilty . . . well, Christ, you won't be the first Vice President to buy a few crucial votes."

"If I ever get in there, the first thing I'm going to do is have that Conyers bastard fired," she said angrily. I laughed, easing some of my tension. Yet something was bothering her. I felt our talk was a nervous prelude to some revelation.

"High motives like that deserve high office," I continued to banter.

She laughed with me, then went serious again.

"Look . . ." she said. Then she stopped. She got up from the table and put her hands on my shoulders, staring in my eyes. I pushed her back gently and saw in her face that she was tormented, genuinely.

"What is it, Anita?" I began to feel panic. I poured a glass of the Burgundy and swigged it like it was cheap California red.

"I've done something to you you don't even know about and now I'm afraid to tell you. I'm afraid you'll leave me."

"Oh, shit . . ." I said, fearful.

"You might be a little more manly about it."

"I don't even know what it is!"

She rose and came back from her bedroom with two shoeboxes and opened one on the table. Inside were reels of eight-millimeter film. I knew it all in an instant. Blackmail movies.

"Us! In the chapel!" I snatched the two shoeboxes from her. "Are these the only prints?"

"Yes," she said. "For God's sakes calm down."

I ran frantically through the two-dozen film boxes, but they were merely numbered. My God! Who else did they have?

"Twenty-four," she said. "You're in number twenty-four."

I found the film box and popped it into my pocket.

"Who are the other twenty-three?"

She sat down opposite me and put her hand over her eyes, then looked up, and blew smoke through her lips, waiting for me to speak again.

If these were blackmail movies, and I had my only print, then I was safe, if shaky and shocked.

"Who's in here?" I repeated. "They're Buffi's, right? How'd you get them?"

She shrugged.

"He loaned them to me. He knows he'll get them back. After all, I need his seventy-five thousand more than his damned movies. He thought if you saw them, you could figure out a way of using them to help kill the investigation."

"He's not getting the one of me back," I said.

"He doesn't care about you. Can they be used?"

I thought a moment. Blackmail: Christ, the whole concept was repulsive. Besides, would Conyers be scared away even if some bigwig told him to lay off? Didn't he hate too well to back away? I dismissed the sordid thought of blackmail. We could only block him for sure by suppressing the facts from him.

She sensed my scruples and insisted, "They could be used. There are important people in there. Why do you think I let Buffi make them: they're *my* final weapon too." Final was right.

She would be committing suicide if she used the films to force a bigshot to move against Conyers. The bigshot, once the contract were fulfilled and he had his film print, would swiftly eradicate Anita's future.

I started to call her crazy. Yet what she said, unprincipled as it was, had at least a plausible quality. But Conyers: suppose he were fired. Wouldn't he work to prove his case anyway—if it were provable—and then leak it to the papers? After all, she didn't have Conyers on film in there.

"You've got Frieden?" I asked. "Who else?" I should have been past the point of hating her for the other men in her life. But I was not. Nevertheless, I thought hectically of Frieden's enormous power, power even over Conyers. Blackmail, my God! "I should be for ever getting mixed up with a weirdo like you," I said to hurt her. "So who else?"

"Chidger," she said, adding quickly. "Four years ago."

"Chidger?" I shouted. I thought of the desert louse, cornbred, always talking God, the FBI and state sovereignty. "I don't believe you!" I said.

She shrugged again.

"But how could you do it, I mean, even to *act* with a filthy bastard like Chidger?"

"If it makes you feel better, he couldn't do anything. He, well, collapsed and got remorseful and climbed out of bed. For my purposes, that's better anyway."

The thought was obscene. That was a one-reeler I would forgo.

"Who else?"

There was Kinsante, as I had already half surmised. And Massein, a senator and king-maker from New York, the liberal Democratic chairman of the Finance Committee; she named a half-dozen more. God, what a collection of political might!

"What a whore you are," I said, almost with awe.

"There weren't that many." To my surprise, she was ashamed.

De Plaevilliers had taken most of the films in his bedroom, which she had used as a rendezvous. Krals had helped. A Frieden classic and the reel in which I starred had been taken in the chapel. Buffi had filmed us through a chink in one of the seemingly opaque panels behind the altar.

"It makes him feel he's a big political deal and God knows what else to look at the damned things and think what he could do to American politics if he wanted," she temporized, keeping the talk on Buffi. "And for me, well, it *is* protection. Besides," she tossed her head, about to dismiss with this gesture, I knew, any talk of morality, "it's only putting on film what everybody else does anyway."

I thought of the tawdriness of Krals and the aristocratic Buffi, huffing and puffing while the little camera purred on.

"But why me?" I asked her.

"He wanted some control over you. Also he thought you might be on the way up . . ."

"Some accolade. And you contributed. Jesus! For money, and . . ."

"I did get him to give up the reel," she reminded me.

My God, what an invasion of privacy for anyone to be filmed like that. My temper flashed.

"To give up the reel! I ought to burn them all," I said.

But *heart deep*, I wanted her, us, to beat Conyers. I hated him and only despised the people in the film boxes. If I destroyed the films, I destroyed her, too, for Buffi would be too angered to help her. He had loaned her the boxes. As she said, his money was the earnest of their return. Could they be used as some desperate last resort? Not by me. I would balk at blackmail, even I.

Anxiously, my gut gave a spasm. I could imagine the walls of my stomach being bathed with squirts of hydrochloric acid. This world of Anita had no relation to my dreams of Susan.

"Did you bring a projector?" I asked.

Anita's concern gave way to a nervous smile.

"Yes," she said. "Buffi sent his along. You don't believe me about the films?"

"I want to be sure," I said half curious, half shamefully, wondering if there might not be something we could do with the damned things.

"Ah," she said, knowing I was partly playing the hypocrite. "Which one?"

"Frieden."

She looked at me to see whether she dared risk my anger by ridiculing my jealousy. I tried to appear stern, now that I had contemptibly approved the survival of the films.

"Which Frieden? He's in two."

The wine, and the shock of the last few days, had cooked out some of my sensibilities. And, in a way, I had accepted her as a sort of whore, as a pimp accepts a prostitute-wife.

"The shorter of the two," I said with remnant dignity.

I set up the projector, then suddenly was struck by the fear that mistakenly I had someone else instead of myself in box twenty-four. I pulled it out of my pocket and threaded it on.

"A curtain raiser," I said, putting the Frieden film box on the table. "I just want to make sure I burn the right reel."

Watching myself as the co-star of a blue movie flickering on Anita's light beige wall was both disgusting and funny. It was hard to care seriously about a movie whose quality was so unremittingly amateurish. Even Buffi, apparently, had his ineptnesses.

The movie began with me looking at the book titles. I recalled the heat of that day, the sun as we walked to where the carp slowly swam, the smell of oil, scorched grass and the roughness of those white, worn statues. There had been the coolness inside the chapel, the leather book covers, and the cutting tartness of the icy Austrian wine.

The scene switched to me standing awkward and shambly beside the table. Anita's image, with wine glass in hand, returned to mine.

The thought, which should have been so obvious, stunned me: she had given me the Spanish fly to make my film performance last longer.

I started to turn on her. But what was the use now.

I could feel my passion rising as I watched her take that tiny sip from the glass. I strained to see her breasts falling free from her suit. The Anita on the film, more openly salacious, seemed more desirable than the woman on the other side of the projector.

"Don't you feel crummy knowing that nut is up there in some little booth panting away while you're humping and grinding?" I asked, exasperated.

She watched the film, not answering for a moment. We were kissing. How ludicrous I looked, pressing against her.

"I don't think so," she replied. "Don't *you* get any pleasure out of knowing someone is watching? None?"

"I didn't know someone was watching," I said glumly. "The answer is 'no' anyway."

"How about watching yourself now?"

"Some. Well, it's interesting more than sexy."

Anita was naked in the film now, the triangle of wiry hair showing as she moved the food to the end of the table.

"Are they all this explicit?" I asked.

"Yes."

"I wonder if Buffi is crazy enough to just take them and blow everybody out of the water with them, you included. You know, get a couple of hundred prints of Frieden and Chidger and all the rest of you and send them around."

That was, of course, a wild notion.

"His cousins would love it," Anita said. "The family would drag out all the black magic business and get him committed to a mental hospital and the good life would be over for him. His cousins would have the corner on the grain market."

The film aroused, though not consistently. I rose and walked around the low table and sat on the floor by

Anita's chair. I softly kneaded her upper thigh. The touch of her firm, real flesh was reassuring.

On the wall, the camera tried to zoom in on our hips, but its lens must have tilted up. I saw the lights and the backs of the books, then it came back to where we pumped away. I did not want to see any more.

"Pedestrian, dot, dot, dot—Martin Dobecker," I reviewed it.

I switched off the projector. I knew how it ended, with me on my back in pain. I began to run it backward on the reel and turned on the projector light.

With fantastic speed I was leaping off her body and jumping off the table. I began to laugh and she joined in.

"That's the way you wish it had been, Martin," she said lightly through her laughter. But I knew this was not true.

I had seen enough blue movies. I did not want to see the Vice President, that footballer gone to flab, humping over Anita's lovely straight body, either forward or reverse.

"When was Frieden?"

"One night two summers ago, during a party."

I was jealous now, imaging the two of them sneaking away from just such a party as I had been to, and there, hushed and breathless, grabbing at each other while Krals filmed away from behind some false mirror.

"Why don't you set up shop in your own bedroom?" I asked nastily. "Christ, I risk my ass for you on this Benn City thing . . ."

She looked up at me from the chair, assessing my anger again, knowing that I wanted her and thus that she could say what she wanted. The reel ran off with its familiar tick-tick-tick. In my ears, I felt the pulse of blood.

"Well, I love you for helping me," she said quietly, not fully meaning the word "love." Ah, how long I had been away from her.

Her elbows on the chair, she turned her palms upward. I knelt by her, kissing her lips, feeling the arousal of culpable passion as her fingers slipped over my ears to yoke my neck.

I stayed the night. When as usual I awoke before she did, my lips sore and my body surfeited, I felt renewed guilt over my betrayal of Susan. Benn City had not gone away either. And the films were a two-edged knife.

At work in the morning, I dissembled with Susan by

laboring steadily on our new cities program. Her worries were my ally in concealing my new treason.

My affair with Susan went on as before. Inevitably, however, I compared her honest caresses and plebeian rapture with Anita's expertness.

Meanwhile, Brendan Doolittle was indicted, as we had feared. Krals made the trip to Benn City and back and arranged for Doolittle to call Anita at a pay booth in the International Club. I stood next to her as she talked softly to the contractor.

What a winner she was in the clutch. He was amenable to bribery. She got off with the promise of $100,000. He could consider it an unsecured interest-free "loan" to help his family while he was in jail. We would turn over $75,000 now through Krals, the other $25,000 when he got out.

This was $50,000 less than we'd feared it would be, thanks to Anita's persuasiveness—and to Conyers' thugs. One of Conyers' young Justice lawyers had made plain to Brendan that a deal was possible. But his pure snottiness had queered it.

I could hear the contractor's voice from the earpiece.

"He treated me like some kind of dirty animal, Anita."

Anita also gently convinced him that if he peached on *her*, no other politician would ever lift a finger for him.

Doolittle had his own lawyer, an experienced Reading court-manipulator, and was optimistic. The case would be heard by a Republican stalwart on the U.S. bench best known for allowing some electrical manufacturers to plead *nolo contendere* in an outrageous antitrust case. The judge's kindness toward poisoners of the economy—as opposed to purse-snatchers or street fighters—boded well for Brendan.

Anita repeated to me Brendan Doolittle's parting remark with a sort of sad wonder:

"How can I lose if I've got the next Vice President of this wonderful, wonderful country on my side?"

Brendan was a hundred percent.

12

The Mass

If Anita scratched up her own money to meet the $100,000, she—we—need not have been in Buffi's debt. But against my advice, she pushed him for $75,000. I agreed to meet with him and her at the Jockey Club where the deal was to be worked out.

It was a place I had come to like for its pretensions. There were the tits and studs of the *Star-News* and *Washington Post* society pages. Among such wasted faces, such shopworn names, I felt almost noble with my brilliant, foolhardy boss-mistress and the incipiently demented, super-refined diplomat who was, in this room of cuckolds, both my cuckolder and cuckold.

"Ah, my old Monsieur Ouroboros," he said suavely.

There was so much good humor, such knowing madness in the Austrian that day. I could not hate or even despise him. I tried to be angry. After all, he had put Anita up to feeding me a dangerous drug and then filmed me demonstrating its effects. But he went on with a theatrically raised eyebrow.

"You have become our lady executive's *avocat de l'alcove*, hmm?" He looked at Anita for appreciation, but her deteriorated French was inadequate to the occasion.

"I have been retained to handle a certain matter for her," I mimicked. He chuckled.

"A devil's advocate. Oh, you *are* one of us, dear

178

Ouroboros. Anita has talked with you about our little
project?"

Well, I thought, here we go. He wanted assurances on
what he was getting for his money.

"You mean this Black Mass?" I said warily.

"No master alchemist should miss it," he said, seriousness showing behind his light tone. Anita watched me.

"Where are you going to have it: in your chapel?"

"Oh, no," said Buffi. "We have consecrated the chapel
on several occasions." He took a bite of his lamb chop.
"We have a special place picked out for my saint's day."
Buffi finished chewing, then said to me with that intensity
which characterized his serious interests:

"You think of Saint Bernard as a sort of dog and brandy man of the Swiss Alps. Oh, no. His real work was
rooting the pagans out of those remote valleys. Read it,
Ouroboros, in *Acta Sanctorum*. And his mother, a Duyn,
dreamed that he was a dog while he was in her womb, a
white and red dog who barked in her stomach." His words
were rolling on toward that descent into sickness. "A holy
man told her that it meant Saint Bernard would bark
mightily against the Church's foes, but actually it meant
he would become the hound of Hell and prophesy his
own death . . ."

I interrupted him, trying to sound nonchalant.

"Don't keep us in suspense about where you plan the
mass."

Buffi drew back from his St. Bernard story.

"I think at the catacombs," he answered calmly.

I was shocked and my face must have shown it. "You
mean the monastery there in Virginia outside Alexandria?"

He smiled assent.

"That's nuts. There are still some monks in there."

I looked at Anita.

"Buffi is an amateur monk himself," she said with a
pointed undertone of anxiety lest I upset Buffi, and the
$75,000.

"Count me out of the catacombs," I said. The force of
what he was thinking struck me. It seemed so anomalous,
sitting in the rich red and black restaurant with the
horsey prints. "For Christ's sake! If you get caught in
there, you're finished as a diplomat and Anita . . .."

"That makes it all the more piquant," he said firmly.

"You're crazy."

"Come, come, Ouroboros," he reproved me.

"It's too much, Anita," I said. Was it just the money?

Her face was set.

"Buffi has persuaded me."

Buffi laughed, crumbling the tension building up between me and Anita.

"If the monks rush in to throw out the worshipers," he said, "we will run out the back like the early Christians."

"It's nothing but a tourist attraction anyway," said Anita, irrelevantly. "It's not like it was all that holy."

"Who else?" I asked. For $75,000 he'd want more than just an Assistant Secretary of Labor and her Deputy.

"A few others," sighed Buffi. He knew he had the cards.

That night, her arms around me after we had consummated such loving indignities as I hardly dared think of with Susan, she said gently, "Come along to the thing. I promise no more foolishness with him after this. I had to do it."

And I thought, well, everybody ought to go to at least one Black Mass, as long as they didn't dwell on the fairyish aspects or the coprophagy. The former, I could avoid. The latter, I suspected, was not Buffi's cup of tea, as it were.

The anniversary of St. Bernard of Montjoux, d. May 28, 1081, Vicar General of Aosta, an octogenarian, was hot and muggy for May. There was no escaping supper with Susan. For two weeks, consumed with guilt, I had said nothing about marriage. But Susan was too smart and, when all her sentimentality was flayed away, too Pennsylvania Dutch and Roman Catholic tough to whine "you don't love me anymore."

I thought about her feelings a good deal, even as I plotted how to betray her with Anita—to whom I was now bound as tightly as ever. If nothing else, Susan must have seen that her affair with me had spared her marrying Conyers.

We had a tamale supper at La Fonda on St. Bernard's night. When, at ten, I kissed her goodnight, passion stirred and I thought, "Well, it's not too late to get out of this Buffi thing." But my heart squirmed when I thought of Anita's long, urgent body. I squeezed Susan's hand and went back to my car.

Despite all the emphasis that Buffi put on style, I was

not ready for the bizarre devotion Anita exhibited to the formalisms of the Sabbat.

At her apartment, she was in a terrycloth bathrobe, smoking. She smelled of British gin and I looked for the martini pitcher.

"S'matter? Scared?" I asked her. The whole thing seemed silly. "Let's just back out—just go to bed."

"Ah," she said, noncommittal.

"I know. You want to be the last of the Red Hot Stabat Maters."

She smiled. I found the pitcher and poured myself a double.

"Who else is coming?"

"You're not supposed to know. Everybody is wearing masks. I'll tell you later."

I started to press her, but she went on:

"I've got a calf's head mask for you. The costumer said it was worn in *Midsummer Night's Dream.*"

"How about you?"

"The wolf costume, sort of."

"Who else will be there? Come on."

"The Krals. Some people from New York. Don't push me."

She sat down, pulling her robe discreetly around her bare legs. The martinis had made her talkative.

"The New York people are just doing it because they're bored. Why not? People re-create Civil War battles and the Crucifixion. Why not a Black Mass? I mean, I know Buffi's crazy, but it *is* different. It's not boring. It's kicky."

I drank a gulp of the strong gin and vermouth and felt exhilarated by its jolt. Kissing Susan had left me seminally lustful. I wondered if there were time . . .

"Hadn't you better get dressed?" I said. "Where's my calf's head? What else do I wear?" She came to me and kissed me, slipping her tongue between my lips.

"We've got to get ready," she said, breaking. "I've got some ointment we're supposed to put on."

"What?"

"Oh, Buffi goes through this ritual thing and so everybody else has to. He'll probably smell you to see if you're salved."

I followed her into the bedroom. She gave me the blue Vicks jar and I smelled its contents. It wasn't Vicks.

She took off her robe and lay naked, face down on the bed. I caught my breath as I always did at the sight of her nude.

"Just a little, before we go?" I murmured.

"No," she said.

I thought for a moment of taking her against her will. I rubbed the ointment on her, breathing so hard I was almost dizzy. The smell of the ointment, however, acted as something of an anaphrodisiac: a mixture of Liederkranz, cinnamon, and something slightly putrid. I took a drink of the martini.

"What makes it stink so?" The thought suddenly struck me that maybe it *was* baby fat. That's what was in the old formulas and Buffi was crazy enough. "What's in this stuff?"

"Goat fat. He said something about goats."

"Oh," I said, "greasy kid stuff."

"Good Lord," she said. "Rub faster. We've got to go."

My hand slid across her back. I saw the flecks of dark pigmentation with which age was speckling her. The flesh of her upper arms draped slightly from the flagpoles of her humeri. At her neck, when I ran my greased fingers beneath her hair, I felt the beginnings of leathery wrinkling.

Part of Anita's vulnerability was her age. And it was her vulnerability that had me trapped between loving and pitying her. I rolled her over and she smiled up. Her breasts lolled flat.

The Vicks jar was half empty when I finished. Anita gave me a cursory rub too brisk to arouse. My skin felt soothed. I recalled uneasily that belladonna was an ingredient in the old recipes for Sabbat ointment. It had an anodyne effect. I touched my shoulder where she had applied it. Slightly numb. Buffi and his wonder drugs. I took another drink of the martini wondering what unpleasant synergism it might have.

"There's belladonna in here," I said gloomily, screwing the top on the Vicks jar. "Save what's left in case you have a cardiac arrest."

I expected her to wear the wolf costume, but she took from her closet only the mask, and from a hanger a linsey-woolsey granny gown. She slipped it over her head. It was a nun's work habit. Her body, braless, looked tall

and humble. She pulled a shapeless black heap of clothing from the closet and handed it to me.

"No," I said, holding up the black cassock and cope.

"For God's sake," she said irritably, looking at her
watch.

She took up the martini and raised it to my lips, stirring
a panicked memory of that last time she had given me a
potion.

"When in Rome . . ." she said curtly.

The martinis had made me a bit giddy. I climbed into
my underwear, then defied her and got all dressed, putting
the cassock on over my suit while she packed her wolf's
mask and a crucifix on an iron chain into her bag.

"When do we get the money?" I asked.

"Fifty thousand tomorrow, the other twenty-five thousand as soon as he can raise it," she replied.

She watched me as I scowled at myself in the mirror.
I looked like Martin Luther. The calf's mask in a paper
sack, I took her heavy handbag while she threw a cape
over the granny gown. From her bag, I pulled out the
cross. It was upside down.

"Buffi follows the book, doesn't he?" I said. I decanted
the martinis into a pint bottle as we left.

The Franciscan monastery was really very well set up
for our farcetta; its parking lot was reasonably secluded.
An Anchor fence surrounded the large tax-free acreage.
Construction was going on, and forty yards from where
we parked a hole had been torn in the fence to let the
construction equipment through.

Our carload—we, Buffi, and the Krals—was all slightly
drunk, but Buffi's "high" was edged with a slightly manic
quality. He looked bulky beneath his cape.

"The kinfolk should be arriving soon," he said nervously.

In the darkness I could see atop the hill the outline of
the pseudo-Byzantine church, built sixty to seventy years
ago, and the nearby dormitory that housed the monks. On
the side of the hill, cloaked now in trees and night, would
be the tourist lure—the "Gardens of God in Gethsemane"
with their fabricated catacombs.

First one more car, then another two pulled into the
lot.

Buffi led the way, incongruously carrying a United Air

Lines flight bag. Behind us some twenty cape-clad figures
climbed from their cars, quietly closing the doors and
stringing out along the fence. In the muggy night, I
sweated inside my cassock. What the hell was I doing in
this nutty scheme? The humiliation of the whole lot of us
being booked by some righteous moralizing cop at a suburban precinct house! And what did I have to gain?
Nothing! Anita, not I, was getting money from the Austrian.

We came 'to the second fence beside the steps that led
upward to the "Gardens." De Plaevilliers fiddled in his
cloak for a moment, then brought out what must have
been a master key and jiggled it expertly in the old gate
lock. This was the back way in. We crept up the cement
stairs to the garden plaza. A signpost dimly directed us to
"The St. Bernadette Grotto," "The Tomb of Our Lord,"
"St. Francis Cell," and "The Catacombs," an eclectic
assortment, even for Virginia monks.

What, I wondered fearfully, would some monk think if
he wandered out for a little open air meditation and found
our band of anti-Christs?

The entrance to the catacombs was through a chapel.
The wooden door gave readily to Buffi's second master
key. He had cased the place well. My heart beat nervously as the leather-padded doors of the chapel closed
us in.

"Right here, Herbert," Buffi quietly ordered Krals, who,
it appeared, would be our watchman for at least part
of the ceremony. The chapel was dimly lighted by tiny
electric candles before an altar to the left of the balda-
chin. How much did a supplicant pay per watt hour? The
church earned even while asleep. Just ahead of me, Buffi
paused, his back to the altar.

To my astonishment, he crossed himself. Then I realized
it had been backward: down, up, right, left—with his left
hand. The kook took his church-defiling seriously.

De Plaevilliers, his cope flared out behind, moved cat-
like now under the main altar canopy, swung open the
gate and went on in blackness. I smelled a hint of incense
as I passed the gate and picked my way behind him down
steps underneath the altar, sliding my hands ahead on
the brass stair railing.

At the bottom of the steps were black padded doors.
Buffi held them open for us and I slipped on inside, feeling

a sudden coolness. In the narrow passageway my hands touched rough walls, cold plaster. We were in the catacombs.

Buffi whispered, "Move on, there, on in, let the others in." I could hear the rest of them coming in, first Lisel Krals just behind us, then the nervous breathing and low coughs of the others. Once we were all in the corridor, the door swung shut and we were in absolute blackness. I felt panicky. Buffi flicked on a penlight; its beam showed the long low corridor ahead. The sides of the tunnel were broken by ovenlike orifices. As Buffi's light swept past them, I could see the bones, held back by chicken wire, and the open stare of skulls. I knew from a boyhood visit they were not real, but the effect was sobering. I patted the bottle in my pocket.

We felt our way, Buffi's pencil of light picking out sunken tombs and dull frescoes: a bird, a fish, faces of unknown saints, the Alpha and Omega surmounted by a Chi Rho. At a final turning, we entered a rectangular, low-ceilinged room. It was an underground chapel with a simple oblong altar.

Buffi moved efficiently to the altar and took the six white candles from their holders. He dug into his airlines bag and pulled out six short black candles of his own.

Behind me the room was filling. I could see the congregation only as bulky shapes. When Buffi had finished putting the candles in their holders, he whispered: "Mask!" and began to light the candles. The calf's head, made of cloth and leather, was stuffy. The other trespassers were taking off their light coats or capes and dropping them at the rear of the chapel. Then, busily, they masked. It was like a second-grade cloakroom.

In a moment the activity ceased. We stood before the altar, a sea of gowns topped by faces of a wolf, a calf, an elephant without trunk, a lion, a goat.

Buffi, beside the altar now, was magnificent. He was clad as an archbishop, from miter to alb. His chasuble was embroidered gold and silver, his pallium velvet black instead of white. The madman had maniples slipped up his wrists, and they flashed gold and silver-white in the candle flame.

In a world of Pop-Tarts, Mustangs, and Enovid, he was a beautiful throwback to the Age of Pre-Brand-Name Belief. Oh, Buffi believed. Self-deluded, probably certifiably psychotic at times, nevertheless he was a believer. There he stood, certain as Adam that he was doing something evil in the eyes of God.

The glow of the candles touched the room's mosaics and the polished marble facings. Beside me stood Anita in her wolf's mask. Was she thinking of Buffi as a fool or lunatic, or as a splendid visitor from another age?

I sensed a sort of awe among those around me. Lisel Krals was beside Anita, clad in novice's white. Her Germanic breasts showed heavily against her chaste cotton gown. Her face was hidden by a grotesque owl mask. The others, about eight men and seven or eight women, were of various ages by their postures and were clad in various ecclesiastical garb—an Ursuline, two female Dominicans, an old, stooped woman in the begging gown of a Poor Clare. The men were in cassocks or button-down-the-fronts. One tall youngish woman wore a corniche and many-layered veil of gauze. I could feel the eagerness.

Buffi worked busily at the altar without an acolyte. He made a quick confession at the altar foot, his chasuble gleaming, then jumped right on into the Introit.

". . . all is a raging riot of blood and murder, theft and deceit, corruption, faithlessness, tumult, perjury . . ." he began. The chapel was warming up from our presence. Cosseted by a gulp from my pint of martinis, I was finding the scene enthralling. I had almost drowned my guilt. ". . . sex perversion, disorder in marriage, adultery and debauchery. For the worship of idols not to be named is the beginnings and cause and end of every evil."

Buffi signaled the congregation to be seated. The old woman dressed as a Poor Clare pulled a flask from her drawstring bag and raised her fawn's mask high enough to swig it. As Buffi intoned his Mass, the others stirred, sought seats on cloaks and coats, and drank.

Who were my companions? I tried vainly to distinguish a mannerism that would identify one. What brought them here? Boredom, as Anita suggested? Did only Buffi really believe?

His gold brocade dashed the light on the mosaics. The candles flickered. He waved his arms, maniples glittering, and made obscene signs with his ringed fingers. Buffi ripped through a richly scatological "Gloria" and a longish "Dominus—Luciferus—Vobiscum."

We were all on the floor now and with the flasks passing

back and forth, the sexuality was stirring. I suppose it was a sign of the generation and the peculiar culture of governmental Washington that there was not one wisp of marijuana in the room.

I saw the pale hand of Lisel Krals creep across the cassock of the man next to her who himself had been paying court to the woman on his right. The man turned his attention to the pendulous form of Lisel. Modestly, I pulled my cope across Anita's lap. As she sipped from the martini flask, I put my hand on her leg. De Plaevilliers was holding the cross upright in his left hand and murmuring the Collect.

"Accursed one, baby killer, bestower of cancer and meningitis and leprosy, give these assembled ones the will to blaspheme the World." I was beginning to breathe hard.

Buffi was getting fired up by his own blasphemies. His performance gave a fillip to what otherwise would have been a conventional orgy. The man next to Lisel was now on his back, pulling both at her and the woman on his other side in the corniche.

Anita and I were petting openly now, a mild pursuit in this company. I could feel the gin working on me in the direction of abandon. But the floor was hard on my tail and I felt frustrated at not being able to kiss her through our masks. Buffi was bowing and swaying into the Eucharist.

"Oremus," said Buffi with low bell tones. "Oremus . . . cum Satana coitu verus." When he turned to prepare the Eucharist, I could see how pale his face was. The Mass was sapping him. There was giggling all around us as our cohorts fumbled beneath one another's habits and cassocks. Buffi was losing his congregation.

He placed the Hosts on the paten and held them up to the audience, most of us supine by now. Ideally, at about this time we should be abominating the chapel and taking him seriously. But the giggling and heavy breathing was drowning out his Mass.

"This is all crazy," I whispered into Anita's wolf earhole.

Here were Anita and I rolling on the floor like a pair of high schoolers, while Buffi was resurrecting a dead art before our eyes. His archbishop's regalia was resplendent, his sacrileges meticulously and elaborately pertinent to his

Mass. How could some twentieth-century parish priest, educated to marriage counseling, to little league baseball, to marching with civil rightists and peace folk . . . how could he encompass this lonely respector of the past and his refined and anachronistic sacrilege?

Poor Buffi needed the terrible hammer of the medieval witch hunters and prosecutors to smash him on the anvil of God. He yearned for some miraculous manifestation of Evil. But Buffi yearned in an age of Billy Grahams and Richard Nixons. Evil was institutionalized.

Through the smell of humanity, good perfume mingled with the ointment on sweaty skins, and candle wicks, I felt a breath of air. I looked back to see one of the congregation rushing through the door, making ooking sounds. For him, it was now just one more drunk.

My hands were already under Anita's linsey-woolsey, moving lightly across her flank and up to the unsupported cushion of her breast. She was reaching for her mask, to pull it free of her lips.

In the candlelight, as Buffi intoned, couples were twisting toward each other on the chapel floor. I could see two already pumping. My mind was on how to get out of my suit, my underpants off and my cassock up. To my surprise, Anita began to try to break free.

"C'mon," I said in an outraged growl. She pushed me off so firmly that I thought she, too, wanted to rush away to vomit. I let her go, angry and frustrated. Instead of running to the door, she stumbled over the supine forms toward Buffi. I watched, amazed and confused, as she slipped off her cope and dropped the work habit to the floor. She stood up there naked except for the wolf's head.

I fumbled for the martini flask. The gin made me reel. Almost beside where I sat now, the owl's head of Lisel Krals was buried in the shoulder of a monk. She lay astride him, wiggling her butt, her habit rising on her fat legs.

Buffi was sweetly chanting a triple Sanctus, while Anita, still naked, clanked a smoking censer. The room was beginning to spin. I thought drunkenly of staggering up and stealing her away from the anti-priest, but was not sure I could move. Should I turn and pull Lisel from the man she rode?

As I sat and considered, I felt a form edging up beside me, smaller than Anita. A thin arm moved expertly across my chest and I turned. It was Poor Clare, the ancient. I recoiled, but the woman crept up beside me and the thin arm pressed me backwards. I yielded. At that precise moment it was more a wrestling match than a sexual encounter. Her fawn's mask hid her face so that her age at this distance was more a matter of conjecture than certainty.

I smelled her rich perfume above the stink of the ointment and the cutting edge of the incense. She was making little sighs over me, her one hand on my chest, the other fumbling to raise my cassock. I took her shoulders in my hands to push her off. But before I acted decisively, she raised my mask above my lips and her own an instant later with the same hand, and dropped between my arms into an embracing kiss. My mask now covered my eyes, and her ginny breath was no worse than any other drunken woman's, her tongue sliding between my lips had no age. My passion rose, wiping out whatever odious memory I had of those thin shoulders and the slack flesh across the bone.

The old woman's lips pushed and darted on mine. Gradually, I began to welcome their touches. I met her nips with kisses. My ears rang. My lust focused on the soft, momentary touches of lip and tongue. Buffi, Anita, were all background, then nothing, nothing at all. I was on the point of ecstacy at those quicksilver touches. With a great swoop, like a match in gasoline, a whoooouumph of passion, I caught flame. I reached under her gown and stroked the buttocks, loose as Jello in a bag.

"Hurry . . . hurry," I gasped as her fingers worked to open my trousers, expert as an old seamstress. With a quick flip of her own gown, she settled deftly on me. The sheer volume of the gin kept me erect. I panted as her lips continued to peck and her tongue dart at my mouth. On the envelope of her tit, the nipple stood out like a dried grape. Those old hands, so practiced in their light caresses, worked up and down across my chest and my hips, my ears.

Without breaking the contact of our bellies, I rolled her over. How light she was. The bones ridged through the skin at hip and rib. We were both gasping for breath, fumbling with each other desperately.

We had rolled off the spread cassocks and were bumping into someone beside us. I cushioned her gelatin bottom in my hands against the marbled chapel floor, feeling again the clinging flesh and skin, velvety with age. I knew if I entered her again I would not last a second, even in such a dried up old catcher's mitt as she must be. I parted those antique draperies with my fingers and found she was as lubricated as a girl. With a great crushing thrust, I plunged into her, hearing in my ears the shrill high "eeeee" of my release. She clawed at my buttocks, finally grabbing them like a ten-pin ball, and with her other hand snatched my calf's head off.

For a split second I saw a monstrous two-head, her old lips and alpine nose just below the fawn's face, then she flung back her own mask and fixed her lips in my mouth, tongue ululating.

My God! It was Buffi's mother! I should have suspected. The white powder was cakey with her perspiration. Her face, save for the old greedy, flaming eyes, looked not just dead, but in the process of sloughing off to the death's head beneath.

But the quintessential "eeeee" still sounded, and the rattle of life, rushing along my spine toward our loins, was all I could feel. I groaned aloud with the force of the first spasm, pressed my lips hard to the mouth that barely covered the skull, and felt her dentures slip.

For a few more seconds, even after I wanted to turn away from her in revulsion, she went on ticking under me, like some old-fashioned runaway time machine whose "off" switch one could not find.

Satisfied, she released my lips and my body. Without a glance of gratefulness or shame, only a brief, hot, birdlike look of curiosity, the Baroness drew her mask over her face, rearranged her clothing and scrambled away, leaving me cold, spent, and dizzy with self-disgust.

"Crispée atrocement," I thought with a gasp of revulsion, "la véritable tête à l'abri de la face qui ment."

I would have left, but I was stupefied with the drink and the traumatic release. Wrapped in my cassock I watched listlessly as the archbishop closed out his doxology, and swung into a blasphemous "Pater Noster." How tired he must be, wrestling with the Almighty this way. Anita, beside him, was perfect in her grace, her tall salved body beneath the wolf mask glistening in the light, the vee of her mount a shadowy forest in the candleglow. In the near darkness, the eyeholes were black and I could not imagine her expression. I sank back, gathering my resolve to leave.

Anita began clearing the center of the altar. I hardly believed it when Buffi, with Anita pushing and tugging to help him, struggled up across the altar, buttocks outward like a child's on a knee.

Anita flung up his skirts and there, white and hairless, was Bishop Buffi's bare bum. I laughed uncomfortably, feeling nauseated for the first time.

Anita lifted her mask and with a brisk little curtsy rendered him the first "osculum infame"—more of a peck than a real kiss. The others struggled to their feet around me. Old fawn-face moved up and gave him the indecent motherly embrace. As she left, she joined Anita and the two of them, backs to each other, held hands and did a slow little jig from the altar's platform to the floor. Anita's compact breasts jounced amid light and shadow. The first of the male guests, mask raised only enough for me to see his strong chin, made a quick pass at Buffi's rear. My God, I thought, Harry Frieden, the Vice President! Another man, in a pig mask, paid half-hearted obeisance to the Austrian's fundament, and he and Frieden jigged athletically off the platform. Obviously, most of them had made the Mass scene before. Now I was sick.

The room was beginning to spin. I was on my feet at last, and there was no reason to stay. I would relieve Krals as the keeper of the gate. I wasn't going to make even a formal pass at Buffi's rear end. It might be part of the classical ritual, but I was not hanging around to see whether they moved to homosexuality as in the old Sabbats.

I slipped into the dark passageway and again felt the rough plaster of its sides. I could hear Buffi's voice, low and intense . . . "Inter omnes angelos Lucifer excelsior . . ." I felt my way to the turn of the tunnel. The last words I heard from the chapel were "Mechlet! Mechlet!"

I opened the leather-padded door and the dim light from the chapel illuminated something in one of the niches. It was the box shape of a temperature-sensing device. My mind played with the idea of lighting a match beneath it. Would that not trip the fire sprinkler system in the catacombs and shower the ritualists in the chapel? I patted

myself for matches, but could find none. It would be a
dirty trick on Buffi anyway. What right had I to play God
and rain on his parade?

My Lord! I thought, Harry Frieden. Crazy Frieden!
Crazy Anita! And how far had I loaned myself to the pro-
ceedings? My guilt over sweet Susan flooded in on me.
Nauseated and heavy-headed as I was, I thought of the
ancient skeleton, that sudden, thrilling lay with Buffi's
mother.

At the chapel exit I passed again the electric votive
candles. They flickered behind their skintight plastic shield
of white and red. This time, I noted the rectangular paper
placard near the banks of little lights. "Each candle, seven
days—$2. Kyrie Eleison." How many kilowatts did it take
to reach God? Whoever had set up these candles and that
placard: were they any less astray from God than Buffi?

Before I opened the exit door, I growled at Krals so as
not to startle him, "Herb, it's me."

He grunted an acknowledgment. I stepped into the hot
night. The stars blazed almost tropically.

"Whatsa matter?" Krals said drunkenly beside me.

"I'll take over. I was about to puke and I have to take a
pee."

"You sober?"

"Sober enough."

"Did Herr de Plaevilliers say it was okay?"

"Hell," I said angry at his sycophancy. "Don't go. Sweat
out here. He's too busy to give permission to take a pee."
I thought with satisfaction of Lisel Krals fatly cuckolding
him in the chapel. But that probably didn't bother him.
It was part of the game.

"Here," he said, pulling at his cassock. "Keep this for
me. Don't leave." He pulled off the tight garment. Beneath
it was an old-fashioned button down clerical robe.
Around his shoulders was a skin, more like the crinkly
skin on a leg of lamb than anything else, it appeared to
me in the dark. But as Krals arranged it to hang straight
and opened the door, I saw it better.

It was a whole human skin, the arms around his shoulders, its front to his back, and the legs reached down to
his calves. The face had been imperfectly tanned and the
black hair was gappy and lank where the skulless head lay
squashed at his collar like some dried out bird pelt.

"Jesus," I said. Krals looked at me scornfully. Without

a word he opened the door and went in. In that thing on his back was real sickness and evil, not just the avocations and neurotic fascinations of Anita, or even the determined de Plaevilliers withdrawal to the past. Swill churned in my guts from my drinking. Off to the side of the church, I bent and stuck my finger down my throat.

Saturday morning contrition! Could I shower away the touches of those antique flanks, the tireless lips, wash my person clean? I was a morning Puritan, the collector of the knowledge of evil, outraged both at the evil and my participation in it. The Lifebuoy still retained a hint of that clean, creosoty smell from its earlier, stronger, nobler vintages.

Furtively, I checked the *Star-News* to see whether the visit had been detected. The paper took small note of it:

Alexandria police said today that vandals, probably teen-agers, broke into the chapel at the Franciscan monastery last night.

Damage was limited to cigarette marks and litter on the marble floor and spilled wax on the altar, police said. An empty bottle of pre-mixed manhattans was left behind by the intruders.

The catacombs have been a favorite area tourist attraction since they were built in 1912 as replicas of the Roman catacombs where Christians gathered. Father Donald Wiley Tunseat, acting superior of the Franciscan Monastery where the catacombs are located, said teen-agers in the past had been caught breaking in "as some sort of adventure, I guess."

Well, I thought, vandals were off the mark. Nobody could accuse last night's tribe of being pagans. My head now ached fiercely. I felt sick every time I thought of Frieden. Likely Anita had talked him into it. As for Anita, even suffering as I was, the vision of her stooping to retrieve a fallen wafer at one point in the Mass, her naked knee flexed and the right breast swinging free, aroused me. If only I could get her away to myself, away from the threat of Conyers' gumshoes, away from the sickness of Buffi and Krals and that lot. I did want Susan, secure in some kid-filled house in suburbia. But now, more, I wanted Anita, crazy old bitch. I wanted to reshape her, recoat her, anneal from her the vile cupric oxides of Buffi and Krals—my God, that human skin.

I recognized the cliché of my delusion. We all want to make over a bad woman. Fueled by my jealousy of all the men who had ever had her, all the men she titillated with her depravity, I wanted to save her depravity for myself alone. I wanted to be her corrupter, her church, and her confessor, all rolled into one big bed.

And Susan? I could not give her up.

June, July, into August, I played a traducing game with the two women and myself. It was when Susan and I were with Ems that I hated myself most.

One afternoon, when both Anita and I had left the office early and innocently—she to a meeting, me with one of the headaches that frequently repaid my infidelity—Susan came to my house.

I was in my bathrobe when I heard the doorbell ring. I saw Susan's face, tense, even angry. My own, I surmised, gave away the feelings for her I had contained these last weeks: guilt, failing love, dissembling.

"Come on in," I said. "I was feeling sick . . ." She slipped by me, looked sharply around, and then turned to me, her eyes hurt, pleading.

"Was she here?"

I could safely play the wronged innocent.

"No one is here. Just me."

"*Was* here?"

"No."

She threw off her light coat. Shamefully, I noted her breasts strain against her trim cotton dress. I did not dare venture the falsehood of my usual pro forma kiss. I knew the game was up and only wondered what had made this the moment.

"You left at the same time. I had to call her at her meeting and she'd already called to cancel it. She wasn't home . . ."

"Susan, she hasn't been here."

"It doesn't matter," she said. "Not really."

"Could I get you a drink or something?" I said asininely.

She sighed.

"I'd hoped to catch her here. I wanted to be done with you both at the same time." Her tone spoke resolve more than bitterness. I had come to expect mildness from her, but then I recalled her matter-of-factness before she came to love me.

"She wasn't here," I persisted. Guilt and her inquisitional air fed my annoyance. She sensed my abruptly disliking her.

"We aren't even friends anymore," she said with a trace of wonder. "After everything."

That clutched me. But in my hostility I was eager, now that it had started, to be done with her. My headache throbbed.

"I'm not worthy of you. I admit I've been thinking too much about work." God, I hated to lie so.

"About work!" she said sharply. "You mean about Mrs. Tockbridge."

My silence was an assent. It detonated her jealousy.

"God damn you! You son of a bitch!" She spoke hotly now. I wanted to step in and snarl that she'd known it for weeks and why was she cursing me now about it. But she stared at me, the tears starting in her eyes. "You're just a shit! A shit!"

I'd never heard her use the word before. In a way it was better, her explosion into vulgarity. The obscenity and anger made us equals.

"You're just one out of an army!" she shouted.

"Oh, I know she's no cherry," I said. I didn't add, Neither are you. It was too unfair.

"There," she said. "You admit you've been with her."

"Oh, Susan, you know that."

She reached into her handbag for a tissue and wiped her eyes.

"Well, that's that," she said quietly, closing the bag.

Beautiful Susan. After such a wrong, only that small flare of temper and it was done. I knew, with an ache in me now, that she was going. At that instant I saw clearly that I was losing a great deal. Feverishly, my mind whipped back and forth between re-wooing her by swearing fealty and letting her walk out forever. I hesitated and the moment passed. She picked up her coat.

"You're just going to let me go, aren't you?" she said, looking at me evenly. "That's really what you want."

"That's ridiculous," I said, only half lying.

"Well," she said, resolved now. "I'll be off."

I felt again that sudden vacuum in my chest.

"What are you going to do?" I said.

"Go home to Pennsylvania, for a while. What does it matter?"

She let me help her into her coat. With compassion, cowardice, what shall I call it, I took her shoulder, but she shrugged off the touch coldly.

Susan paused at the door. Her eyes were teary now.

"Were you seeing her during the days in autumn when . . ."

"No," I said, tears coming into my own eyes now.

I thought again of Ems and of Susan's hair blowing. Then, in my mind, I saw Anita, squatting in the smoke-filled underground chapel as Buffi incanted.

"Why did you stay with her so long when you knew what she was really like?" I asked. But she turned her eyes from me, opened the door and walked away very quickly to her car. I mixed myself a bloody mary with V-8. My air-conditioned living room felt chilly. I moved a little closer to the radiator as if its cold surface would warm me.

CHAPTER

13

The Advance Man

This was election year for a third of the senators and all the congressmen. It was the year when Vice President Frieden must do for the Republican Senate candidates what he hoped they would do for him in two years when he campaigned for President. Most importantly, it was a year when Anita, by speaking to her fickle and determinant half of the electorate, could build strength for her own ambitions while seeming to be working selflessly for the party.

The Conyers matter seemed quiescent. We had successfully bought Brendan Doolittle, his key witness. From prison, he got word to us that Justice's interest in him had slacked off, a good sign. The case folders on Benn City were back in the General Services file, and had not been withdrawn again. But the narrowness of Anita's escape still nagged her. Now with a genuine if long-shot chance at the Vice Presidential nomination, she made her life more orderly. She did not break off with Buffi. He still owed us—her—the $25,000. But she convinced him that the public spotlight was too intense for her to trifle with his odd fancies.

The Austrian accepted grudgingly. As Anita spent more time making speeches, Buffi drifted more frequently out of town. In Buenos Aires he had found some faded, right-wing Hispano-aristocrats who were already copractitioners of witchcraft.

Once, at the Provençal restaurant, I saw him with a
pale, young Latin woman. He signaled me over and introduced me to the young Duchesa de somewhere. When
I looked closely I saw that she could not be any more
than eighteen or nineteen under the makeup. Her eyes
assessed me darkly.

"Monsieur Ouroboros is an old friend," he said to her,
then with his light sarcasm, he added directly to me: "You
are taking good care of our mutual friend? We will want
to see more of you when the elections are over." The
"you" was collective. The tone, I felt, ominous.

Anita, when I was with her, was trusting and friendly.
She leaned on me and I labored my ass off to get her
speeches written, her sponsors lined up, her jobs at the
Department handled so they reflected her presence even
when she was out on the hustings.

Whether it was Anita's appreciation of my help, or the
waning of her relationship with Buffi, or even her menses'
impending end, I was touched by her need of me. When in
town she was almost awkward in inviting me to a "business lunch" that would permit us to eat together in some
unromantic restaurant like Harvey's where, amid the mem-
ories of famous and crooked politicians, no one would suspect a scandal.

During those short days of respite between political
drives into the South, the Northwest or New England, she
talked of her husband and her sons, and I of my past.

"The psychologists would say I married my father," she
said. "I guess he was like my husband, witty, weak about
women. If I've done one thing for the boys, in their teens
anyway, it was to cut them loose. I knew if I weren't
careful, I'd make them into the same kind of lap puppies
their father and grandfather were."

"You mean you were too busy by that time to pay any
attention to them," I ventured with a laugh. "You made a
virtue out of . . ."

She interrupted.

"Maybe, maybe so. Maybe that's part of it." She was
sipping a Guinness. Someone had told her she needed iron
on the campaign trail. "Well, I did think of them, the
kids. I wish . . ." but she changed her tone. "No, I'm glad
they're away. Christmas is enough. It's one thing to wear a
false face for everybody here, but for the boys . . ."

I must have started.

"Oh, not you," she said, reaching as if to touch my hand then drawing back lest it be seen. "No false faces for you, Martin."

The real election madness began in September. Our appropriations had come through about as we wanted them. I was free to take off days at a time to work for the Republican National Committee. I was careful to have the Labor Department payroll section drop me on my political days.

My life without Susan had less companionship, but it was less a lie. The symbol of it was Athanor, unfired in the cellar. But if in personal ways there was a cold-brick quality to my existence, there was plenty of heated activity in my public endeavors. I was being roughly seduced ever deeper into the power bag.

I served as Anita's "advance man." It is a specialty little known outside politics. The advance man sets up sponsors, arranges auto leases, implores local dignitaries to share the candidate's platform even when the speaker's views are abhorrent, threatens the county or city pols into action, issues preliminary statements to the press in the name of the campaigner. He arranges hotel space, rally space, reception space, passes out favors to get civic, management, union, ethnic, religious groups on hand for the speaker.

When the campaigning dignitary arrives, the advance man turns over the reins to the staff which travels with that notable, and rushes on to the next stop to repeat his advance work. He sleeps none, drinks too much, and if he is worth a damn, gets a craftsman's pleasure out of the hitchless show.

My work was for Anita, but often it meshed with Frieden's campaigning, as in Indiana, a test ground for our party. A Frieden Republican was running for the Senate.

He was up against a downstate Hoosier Democrat incrusted with money, backed by the governor and his patronage of eight thousand civil employees. Our man, the would-be senator, was Russell Eliason. He was young. He was liberal. He was rich, the scion of a sheet-steel fortune. He had a good record as a two-term congressman. He was a nitwit.

Anita and Frieden were to do the two-hundred-dollar-a-plate dinner for Eliason's war chest in Indianapolis. I worked from a motel room, trying to fill up the hall. Only two-thirds of the seats were sold and there were two days to go.

"I thought I'd pick up the tab for about half of those two hundred and fifty," he told me superciliously on the telephone. "I'd like to see some of the junior executives from the company at the affair."

I was tattered by work. Somewhere along the distant road from my cubbyhole to this dreadful city, my timidity had worn away. If self-confidence had not taken its place, at least irritation had.

"Mr. Eliason. Please. Let me tell you frankly that you had better forget the junior executives if you want anybody out here again to speak on your behalf any bigger than the chief of the Commerce Department garage."

"Well . . ." he started nastily.

"Look . . ." I cut in, but he was nothing if not rude.

"I don't want *any* empty seats!"

"No, nor do the Vice President or Mrs. Tockbridge. But, Mr. Eliason, no junior executives. You want black faces in those free seats. Make sure a couple of them have been arrested for demonstrating someplace."

"In the past . . ." he began stuffily.

"In the past you were running from a nice lily-white suburban district. You didn't need those black Gary votes."

"All right," he said, getting the point at last.

Next, it was the state chairman, wanting free seats for the county political hacks.

"What about the unions?" I asked him.

"The Teamsters took a table."

"Who else?"

"We didn't push."

My stomach wrenched.

"Oh, my God," I groaned. "Listen, this administration has got the best Republican labor record in a century. Why *didn't* you push?"

He was intimidated, but not to the point of reasonableness.

"Marion County has never been a union county."

"Look," I said. "Hire a plane and fly the union leaders down from Lake County if you have to. Explain to them that Mrs. Tockbridge interceded last month on what she regarded as an unfair Taft-Hartley prosecution against one of the steel locals."

"There wasn't any prosecution?" the man said cautiously.

"Christ," I said, yearning for the explosive power of the true bully. "You can bet your sweet ass there will be if we don't get a vote of gratitude this Friday night from Lake County."

I was, at last, discovering the uses of power.

Anita and Frieden were to speak Friday afternoon at the James Whitcomb Riley Liberal Arts Memorial Center (built mainly with federal funds) at Butler University. The president of the university was willing to share the platform with a liberal Republican, but only to honor the man all Indiana knew simply as "The Poet."

"Are you sure there will be no political coloration?" the educator sniffed.

"No, only at the two-hundred-dollar-a-plate dinner Friday night," I told him. "You're going to be there too, I hope."

"I'd like to, but . . ."

"Mrs. Tockbridge, in Congress, and the Vice President as a member of the Advisory Committee on Education helped push through the Riley center. The Vice President is thinking already of additional federal funds for the colleges." I put it bluntly.

The pompous don still balked. I recalled to him the warning of "The Poet."

"The Gobble-uns'll git you ef you don't watch out."

Then it was contacting the student GOP leaders to meet at the Claypool and help turn out the kids at the dedication, finding a printing firm to deliver a last-minute dinner program and goosing the big unions. When the Machinists turned us down, I called Washington to remind their international headquarters of past favors. Ten minutes later, the big local in northern Indiana called tersely. All right, they'd be there. I spent half the night writing Anita's two speeches, then got two hours sleep. I dictated the schedule stencil for the press and radio.

"10:45 A.M. Arrival, Indianapolis, Weir Field: Vice President will speak briefly. (Text attached, for PM release, Friday.)

"11:20 P.M. Depart from Claypool Hotel. (Press bus available . . .)"

It had been hellish, having Frieden's office phone me the airport speech, switching to Hertz at the last minute when we learned a big contributor had an interest in it, firing a nonunion technician and bringing in a union one to set up the PA system at the dinner.

I ate an enormous breakfast on Friday morning so that two spicy bloody marys would go down harmlessly. Thus, though exhausted, I was hopped up when the big Vice Presidential Air Force Two put down on the runway.

Damned respectable crowd for Friday morning, I thought. Mostly college kids, but we'd bussed out a big load of Negroes from the community center on College Street, plus several busloads of 4-H kids. And there was a good turnout of simple Hoosiers who suspected the Vice President might be in the White House two years hence and wanted to see him.

Catch him now, I thought. No man in his right mind would ever want to come twice to Indianapolis in the same decade. Even the Democratic governor was on hand, a Roumanian-American named Reschiu. I'd had to promise him a few minutes personal chat aboard the jet before Frieden got off in order to get him to the airport.

The fat little politician could already savor the write-up.

"Before the Vice President left the big Air Force plane, he spoke privately with Governor Reschiu in the jet's conference room"—something like that was, I suspected, running through his head.

Reschiu, intimate of the famous.

The plane pulled up to the terminal. The band struck up, "California, Here I Come." The kids pushed forward. Inside the wire fence, my Secret Service walkie-talkie looking very jazzy, I was sure, I listened to the cop voices.

"Dapple will deplane first . . ." That would be Anita's code name, "The governor, what's his name, Risher, will ascend forward ramp to meet with Dogwood," that would be the Vice President. The door opened.

Dapple came down the ramp on the arm of the pilot, a tall Air Force colonel, she so tall herself, yet deferring despite her rank to him as a man. Oh, Dapple, Dapple Anita. I watched half-bombed by the bloody marys as she gracefully held her tailored skirt down with kid-gloved hand when the wind caught it for an instant.

There was a shiplike majesty about her as she sailed toward the stubby Roumanian-American governor. First her hand went out, then she pecked him with a kiss as if they were old friends instead of political enemies. Taking his arm, she allowed him to lead her back onto the airplane so that he could talk with the Vice President.

And when the three came down the ramp, Anita, with her clean carriage, those strong, sharp facial lines in the sun, between the Vice President, golden Harry, bright Phoebus Adulterer, and the glowing fat man, then surely part of that cheer was for her beauty, tall and sure.

I loved her then not just for her person, but for the trust she had in me. She had given me that sweet power: the means to get things done, to make things move, to bring order from disorder. That was the exultation of power: the ability to say, "This is the way it's going to be done. Do it!"

Power! I did not need Anita and Frieden to hail me to know that they noticed how well I executed my mandate. The crowd cheered, tried to break through the police lines. The autos waited in a neat line to take them to the hotel. The press room phones all functioned. The proper dignitaries were on hand.

The crowd surged again as golden Harry and Dapple Anita trooped the ranks of greeters, shaking hands, touching children. A young mother held up her baby.

Quickly Anita took off her gloves, tucking them haphazardly into her neat suitcoat so she could hold the baby in her bare, certain hands, push back the baby's wind-strewn hair, not with a glove, but with a mother's naked hand.

I almost swooned with joy and self-pride when I saw that a TV cameraman, shouldering past the Secret Service guard of the Vice President, had caught Anita's little gesture. Lived there a film editor with heart so hard that he could prune that sprig of humanity and showmanship? I accounted it a personal victory when I saw the scene on the seven o'clock local news that night in my motel room.

I flew back to the Capital next morning with Anita and the Vice President in the forward cabin of his plane. He had his own press man aboard to pamper the dispirited White House press corps members who had been lugged out to the Hoosier state and back in the rear section of the plane. A few free drinks, a few confidential-sounding words about matters of public knowledge, and the reporters could puff up their little "situationers" into appropriate omniscience. Ah, the hyena press, I thought, swapping

Frieden-told-me stories at their seedy National Press Club.

Yet, yet, Frieden was even more despicable. What would the press write if they knew of Frieden prancing back-to-back and a do-si-do at Buffi's Mass? The Vice President of the United States! His part in the function and debased sing-alongs of Buffi, even though I, too, was contaminated, still managed to afflict me.

I glanced at him. He was full of his Indiana triumph.

"Anita says you singlehanded the whole thing," he said to me agreeably, sitting back with his morning screwdriver, fresh California orange juice and vodka.

"Yes sir. Thank you."

"She's living high off the hog, using a Deputy Assistant Secretary to advance for her," he said.

"I prefer to call it 'coordinating your visit,' " I said with light deference.

Anita looked up. Oh, light-blue morning eyes! I thought.

"Why don't you tell him what you told me, Mr. Vice President?" she said. *When* told her, I wondered? While I slept, had she posted to his bed? I pushed back the jealousy.

"I told her," said Frieden, "that any Easterner who can turn out those Indiana xenophobes like that for a Californian ought to be running for office instead of running for office holders."

I forced a chuckle.

"How does the state look for November?" he asked.

"The state organization stinks," I said.

"They all do when they're out of power," he said glumly. "I can use Indiana. How did you get the airport turnout?"

"College kids mostly. They want to see you."

"I remember the way college kids got fired up by McCarthy in Sixty-eight," he said. Then he smiled winningly. "I could fire them up if I were as smart as he was. I'm not."

Anita looked at him with warmth. I recognized, as I had at the party, so long ago, that look of lovers. Now, it wrenched me less. That Anita was a courtesan was bearable in the context of her other transgressions.

"We are touched my your modesty, Mr. Vice President," she joshed him.

The Air Force steward, his uniform a mixture of airman and bellhop, brought us another round of screw-drivers. The morning sun was bright, endless. Down below, the cumulous clouds boiled up like instant mashed potatoes. It was pleasant up here with these two uncommon people.

"Will your Tarot cards tell the Vice President whether he will carry Indiana?" Anita asked me, still jesting. With him she let down some of her caution, allowed her two lives to overlap as they did in our own relationship.

The big blond man smiled. His interests were eclectic. His curiosity was boundless. Perhaps these helped him keep so young and thus so attractive to the young.

"Do you have them here?" he asked.

"No, sir," I paused. How much of my peculiarity did I dare give away? I thought of the blue movies.

". . . organization," the Vice President was saying. "You can have everybody from the Klan to the Black Panthers but without organization you can't even carry Vermont." He beamed at me and I put on my modest alert look. Anita butted in:

"If you are thinking that my strong right arm, Mr. Dobecker, would make a good organization planner for you, then you will have to pry him loose with a Presidential order."

Golden Harry tapped me on the shoulder.

"Don't fool with politics. Stick with labor law. Keep this politics thing just as a sideline. Stick with the Department. We need people like you there. Every administration does."

I noted that Frieden had said, "stick with the Department," not "stick with Anita." I would have to sound her out later on just what he meant. Things were cooking between Labor and the White House. For one thing, old Woeckle, my ex-boss, was at the White House now on loan, as he had hinted he would be a year and a half ago.

The Vice President downed the last of his orange juice and vodka. He rose, patted my shoulder again, and turned to the rear of the plane.

"I want to have a few words with our friends of the press," he said. "They'll need a little story freshening, I'll betcha."

The press: Harry and they used each other, as symbiotic a pair as a goat and its intestinal bacteria.

After we had landed, I watched the Vice Presidential

Lincoln Continental pull into the runway with its dog star Pontiac full of Secret Service men behind it. I got into the Lincoln's front seat and our party pulled past the low buildings of Andrews Air Force Base and onto the parkway.

Why deny that when we pulled up in front of the Labor Department, where I had some Saturday work to do, I felt undeniably big league? How I hoped that some of my former colleagues from the Labor Solicitor's office might be glancing out their windows to see me as I got out and said a few parting words to the Vice President before slamming the black door.

Anita Benefactor! She had given me love, her own in her way. And she had even thrown Susan into my arms. Now Anita saw to it that when I was not on the road working for her, I had the ornamentations of Washington stature.

My "debut" at the White House was a dinner for the president of Argentina whose labor government, if precarious, did give Anita an excuse for getting a sub-sub-Cabinet officer invited.

My feelings, as I drove toward the White House's southwest gate, were anxious and childish. Surely, in that place of the mighty, where antennae were finely adjusted to sense the fraud and the crook, I would be exposed.

Nervously, I fantasized the scene of finger pointing, as in a dream where one is at a party wearing only underpants. They, all of them, would divine my part in Anita's feral black magic activities and in the cover-up of her bribe-taking. They would know my betrayal of Susan, my nasty hopes that Anita would become Vice President and make me Labor Secretary or be named Labor Secretary and give me her present job.

I tapped my tuxedo pocket to assure myself that the card was there which would admit me to the White House. At the sentry box, I pulled it out and felt my fingers grease it with sweat as I handed it to the White House cop.

He glanced at the card, then, I thought, hostilely at the shiny old Morgan (I had thought of but not yielded to the temptation of renting a big car). With some residue of guts I gave the Morgan a burst of gas as I left the sentry box to park.

In the foyer, dress-uniformed Marine bandsmen played

a gooey medley from "Oklahoma!," sentimental favorite of the President. At the East Room, the usher announced my name over a loudspeaker. Surely I would be found out now. I made for the nearest waiter with his silver tray of drinks and resisted my nerves' call for a martini, selecting instead a sherry.

I knew no one. Where was Anita? I made my way past the groups around the famous. Old Senator Borchlind's weak face (he was chairman of Senate Foreign Relations' Latin American subcommittee) was hemmed by the olive and swarthy heads of diplomats, bears at the honey. Undersecretary of State Christopher, that great gray-maned lion, had his coterie of assistant secretaries and Latin women. The Vice President . . .

At least I knew him. He stood beneath the picture of Herbert Hoover, substituted by the President for that of Andrew Jackson in one of the few controversial acts of a bland administration.

A sense that I was being stared at chilled me. I turned to see who it was and noticed first the fat Attorney General, rumored on his way out. He had suicidally shown the courage to press an antitrust suit against some big steel companies and to make some noises about breaking up the auto industry. However, it was not he who stared, but the man behind him, taller by a head. For an instant I did not recognize him as Roger Conyers.

My horror of being found out had come true. Conyers detached himself from his chief, circled the group and made for me. I reached for his hand. He took mine as if he were touching tubercular meat. I glanced down to see whether he wiped his hand on his pants leg.

"How are you?" I choked out, noting my voice had an agreeably urbane sound despite my panic.

"The boss wanted me to get a look at the inside of this place before we're all kicked out of the administration," he said, also lightly. My heart leapt. Did that mean he was leaving too, with the Attorney General?

"Why don't you move over to Labor?" I said with safe mock friendliness, suggesting the impossible.

"Oh," he said, with a tiny edge now. "Actually, I'm sticking it out at Justice if they'll have me. The boss is getting assurances for me on that."

The ice set into my heart again. Still, maybe I could

get him fired, now that the lard-assed executioner, the shield that protected him, was going.

"How's the Naniglione thing going?" I said neutrally. A labor thug, head of a criminal "family," had been convicted and the papers reported Conyers argued the case on appeal.

"We're hopeful," he said, then he stuck his cold Irish shiv into my guts. "We aren't giving up on *any* of them, not on one." That was all. But it was enough. It told me what I had feared. Anita's case was not closed. Did my face betray my descent to terror?

His little phrase had shattered me. I wanted only to take it to Anita, now.

"Well," I said. "Good luck." It sounded so lame, so much the surrender of the ox to the goring bull. He had ripped me with sublime and vicious precision. I was goddamned if I were going to let him enjoy it. I would plant my horn in him, too, to let its infections fester and rot as his would in me.

"Say, do you ever hear from Susan?" I asked off-handedly.

His blue paranoid eyes flinched as if he had been bitten by a snake. My heart beat rapidly but I continued to smile pleasantly. I had bombed him with the consummate weapon. I allowed the remembrance of what a good lay Susan had been to shine out on him from my eyes. Yummy, yummy, my slight smile said. Sweat, you motherfucker!

"No," he said, biting it off like an animal would a foot in a trap. Conyers trusted himself no longer to contain his hate. He wheeled and was gone. I had cut him, but my lips were coated with a scum of anxiety. I looked for Anita. Failing, I continued on toward the Vice President, shaken by my encounter with the wolverine.

Frieden's friendly greeting to me told those around him, "Here is a comer." Poor Golden Harry. Conyers' investigation could spread from Anita to him. Its wavelets could drown his hopes of being master of this very house where he now chatted and smiled. Or could Conyers somehow be stopped?

Ordinarily, at such a party, Anita's entrance would have thrilled me. She walked in, stately as an elk leaving a lake. Rapidly now, as I approached her, I ran through the names of those who could ruin her—us: Buffi, Krals, Susan, ourselves. Doolittle. Was that all? I looked at her.

Head up, a dark green ankle-length gown setting off her height, she was regal. Only I knew her stripped of the long kid gloves, rid of the silver handbag and shoes, and the pearls that lay on the high chest of the gown. Oh, others had taken her. Frieden, perhaps others at this party. But had any of them known her, mended her when she cracked, counseled her and comforted her at the risk of becoming her criminal accomplice. I saw the flick of her eye that acknowledged my look of concern.

She was cordial, slightly condescending to me lest she cause the senator and army chief of staff, who stood with her, to speculate about us.

"Well, Mr. Deputy Assistant," she said, extending her hand.

"Hello," I said with suitable eunuchry, then nodded at Senator Kirsted, and bowed slightly as Anita introduced me to the general.

"I didn't want to butt in, Senator, General," I said, diffident as Rigoletto. "Just wanted to let the boss know that I'd have to get her aside for a minute later about one of the Northern projects."

Without meeting her eyes, I knew she understood: Benn City.

"When I was a housewife," she said without a hint of alarm, "I only worked an eighty-hour week." The two mighty men laughed appreciatively and I Stepin-Fetchited away. I skirted the clumps of people and risked a martini. Nothing worse than Conyers' imprecation could happen now.

There was a murmur in the crowd and I glanced toward the foyer door and saw the familiar florid face of the President rising above his black tie. Beside him was his dumpy downstate Illinois wife.

The Argentinian president, short, his dark face measurelessly compromised, stood between them. I shambled into the reception line with the hoi polloi behind the justices and Cabinet members and legislators.

It was a meal I should have enjoyed, Konstantin Frank wines in hand-blown, smartly primitive glasses; a light ice-cold soup of many vegetables; pompano, rare roast beef and long, pale asparagus, a bombe glacé. One after another of my gold-rimmed Presidential-sealed plates went back unemptied.

At the toasts, I found Anita with my eyes. Her face was dynamic, teeth white with smiles for those around her. My apprehension sat heavily on me.

Back in the foyer after dinner, a cognac in my hand, I gloomily thought of Conyers. Could I desert Anita and bind myself to the Vice President? She could take the rap without bringing me in. It was her crime, not mine or Susan's. Why should I get myself any more deeply into this mess than I was now? If she wanted Conyers destroyed, let her try to destroy him on her own. I could move up now independently of her, through Harry Frieden, my new patron.

But would I desert her? Could I?

Anita in the green gown. It was five, no six nights, since I lay with her, in the Brown Palace in Denver where I had advanced her speech to the Federation of Women's Clubs. Fresh from her talks to the frowsy female leaders of the national luncheon circuit, we had made gaspy kooky love in the grand old hotel. After so much, could I revert to my old cowardices, leave her to be chewed up by Conyers without even a fight from me?

"Jesus, Jesus," I murmured to myself.

I wandered to Frieden's group toward which she, too, moved.

The Vice President was talking about his tour of South America a year ago, but he caught me with a glance that told me he had something to tell me. His story finished, he took my arm and eased me from the group, leaving Anita behind for the nonce with his wife, a frail, demure woman with ashen hair and an aristocratic, impenetrable expression.

"I've thought about the job you did for us in Indianapolis" he said. "I want you to call my secretary, Sara, and get us a meeting set up."

I was startled and must have shown it.

"No, no. I'll fix it up with Anita. It's not a highway robbery, I want to do some talking with you bright young subcabinet people in the next two years, lots of talking."

"Yes, sir," I said. He led me back to the group. It had been terribly short, these explicit words among all the horseshit. I was unnerved. What he was telling me was that he was going to put together his own administration in

two years and had picked a part for me in it if I lived up
to first impressions.

We joined the group and Anita turned a questioning
eye on Frieden.

"I may want to borrow him for a bit, Madam Assistant
Secretary," he said to her jovially. I saw her lips pinch.
"We are going to do some other shuffling, too, that will
please you a little more." He was telling her that she was
going to move up to Labor Secretary. A half year, maybe a year from now.

I looked at her, her eyes animated with the secret he
had imparted to her, yet clouded with fears of what I
would be telling her. The Vice President turned back easily to his Latin Americans.

On a low bandstand in the corner, the Marines were now
playing a stringy version of "You Can't Hurry Love," their
concession to the latter half of the twentieth century.

On the dance floor, Mrs. Frieden, wan as ever, was with
the President, following his jerky Illinois two-step. I saw
Anita, dancing with a Latin diplomat. The man was tall,
handsome. I waited for the music to stop and went to her.

"Forgive me, Mrs. Tockbridge," I said. She introduced
me to Ambassador del something. "I thought I ought to
get your okay on . . ." She excused herself for the moment
with a sharp smile at her partner and joined me at the
edge of the dance floor.

"Conyers is here. He came up and volunteered that the
case is still active."

"What's he got?"

"I don't know. Where can I see you tonight?"

"Tomorrow," she said, then abruptly changed. "No, tonight. I'll call you."

"I'm paranoidish about phones," I said, half reasonably,
half wanting to be with her that night.

"Then, listen, do you think it's safe . . . ?"

"Yes," I said. "At my place. Leave when you can."

She smiled at a senator, then turned back to me, her
face serious.

"That goddamn cop," she said. "If you hadn't stolen
Susan . . ."

"Oh, horseshit, Anita," I snapped at her, maintaining
my phony subservient smile. She switched subjects.

"And on the night when Frieden's promising me Labor.
Goddamnit!" She was almost tearful with aggravation. I

led her back to the Latin. *He* could dance with her now. *I* would dance with her in bed that night, come Conyers or hell itself.

As I left, I noticed Ming bowls and plates, pale preciosities in the foyer's glass exhibition cases. I had longed at one time to study the bowls of the T'angs and Mings. That world of beautiful, useless things, of Athanor, and Baudelaire, of soap temples and tinny arias seemed remote tonight.

Anita reached my house shortly after I did. We sat in my small living room, cursing Conyers, scheming how we could undercut him.

"Look, Anita. You've known from the beginning . . . if you tell Frieden you're in trouble with Justice, then even if he kills the case for you he's not going to want you on his team."

She looked somber, nodded.

"Much less as Vice President," I finished.

"You're saying we should try to ride it out," she said.

"Yes," I said. "Unless it's clear your game's up."

"Then?"

"Then, we really start to worry," I tried to joke.

Once more we went over the names of those who might betray us. I watched her smoking, the supple body rippling the fabric of her evening dress.

Finally I said, "I'm tired, let's go to bed. We can talk about it there and then sleep on it and get up tomorrow and talk some more."

"I don't want to go to bed." She lit a cigarette. "Besides I can't go home in the morning in an evening dress." She looked at me wearily. "Do you really want to go to bed?"

"Yes," I said.

When, exhausted, we turned toward each other, the freshness that had made us so good together was gone.

In the morning, I fixed an omelette. The eggs firmed and crinkled in the iron pan as I forked them toward the center. She ate, wearing my bathrobe.

"Buffi scares me," I said. "Suppose he gets crazy enough to talk?"

We had discussed it dozens of times. It was a big worry.

"He won't, don't worry," she said.

"Krals?"

"We've been through all that."

"He's crazy too," I persisted.

"Not that way."

"How about that human skin?"

"He's loyal to Buffi."

"Anybody who could wear a human skin. Where the hell did he get it, anyway?" Then I thought of Anita at the altar. "You're *all* crazy," I added quietly.

"*We're* all crazy," she corrected me, and sighed. "He tanned the skin. When you finish your eggs, I'll tell you." She seemed glad to talk about something else. We smoked over the coffee.

"He and Buffi dug up a body," she said. "Really. Down in Louisa County."

"Oh, my God," I said. I could imagine them. She laughed at my shock. The breakfast and almost no alcohol in her system from the night before had her in fairly good spirits, despite the bad omens.

"They dug it up and Krals got one of those little pamphlets from the Department of Agriculture. Buffi showed it to me, the pamphlet, I mean. Those things tell you everything, how to kill bugs, wean children, dress rabbits. This one told you how to skin and tan a sheep."

It was too much. "Jesus." I had to laugh.

"Krals lives out in the country in a renovated barn. He tanned the skin out there in drums with all sorts of chemicals."

I imagined the sculptor busily soaking, bating, and pickling his skin. I recalled from some old memory hole— "fat-liquoring."

"You know why he did it?" she asked.

"No."

"He says the old sorcerers wore human skins to turn themselves into werewolves . . ."

"You're all like kids with a nutty game. It's going to get the whole bunch of you in trouble."

"The whole bunch of *us*," she said.

"Where's Buffi now?" I asked, and then we were back worrying about Conyers. We went down the list again.

This time she actually wrote them down. As she bent over the paper, I pulled the Tarot deck from a drawer and shuffled the long rectangles.

"Here," I said, trying to perk her up, "let's find out what's going to happen, once and for all."

"I wish they'd do it," she sighed, inspecting the cards.

"They tell you what you read into them," I said. "I'll read in something nice for you."

She looked at me dubiously.

"Pick a card below twenty-two," I said. She chose twelve and I peeled off the twelfth card and laid it down. We went through the thing four more times until I had a lozenge around the middle card, the synthesis card.

By this time Anita was worried, staring at the unfamiliar figures on the bright, simple cards. But she seemed in luck at first. The Chariot meaning success, another "luck" card, the Wheel of Fortune and, as God is my witness, Temperance, standing for good management, made up three quarters of the lozenge.

In the "negation" position was the frightening Hanged Man, his left leg figure-of-foured behind his right as he hangs upside down from a T-cross. But the card is so equivocal that I had no idea what I should indicate it stood for. Something to do with "lack of ordeals" and, I thought whimsically, "false prophecy."

I explained my way through the four lozenge corners rather pedestrianly, trying to figure out the middle card, the Pope. "You seem a little fuzzy," said Anita, not wanting to hurt my feelings. "All this sounds too good to be true."

The Pope alone stood in the "synthesis" position. The reader, called by fancy folk the cartomancer, was supposed to use the card to draw together all the others. The Pope itself means "inspiration" or sometimes "need to conform." I took a solid gulp of coffee and contemplated the thing.

Then it hit me. I was playing in the wrong ball field. Toying with the old modes, the old interpretations, I was letting the crude fact of the card itself go by.

"Oh, shit," I moaned.

Anita looked up, startled, her lips pursed in a childlike expression of trepidation.

"What's the matter?"

"The Pope. Catholics. It's Conyers," I said. "All the rest of this stuff is bullshit." I folded the five cards back into the deck and put it up. "It's no fun when reality steps in," I said.

Gradually you learn to live with a criminal prosecution. I recall the bright, chipmunk face of Bobby Baker, the onetime crony of Lyndon Johnson, alight with amusement and wit in front of the Sans Souci restaurant even though he was under indictment at the time. So with us. We feared, but we did not know where Conyers stood. So we permitted ourselves to believe the best: that he had nothing on Anita, that his colleagues knew his case grew out of jealousy over Susan, that Conyers had seen the folly of a lover's vendetta and would desist. Almost as if in concert with our hopes, we got no hints of new activity by Conyers. Like some unpredictable disease, his prosecution seemed to be in stasis.

Our own efforts to make a case on Conyers had been fruitless as I knew they would be. Kinsante had obtained the file for Anita. Wearing gloves, out of an overabundance of fears over our fingerprints, we had gone through it. We might as well have been trying to incriminate the Archangel Michael.

When I was not on the campaign trail, I worried over whether to escape from the sickness of the political world. But then the power Anita had given me would seize me and I would feel saccharinely sentimental over her dependence on me. The home stretch of the campaign came in mid-October and left me no time for temporizing.

The Vice President's own staff was swamped. Increasingly, he used me for advancing. It meant lining up Cleveland for him, then Topeka for her the next day, and on, night flight after night flight, to Tacoma, or Santa Ana or Louisville.

There was a thrill, to be sure, in speaking with the voice of the man who was to be the next President. The majesty of the word! When the mayors spoke with me, I knew they felt they were storing up largesse for their cities with Frieden two years hence when his hand would control the money valve.

Whenever the Vice President's plane touched down, it was I who was first up the ramp to brief him for the crucial minute or two before he stepped out to be greeted by the city fathers. He listened to me intently, sopping it up.

"The mayor wants a promise that the President will stop by, just once, before November. He also wants a word personally with Bolitch"—that was the NASA administrator—"next week to talk about the environmental planet lab location. Finally, he wants a shot at the Western District appellate judgeship if he doesn't get elected."

"Shit," said Frieden, "he wants the moon."

"He's got yea or nay on a Senate seat and three congressionals. If Cleveland goes Democratic, if he doesn't turn the regulars out November fifth . . ." I didn't need to finish.

Frieden pulled his coat down over his big chest, his face screwed up in thought.

"Okay," he said. "Call Turnbull"—the President's appointment secretary—"See if he can get it lined up for him, maybe on the way to L.A. next week. Just an airport stopover, huh?" Then Frieden was on his way out, the great-to-be-here grin already forming.

I was never wrong on the briefings because I worked my ass off to be right. I had his total trust and was flattered: me, relied on this way by the Vice President.

Advance work for Frieden had a powerful rub-off back in Washington. I was gradually shifting from the Labor Department's to the Vice President's employ. Still, when Anita was on the hustings, I went to the Secretary's weekly Labor meetings in her place. I got deferential nods even from the assistant secretaries who outranked Anita, and sometimes from the Secretary himself. They had all been in town a long time.

I kept it low key:

"I believe Mrs. Tockbridge would agree . . . Before I speak for Planning, I'd just like a quick call to Mrs. T . . . On this I know Mrs. Tockbridge is one hundred percent."

That's the way I said it, although I knew the other conferees were aware that on many items I was making a spot decision and rubber-stamping it with Anita's approval and Frieden's backing.

Naturally, the newspapers found out I was politicking. I was surprised, even a little hurt, that it took them so long. *The New York Times* was the first to call.

I invited him in, a man named Baney Stoffers. His presumption was nauseating, particularly in view of his stupidity. I had read his stories for years. It was a marvel to me that the *Times* kept him, until I met other *Times* reporters and realized he was a cut above the rest.

"How do you square out your political work with keeping your shop in order?" he said, trying to arrange his baggy, florid face into a perceptive expression.

"By using my annual leave."

"What about the Hatch Act?"

"I've had to give up Civil Service protection, really, in taking this job. And I think the courts would have to say . . ."

"But it is uncommon."

"I've taken the precaution of going off the government payroll, Mr. Stoffers, when there could be any question."

I felt at ease in the reasonably big office with its new modern desk and my Rossant and Grenquist sketches, risked despite Labor's devant-garde attitudes. I buzzed my secretary.

"Can you find those leave slips, and the payroll, too, please?" I had them all in a big folder awaiting the arrival of the reporter. He wanted me to have them Xeroxed for him.

"I don't mind you taking notes on them really, but I think running off my pay records for you . . . it's a little lacking in style." With a disagreeable grunt, he set to work making notes.

"You know," I said, interrupting him at one point, "whatever work I do is related to the Vice President and Mrs. Tockbridge's role in getting the message of their jobs out to people in the states."

He was stupid, but not stupid enough to gobble that up. I watched his turkey neck swallow as he looked up to answer.

"Maybe *they* should show some of your meticulousness in getting off the payroll when they go on the stump," he said.

When his story came out, I was pleased to find myself only among the also rans. Most of it was the junketing of more prominent officials, including Mrs. Tockbridge.

We won in November. By then, I was exhausted. I flew to Sint Maarten in the Caribbean, to loaf and fish for a week. It was lovely, the big tropical fish, snappers, and triggerfish, hinds and even a sluggish shark, struggling against the line as they came up through the clear blue water, first as wavy pink or gray shapes, then threshing at boatside.

One night, after lobster and a bottle of pale yellow wine, I walked in the Dutch town until I was too tired to walk any longer. I thought more of Susan here, because it was so clean, such a clean life. You paid the fisherman and the inn and the restaurant and it was a deal completed, money for services.

Susan had been infected with the power thing, too, in a way, but now she was out of it. Where, I wondered? I thought of calling her, finding her through her mother and browbeating her into flying to meet me. Instead, I called Anita and invited her. She said, rightly, that it was a foolish thought, however pretty. I changed my reservation and went home a day early because I wanted her.

My first job back at Labor, now that I was soon departing (the Vice President had told me as much), was a political one—to chart the places where Anita had spoken and relate them to the returns. I used voter profile data to see particularly how the women voted. It was dubious evidence, but it indicated we did well where Anita had campaigned.

She showed it to Frieden and the next week he called in person and asked me to help his staff get up the same sort of tables on him, only in greater detail.

Elections over, Washington went through its biennial transformation. The losers went home or set up consulting offices as lobbyists or worse. The Attorney General resigned with the usual gavotte of letters about urgent personal problems. We heard nothing more of Conyers. Either he had hit a snag or had failed to make his case and given up.

The Vice President, using my voter tables as evidence, took considerable credit for the off-year win. His eminence was vouched by a feature story in *Parade Magazine,* full of his wife, children and dogs. *Good Housekeeping* traced his boyhood—there was his determined young face beneath a yarmulke. A TV hour special on him used his native California as a setting for his views on air pollution, birth control, and poverty.

The President announced that come spring, Harry would be coronetted with a trip to Peking and Moscow to show that the Grand Old Party of Peace was mending all fences.

I knew I was on the rise. Frieden called me in frequently now for opinions on Labor and labor. Anita was almost a certain bet next year as Labor Secretary: our good Secretary-professor was flagging at last.

For me, that could mean the Assistant Secretaryship.

And if he picked her as running mate? I would be a Special Presidential Assistant, or conceivably, later on, even more. When I dreamed such dreams, which was often, there was a headiness I had never imagined before.

My fortunes were tied to Frieden's now. Once, with Anita in bed, I asked her whether she thought the star of a blue movie should become the world's most powerful head of state? We laughed. Why shouldn't he? I thought. Better a man whose curiosity or lust or simply eccentricity had put him at a Black Mass than one whose penchant was barbecued Southeast Asians.

And yet, and yet. Sometimes, those terrible old timidities overcame me. At home, when I went down cellar steps for a hammer and a nail, there was Athanor, undusted, unused, a child's forgotten toy. The old yearnings began: for privacy, for family, for a wife who would tolerate the peculiarities of my simpler days. I stood in the cold basement. The remembered desires danced in my mind, there beside the dumb alchemical furnace where I had seduced Susan and never tried to fabricate the Philosopher's Stone.

Anita telephoned me one night so summon my talents from the past into play.

"He wants you to come and bring your cards," she said.

"Who, Buffi?"

"No, you know." She was still cautious on the phone. She meant Frieden.

"Where?"

"I'll drop by for you. In a half hour," she said.

The Vice President's house in Wesley Heights had a piked fence around it almost like the one around the White House. A Secret Service man came out and buzzed open the gate. A maid took us into Frieden's library-den. It had the staple law books, bound *Congressional Records*, *Congressional Quarterly Almanacs*, plus a shelf full of Books of the Month and a shelf of bound *National Geographics*.

Frieden came down a few seconds later. Just out of the shower, sorry not to have been at the front door, garbed in slacks and a University of California Athletic Department sweat shirt. Anita and I sat on his leather couch while he made small talk, fixing us drinks. His desk was full of trophies of politics, an African-carved elephant, a gold-wash orange tree with a plaque at the bottom, a

Great Seal of Japan in lucite from an Imperial Coronation.

The Vice President was nervous and it made me nervous. For the dozenth time I knocked my coat pocket to make sure I had the fat deck of Tarot cards.

"Bitter lemon and vodka, right, Mrs. T?" he said. He poured himself a straight bourbon on the rocks. I took the same, knowing I shouldn't.

"Well," he said. "I told Anita I wanted to take you up on your offer on the plane." I was almost sure I hadn't offered to use the Tarot cards with him, but no matter. "I thought I ought to go into the home stretch with some scientific findings."

He chuckled uncomfortably, like a man bargaining for a dirty picture.

"I'm not that good at it," I said. "You ought to get an expert if you want the real McCoy." I knew he wanted me to do it because I would not betray him.

"Anita says there's none better," he went on, still nervous and hearty, but dropping the "Mrs. Tockbridge." The print of my sweating palm was on the maroon box of cards as I pulled them out.

I shuffled the big oblongs. "I need more room, sir," I said, gesturing at the coffee table. "I'll have to deal them out on the floor."

Frieden pushed back the coffee table. Well, I thought, here we go.

"I'll have just another little nip of that bourbon, sir, if I may," I said.

I hated like hell to tell his fortune with the Great Game, which meant using sixty-seven of the seventy-eight cards. It drained so much out of me and was just as fraudulent as the abbreviated five-card version which I had used with Anita. But out of respect for Harry Frieden's office, I could do no less, I thought nastily.

We sat beneath the Tensor light from his desk. I began to lay out a five-foot square of cards with a circle of them inside. The right-hand part of the circle is the past, the top the present, and the left-hand the future.

I was dealing out the past when Death popped up and Frieden said abruptly, "That's Death!"

Trying to concentrate as I was on what lay next to what, I didn't have time to stop and hold his hand and tell him he was lucky Death was in his past. That was only a grandfather or parent or somebody.

By the time I had dealt the last few cards of the future, I was feeling a little woozy from the mental concentration. I took a quick sip of whiskey.

"Could you move the light off a little?" I said. It was turning the cards to blurs. "It's too hot."

The gleaming black of a trump called The Tower turned a bit duller as Frieden shifted the Tensor. The Tower meant "ruin" and "deception."

Anita whispered to Frieden:

"Don't say anything, Harry, he's trying to memorize them."

The Vice President's face was just outside the Tensor's glare. Red from his drinking, in his collegiate shirt, he looked like a returning alumnus worried about his heart.

"You asked me about Death," I said, surprised at the reasonableness of my voice. "It is in your past, some friend, not a lover. I read it with the nine of pentacles and the Jack of rods, these cards here. Together they mean this dead dark-haired person assured you of a durable fortune."

"My grandfather!" he burst out. "Gahud-damn!"

My heart jumped and I began to sweat.

"He was a dark-haired man?" I said softly.

"Yes," said the astonished Frieden. "He had a clothing business . . . a good, solid business."

I moved on through the swords suit that dominated his past. There was the dreadful ten of swords, a card showing a dead man with ten swords stuck in his back beneath a black sky. It meant uneasiness about friendship.

"You learned insecurity at your mother's breast," I told him. "See these cards in the cup suit. They mean love. The two of cups, here, means 'one of the couple has caused obstacles.'" It could be his mother or his father. "It is your mother," I said, figuring that Jewish mantisism could apply to Harry.

"Oh, yes," he said with a little grunt of pain, hooked now.

"Here," I said, "this card, the eight of swords. It means your enemies were successful in part. I do not wish to get into your early family life, Mr. Vice President, but there is an effort here, perhaps, to hold you back . . ."

"Ummn," he said.

We moved around the circle toward his present. There was a major card, The Lovers, meaning passionate love, near the Queen of Pentacles, a woman with light hair, either indifferent or unfriendly to him. I pointed out the pairing to him.

"Could that be my mother, too?" he asked. "She was light-haired. I got my hair from her." He was puttyish now, disturbingly so for the man who would be the next President.

"I don't know, sir," I said. The next card was a three of rods. "Initial success. The woman we are talking about would not be your mother. Probably a girl in your teens?"

"Yes, yes," he said, pleased not to think of being passionate with Mom.

I worked on through the last of his past and then into his present. It was full of cups and pentacles and rods, almost all good, with achievement cards like The World, and The Chariot. The cups concurred with what I already knew of his love life: active.

"I'm just going to let the cards say it, Mr. Vice President. I don't want to embarrass you before Mrs. Tockbridge. I see here some pretty salient evidence of a man with a nice eye for the ladies." He heh-hehed. My stomach wrenched as I saw his proprietary look at Anita. The fart.

There in the middle of the present, astride it like the Colossus, was the King of Cups. Old lover boy himself, light-haired, judge or clergyman. Since there weren't any Vice Presidents in medieval times when the cards originated, it had to be the Golden Jew himself. Around the King were aureoles of success, difficulties overcome, a few losses quickly made up with gains.

I took a gulp of the bourbon before I entered the future. It was one gulp too many for a man who should dissemble: Frieden's future picture was awful, a horror story.

The bad cards were all there. The terrible swords suit was back in spades, so to speak.

"I'd rather not go into the future," I said abruptly, my smoothness all gone from the influence of the bourbon. "I feel queasy."

"What do you mean?" He was suspicious, even angry at the peremptory tone.

"It's not a happy picture," I said. "Of course, the whole damned thing is just a deck of cards . . ."

"No, go on," he half wheedled, half ordered. "I want to know."

Even through the fog of my hootch, I sensed Anita tensing. I wondered vaguely if she feared I would do something foolish now. Or was she genuinely and superstitiously interested?

"Well," I tried to stabilize. "I don't want to be the bearer of bad news. But you have a tough go in the next few years. Just look at those swords. Look at the Moon, there." The glistening cards shrilled at me like Harpies.

The Moon meant false friends, enemies. Right by it was a weeping man against a tatter-clouded sky, five fallen swords around him: the enemy triumphant. Farther along were three swords piercing a fat red heart: hatred. I explained it to him as gently as I could.

My head swam. Poor Harry, if they were right!

Now, only a small part of me snickered. "These cards are trying to tell you something about dates, and something extremely important about your enemies," I said.

I was tired now. There, toward the middle of his future was The Pope—Conyers—among the Moon and its satellite horrors. Well, I thought, if you use damned near the whole deck, it had to turn up somewhere. Still, it chilled me.

"This card, The Pope," I said to him, lacquering over my acute anxiety. "It means . . ." But the bad news had built up a resentment in Harry that burst out.

"The Catholic vote! Goddamn them, the bigot-bastards. They almost beat me in California." His outcry snapped me back to reality. No, it *was* laughable. Just a big superstitious kid—and he was going to be the next President. But my ridicule was edged with fear. Catholic vote, my ass! Roger Conyers, just as in Anita's Tarot, was Frieden's—and my—real nemesis card. I tried to shake off the thought and went through the rest of the cards perfunctorily, depressed by my own flight of superstition.

Done at last I stood up, bladder heavy, arms and legs stiff from squatting and sitting. My eyes throbbed. My head hurt.

"Whew," said Harry, glad to be done. "With a future like that, I'd better live for the day."

I limped off to the bathroom, leaving him with his thoughts and Anita. When I came back the Vice President was sunk gloomily in his chair.

"Heavy sleeps the head," he groaned.

"It's just a parlor game," I told him. I wanted to go to bed now. Thoughts of Conyers preyed neurotically on my mind.

"I wish the picture had been brighter," Harry moaned.

"Well," I tried to console him, "if you take seventy-eight cards and a quarter of them are actively bad news, you're bound to get some bad news."

"But why in my future? My past wasn't all that happy."

"You want me to stack a deck for you and try again," I risked. Frieden gave me a cloudy smile.

"That's the nice thing about you, my boy," he said. "You wouldn't stack a deck on me. God," he groaned again. "What a fortune!" He poured himself another drink, a strong one, and rolled a sip around in his mouth, brooding. "Well," he sighed finally. "That's that."

Then, as if he had made up his mind to try to shuck off his woe, like a chameleon its old skin, Frieden grunted and turned to Anita.

"While you're here, let's talk about how long you're going to keep Martin tilling the fields of Labor, Anita." Even in my funk from the ordeal of the cards, I felt a lift. He was going to talk about my leaving Labor, going to work at the seat of power.

"The President is stepping down in two years," he said. "That's no secret, I guess. I want, he wants, a few of my people in there for a year or so before he steps down, transition men . . ."

Harry was going to make me his man at the White House. Jesus!

". . . someone to keep me up-to-date on a staff level, as opposed to a policy level. I'd need Martin there soon," he said. Anita looked distressed. I was touched to see it.

"I'd really like a little say on timing, Mr. Vice President," she said, a rare trace of whine in her voice.

"Anita, Anita," he placated her. "You're looking like a good bet for a Cabinet post. And here you are unwilling to help out an old man in a spot, an old man with a terrible, terrible future to judge by the cards."

He was half jesting with her, but implicit was the same promise of advancement for her that he had given me at the White House that night. Anita, for a moment, was wistful. Her face in the masculine light of the den was not young and sprightly.

"I wish I could tie you to it, Mr. Vice President. You're taking away my right arm, and giving me a pretty vague promise . . ."

"Not that vague," he said. She started to press him, but left it at that. Frieden turned to me again.

"So?"

"I don't know the President," I said. I felt the familiar clutching of noninvolvement. Run! was my instinct. Run from it. "He doesn't know me."

"Oh, he'll like you. My God, he'll be lucky to get you," said Harry.

With Anita I felt, if not secure, at least informed. Crazy as our relationship was, I could cope in it and now I clung to it. In her eyes, I saw something fearful, too. I felt remorse at the idea of leaving her, and besides, it would leave me even more vulnerable to Conyers' villainy.

"You don't want me to go, do you?" Did my tone give our affair away to the Vice President? Would he care? Yes, I thought, he was the sort of man who wanted everything for his own.

"I don't want to keep you back," she answered, masking her anxiety. She looked at the Vice President. "Why don't you let him stay at Labor a few more months? You can borrow him, can't you, for liaison?"

"Now, Anita," he said. I hated the domestic tone. As if she were a chattel, simply because he had screwed her. "Martin's not a goddamned anemone. Don't stick him on one rock like that. Let him move on."

She had a lot at stake in not bucking him, but still she persisted. At that moment, I loved her. She had made a man of me, now she made of me a valuable man, even in my own suspect eyes.

"Well," she said finally to Frieden, not really yielding, "let him think about it. Okay?" She turned to me. I saw anger in her eyes and it dispelled my soft love. "You obviously want to go." It had the cut in it of the woman scorned.

As it worked out, Anita had her way. She got Frieden to put it off a month or two.

We were lovers again, even friends.

She had not seen Buffi for weeks. His Black Mass, with its foreignness, in retrospect did not seem so pitiful, so crude. Mostly, now, I recalled him bobbing and sweating with his exertions. He believed, therefore he was.

I considered him against the federal timeservers who neither believed nor thought, and who, therefore, were not. Accepting de Plaevilliers in that way, albeit as mad, made him more bearable. And Anita less exotic in being attracted to him.

Anita and I made love in those weeks at her apartment, talking politics, drinking fine clarets, as comfortable as married lovers. After breakfast I left her to change my suit at home and to meet her again in the office.

One day Anita said she had to see Buffi and wanted me there. My first thought was that she had tired of my normality. She saw the green flare in my eyes and tried to assure me.

"He's going to make a big fuss about the money. He just wants to believe he's still got some control over me before he gives us the last twenty-five thousand."

"I thought the Black Mass was all we had to do." I was in her office, drinking coffee and checking off a list of projects I was setting up against the time when I would no longer be with her.

She shrugged, straightened her wool jacket with a pull. The octagonal masculine pocket watch on its holder jerked and I smiled. She looked up with a question, the pouty lips parted slightly.

"I was smiling at your watch. It was the first thing I saw about you that I knew made you different."

Her eyes held a fond moment of memory. She let one corner of her full mouth stretch toward a smile.

"Poor Martin. You had no idea how different."

"So, Buffi?"

"He wants us to meet him Friday night."

"Another Black Mass?"

"No, at Krals'."

"Home movies?"

"God," she said in mock terror. "I hope not . . ." There was a twinge of concern in her voice. "He sounded funny on the phone."

"Funny?"

" 'And how is Monsieur Ouroboros and his lovely succubus?' " she drawled in imitation.

"Arrgh."

"You'll go?"

"What's he want? Don't you know?"

"No. Honest."

"Sure," I said. "I'll go." We were pals, Anita and I, what the cops call confederates in crime.

14

Buffi

Krals lived beyond Fairfax City. We drove out in Anita's Buick, the heater keeping us snug, listening to *Tristan* on WGMS-FM.

"Have you ever thought we'd make a fairly good married couple with a few of our kinks straightened out?" I said to Anita.

"Well, the question doesn't arise," she said practically. But she reached over and took my hand.

"Do you wish it were possible?" I persisted.

"Well, I wish I were younger."

"If you were, would you love me? I mean now you *are* dependent and . . ."

She interrupted:

"No. If I were younger, I would be ambitious the way I was then. I would know enough to leave you alone."

"Why?" It was rare she would play this fantasy game.

"Because I would have wanted someone to help me politically." She lit a cigarette. "You would have wanted a housewife and a mother and a drudge, probably." She took my hand again, then let it go. "I'm tired of this sort of speculation."

We drove on silently.

"Besides," she said as if some switch had turned her on again. "You would have fought me. Wanted me to get interested in your furnace and your operas. My ambition and your trying to force me to be something I'm not would have been a mess."

I thought for a moment of protesting, not because she was wrong, because she wasn't, but because I sensed she wanted to be challenged. I had let her deny a part of her femininity without objecting.

We drove on for awhile and when she spoke again we were back into our old concerns.

"Will we luck through, on Conyers?"

"Maybe," I said. I had been thinking about how we could fight him. I knew it would only be in close combat. Only when he was on the brink of something calamitous for us would he be vulnerable. Only then would we be able to use his cankerous love for Susan against him, or trap him into some unethical legal practice that would destroy him at Justice. Rather than get that close, I prayed, and often believed, it would blow past.

Just south of Manassas, we turned into a rough Virginia state road. Two miles, and we turned again into Krals' dirt drive. The headlights blazed on the skeletal stalks of weeds, his only crop.

Krals had let the farm go to hell because he wanted the land only for its privacy and space. The barn hulked at the end of the road. Near it were lights from his small house. The yard was an uneven area where cars had packed down the dirt. Buffi's black Jaguar was in front of the house. Once I had wondered why he did not drive a Mercedes. It was because he hated the Germans.

I was unprepared for the faces. Lisel and Krals were pallid, the summer tan all gone now. And Buffi, in the few months since I had seen him, had crossed the watershed into old age. His trips to the subequator had hastened his rot. His skin was withered: lizard skin.

Buffi, as I knew he would, greeted me with his "Monsieur Ouroboros," and a smile of bad teeth. Curiously, his voice warmed me.

"Dear Ouroboros," he said, "envisioner of pelicans and refiner of antimony: see, I have been reading up in your field." His failing face beamed on me. His eyes looked worried, almost crazed as if he carried in him a growing cancer. Yet, again, curiously, I was touched. The man liked me.

"Buffi," I said, using his nickname as I rarely did. "I have gone over to politics. Athanor is neglected."

"And taken our Anita with you into the *Beamterstadt,* into the City of God," he said. Krals' expression of yearning over Buffi was disgusting, that of a dog. Lisel came in with drinks and Krals' eyes hooded out his concern for de Plaevilliers.

Anita, I sensed, wanted to get to the $25,000 and go, but Buffi was making an old woman of himself, teasing her along because he knew he had lost his investment in her.

"Anita, I am flying to Buenos Aires this spring to help my friends celebrate Easter. I want you to come with me. I want them to meet you."

Shit, I thought. He may get serious about something like that, an Easter Mass. I thought of the pretty Spanish girl at the Jockey Club. Why not use her as acolyte?

"Buffi, Buffi," she said. "I am going to be fighting the budget battle. I . . ."

"*Every* weekend?" he interrupted querulously.

"We'll see, all right?" she answered appeasingly. Anita and I made small talk, wondering what Buffi had brought us out for. Everyone had a second drink. Herbert hit the bourbon on the rocks hard and insisted we see the sculpture in the barn. I wondered nervously what the hell was going on.

The barn was a strange twilight world, an immense cavern, lit only by a trouble light inside the door. I could see crouching statues inside, hulking and uneven. Krals turned on the lights. Above us, the fluorescent tubes flickered, giving the statues erratic life for a moment, before the tube light steadied and the huge forms were still again.

The barn held a half-dozen enormous figures, some finished, all grotesque, demonic, a goat-headed god, a dragon, a man-shark.

Krals led us to his major work-in-progress. Gleaming white in plaster, bigger-than-life and ready for a casting. It was not a werewolf in the grand old Lon Chaney tradition: a man with some wolf attributes. Rather, it was a wolf with some features of a man. The thick thighs and neck were those of a man, but the maw of the horror, the lower legs, buttocks and loins were those of a wolf. It had the unlikely grace of an Artzybasheff drawing.

Krals' face, in the light that now splashed the barn, was a mirror of desire and hopelessness as he looked up at the white plaster monster on its stand. He had sculpted himself as God.

Buffi and I walked back to the house together.

"Yes," he hissed in the cold air, "Herbert is studying to be a werewolf."

Inside the house, he finally told Anita and me what he wanted.

"I will be able to help you," he confided. We tensed. He had already promised us the money. We, she willingly, me half reluctantly, had gone to his damned Mass. What was the new tab?

He looked at his watch. All my fondness for him dried up in my fury at his manipulation. "Monsieur Ouroboros, I want you to help me and Herbert with some boxes." He smiled, the blackening teeth sinister now. "I must get it done by tomorrow."

Was he robbing something from the embassy?

"What boxes?"

The tension in the room almost smelled.

"Nothing of value. We only want your brawn, not your brains. It is not a jewelry robbery." He was a cute rat.

"Look, I want to know what it is."

Buffi's face firmed. He was determined that I would play some role in whatever corrupt venture he had in mind. He wanted me and Anita back.

"You will not help?" he asked quietly.

"No," I said.

"Then the party is over," he said petulantly. There was no doubt of what that meant. No $25,000. I saw Anita's face freeze into old-woman lines. Christ, why couldn't she use her own $25,000? Yet, here was Buffi with the money on him, no doubt of that. We could be done with it, perhaps tonight.

"How big a criminal violation is it?" I asked him nastily. He saw I was weakening.

"Nothing. Oh, perhaps like spitting on the sidewalk, Monsieur Ouroboros, or like fornication. On the books, as you say, but not enforced."

"What is it?" I persisted.

"Come along," he purred. "After it is done, you and Anita will have your full wages."

I pushed him some more, but the money, so near now, had beaten me. We left Lisel, who knew what it was and whose eyes were guarded, and Anita, who did not know.

As we got our coats from the closet, I saw, with a riptide of sickening recollection, the human skin, hanging like some butcher's scraps, inside a heavy plastic bag.

"Jesus," I shuddered. Behind me, Buffi laughed.

"He has seen your Saint Monica's wrap, Herbert."

We took Buffi's Jaguar. With its diplomatic plates, he could assert his immunity if we were stopped. It was an uncertain umbrella for me and Krals.

De Plaevilliers drove with a flair. The car slipped down the dirt road and on toward Brandy Station.

"What the hell are we up to, Buffi?" I asked him with irritation. "Christ, let's have it. I'm tired and it's too far back to walk, you know." Speaking out eased my pain.

"We are visiting Fauquier County by night," he said lightly. "Krals and I are friends of the county. We are transplanted Virginians." I grunted sourly. Another forest, scraggly with second growths of pine, and the Jaguar slowed. Buffi turned off his lights, looked out at the trees, then drove on in the dark. I was distressed again, sweating, hating Krals' beast loyalty, detesting all foreigners.

Miles down the road he turned in at a driveway. I saw the battered little box of a Negro church, its steeple no more than second-story high.

Oh, Jesus, I thought. He's going to break into a church and desecrate it or some damn thing. Housebreaking! My nerves began to stampede.

"No soap," I said. "I'm going up the road."

"Get out then," he barked angrily.

We all got out and I started to walk, cursing him and his lousy money. But he did not walk to the church. Instead, he opened the trunk. I watched him from up the road. Silently, he and Krals took two short shovels from the trunk.

Then I remembered that dreadful line he had thrown into his Black Mass, "Puerorum pinguedine e sepulchris eruta. . . ." Something to do with dead babies. It may have been goat fat at the last Mass. But Buffi was going to dig up a dead baby to make witch ointment out of its fat for his Brazilian experiment this Easter.

"My God," I said to myself, and began jogging up the road, sickened. We'd been gone thirty minutes, that would be twenty miles, halfway to Culpeper. I was nowhere. If I found a telephone in a farmhouse or some little town like Catlett, then the taxi driver I summoned might well tie me to the grave robbing when it was discovered. I slowed my jog to a walk. Another hundred feet and I heard running footsteps behind me. It was Krals.

"He says to show you this," said Krals all out of breath. I saw the wad of bills in the big spatulate hand. "Look. Don't be a fool. Help us just a little. He'll give in. I know him."

I turned and started walking again.

"I know him," said Krals urgently. "If you back out now he'll never let her have the money. You are six miles from anywhere. The farmers will set the dogs after you anyway."

It was clear enough Buffi wanted me to have a hand to the shovel. Possibly, too, he feared my disgust would lead me to blow the whistle on his whole nutty business.

"How long will you take?" I was thinking of that walk into nowhere.

"A half hour if you help. Herr de Plaevilliers gets out of breath easily."

"Krals!" I shouted at him. "Are you crazy? I mean, you must be to let him make you dig up some poor damned baby. And cook it! You plan to cook it! Jesus Christ!"

My instant anger triggered me to action. My temper blew. I grabbed the big handful of money and tried to wrench it from him. With a quick wrestling fall, I threw Krals over and fell on top of him, still grabbing for the money.

"You dirty bastard," I screamed at him as I pulled at the money. But if his face had gone to hell, his sculptor's arm hadn't. He hammered me on the face and I fell off him and into the dirt. Stunned, I saw him picking up the money that had fallen to the ground.

I was exhausted, and now my bruised cheek throbbed. Why should I go walking off into the night? Didn't Buffi have enough on me, and on Anita, on everyone, to destroy us, without this even mattering?

There was my role in the Benn City fix, too. Oh, he knew enough.

I thought of the disgusting load we would have in the trunk. But $12,500 an hour—Krals' half hour estimate was, of course, a lie. It would take two hours. $12,500 an hour! The kid was dead now. No, I couldn't do it.

"No, I can't do it," I said.

Krals growled from above me and turned away.

I sat miserably in the Jaguar for an hour, fearful and humiliated, hating myself. I tried to think again of how Anita would be that night. My cheek ached. A costly piece. I thought of Susan.

Finally the loneliness and cold were too much. I got out.

A country sharpness in the cold air filled my nostrils. I walked around the wooden church and saw them in the darkness before they saw me. Krals, shortened in the hole, was digging. Buffi was upright.

They heard my step and both froze, tense as rabbits.

"It's me—I," I called softly. Krals went back to work.

Buffi sloppily pushed Krals' diggings back from the hole. I watched the diplomat for a few minutes. He was awkward at it, ineffectual.

"Here," I said, taking the shovel from him in my gloved hands and going to work on the dirt Krals had piled up. Krals paused in the hole. He was panting.

Buffi pulled out the wad of bills from an inside pocket.

"Here is a down payment for the first half hour," he said with a comic flourish. "You are better paid here than in alchemy or government, Ouroboros."

I counted out the $500 and $100 bills. It was $12,500. I put the money in my pocket. In the hole, Krals worked vigorously at the loose dirt. I thought about the contents of the coffin toward which he dug.

"This is sick. You two really are sick," I said wearily.

Krals was all but exhausted from shoveling. If I waited for him to finish the job, the danger and anguish would only be prolonged. At last, I spelled him, and it was I who hit the coffin.

It thudded as hollowly as in those old horror movies. I climbed out, my suit covered with mud. They could finish the job.

Suddenly, I heard a rustling near the church and a gasp. All three of us wheeled.

A shocked Negro voice, "What's this?" came out of the dark. Panicked, fearing a shot, I scrambled into the muddy grave. Two forms were in the shadows of the church. Krals snarled a curse and ran at them with his shovel while Buffi and I stood paralyzed, one in, one beside the grave.

The two men screamed and fled. Krals puffed back.

"Look!" I warned. "They're going to the cops."

"No," said Krals, panting. "It's all right. They ran. They're just stupid blacks." I climbed out of the grave.

"Maybe they took the plate number," I said, pulling at Buffi's coat. The urgency gripped me like a thumbscrew. "We've got to get our asses out of here."

"It'll only take a minute," Krals snapped, jumping back into the grave and pushing his shovel at the crack between the coffin lid and the rest of the box. The scrape sounded deafening.

"Buffi," I said frantically, "for Christ's sake, tell him!"

"Let's go," ordered Buffi, grabbing up a shovel and walking briskly.

We piled into the car. My mind worked frantically.

"We've got to get to Krals' house without getting picked up by the police." My own safety was at stake now. I had no diplomatic immunity. God, God, caught as a grave robber!

Buffi was driving with no lights, 50 miles an hour on the shadowed road. I clung to the seat side as we rounded a corner.

As we hurtled on, I began to relax. Now, I thought, we could make it. My anxiety began to lift. I would get the other half of the $25,000. There were headlights burning up ahead, and the pendulum swing of a red light in the road; a cop, signaling us with his hooded flashlight.

"Turn it, Buffi," I yelped. "It's them."

He braked the car, downshifting as he did. I flung my arms against the dash.

Down to half speed, Buffi hit the brakes hard. I clung to the passenger bracket. Buffi clunked into low with a metallic ring and bounced onto the narrow shoulder with just enough room to turn.

Buffi was in second now, the Jag giving out its whine-and-roar. I latched my seatbelt.

"Du Blaeder," he growled at the car with satisfaction. I was sick with worry. Police cars had radios. They would block us at the other end of the country road.

Buffi was in third, doing 65 already.

Far behind us, the police car was in pursuit. In my back, precisely between my shoulder blades I sensed the exact spot where I was sure a bullet would strike. The skin on my back seemed to writhe.

Buffi had the Jag at 80. We flashed through the tunnel

of dark beneath the huge old roadside trees. One bump would throw us from the narrow road into a spectacular end against one of them.

Krals, too, was paralyzed. I could see the puffy white of his face when I turned to glance at the police lights.

Buffi, braking, ripped around a slow curve. The car swerved almost out of control. I was imploring God to burn out the Jag's gears so the car would decelerate to a stop.

"Buffi," I gasped, "for Christ's sake. Let them get us."

Buffi did not answer. In the dash light I saw the fixity of the pallid features, lost in a dream of speed. My life or Krals' or his own meant nothing to him.

I pivoted, feeling the tight belt cramping me in the gut. "Krals, where's he going?"

"I don't know." His hands were pressed against the back of the seat.

"Put your seat belt on, you damned fool." I told him. The command moved him into action.

We were at the top of a hill and rollercoasted down. On the other side of the shallow valley, a car approached.

"Oh, Jesus," I said. There'd be a bridge, a narrow one, at the bottom. The other car's lights slowed. At least it was not racing us to the bottom. Countrywise, its drive must have recognized that our lights, blinked off and on as Buffi needed them, meant a car out of normal control. The driver approaching us seemed to be pulling to his extreme right.

We were almost to the rickety wooden bridge. With an enormous clackety-clack we struck the asphalt-coated wood. For a breathless moment I thought Buffi would go off the road. His lights caught the side of the other car, an old sedan, in their glare. As we flashed by, I saw the driver's terrified black face, white-eyed and white-toothed, in three-quarter profile as he strained to keep his still-moving vehicle on the road.

Looking back, I saw him jounce off the shoulder and into the ditch, then lurch back up and stop hard against a rugged wall of underbrush and low trees.

The police car was over the hill and on the downgrade. Blessedly, I saw the outthrust funnel of its headlights decelerate.

Of course! The officer's duty was to the injured, first.

A cardinal rule. I almost wept with relief, incongruously and genuinely touched by the policeman's devotion.

"Slow down, Buffi! He's stopped for the wreck."

"Wreck?" he said. It was his first word during the insane race.

But he did slow. I quickly told him what had happened.

"Yes," he said. "Well, we can make it back to Manassas on these back roads. Or I can cut all the way over to Route Twenty-nine."

I saw a glitter in the mirror at the same time Buffi did.

"Just local traffic," I said hopefully.

I was ready to be caught rather than risk another such ride. We could pretend a drunken, basically harmless, if macabre, stunt. Buffi would be sent home to Austria or to Buenos Aires. Krals and I would take forfeitures on disorderly conduct charges and I would lose my job when the newspapers played it up. I had come so far for this!

Buffi jammed down on the accelerator.

We roared off. Within seconds a red-top was blinking on the car behind us. Another—or the same—policeman. I thought of grabbing the wheel, doing the dramatic. But that was asking for a crack-up. I prayed again, telling God all the things I would never do again if He let me get out of this.

The police car gained. I heard a *thwat*. The thought of a flat tire shocked me with terror. But then I knew. The unmistakable report of a shot had overtaken us.

"They're shooting. For God's sake, stop!" I shouted. Krals screamed. He had his hand to his hair. His lips were as pale as his skin.

"Where are you hit?" I gasped at him.

"Dem Kopf," he shrieked. I looked at how high the window was above his head.

"You got hit by glass," I bolstered him. He pulled his hand away and almost fainted at the sight of the blood.

"Look," he thrust it at me as if it were my fault.

"If it had hit you in the head you'd be dead." I heard a third *thwat*. Cringing, I listened to the groans of the terrified Krals, and, as if far away, the siren whine of the pursuing car.

Buffi, by risking enormous speeds, had gotten us out of pistol range. At a fork, without slowing, he bore left.

We roared past the sedate two-story dwellings of a crossroads village, everything dark.

Buffi slowed to a moderate 60.

"We can still make it," he said. I closed my eyes with fatigue and prolonged fear. Behind me, Krals whined loudly. His face was bloody.

I thought of how we could put together a stolen car story. Could we smuggle the broken-windowed Jaguar into some alley and desert it? Shouldn't Krals and I—or at least I—abandon Buffi right now? After all, the government couldn't prosecute him—at worst the little scandal would rock him from the country.

Buffi had begun to unwind.

"Anita will wonder where her gallant chief counsel is," he began with a light touch of nastiness. I prepared an answer as he turned back to the road. But I saw his lips flinch from the teeth in a spasm of terror.

I screamed, hearing the cries of the others as I did.

Directly in our path were the woods. Somewhere behind, Buffi had neglected the sharp-turn warning on the country road. I threw my hands in front of my face and felt him swerve violently.

Then my body was wrenched. The seat belt garroted the wind from me and I passed out. When I came too, I was alone in the car, which rested on its right side. My leg, aching from its old twist, was beneath me. My right arm was above my head.

I tried to move, but was held back by my belt. When I undid it, I felt an agonizing soreness in my hips. Every movement was anguish.

"Buffi," I said in a groan. My breath frosted before me. He and Krals, I thought, had escaped and left me for dead. I stood up on the scratchy weeds through the open window. My ankle barely supported me. I clambered up the seat and out the driver's side. The door was crushed open against the car. The night air was biting cold on my hot face.

The car was in a sparse woods. It had caromed off the road, tumbled, and slammed into a tree.

"Buffi," I yelled. I saw Krals come stumbling out of the underbrush.

"Come. Gott! Gott!" he said frantically, uttering beastlike grunts of pain as he helped me down from the side of the car. "He's hurt, he's hurt." His voice was high and urgent, hardly his own.

I limped, my left ankle agonizing as Krals tried to hurry me on with a rude grip on my arm.

Buffi lay on his back. My hips shot with pain as I bent to him.

Blood had come up from his chest in a quick gush, and his mouth and neck were claret-colored from the veinous bleeding. His eyes were shock open. I tore at his coat, then his shirt, the fine fabric giving while the buttons stayed anchored. His chest seemed flattened and lumpy beneath his undershirt. The car must have rolled completely over and come full weight on his chest as he fell out. I looked at Krals.

His face twisted in childish expectation of the worst. He waited only for me to say Buffi was dead. I had to do more than that. All that was left in me of decency demanded I do more.

I picked up the lifeless wrist as if to seek a pulse. I knew the vanity of it. Krals was kneeling now, feeling at the other wrist. I reached over and put my hand on the sculptor's.

"Herbert, he didn't feel a thing. I swear it. You can be grateful for that." Krals' body shook with sobbing. I gripped the top of his hand.

"He didn't feel a thing," I repeated.

I was getting cold and I ached. When Krals' shaking eased, I slipped my hand carefully into Buffi's coat and pulled out the rest of the bills. Krals tensed.

"He'd want us to get out of here," I said quietly. Krals looked up at me with hostile unbelief. He was paralyzed by his master's death.

"Buffi would want you to get back to Lisel, Herbert," I said with irritation now. I was getting cold. My ankle would not carry me back to Krals' house without his help.

He started to take off his muddy coat and spread it over Buffi's face.

"Don't be a jackass, Herbert. They'll trace it." I struggled with Buffi's coat. Krals picked up the body slightly and I got off the coat and covered Buffi's head and shoulders.

"We can't leave him here," he simpered, sitting down.

I whipped back the coat from the bloody mouth and staring eyes.

"Tell him," I implored the corpse. "Tell him, Buffi! Look at him, Krals. Can you think for a moment if that poor dead mouth could speak that it wouldn't be commanding you to go? Commanding you! Tell him, Buffi, for God's sake, to save himself." I pulled the coat back over the head and growled at Krals.

"Now, for Christ's sake, let's get going."

Back on the road, the two of us trudged toward Manassas. We left the road when we saw the lights of cars through the trees or heard a motor away off in the cold night. Up above, the stars were failing. There, dumbly, were The Twins.

Buffi and I, Castor and Pollux, Krals and Lisel, Anita and Susan, all, all of us, I thought, lost in a straight world where the Polydeuces were wild. I resented this straight world. I resented Buffi's death. I would miss him, did miss him and his queer faith.

Buffi, Buffi. He had gotten me into this mess. Now he was dead as Yorick. That awful face, bloody-chapped. Doing this insane thing, he had died. The world beneath those fading stars had no place for Buffi.

God, I was miserable in the cold. Longing for my snug cellar, I groaned aloud for the simplicities of my old life. Real tears of self-pity ran from my eyes.

Krals' wife was nearly frantic when we got back. At the Mass she had been as casually lubricious as a sheep. Now she fell on him like any blubbery German hausfrau. As for me, I could see relief and concern in Anita's eyes. I nodded that I had the money.

While Krals sat nursing straight whiskey, I told them what happened. Thank God I had shoveled with my gloves on. Would my prints show up on the dash? That could be explained. I thought of those damned blue films at Buffi's house. I cued Anita and she painstakingly explained to Lisel and then to the still stunned Krals that, for Buffi's sake, the films must be removed when they went over to tell Buffi's mother.

Anita drove me home, both of us nervous and gloomy over the death. She helped me into bed and rubbed some Baume Bengue on my aches. Then she crawled into bed with me. I suppose that if I ever loved her purely it was then, for with her car out front, she was taking a genuine risk on my behalf. We spoke glumly of Buffi, yet not without relief. At the end, I was too tired and too worried about myself and too full of my own misery and the burning of the salve to think of lovemaking. The foretaste of sex with Anita had sustained me when I needed sustaining. The act was beyond me.

The *Star-News* had a big story on it. It was Saturday and a light newsday so there it was eight columns across the front page:

"Austrian Envoy Dead in Bizarre Police Chase."

Not bad for the *Star*. They made it into a sort of tragicomedy: unpredictable millionaire who threw all those wild parties going out to dig up a corpse, no doubt on some foolish bet, and then dying after the police chased him. The story mentioned that one, possibly two, of his friends were with him as witnessed by the two Negroes at the church, and the two shovels in the car. The police were looking for them, but no clues. I thanked God again for the gloves.

Krals recovered the films and dutifully gave them to Anita. The Austrian Embassy had Buffi cremated, and put the urn in Gawler's for an evening. They had a guest-book there, and the old lady sat with her son's ashes all evening. I heard his friends stayed away in droves. No one wanted to be suspected of being his graveyard accomplice. Anita and I were among the many missing.

CHAPTER

15

To the White House

It fell to me to make the final $25,000 payoff to Brendan Doolittle. Krals, queer enough at the best of times, was now completely unpredictable. He had tried to transfer his dependency to Anita, but she wisely had rejected it. The rejection just made him more neurotic.

I meant to destroy the films. But she sat on them like Fafner with the Rheingold. They were her Doomsday machine. I made no issue of them with her for the time being. My own film debut was long since destroyed.

I say the payoff "fell to me." Up to then, I had not actually passed money, although I was so deep in the payoff that if a charge of principal could not be made against me, still I was clearly guilty of five or more years' worth of felonious conspiracy. As our horror at Buffi's death dwindled, I was wrapped up more and more with Anita's political ambitions and with my own. It was imperative that I feel out Brendan to make sure that he was solidly shored up against any revelation of the old Benn City case. Not only Anita's and my career depended on it, but our freedom.

We had heard nothing of Conyers since the White House party. I was almost sure his case was moribund. Yet I also knew that vengeful corseworm was still at work. I worried about tapped telephones, shadows, bugged bedrooms. From a pay booth, I got Brendan Doolittle at his home. He was out of Lewisburg a week.

It was very cloak and dagger, handkerchief over the phone.

"I'm a friend of the friend who helped you with that initial adjustment," I said to the unknown voice and to however many unknown listeners there might be.

"Yeah?" he said cautiously. I was struck by the coarse rasp of his voice. "How do I know it's you?" I had already figured it out.

"Take the first letter of the second word of where you talked to a special friend before." That would be the C in International Club. I could almost feel him thinking it through.

"Okay," he said. "I have it."

"That letter's place in the alphabet: figure it out." That would be three. I gave him a few seconds to think.

"Okay."

"Triple it and add one. That's what time to call me at the number I'm going to give you in the same code."

"Okay."

"Multiply the original number four times: that's the day of the month, to call." That would be the twelfth.

"Okay."

"Now the phone number itself. Ready?"

I used other parts of International Club as a code to give him the number to call us.

"If it's busy, try again. Make sure you call from a pay booth, okay?"

"Okay," he said.

On the night of the call, I met Anita at the International Club. We had Vodka Negronis for kicks. My stomach was upset by the first one, but settled during the third. About five of ten I tied up the booth. Brendan called on the dot at ten.

"How do I know who you are?" he said. I disliked his harshness, the crude construction worker turned corrupt contractor.

"You've got to trust me," I said.

"No, you've got to trust me. Put her on."

I didn't want to, if only because I didn't like to be ordered around by him. But I didn't have any choice.

"Okay," I said. I left the telephone and nodded at her where she sat in the bar. She rose as if she were making an exit from a business conference. I watched her, the black suit, the old octagonal clock still her focal jewelry.

It was just as if she were walking from that hearing room so long ago. She took the telephone.

"How are you?" she said. I took the phone back.

"Enough?" I asked.

"Yep," he said. "I'll never forget that voice."

An angry bolt of jealousy shot through me. I looked at her with fury and she stared back at me curiously.

"Can we mail it?" I asked, knowing how he would answer.

"No," he said. "Not unless you'll make it good if it's lost or grabbed." That meant either he came to us, or we to him, or we met outside either of our towns.

"Okay. Can you shake anybody that might be following you and meet me out of town?"

"Yeah."

We agreed to meet at Duchamps' urinal in the Philadelphia Museum of Art. It was the least likely place I could think of. I had to tell him twice before he finally got it. I have always had a weakness for Surrealism and Dadaism and I didn't think it would do Brendan any harm.

"I'll be wearing a United Givers Fund button in my lapel," I said.

That Friday, I bought a ticket to New York on the Metroliner. At Philadelphia I waited until the last moment, then crept out, and watched the train pull away without any more people stepping off. I, at least, had no tail.

Arriving early at the museum, I sat on a ledge, gloomily watching the ponderous and minute turnings of the Calder mobile. After a few minutes I walked into the world of Dadaism.

Doolittle was already there. I recognized him from Anita's description.

"Great stuff, huh?" I said. He seemed more nervous than I. Doolittle's prison paleness gave a fish-belly sag to his pompano face. Could Anita have gone to bed with that?

"I'm more of a classical guy myself," he said.

"Like who?" I asked.

"Don't shit around with me," he said, suddenly tough. "Where is it?"

"I'll give it to you in the men's room. Listen, she's got a couple of questions first."

"Yeah?" he said, suspicious. His nondescript gray-green eyes went hard as agate. He drew up inside his oversized clothes. "If it's gonna put me back there, the answer is 'no.' I did it for six months, baby, for a lousy hundred grand. I wouldn't do it again for half a million."

Now it was my turn:

"Come off it. If you'd testified against her you'd have missed prison, but you'd have been finished. Just a stool pigeon that nobody'd trust anymore."

He shrugged.

"So what's she want?"

"Does anybody have any idea, I mean any idea at all, about any of this? Your wife?"

"No."

"Has Justice tried to talk with you recently?"

"No. They gave it up while I was in there." He looked pleased, his face reflective. I could feel him reliving tough-guy talks with the agents, the Justice Department lawyers.

"So, it's just you and me and Anita?"

"Right," he said, then fixed me with disgruntled eyes. "You know, lover boy, if you're talking about a setup, I mean having me trucked off because I'm the only one who knows, then you can forget it. I have it arranged so that if I die unnaturally, then there's a 'to be opened' envelope. And that's a threat."

The thought chilled me. After all, we weren't killers. The bastard had a time bomb set for us.

"Suppose you die naturally?"

"Then the lawyer will destroy it."

I had no recourse. I had to trust in him and luck.

"That's a shitty deal," I burst out nevertheless. "You could fuck us all up by getting hit by a car."

"Baby," he said patiently. "The lawyer knows when he's supposed to cut the stuff loose and when he ain't. No damn bells are going to ring if some drunk runs me over."

Brendan was proud of his counsel, and his counsel's clients.

"Every big hood in this state is alive because of that guy. If one big boy hits another, he knows the message gets sent out. Those little sealed envelopes are life insurance. Mine, too. So stop worrying."

I turned the money over to him in the men's room. While I stood urinating, he counted the money in a stall.

He came out and nodded, a small, brave, and venal little man in a suit too big for him.

"If you have to call me again," he said, "use the letter D as the takeoff point. 'D' for Doo-champs."

Harry Frieden called me in late January to say he had a place for me in the White House. If I passed muster in an interview with the President, I would start to work as soon as I could wrap things up at Labor.

To my joy, Frieden said I would be working under Wo-eckle, who had been at the White House now about six months. Like me, he had been jarred from his cubbyhole, a decent man reborn into new power at the end of his life. Power! My heart sang with it.

A few days later, I met Frieden in his Executive Office Building suite. He was busy, glad to see me, and eager to get me introduced to the President so he could get back to work. We walked across West Executive Drive and in through the West Wing.

The President was having coffee in the big oval office. I skirted the Presidential seal on the floor and gave the florid-faced man a hearty grip.

"Sugar and cream?" he asked and buzzed us in some coffee. Harry was more businesslike than was his wont. I could see why Washington thought of this as a no-horse-shit administration.

"I want to get right back to work on the oceanographic meeting at noon, Mr. President, if that's all right?"

"Fine, Harry," he said. The bass growl, so familiar, that I had heard personally only at that brief supper earlier in the winter, did thrill me. Wasn't it natural to be awed in the office of the man who could push a button and destroy the world?

"The Vice President thinks highly of you, Mr. Dobeck-er. He wants you to be his liaison man here," he smiled. There was a rush of warmth in me as he turned on that smile: the big daddy smile, the chairman of the board announcing an increased dividend.

"See," it seemed to say, "I'm already trusting you. We haven't even announced I want to step down next year, have we, and here . . ."

He turned off the charm and got down to the business at hand.

"One question: why so long in the Labor counsel's office?"

My palms began to sweat. I would have thought he'd have checked with Woeckle on that. He probably had. Frieden had told me, though, that the President always obtained his own resumé on prospective aides. I hoped he had gotten my grades at Lehigh.

"It was an interesting job. I had a good boss . . . Mr. Woeckle, you know. And I guess my ambitions just took hold a little later than some others." I felt craven.

"And . . ."

"And the Secretary was looking for someone to help out Mrs. Tockbridge, so . . ."

"A sort of tide in the affairs of men thing, huh, a light under the bushel," said my interrogator.

"The switch wasn't that dramatic," I said. "But I've liked it. Even the sixteen-hour days."

He laughed.

"Well, it'll be all of that around here."

I wanted to kiss big daddy. I was in.

"I'm rather humbled by all this," I said honestly. He did not see my unworthiness, did not see I was a hypocrite, a criminal. He was trusting a man I was not.

"Well," he said, "you will learn our ways." Almost nostalgically, he added, "Although Harry will have his own ways as I had mine when I came here." Quickly, the decisiveness clicked on again. "I'll be seeing a good deal of you. We'll want to get you in here as fast as Labor will let you go."

I thought it was all over and began to screw up my face for an impressed but strong departure. But there was something else.

"There's not going to be anything in that divorce that will hurt the office, is there?" A less wise man than he would have hastily added, "I'm sure there isn't," to let me off the hook. The President simply waited my answer.

"It was a bad time, sir." It was easy to show candor on this small mote in the rotten eye of my past. "The divorce was uncontested. The grounds were separation. My wife married the man in the case. I gave up our daughter and continued to pay support." I sighed. A momentary picture of the little girl, listening at the zoo as I tried to explain the reticulation of the giraffe, came to mind. Then I thought of Ems. "If there are other details necessary," I said, "They can be provided."

"No," he said. I had the feeling he already had them. The thought made me sick. If he had them, why not the hints that Conyers had developed? But, of course, Conyers was not that way. He would rather let me get the job, then explode me out of it. The higher Anita and I rose, the more satisfying our destruction.

"Anything else I ought to know?" he said. No wonder the nation thought of him as a father. He was a walking candy cane and birch stick combined.

A vision of Anita squatting at the obscene Black Mass came to me. Oh, what a tale I could tell, I thought, seeing in my mind's eye the Vice President in the movies.

"Well, I wouldn't say I've been more of an angel than most men, Mr. President," I said. A man's man. Had I carried it off? What was the President thinking of? Walter Jenkins, Sherman Adams?

"Fine," he said. "I suppose I should leave that sort of question to the security check. But I'm old-fashioned in some ways. I like to see how people react."

He had irritated me and I wasn't going to leave it quite at that.

"So how did I react?" I asked with a smile, polite but direct.

"You pass," he said rising. "I'm glad to have a six-teen-hour man aboard."

There it was: the red face, neck wrinkly above the buttonless collar and figured tie, the eyes quick as a big-time banker's. My new boss.

I would work hard for the President. Harry Frieden was a sort of governmental co-conspirator. I knew too much to really respect him. But not this one. This one I feared. He had been as bad as any Republican fat-cat politician in his day. But the Presidency had burned out a lot of the impurities.

I left his office feeling euphoric and slipped out the South Gate. Anita was off on a speech. I called her long distance as soon as I had crossed the Ellipse to our offices.

It was a parting for us, I knew. But the thought of the job was too exhilarating at the moment for me to consider what it would do to her. Not she.

"Is it final?" she said tensely.

"I'm sorry, Anita," I said, fearful now not so much that she would be angry at me, but that she might try to queer it.

"Goddamnit," she almost cried. "I knew that Harry was going to, but he said he'd wait . . ."

"He did for a while. Besides, I'll only be working over there sixteen hours a day," I said. "The rest of my time is all yours."

"Very funny."

Our love, or whatever it was, was woven in with our criminal conspiracy. When we were not wallowing in our fears, we were rolling in bed, a kind of loving. But it was a loving that was based on our seeing each other daily.

At home that night, for the first time in weeks, I went to Athanor. With a moist cloth I rubbed the dust from the furnace's shiny brick sides. I had never fired it up with gold and mercury. Susan and I had never executed my old formula to "envision the pelican," as Buffi and the alchemists described it. I had made it to the big time, but I missed her. Outside the window, it was snowing, the big onion flakes flurrying around the streetlight like moths.

Upstairs, I popped a split of sparkling Burgundy and drank it with a toasted ham sandwich. *Turandot* was on the stereo. Outside, the snow had covered everything and was still sifting down. The wine was soft, too sweet.

"Nessun dorma!" sang the voices from afar, somewhere way out beyond the snows, in an Italianate Cathay. "Nessun dorma!"

For my first week in the new job, I was insecure. Familiarity washed out the fears. I saw how many details went untended, how many decisions were made on expediency and were then covered up with statements about "after weeks of study" and how many pure goofs went unrectified simply because the White House was no more efficient than a factory or a kitchen.

My purpose from Frieden's point of view was to learn the workings of the White House the better to serve him in the future. My classroom was Bertie Woeckle. With my talent for wrapping up minor problems, I was helpful to the former solicitor. Forced now to make policy decisions, the fat old man heaved up sighs of apparent resignation, then blossomed forth with wisdom and acuity. While he worried and mumbled over policy, I drew up lists of labor leaders, for example, who could be browbeaten into accepting the White House's workmen's compensation amendments.

Using such a roster, Woeckle ran down the names with his thick finger, jotting on yellow foolscap a smaller list of labor men actually to meet with the President.

We spent no more than five minutes on these matters with the President. Woeckle put the case succinctly.

"Martin and I have twenty-four possibilities for your meeting. We think it ought to cook down to no more than eight." Woeckle handed him the twenty-four names. "When you finish, Mr. President, we have a decision for you to make." The old caution was still in Woeckle's voice, but the words were crisper.

The President raced down the list, then looked up, sharp eyes waiting above the pouched skin for Woeckle's question. Woeckle put it to the President with the same sort of diffidence he had shown me just before I left his office for Anita.

"Martin thinks the Ironworkers can be cut out, letting the Steelworkers cover them because of their community of interests. I think they ought to be included because Mihalik was left out of the last meeting, on minimum wage, and is feeling very feisty about it." He sighed. "The best argument against my view is that if we cut out the Ironworkers, we can have one more smaller union, to keep the little fellows from smarting too much."

Woeckle's arguments, fairly stated, won. Sometimes, when he was more sure of himself on an issue, he would overrule me himself, generally with a long explanation. Working again for this decent man was like drinking spring water after trying to quench my thirst with Marsala all' uovo.

The sixteen-hour day was no exaggeration. When I finished my work, as often as not I called a White House car to rush me to the Vice President's Senate office. There, either he or a staffer would brief me on what "input" they wanted with the President on labor matters, health, education and welfare, or even commerce.

Sometimes, the car would whisk me once more to that turreted fieldstone house in Wesley Heights. I had come to like Frieden's withdrawn wife. Perhaps in me she saw and liked some shred of the timidity that persevered from my *Labor Notes* days. She made a point of fixing me a bourbon and water herself before the sessions with Frieden began. Oddly, I found her delicately sexy, and it may be that my small, incipient lust was not unflattering to her, married as she was to an overaged line-cracker.

With Frieden, he too already tired from a long day, it was all business on such evenings. Yet, he trusted me with feelings about the President that jarred and unnerved me.

"Goddamn Vernon," he fumed, pouring over some sheaf of paper with the White House seal. "He's dragging his ass on the water problem in California again. He thinks I don't know it's because of the banks. Goddamnit, Martin, any politician that would suck up to the banks in California would cornhole the national bird. He could *lose* me California on water. Now, get that across to his staff, okay? You know, but with your fine Italian hand, or whatever in the hell race Dobecker is."

"German," I told the Golden Jew with a smile. "On my father's side only." And he would bang the desk, smile himself and say, "Ah, you sly son of a bitch. Well, get him going on water, okay."

And next day I would laboriously draft a memo for Harry to sign on the 160-acre land limitation, water rights, river trespass, Indian treaty waters, and water tables in the western United States—including California.

Frieden made certain that I was at the Cabinet meetings so we could compare impressions later.

In the sunlit room, I sat back against the wall with the other staff assistants, away from the Cabinet table. Behind the gray heads at the table, the White House south lawn stretched snow white and perfect out to the Ellipse and beyond to the thick shaft of the Monument.

We were, in that room, the board of directors and officers of the nation. And I was acutely aware of it. When, in the minimum wage session, I heard the Labor Secretary accept the Vice President's view that we should demand a 25-cent increase instead of 20 cents, I knew it had been my arguments to Frieden and his to the President that had determined the issue. So in two years, the poorest workers would get $10 more a week instead of $8, and $520 a year more instead of $416. Yet some workers would be fired because the $10 was more than the employer would meet. Federal wage cases would be prosecuted, be decided by appellate courts. Debate would bubble on the Hill—through Frieden, I had done it all! I was mad with delight.

But my successes were indirect. I longed to sit in the seat of power, not just to recommend. That, I knew, was the disease that newspapers, only sensing its virulence, called Potomac Fever.

Often now, I actually held and used the power of the Vice President. Pressing the White House budget hopes with old Joe McFadden of House Appropriations, I could feel his antique and canny mind worrying over what the budget would mean to Kansas, the Midwest, and the nation, in that order. McFadden did not dare to buck me, representing Frieden as I did, and because McFadden heeded me, the lesser committee members deferred to me. Ah, that was champagne.

They all knew, and softly, softly, I drove the point home that now I spoke for the Vice President on whether great buckets of federal money would eventually go to their districts, or whether they would get only cheap, dry promises under President Harry Frieden. There were other emoluments.

The heads of minor agencies sought me out. What did I think about a less liberal replacement for Alvin Robertson on the Federal Trade Commission? Why was the budget being cut 10 percent at the Interstate Commerce Commission, but not at all for Federal Aviation. Couldn't I put a call into the Budget Bureau and find out?

Even Vernon MacGregor himself called me in from time to time when Frieden was temporarily out of pocket.

"Martin," he might ask me, "did Harry personally see the third paragraph of that memo on water problems? I think it's too damned strong, as stated, but if he wants it badly enough, I'll send it along that way to Interior and EPA."

Then, still nervously, I would answer him straight, "Yes, sir. That's his personal rewrite job on my draft." MacGregor would grunt, give me a friendly smile, and initial the memo that would change the water distribution for a million square miles in the West.

The controlled excitement of power was like nothing else, except sex. It was less explosive than lovemaking, but headier, more awesome, more kinetic and long-lasting. And I was at my pinnacle. As the days went on, I imagined myself under President Frieden and Vice President Tockbridge as one of history's youngest Labor Secretaries. But, cautious, I planned a cautious game, minding modest ways and gradually working at labor and other policies to assure Frieden the votes he needed for election in eighteen months.

Once, at Anita's, when I came to her past midnight from the White House, I asked her for the films. Because they were a danger to Frieden, they endangered my career, too. Now, Anita could drown without it touching me or the Vice President.

Anita was wrapped in an old robe, striped like a Joseph's coat, and turned from me to the window.

"You won't need the films," I told her. "You can't really use them to *do* anything with, only to *undo* things. I mean you can't use them to get the nomination, so they don't have any leverage."

"Oh, Martin," she said with annoyance.

"Look, you've already got the Labor Secretaryship sewed up, believe me."

"How do you know?"

I laughed. It was a change for me to be closer to the inside workings than she.

"Because the Secretary is leaving in a couple of months, a half year at most, and nobody over there is talking about who should get the job. We know it's been settled between the President and Harry."

"Yes, but how do you know it's me?"

"Don't ask. Trust your lawyer." Woeckle had told me, certain, if distressed, by his information. He was never wrong on such matters. "I'm guessing Conyers can't make his case," I added.

She sat down in an easy chair and sighed. The prospects of the Cabinet post should have thrilled her.

"I feel crummy ever since Buffi died," she said. "I miss him."

"What does that have to do with the films?"

"They're insurance," she said.

"Come on, Anita, You can't use them without ruining yourself. With Buffi alive, you could have risked them. He'd have taken care of you. Let's get rid of them. If they ever get loose, you know, a safety deposit box search or robbery or something, they'd mess up everything, including you."

"You mean they'd mess *you* up," she said finally.

"They'd wipe out your sponsors, me and Harry. Except that you don't really need me anymore, do you?"

"Poor waif," I said, sarcastic.

"No," she went on with asperity now, "you've got yourself fixed up there with Frieden and Woeckle and the President and I'm down on Constitution Avenue wondering what the hell is going on."

"I tell you everything," I said. I took her in my arms. But she broke to light a cigarette.

"No. If I let you burn the films, there goes my insurance or whatever you want to call it. It may seem like dirty work to lily whites like you."

I did not like being made to feel the Puritan.

"I'm bored," she said quietly, knowing it would hurt me. "Sometimes you bore me."

I shrugged, angry, and wheeled to the chair to get my overcoat.

"Find somebody who doesn't," I said. There would be plenty of women I could date now, if only I had time. "*You* don't bore *me*," I said, to make up for my guilt at the sudden thought of leaving her. "Only when you act like a fool."

She came over to me as I buttoned my coat.

"Look, I won't let you have them," she said calmly. "I've given in to you before. Now just let me have my way on this, please." She began to undo the coat buttons. It would be cold driving the Morgan across town at 1:00 A.M. So I stayed.

More and more it was like that, flare-ups that we mutually squelched, not so much out of regard for each other, but because we were aware of the vacuum that severance would leave in our lives. That night, after we had made love, I lay awake for a few minutes, thinking how our liaison restricted me. Why didn't I let it dry up and blow away. The Conyers thing seemed to have passed. That gone, no demand except my lust kept us together.

She had, in a sense, been my Mephistopheles. She had provided a taste of power and then helped me to make a meal of it.

But I no longer needed her much, now. An ingrate, I was like the rest of Washington. Except that perhaps the disloyalty lay a little heavier on my head.

We saw each other less frequently after our argument over the films. I began to imagine other women—not

Susan, but rather some affairs simple and without intensity. I wanted a diversion that would not hinder my work at the White House or diminish the almost sexual thrill that I felt in the rhythms of those high places.

On a Thursday night, at about nine, Anita called me at home. I was so far removed now from the weird old world of Buffi that what she told me made me think she had gone mad, that her breakup at Labor had exploded again in some psychotic and surrealistic way.

"Krals is trapped in the Capitol," she said.

"Huh?"

"Martin, he's in the Capitol!" she nearly screamed. "He attacked some secretary in the hall of the Old House Office Building . . ."

"What? Krals?"

"Will you listen?" she pleaded. "He's been funny ever since Buffi died. He went up there in his goddamned skin."

"The human skin?" Now I was screaming.

"He tried to bite her."

I still couldn't believe it.

"The girl got away," Anita was going on now. Well, it was true. "He called me from some office he broke into. He's got control of himself. I mean he sounds like he has. He knows the police must be all over, looking for him."

"The girl?"

"He tried to bite her, I told you."

"Oh, Jesus . . ."

"He's afraid he bruised her throat . . ."

"Unh!"

"Can you . . . ?"

"No, for Christ's sake. Let them catch him. They'll put the crazy son of a bitch away. He needs it."

"Martin!" she exploded. "He could finish me, us. Benn City. And the films. Everything!"

"He'd never tell." I felt the sweat run into my palms and looked at them. A shiny streamlet was in each palm line.

She was calmer again:

"They'll get him over to Saint Elizabeth's and he'll talk to some damned psychiatrist, some government psychiatrist. They testify, you know. They testify, you know, about the patients."

"They'd think he was crazy." But I knew it was easy enough for a doctor to tell when a clear cut hot-and-cold psychotic like Krals was being rational. "What the hell could I do?" I whined.

She knew I was wavering.

"Well, damn it, it's about time," she said.

I would be risking everything: my new job. Everything! But if Krals were caught . . .

"He left his clothes in a men's room before he attacked the girl. All he has on is his skin. I mean the dried one. He needs clothes to get out."

I was incredulous. It was fantastic.

"Christ, Anita. They won't let me in there if they've got a madman loose in the building." Now I was wasting time. If he were caught, I thought again, she was right, we'd be cooked. As a White House aide and sometime assistant to the Vice President I had every right to be in Frieden's Senate office, any time, day or night.

"What room is he in?"

"The upholstery shop." I thought a moment. Would that be in the New Senate Office Building? "How'd he get over to the Senate side?"

"He worked on the East Front sculpture, remember? The whole basement is tunnels, he says. You just have to find him and give him some clothes."

I balked again. How great was the danger of his telling? Plenty, I thought. He had no love for me. He might even lay Anita's part in bribing Brendan Doolittle on me. And the movies: Good God! Krals was head camera man in that little film festival.

"This could finish me," I said lamely.

"So could letting him get caught."

"*Arrgh.* If he calls, tell him I'm on my way. Try to make sure if he *does* get caught that he shuts up, Anita. Please, sweetie," I pleaded.

The Keystone Cops at the Capitol were almost totally untrained, most of them either political sub-hacks or college kids picking up change while they went to school. I would explain I'd been called away from a party to draw up some material for the Vice President. I had my Secret Service pass and the key to Harry's office.

The night was bitterly cold. The damned Morgan didn't want to start at first. In my attaché case was a shirt, a tie, socks and black sneakers, the only shoes that would fit in it. I wore two pairs of pants. Also I had a razor.

I turned off Massachusetts Avenue and sputtered toward the brilliantly lighted dome of the Capitol. I would first go up to Harry's offices on the fifth floor in case some wise cop checked the elevator lights. Then I would creep down the stairs to the basement.

In front of New Senate two police cars were parked. A Fifth Precinct cop stared at me suspiciously as I opened the big bronze doors with the bas-reliefs that look like Bobby and Teddy Kennedy even though they were built before either of them ever got to the Senate. Inside, three Capitol police were standing, looking nervous rather than suspicious.

"What can we do for you, sir?" said the corporal among them uneasily. Obsequiousness sits heavily on that low forehead, I thought.

"What's going on here, the police outside?" I asked with verve, despite my fear that my running palms would streak the attaché case. "I'm from the Vice President's office," I added with a touch of scorn, digging for my pass.

The three shuffled into attitudes of sorry militariness.

"A secretary, sir. Some ape jumped her in the Cannon Building."

"Rape? A Negro?" I said with suitable outrage.

"No, sir," said the corporal. "A white man, I didn't mean . . ."

"Inside the Capitol buildings? My God!"

They looked intimidated. I thought they were going to explain where they had been at the time of the crime.

"Yes, sir."

"What happened?"

"He bit her throat. Some weirdo. He had his clothes off. Choked her unconscious." Crazy Krals, I thought.

"Did you catch him?"

"No, sir. He must've run out. They've got a citywide alarm."

"I've got some work to do." I showed the corporal my pass. "Say, I wonder if you'd keep an eye on my car. Across the street. Just a quick look or two, huh?"

"Yes, sir."

"Any chance he's over here on the Senate side?" I asked.

"No, sir."

I kept my hands steady as I gripped the pen and signed in.

"I'll be upstairs, or over at the Capitol office for a few minutes. Call me, huh, if you catch the guy." I feared my lips would turn to blubbering fat from fear. "The Vice President might hear about it and I'd like to reassure him."

The three police bobbed their heads. They understood the principle of answerability to patrons, total accountability and total subservience. Inside the elevator, I leaned my head against its cool metal wall, waiting for the weakness to leave me. My plan was to let the guards think I was working in the Vice Presidential suite in this New Senate Office Building, but to sneak Krals over to Frieden's smaller Capitol office which was closer to all the Capitol's secluded exits onto the grounds.

I turned on the lights in his suite, then crept down the hall to the stairwell and descended. I reached the basement and made my way through the empty halls to the wooden door of the upholstery shop. Its latch was ripped loose from the wood of the doorjamb.

I paused, my heart beating in my ears. Were those voices behind me?

"Krals," I hissed frantically through the vents in the bottom of the door. He popped it open a crack and I spotted those wild, crazed eyes in the rotting face. When he saw me, the tears gushed up and he sobbed.

"Krals, they're down the hall. Come on."

"Clothes," he whined. "I left them . . ."

"Shut up, Herbert. They're coming! I've got clothes. I've got a place for you to dress. Come on!"

He slipped out into the hall. Frightened as I was, it was a shock, the anguished face atop those powerful shoulders. His gut, a corpse gray, hung down almost to his loins.

The maniac still wore the nauseating hide. Its hideous lank locks spilled on his shoulder, and the arms were tied around his neck. It hung down his back, a parchment-thin caveman mounting him in buggery.

"Throw it away," I whispered as we walked down the hall, me on tiptoe.

"No," he grunted back.

"You asshole!" I said to him angrily.

The mania sprang into his eyes like an electric spark.

"I'm cold, give me your coat!"

"Fuck you," I hissed, hating him for everything.

We walked down the hall and ducked around the corner, I in my executive garb, attaché case in hand, he in the grisly costume that had failed him in his try at metamorphosis.

At a "Stairs Up, Stairs Down" sign, I opened the door. A blast of heat and a steady rumbling noise rushed up the steps. We crept down. The Senate, so meticulously maintained for public eyes, became its true self at subbasement level.

The creamy plastering gave way to whitewashed cinder block as the stairway narrowed. Krals, his heavy hams rising and falling—I had never realized how ugly a man's ass was compared to a woman's—stepped briskly.

The subbasement seemed to stretch endlessly. We half ran toward the Capitol and the safety of Harry's office.

The basement stank of mucilage and dusty debris. We hurried on past old file cases, their keys dangling from pull handles.

At another turning, I strained to hear. Back there, past an underground desert of broken door frames leaning against the wall, there were human voices. The huge heating fans near us all but drowned them out.

"Let's go," urged Krals. He began to jog, padding on his spatulate feet. Suddenly behind us I heard a yell.

"Hey—aayyy-aaayy-aaay."

I broke into a run, my shoes ringing on the cement floor. I looked back. There was no one behind us except our long, spastic shadows.

We rushed on past the smell of wet concrete where a wall was being patched. Behind us now were the calls of more than one voice.

"Oh, my God," I said. This was it. We were caught.

Krals banged open an "exit" door and we rattled up metal stairs and into another hallway. It was the familiar world of the building's basement down the hall from the restaurant kitchen. Once past that, we would be close to the subway tunnel leading to the Capitol.

I raced behind Krals now. Suddenly a woman came through the swinging door from the kitchen. Even as she shrieked, Krals shoved her backwards and the door swung in with her weight. I dashed past, seeing inside for an instant the shocked face of a chef, whose hat was like long white hair on end.

We burst into the restaurant-cafeteria, fully lighted but

empty, chairs on tables. The mirrors reflected Krals'
churning arms and desperately frightened face. My own
reflection seemed sleek as a bird's.

Ahead were the heavy glass doors with black letters at
the top, "Subway Cars to the Capitol." They sprang open
as Krals heaved into them. I heard only the rasp of my
throat, pouring down air.

Krals ran full speed along the walkway beside the
tracks, the human skin flapping out behind. I was having
a hard time keeping up.

The lights in the tunnel were dim. Yet it could be a
trap if someone had phoned ahead. The guards could
block off the Capitol end of the tunnel and the fork back
to the Old Senate Office Building and trap us like rabbits
in a hollow log. Panic pumped in me. I passed the gasping
Krals.

A wild clanging echoed in the subterranean tube. Someone had pushed the call bell hoping to get a policeman at
the other end to cut off our flight. Krals' face was so red
now that I thought he was going to collapse.

"Come on, Krals," I gasped. We were scarcely a hundred yards from the steps that led up to safety in the in-
nards of the Capitol, the beehive of hiding places that
the tourist never saw.

Suddenly, the lights flared. The bells were still clanging wildly, but above them I heard the pulsing roar of the
subway car motors coming to life. They were going to
hunt us down on wheels. Krals lurched to a column for
support and began to vomit.

I was ten yards past him now. I could save myself. Unless someone had seen me behind Krals.

"Come on," I growled back at him. Christ, I hated him,
hated him for getting us into this mess. The steps were
just ahead.

He was erect now and running again. He went down
on one knee then rushed toward the steps again, a lunatic
in two human skins.

Behind him, the subway car was gathering speed. Krals
looked back. He clutched his naked breast and staggered
on.

"Krals!"

I was at the top of the steps. He looked back as the car
rounded the corner. In its front seat were two of the

Capitol cops. One of them wrestled his pistol into a steady aim at Krals.

Murderer! I thought. Poor Krals!

The gun roar filled the tunnel. Krals stumbled but ran on. The shot had missed. He rushed up the stairs, out of the bright light and into the Capitol basement.

We ran into an elevator foyer that opened on the oldest part of the Capitol, its original foundations. Another shot shattered the glass doors behind us.

The police were too close behind for us to go directly to the Vice President's office. I jabbed the third floor button of the "Senators Only" elevator. If our pursuers saw where the elevator was they would think we had fled upstairs. It would give us vital moments.

I grabbed Krals' sweaty arm and pulled him toward one of the narrow corridors. We ran past the immense stones of the ancient foundation.

I swung open a door. The room reeked of decaying firewood thrown haphazardly. Could we hide there? We jogged on, too fatigued to run anymore. The close air filled my throat. The passageway sloped upward.

In front of us was a door, a loading port for trucks. It was glass and cross-hatched with wires and it led to the outside. We rushed to it, but it was locked. We could break the door and be out onto the Capitol grounds, but police would be all around this part of the building.

"Krals," I commanded. "Break open the door."

Without asking why, he hurled his bulk against the wood. It did not give.

"Smash the window," I said. "There," I pointed to an overturned desk chair. He looked at me curiously.

"Break it! We'll make them think you've broken out of here, they'll quit looking inside," I said. He slammed the chair a half-dozen times through the pane. The clattering sounded like construction work.

"Hurry, for Christ's sake," I hissed. He finished finally and looked at me.

"You've got to put that goddamned skin outside, like you got rid of it. You've got to, Herbert! The cops back there know you had something around your neck. The girl and the woman in the cafeteria probably saw it too. If you throw the damned thing outside, they'll believe you've left the building."

I looked to see if his mad stare would replace this one of slightly bewildered trust.

"You've got to do it, to save yourself. To save us," I said, shaking his arm.

He slipped the crinkled arms from around his neck and gave me the skin.

The thing was slimy with his sweat. I felt sick touching it. I stepped up to the chill of the window.

I hooked the mouth hole onto a jagged edge of the window. I tore the skin, then let it dangle on the outside of the door as if it had been caught on the glass and been deserted.

Krals grimaced in agony. I dragged him down another corridor. Under the rotunda we went up a flight of stairs. I knew where we were now. We darted past the old first Senate Chamber, up a queer circular staircase. Then we were there: on the second floor, the small reception office of the Vice President, a few feet from the Senate chamber.

Poor Krals collapsed on the floor, his body running sweat. I fell into the Vice President's chair. I tried to think of how we could get from here to my car, or to where we could get a taxi. But there was nothing we could do until morning. My mind swung between panic and exhaustion.

On the floor, Krals snored. I waited in terror for a knock on the door.

After a while my anxiety eased to a dull gnaw and I called Anita. In the morning, I said, I would try to get us out.

Krals awoke about 6:00 A.M. and I made him shave. The shirt and pants were too tight on his barrel body. But with my coat and shoes, we should be able to mingle with the arriving secretaries.

We plotted our departure—at 8:30, before the Vice President's staff would be here. Thank God I knew their habits. When I had Krals looking as human as possible, I talked to him seriously.

"Herbert, you've got to go back to Austria. The FBI will get you if you don't. Fingerprints or something." He was controlled now.

"What the hell got into you?" I asked him.

But he only shook his head, lost in gloom. I imagined him bolting down the aconite, cinquefoil, and God knows what they were supposed to use to become werewolves. The miracle was that he hadn't killed the girl.

We pulled off the escape from the building without any trouble. I walked with him to his car which, thank God, he had parked six blocks away.

"What shall I do?" he asked me, all the hate gone now in remorse.

"Go back to Lisel and start packing to go home to Austria."

Krals began to cry.

"I love it here."

"It's no place for werewolves, Herbert. If they catch you, you'll be in jail for the rest of your life."

He reached sorrowfully for the door handle.

"Look, Herbert. I can tell you that Buffi would rather have you go home." I paused for a moment, then added with a crocodile-tear catch in my voice. "That's where he is now. That's where he would want you."

I called Anita from a pay phone. I could hear the gratitude begin to come into her voice. But I was too tired to enjoy Lady Guinevere's compliments.

"Look," I said, "just get Lisel and Krals to go to Austria. Make that your project for the day."

The *Post* had the story on the front page, but it lost some prominence through the coincidence of a Presidential announcement on the second-generation Antiballistic Missile Program.

There was no hint in the article of an accomplice. How many times, I wondered, before we got caught? I fell on my bed without brushing my teeth, dreaming of blacks and whites with machine guns.

Awaking a few hours later, I did some calisthenics from a tattered old Kennedy administration booklet and then went down to Athanor. I whisked off the dust with the calisthenics booklet. Someday, if the work would ease up, if I could slough off Anita, I could purge my spirit of the sicknesses of Buffi, of Krals, of the Vice President. If, if, if that life would pause even, then I could come back. The heating-unit system made the basement warm. I thought of that day with Susan on the floor.

If she came back, we would make a day of it, drinking champagne, laughing, firing my creation. And when our Philosopher's Stone turned out to be only an off hydrate of gold of some coarseness, then so what?

My joy would be in doing the dance steps right. In mere adherence to form, there was sweetness. I longed for order, Susan represented it.

The Krals incident pushed me into dread. There were so many more clues now for Conyers to find if he were still looking. I brooded over the ways he could discover me and destroy me. He might exhume Tapir and find the hypo mark in Tapir's old embalmed butt. Could he not get my fingerprints from Buffi's cellar chapel and find a trace of the Spanish fly in his ciborium-safe? Had I left a print on the backboard of Anita's bed, or on Buffi's car, or in the monastery's catacomb chapel? What about telephone taps and electronic bugs? Did he have a voice print from my call to Doolittle in Benn City? Or had someone seen me with him in the Duchamps room? Suppose Conyers noted that I had signed into the Senate Office Building on the night of the Krals attack? I knew I was verging on the paranoid.

I had reached forty-seven specific instances where Conyers might have found me out when I felt the wings of panic fluttering over me and I knew I must talk with someone or else take up with a psychiatrist. I called Anita and talked it out with her. It did not tempt us together, but it partially shrove me.

"You're getting like Lady Macbeth," she ended, with one of her rare literary allusions. It wiped out much of the therapy.

CHAPTER

16

Susan

Susan called me at home one night in late February. Her voice was crisp, polite and steady as it had been in those halcyon days when I was wooing her. For a moment my pleasure at hearing her voice overlaid my certain knowledge that there was trouble—and not just for her but for me or Anita.

She broke into my quick questioning of where she was and how she was.

"Roger's men, FBI agents, were by this afternoon." Then she paused. "I wonder if it's okay for me to talk, I mean tapping and all."

My breath boiled out in terror. Conyers was reopening the case! My fears had been real then. Of course she was right. The fear of bugging was no longer mere paranoia.

"I don't know." I started to figure out a page in a book she would remember, to give us a starting point for a code we could converse by. But she was going on.

"It doesn't matter. I have to come to Washington. They want me before a grand jury."

My temple ached with the shock. I thought I was suffering a stroke. Suddenly I felt as I had in all my great anxieties of the past—that I had to urinate.

"Susan," I breathed finally. "What did they say?" A grand jury! They never went to the grand jury until the preliminary investigation showed some kind of criminality.

264

Whose? Mine? Susan's? Anita's? or what combination of the three of us?

"They want me to testify tomorrow."

"Where can I meet you?"

"They're taking me there direct from the train." God-damnit! Conyers must have something. He was rushing her right past me, wanting to make sure she had no time to consider a strategy. And if I did try to talk with her the morning before she testified, wouldn't it get me too close to trying to influence a witness? But her voice had strengthened. She was pleased I had wanted to meet her. Had she really thought I was bastard enough to let her go through it all alone?

"We'll have lunch," I said. "After you testify. Okay?" I could safely talk to her then. And she could tell me what they had asked. "Now, what's happened so far?"

The two FBI men had watched her come home from her marketing, she said. They knocked on the door only a few minutes afterward. They had gotten right to it, both young and quick agents from Villanova or Fordham, I'd bet.

She'd noted their names and I would check them out, of course. They said they were on a construction case in Benn City and wanted her help. Some papers were missing, papers they thought had gone to Mrs. Tockbridge's office when Susan was secretary. The ruse was too obvious. Susan had known what they were up to. They wanted to prove the papers had been destroyed.

"So I told them I had never gotten the papers, never had them," she told me. I started. A lie! She never should have lied, just "forgotten."

They kept pressing her. Hadn't she gotten some papers about a contract from the procurement offices at HEW?

No, she said, she hadn't.

You shouldn't have lied, I said again to myself. Why couldn't she have said, "I just can't remember." That's what kept Jimmy Hoffa out of trouble so long.

I thought it out. Was she stuck with the denial, or could she say now, well, I can't remember whether I got any papers.

I asked whether there was anyone who could prove she saw them, who could testify to it, besides Anita. She thought not. Well, did she want to stick to her story—I did not say "continue to lie"—or could she belatedly and conveniently forget? She wished now she had not said she hadn't seen them, but now that she had, telling the second lie, saying she forgot, would give Justice an airtight case against her of making a false official statement, a felony.

"That's still a helluva lot less serious than perjury," I said.

"I know," she said worriedly. "But maybe . . ."

We turned it over and over, but I could think of no advice to give her, or at least none that would not later incriminate her in further lies, and me for obstructing justice.

"Listen," I said. "This sounds nuts. But I'll be glad to see you. I wish . . ."

She interrupted.

"Before you hang up," her words were coming nervously again. "There's something else. It isn't your problem. Really, I had adjusted to it and reasoned it out." Her voice was terribly tense now. "I had planned for you not to know."

Well, shit, I thought. He whom the Gods would destroy. And yet, in that split second before she told me what I had already divined, it all seemed logical. If Conyers were out to cold-cock me, at least there was a justice in having physical evidence before me of Conyers' cuckoldry.

It never occurred to ask whether the child was mine.

"Jesus," I said. "Well, we'll have something to talk about on that, too."

"I hadn't wanted to tell you," she repeated. How precisely in these crises do we say the clichés we are expected to say. Annunciation! I stammered:

"Listen, I don't feel bad about it. I mean, I'm sorry, but . . . Look, does it seem too crazy that I don't feel bad about it?"

"No," she said, waiting.

"Maybe we can talk about marriage?" I didn't want to marry Susan, or anyone right now. My hesitation must have given me away. She knew me well.

"No, I don't think so," she said. "I've worked that out in my mind too."

"You're feeling all right?" Ah, how maudlin.

"Fine. It's been easier, I mean physically, than with Ems."

I thought of that beautiful little girl.

"Will it work out with Ems?"

"Yes, I think so." She was talking fast again, but less nervously. "In a small town these things work out easier. I'm a local girl who went to the big city and got pregnant. That kind of story is part of the folklore of Myerstown. The sort of thing they expect. So there's the whispering for a little while. Then it's filed away and forgiven, if that's the word. Look, I'll tell you about it when I get there."

But I didn't want now to break off the call with her. Some of the old tolerance between us was returning. And she was all there was between me and the anxious thought of the grand jury.

"And your mother? What does she think?" I asked.

"Ah, my mother. She has made a very big thing of forgiving."

"I never liked her." It was easy now that we were talking about her mother.

"She'd rather have me pregnant than married to you." She stopped as I remembered her doing so often when she had something important to announce and wanted to be sure she said it just right.

"I may be getting married."

The shock dismayed me. It was, after all, my baby.

"Oh?" My disappointment must have shown. She laughed with more humor than warmth.

"From Reading. He knew me when we were in school. He's a widower, a doctor."

"Ah," I said.

"Yes, we small-town Catholics have gotten very liberal about marrying fallen women. He's Catholic."

"And he has . . ."

"Four kids."

"That was all fast enough," I said. It hurt that she could have consorted in such haste with a man of substance.

"Well, if it makes you feel any better, it was rebound."

"Yes," I said.

"Oh, come on," she said. "You want everything, Martin. You want me to say you were my grand amour, and so you were, and look where it got us . . . got me, rather."

"It's getting you married."

We said goodnight, both worrying again about the

grand jury, but I felt she had stirred some old warm mix.
Lust? Some of it, but also in me a protective outrage at
those FBI men boring in on her, and she so pregnant—
with my child.

There was no one to talk with now but Anita. I called,
but then remembered she was giving a speech in Kansas
City. Where did she stay in Kansas City? The Muehle-
bach, of course. I called there and she was registered, but
out. I left an urgent message.

At 3:00 A.M. she called. I had gone to sleep only fitfully
and there were terrible moments when the telephone
seemed to sound in my dreams.

Then I looked at the clock and knew it was Anita.

"Who are you shacked up with out there?" I asked
jealously. I knew instinctively she had called the hotel
desk for any messages and was actually now in someone
else's room. Her bed partner lay there between the night's
initial intercourse and the return of his passion. Oh, I
knew how it worked.

"What do you want?" she said coolly, ignoring my
question. The man would be lighting a cigarette for her,
well screwed and pleased with himself and with the discovery or rediscovery of what Anita could do for self-
esteem.

"I've been waiting for you to call all night. You'd better get your old ass out of bed and get home. Susan's been
subpoenaed by Conyers." I could hear her catch her
breath. At least there was that satisfaction.

"How soon do you need my comments, Mr. Secretary?"

Need my comments, Mr. Secretary, my ass! So it was
true. She was with someone she couldn't speak in front of.
I wondered who it was. I hoped it was Harry. Better the
certain evil.

I was astonished at my fury at her. Partly it was that
she had brought this on our heads, but partly it was raw
jealousy. I had accepted only intellectually that she would
be looking for new men, now that our affair had disinte-
grated, our mutual and complex fidelity done with.

"Susan goes before the grand jury tomorrow . . . today.
Call me from another phone. Now," I snarled.

She thought a moment.

"How serious is it, really?"

"Plenty."

"I'll get back to you as soon as I can get my notes together, Mr. Secretary," she said.

"Okay," I replied, defeated in some way, almost in tears of anger, desiring her now at this awful hour of morning simply out of animal jealousy.

Yet, when love failed, as it had with my wife and with Anita, even amid the acrimony, some old hold remained. I wanted Anita to win, to escape Conyers, too. We had forged a contract of sorts and she had carried out her part. She had given me love, when I had thought myself unworthy of it, and certainly she had given me sex and power, even pride. And for my part, I had given her—what had I given her? Friendship. And my soul, if I wanted to be dramatic about it.

How well I knew her. She would be explaining now, tensely I was sure, that she had to go back to her room. Harry, if it were he, would be marveling that our Secretary was still up at 3:00 A.M. on business. I wondered had we been tapped? How dreary it was, this wariness. We had become a nation of telephone paranoids, I mused, wearily, as I waited. There had been our plan to get telephone scramblers. But did they work? Wouldn't it have been much easier simply to be honest?

By now, wrapped in her dress, hair brushed quickly, Anita would be returning to her room. And so it was: the phone rang.

"Are you okay?" I asked her.

"No. I feel scared as hell," she said. I sensed she would be all right from the strength in her voice.

"The jig may be up," I told her. "If Conyers has enough to start calling witnesses, then he may have enough to ruin us."

"You mean to indict and convict us?"

"I don't know. If he just cares about ruining us, he doesn't need enough to indict. All he needs is enough so that he can leak it out that we're under investigation. Then we'd have to quit. He's asking Susan about the papers, so he probably knows what's in them."

"Oh, Jesus," she said.

"To indict, he might need the papers, some papers anyway. But even without them, he can make a good enough case by getting some jerk at HEW who remembers them to confirm they existed. Then he goes to the

AG and says, 'Look, shouldn't you ask these people, or have the President ask them, what gives?' "

". . . so we'd have to go," she interrupted.

"Except that I think that bloodsuck wants more than for us to just quit. He'd like to jail me, you, too, maybe."

"*Unk,*" she said, picking up one of my expressions. I laughed sourly.

"We'll know something more after they talk to Susan. Their questions in the grand jury will tell us something."

She paused, then said almost with wonder:

"It's that bad, isn't it?" Then there was the conniving pause, and she breathed out, "How much of what he has would be on me personally, and how much . . ."

Ah, Anita. Even now, with the hooks deep in our hides, she wanted to see whether hers would pull out.

"Come on, Anita," I interrupted her. "You knew all along you might get caught." Before she belabored me more with her selfishness, I went on.

"Susan's pregnant."

"Pregnant! Ah, you dumb bunnies." The earlier rancor was all gone. "Is it too late for an abortion? Yes, it would be. Why didn't you . . ."

"Look, that's not your worry, Anita. Okay?"

"Okay," she dismissed Susan. "When will you call me?"

"After Susan testifies. After I decide what can be done."

"What about . . . What can I do?" she asked, nervous, the old self-protective tone back in her voice.

"You can expect the worst," I told her.

When we had hung up, I lay awake, fretting and tatting at the possibilities, all of them blown out of shape into nightmarish fears. How much did Conyers know? I did not underestimate the venom of that scorned man. I had seen his hate, raw as a shrapnel wound, at the White House that night. What a witch trial judge he would have made. He was the particular sort of virtuous man, full of floating hate, whose belief in his own right-thinking could surround the pressing or pulling to death of a witch with a sense of a job well done.

I knew how he'd gotten it this far along. His FBI sleuths had done the timeless detail jobs of the secret police: checking out old long-distance toll bills for calls between Anita and Doolittle; piecing together the dates Doolittle cashed and deposited checks; the dates he paid his major creditors; bullying with ominous politeness the clerks who had once worked for Anita; questioning Public Health Service contract officers for rumors, reports. And so on and on, piling up circumstantial evidence—the police ants—all leading up to the federal grand jury, where we were now. There, Conyers was painstakingly building his case before the twenty-three jurors in the hot, cluttered room. They would hear the FBI agents with their biased stories first. Then Susan. Obviously Conyers had summoned her to establish that the incriminating letters linking Anita to Benn City had been destroyed. Perhaps Anita, Doolittle, I, would be invited or subpoenaed to seal our guilt by taking the Fifth Amendment before the grand jury. Then, depending on what he'd come up with, the indictments.

I imagined myself a loathesome figure in the dock before the trial jury, before the thirsting reporters, the courtroom audience.

I saw myself humiliated by the guilty verdict, head bowed in front of a merciless judge, I heard the sentence: Ten Years. I envisioned the failed appeals, the inevitable lock-step to the penitentiary.

In the rumpled bed, I twisted to escape such thoughts. Why was I acting like a sheep, awaiting Conyers' knife in my neck? Within the black vacuum of night, I was regressing to the Martin of the cubbyhole. When I looked at my craven self clinically, I began to grope upward. The pressure of my trepidations eased.

Instead of writhing about in nonspecific guilts and forebodings, why not look at the damned thing legally? Goddamnit, I was a lawyer. What, actually, could Conyers charge me with:

Well, there was the false statement on Pauhafen's death, if Conyers wanted to go back far enough; trespassing at the monastery, probably a misdemeanor (maybe there was some old Virginia statute against practice of witchcraft, too); digging up the grave; failing to report Buffi's death; harboring Krals, a man sought for attempted murder. All these were crimes Conyers wasn't likely to discover, or if he did, he would have trouble prosecuting.

But it was the offense involving Anita's deals with Doolittle that he was working on. I numbered the counts he might get me on:

My passing the $25,000 to Doolittle, a bribe, a felony.

Conspiring to bribe by helping to arrange for Krals to pass the balance of the $100,000 to Doolittle.

Misprision of a felony, that is, knowing about Anita's numerous Benn City crimes and failing to report them.

And if Conyers couldn't make any of these, he still had publicity for a weapon: the leaks he could make to the vulture press that would get me out of the White House just as surely.

All right, I said in the night, there are the dangers, clean and neat as a rap sheet.

But all that was assuming I just sat back and let it happen to me. Passivity was the one sure way to Lewisburg. What were my own options? I listed them on the foolscap of my mind:

One, I could turn turtle and let him have his way, either with a trial or with a cowardly guilty plea to something to get me off lightly. I snapped off that thread of thought. I was not going to jail that easily.

Two, I could strike a deal to save myself at the expense of Anita and Susan and Doolittle. Maybe Conyers didn't have enough to indict me, only the others. Could I help him to push Anita under? If you wanted to be a moralist about it, she deserved whatever she got. But not Susan. Never. Besides, he wanted me. I would be destroyed as fully if I turned stool pigeon against Anita as if I pleaded guilty. More, because then Conyers would have castrated me as well as getting my admissions of guilt from the witness stand when I publicly hanged Anita with rope I had helped braid. No, it was unthinkable—and impractical.

Three, we could use the films to blackmail the Vice President into forcing out Conyers. Where were my scruples now? But even if it were a sure way of keeping us out of jail, it would polish off Anita with Frieden, and perhaps me, too. We would wither saplessly on the governmental branches. I shelved the idea.

Four was the midnight unmentionable. We could get Doolittle to have Conyers killed by one of his gangland friends. It wasn't even tempting. I could never do it. It was an infantile fantasy of revenge. It was also risking life imprisonment.

I mused on other fantastic possibilities: fleeing to Greece, going underground. Then, finally, I turned to look brute fear in the eyes. I could try to fight the son of a bitch.

That would be option number five. Since the other four wouldn't work, five was really the only pragmatic thing to do. The question was how.

I realized I was boxed into bravery by default. How ironic it was: three years ago, if it were conceivable I could have been in such a mess, I would have surrendered without a twitch of spirit. Now it was too late for that. I had undergone an alchemical change.

I had fought the armed street urchin, screwed Dapple Anita, bullied mayors and senatorial candidates, unionists and corporations. I had lied to my President in his face, and to the police, and intimidated some of the mighty on Capitol Hill. Even if I wanted to, I could not return, could not become again the carrier snail.

And anyway, why should the son of a bitch get anyone? Why shouldn't *we* strike him? Yet, how could we, I wavered, him with his legions of pliant FBI. Somehow! We could strike him where *he* was weak. There were spots in his peatsmoke-hardened skin where we could stick a rusty nail. He was vulnerable in his piousness, his ambitions at Justice, his wolfish love and jealousy for Susan that was in his fibers like his Church.

But how could I use his weaknesses? We had to blackjack him not only into killing the case completely, but into remaining forever silent about it. What had that shanty Irish Savonarola ever done shameful enough to give us that kind of crowbar leverage? I answered myself: nothing. His file had proved that to us.

Then we must make him do something shameful. Catch him in bed with a bimbo? Not likely. Use Susan to entrap him somehow? I dismissed the idea. If not sex, then something in his job might compromise him. Suppose, I mused, I offered to plead to a charge of which both Conyers and I knew I was innocent, pretended to go for my gutless option number one. He'd lunge for that like a hungry dog for raw beef, just to get me. I knew it wasn't Anita he was after, or Susan, or Doolittle. And this would let him avoid a trial, avoid exposing in a formal trial his emotional stake in getting me.

But even if he fell into the trap of letting me make a phony plea, I would have to be able to prove he knew it was phony. And it would take very solid proof to ruin him as a lawyer for the rest of his life.

To get that proof, he would have to confess his guilty knowledge to me in some way even as we struck the deal, or confess it to some totally trusted confidant. How the hell was I going to get that? He obviously wasn't going to give me a signed statement. Then, I gasped: those long-ago frogs I had recorded when I was a youngster as they belched their deep voices into the fat, round microphone. *"Err-gut,"* I said aloud.

I rolled it all over and over in my mind. About dawn, I could lie in bed no more and went to the window. The dirty snow was heaped in mounds under the streetlights. It had been a horrible winter, cold, slushy, icy-streeted. But the mess had begun to melt the day before. At least Susan would arrive in sunshine.

Later, at the office, I worked wearily, wondering why. Would I be forced to quit? The slightest stigma on me from Conyers would compromise the White House. And if his case were this far along . . .

Goddamnit! I wanted to stay! If it got too close to me, sure, I'd quit before it hurt Woeckle, or Frieden, or the President. Part of me, even now, was ready to leave it, to cut away the tentacle hold it had on me—but not yet, not yet.

I worked at the legislation on my desk until it was squiggles of corrections in fine-tip ink. I prayed the secretary would be able to wade through them. In between bills, a vague plan began to germinate in my mind. But as soon as my secretary told me Susan was on the telephone, the sweat was in my palms again.

"I did what I said I would," she said between sobs.

"You denied you ever saw them?"

"Yes."

"And?"

"Roger came up to me afterward . . ."

I imagined the nasty son of a bitch walking up to Susan, hating her for being pregnant, yet still wanting her with that animal hunger of his. *His* belly would be full of anger and revenge.

". . . and he said he had evidence that I'd seen the papers."

I shut my eyes. That was the end of Susan. He would not be bluffing about that kind of evidence, never.

"What did he say, Susan?"

"He had a transmittal slip, and when I said that only meant it got sent from some office in HEW, he said, yes, but the girl who sent it got burned once for losing documents and kept a log of everything transferred out of her office . . ."

I felt sick and put my left hand to my throbbing head. That's it; Susan is caught. And he'll use her as a hostage for me, and for Anita. Unless I could put the vengeful son of a bitch into the kind of trick bag he had us in!

"He showed it to me, the Xerox of it, and it said, 'documents turned over to Mrs. Bieber for Mrs. Tockbridge' with the date."

I rocked in the chair, my head bobbing back.

"God," she said, "how could I ever have thought of him as a husband? He is so goddamned pious, so vicious."

She told me how Conyers, after showing her the Xerox, had given her a line about her being only a small figure in all this.

It was an ugly business.

"He asked me if I'd talked with you before I testified."

"Ah?" I gasped.

"I said I had, on the telephone. You don't think I should?"

"No," I said, then added, "it doesn't matter." He was wrapping us in his coils now.

I told her to meet me on the Mall side of the National Gallery.

Susan was at the bottom of the gallery's marble steps. I had forgotten that she was so pretty. In my mind, I had preserved the vision of a plumper face. And even now, this heavy body, loaded as it was with our bastardy and the necessary newly expanded tubes and juices, was still, because so familiar, attractive.

Her face was full of hope when she saw me—so full of belief that I would find a way out. Did she sense immediately that Anita and I were no longer lovers? I jumped from the car and ran to her. Hugging her, I felt the thrust of her belly and I kissed her warm cheek. She needs me, I thought. The basic equation of love. And of cannibalism.

"Well, so here we are," I said stupidly. I took her bag.

"So, hello," she replied. Both of us were awkward.

"You're looking pretty. It all becomes you," I lied.

"I can think of better ways to pretty up," she said. I helped her into the Morgan, seeing a white flash of thigh. She had never really learned how to get into the sports car.

"What did he say about you being the little fish?" I asked her when she had recited again what happened. Now, easily, all of a sudden we had picked up where we parted those months ago. I drove toward Hall's, feeling that if we were being followed, I would soon know it on the semideserted Southwest streets.

"He said he knew I was only acting for my employers, meaning you and Mrs. T. He said if you wanted to come forward with any information, he would welcome it." Ah yes, he'd love to get me to turn myself inside out as an informer. Susan put her hand on mine where I gripped the polished wooden wheel. "Martin, the grotesque thing is when he's talking to me, he looks at me the same way he did, that old look . . ."

"He still loves you." ·

I knew that was why he was roughing up Susan. I rolled down the window for fresh air. We were in a shoddy section of the Southwest. The Negro kids, bundled up in short-life, overpriced jackets, played in front of their public housing blockhouses.

"What he's saying, Susan, is that he has got you now. He can make a case of perjury against you because he trapped you. If you'd said you'd forgotten, he had the false-official-statement charge. He was saying that if I have information—if I put my neck into the noose, he will let yours out. That's the way his jealousy works."

"God, God," she groaned.

That clearly was Conyers' plan. If I took the rap for Susan, she would be disgraced and I imprisoned. If she and I pushed the blame off on Anita, we would both be disgraced—a pair of stool pigeons—and Anita would do a very little time in some women's house of detention.

That was Conyers' ultimate dragon, to turn me into a cheap squealer and Anita into a jailbird. And why? Jealous, paranoid revenge!

We pulled into the lot beside Hall's. The restaurant looked out over the confluence of the Anacostia and the Potomac. Their frozen surfaces were littered with ice—dirty gray-white chunks stretched from shore to shore. Like elephant hides, I thought. The day was noiseless except for the faint whirr of two helicopters far away in the moistened air.

The room was warm, familiar. Its green tablecloths and dull coral walls, and the baby grand piano bar, unused now, seemed as constant as a Vermeer interior.

I helped her out of her coat, seeing her belly press against the soft brown flannel of her maternity jumper. Her blouse was ivory-colored and silken.

She saw, or felt, me noticing and looked back as if to say, "Is it all right?"

"You look lovely," I said. "You made the dress, didn't you?"

"Yes," she said, pleased.

"I like it." I took her arm through the smooth cloth, feeling her firm upper arm with a wallop of sensuality. And suddenly, I felt a surge of joy. For all of the terror of being caught by Conyers, and for all that Susan's belly was swollen, her breasts, already heavy, now overfull, still I recalled the ardentness of that day by Athanor. She twisted her ungainly body, big-hipped, between the tables.

There were seats by the window. Susan looked up quickly again at me as she sat, wondering if I had noticed how sitting accentuated that bulge on her midriff.

"Well, it won't be there forever," she said. She paused. "I wish I could bring myself to reproach you. God knows I did the first few months."

"Why didn't you call?"

"Ah, that was no way."

"You mean you were afraid I'd do right by you?"
She flushed. "That, mainly."

"And you were hurt about Anita." Why, so often, did I articulate for her what she herself thought? Yet we had built our relationship of that, found it even comfortable.

"Well, I was a fool to like you," she said with some heat. "It was a dirty trick, you talking about marriage and seeing her. Ah, you're a bastard, a real bastard," she added sorrowfully.

"Why couldn't we have talked it out instead of you just marching away?" I said. "Why didn't you stay and fight if I was worth anything to you?"

She shrugged and said nothing. I looked at the quick, intelligent face, the eyes down now.

"You would have won, because you're prettier," I said,

reaching across to touch her hand. She looked up with a smile.

"That's a sweet little lie," she said.

"You were better in the sack," I lied again in a whisper.

"Oh, come on," she laughed aloud now. "It's a fine time for that."

I ordered us a bottle of overpriced Rhine. It was just the way I wanted it—a little colder perhaps than it should have been. Susan had her nose buried in the menu. The sunlight hit her gold wedding ring where her hand rested on the paper placemat. She had taken it off when we went together. Now it legitimatized her. I turned back to the menu: the clams casino that I knew would have all the garlic I wanted and the soft-shell crabs that would be succulent and rich.

"I can see why the condemned man enjoys his last meal," I said.

"More the condemned woman," she said, looking up.

I met her eyes, none of that spectacular light blueness that dazzled in Anita, yet honest and wise. Oh, I could not let Susan go into court for me. But it was hard to make the commitment to her, so hard because in practical terms I would suffer so much more by a guilty plea than she; if that's what it had to come to.

I took a draught of wine, damming a wave swell of tears. Oh, goddamn, I thought, I could be sitting here, married to Susan, drinking this cold wine and looking forward to clams casino on heated rock salt with no more guilt than a pig. And here I am caught in lies, scheming like a jailed medieval poisoner because another woman, a crazy and aging tart, stole some money once that never had anything to do with Susan at all.

"Oh, Susan," I moaned.

"Stay out of it," she said quietly. "He wouldn't do anything much to me."

But this was a lie. Susan had betrayed Roger Conyers, treated his manhood like a questionable joke, and he was as vengeful as Klingsor. He wouldn't jail her, that would not be his savage mode of love, but he *would* indict her, lusting for her even as he did it.

"Oh, hell," I said. "He'll drink some blood one way or the other, yours or mine or Anita's, or Harry Frieden's if he has a clue about him."

She touched my fingers where they held the wine stem.

No matter how much guts the doctor had, he might not want to marry her if she were to become a convicted felon. Then who would give my little bastard a name?

Looking out into the sunlit day, I saw a big tree by the Corinthian Boat Club next door, naked of leaves, bending over the moored boats. The flowers in Hall's lampposts dead, drooping strands almost down to the cold, wet patio. In summer, I had drunk this same wine beneath the subdued outdoor lights.

"When are you going to get married?" I asked.

"Why?" she asked cautiously.

"You mean it depends on what happens here?"

She said nothing. Then, with an imploring look, she said: "Why can't . . . ?"

"Anita? No."

But why not? One last time I seriously considered it. If I couldn't sacrifice Susan, why not eat a little shame and throw Anita to Conyers? And yet the answer was always the same: that was what Conyers wanted, not so much to imprison me, but to uncock me, make me a eunuch, as I was before it all began.

"It won't do, Susan. Conyers wants to get me where I got him, in the pecker." She looked around furtively to see who had heard me. I had forgotten that persistent Puritan streak in her. I laughed and she joined me. And in that laughter, I put the seal on my resolve. I would fight Conyers, not sell out Anita or Susan.

The clams came. They sat in beauty atop their rock salt. After Susan had speared one, I forked one up from my side of the plate and dipped a piece of black bread in the melted butter. Then I sipped the wine, chewing it all together.

"I never felt comfortable with her," I said, remembering that so many meals with Anita had been edged with uneasiness, jealousy, floating anxiety. "I feel I'm home now, with you."

"Oh, it won't be the same for me with someone else either," she conceded.

I ate another clam.

"The apotheosis of the bivalve," I said safely. I had been pouring large quantities of wine. The bottle was empty. I ordered another to go with the soft-shell crabs. Yes, it would make me tipsy, even drunk. I got up to call the

White House. It was a rare light day. How many more days of any kind would I have there, I wondered.

The thought depressed me. I recalled the Cabinet room in the morning, the snow clean-looking out the French windows and the thick atmosphere of power almost visible in the room. Those faces from newspapers' front pages, deliberate or laughing while the President spoke in his midwestern flatness, gesturing with a document or a pencil.

"I ought to be worried about toxemia," Susan said as the waiter poured her a glass from the new bottle. There was the old primness in her voice that had made her seem so sexy when she yielded.

"You better be worried about abduction," I replied, touching her leg under the table with my calf. She laughed, the final clam still in her mouth.

"Oh, my God, what a thought," she said.

Yet it hung there between us, shining, dulcet, loving, the memory of passion, through the long meal and the long talk. It was midafternoon when I paid, the cognac still warm on my tongue. There was no going back to work now. Had I ever in all my government days simply taken off? Yet how blithely I was doing it now.

I bundled her coat onto her jumper and the sight of her strong, tapered legs was exciting. I wanted to laugh at my lust for her.

We walked to the river bank. The air was still fresh, the sun warm on our faces. Beneath our feet, the snow was only about an inch deep, wetting me through my shoes. Susan had providentially worn slip-on rubbers over her low pumps.

From the confluence, I heard sharp cracks and knew what was happening, for I had seen it before, years ago at Hains Point. The ice on the river was breaking up.

The big rough rectangles of ice thrust then dipped back into the river as another rectangle pushed up from behind. The floes lumbered downstream, cubistic and mythical sea animals humping each other, rising from depths to mount the animal ahead.

Susan and I held hands tightly, watching the spectacle. We could hear the reports of the ice breaking all the way from the opposite shore now. The rivers were moving down to the bay. Moldau music in my giddy head. Despite all the grasping, vengeful tentacles of Conyers and his bunch reaching for us now, still we had not reproached one another. It lifted all my anxieties.

"Oh, Susan," I said. "We could have made such a lovely go of it, given a little bit of difference."

She pushed her head into my shoulder and I turned her away from the two rivers and kissed her lightly on her parted lips. Neither of us doubted where we were going. And there was time, all the way to morning. I drove the Morgan carefully along the river toward home.

Inside my house, I kissed her, deeply this time, feeling her stomach against me as she moved her hips slightly to make contact with my horniness. How hot I was for her! I reached through the rough cloth of her shift top and felt the breasts.

"Oh, Lord," she said, more resigned for a moment than passionate. I assumed she was thinking of her doctor-fiancé.

"We never tried out Athanor," I said.

"I would have liked to," she said.

"Will you stay? I can get the gold."

She stepped out of my arms and sat down in an easy chair.

"It's such a silly thing," she said.

"Will you stay?"

"Oh, God, I don't know."

She moved back to me awkwardly, and kissed me on the lips. I pulled her in, accustomed now to her swollen abdomen, and again she rubbed in close to me.

"The doctor has been circumspect," I said, panting.

"Ah, this is dumb," she said.

I led her to the stairs and she went up first, her behind a little larger, Maillol curves moving with the rising of her thighs. I put my hands on it.

"What a lovely sweet ass."

"You haven't changed," she said, then added, "Well, I guess I'm glad of that."

"Didn't you think we would come to this?" I asked as we reached the top.

"No," she said, "not really."

At the top, she turned to me and we kissed again. I slipped my tongue for a moment between her lips.

"Oh," she said surprised.

I wondered what kind of silly bastard she was marrying.

"Does he hold all this up to you?" I asked. "I mean, does he play martyr?"

"Well, sort of," she said, not breaking, but continuing to press her belly to me. "He loves me as a kind of romantic vagabond who left Myerstown, lived an exciting life in riots and in far places, and came home done in by my adventures. He thinks he is marrying something very exciting."

"So do I," I said, touching her breast ever so lightly.

"Ah," she said, pleased now. She broke for a moment. "But at another level, he knows that I'm a good Pennsylvania Dutch housewife who will be hardworking and true to him and grateful." She paused, then gave me a pecking kiss. "He loves me a little like I loved you."

I held her hand and led her into the bedroom. Had I known she would be up here? Otherwise, why had I made the bed?

I kissed her and she turned around, swinging her body so that her loosened bosom pressed up against my suit. I took off my clothes, turning my back with some delicacy so she could get out of her underwear.

She was between the sheets and I climbed in with her, the two of us on our sides.

"I've forgotten whether it works this way," I said, panting now. I snuggled in to kiss her.

"It doesn't matter," she said, wrenching her mouth up against mine and taking my head in her hands. How passionate she was.

Her stomach was unusual, pressed against mine lightly, but not really unsexy. We kissed and I reached to her right breast, lolled on the bed, supported it slightly and found gently its nose.

"Are you sensitive?" I said.

"Not too."

"You're sure this is okay?"

"Yes, it's fine."

"God, you've a lovely pair of tits," I said. "Like fresh bread or something."

"Loaves, loaves," she said, reaching down along my side and then slipping her hand onto me. I almost came, but directed my thoughts to the ice breaking up on the Potomac. The distraction saved me.

"You'll have to not do that," I gasped. "I'm too hot."

"Oh," she said. "That's sweet." I remembered that my

wife had found it difficult to believe that she could be both seven months pregnant and arousing.

I stroked Susan's tail, still something to sing "The Star-Spangled Banner" about, so shapely.

"That's nice, too," I said. "I did you a favor."

"My God," she said, pulling me closer to her with a half laugh.

We lay together like that, working our tongues in each other's mouth until the passion gripped us both out of our minds. I started to mount her, reaching down to spread her nether lips. "No, no," she whispered, and pushed me off, turning her body as she did on top of mine. Quickly she slipped me into her, half crouched over me, still kissing me, her back arched and her full breasts drooping on-to my inflamed chest.

She must have been away from it for a long time, be-cause a couple of deep pumps, the big belly lodged against mine now, and I could hear those little noises in the back of her throat that I remembered so well. Thank goodness, I thought, thank the Good Lord for this nice gift.

I opened my eyes. Through the window, the sun still shone brilliantly. The ice had broken in the Potomac and I had just had a lovely, lovely screw with a woman I loved, and soon I was going out to fight Conyers and maybe I was going to jail.

"You're a very sexy unwed mother," I said, holding on. I did love her now.

"Listen," I said. "Why don't we at least think . . ."

"No," she said. "No. I have it all set out." She kissed me. "Just enjoy it, if you do enjoy it."

"God, it was lovely."

"It was as nice as when I wasn't, wasn't it?" she said.

"Yes." It was true. "Better."

"Why was it better?"

"You're more passionate."

"I'm a little soft down there, aren't I?"

"That doesn't matter."

"I'll be firm again," she said.

I didn't answer. It was a saddening thought. She'd have a firm quiff again, but not for me. She must have sensed my thought.

"I'm crazy to marry him," she said.

"Because you love me."

"Yes."

"And I you."

"I should have gotten a diaphragm," she said. "The Church." She sighed, "My God, they'd rather have you in a mess like this than put a little rubber jar ring in your stomach."

Toward dusk we got up. She called her doctor friend and her mother, her tone so different to each of them. I did not want to listen, but I heard bits. "Yes, it's going to be all right . . . no, really all right, better than I'd even hoped . . ." to him. And to her mother, "Did Ems say anything . . . oh, not as cold as up there, in fact, the snow's melting . . . no, I called him . . . yes, I told him . . ."

I built us a fire in the fireplace while she went down and looked at Athanor, and we had some of that Campbell's soup, the cheddar cheese kind, so damned good after the heavy lunch, and we drank a little of the cold beer I had in the ice box.

The problem with Conyers came back, but freed of the anxieties that generally accompanied it like Furies.

"Susan," I said, "tell me about Conyers. Does he really confide in anyone? Anyone at all?"

She reflected a moment, then said, seriously, "No, not even when we were . . . Why?" she asked, then interrupted her own question, "Except for his priest. He said once his priest was his idea of a psychiatrist. Now, why?"

I thought of the witch trials, how the Inquisitor used eavesdroppers outside confessional booths to gain admissions from victims. The subtlety of the Church. Nothing had changed that much. Conyers was our Grand Inquisitor. I could be his. There it was, if I dared to use it!

"When does he confess? I thought confession was old hat."

"Not for him. What are you up to?" She looked sternly at me from her chair where she sat in my sweater and my workpants, my ski socks pulled up to her knee. I laughed at her.

"Where does he confess and what time? Really, it's important."

"Saturday. Almost every Saturday. At five. Saint Bridget's out where he lives, in Northwest. Martin, what is this?"

I took a sip of the cold beer and leaned toward her.

"I'm going to try to mousetrap him into letting me plead to a crime I didn't commit. Say suborning you to testify falsely, or a false statement to a federal official.

He'll know it's wrong—unethical. Sometimes a prosecutor will do it, but getting caught at it is the worst thing that can happen to a federal prosecutor. Follows him all his life if it gets him a censure from the bar association. But I think he wants me badly enough and I think he's scared enough of how bad I could make him look in a trial to risk it. And it would be logical for me to go along because it would get me off easier."

"God, it's nuts. He'll never do it," she said. "And what's the confessional . . ."

"If I read him right, he'll confess to his priest to making an unethical deal with me. Maybe he'll say the whole prosecution is based on jealousy." I started to tell her about those long-ago frogs, but instead just blurted it out, "I'm going to bug his confession."

Wild as it was, I had not expected her to laugh.

"Martin, it's nuts," she repeated. I was annoyed with her.

"Have you got a better idea? Look, I can't let you take the rap. I won't let Anita. There's no way we can use pull to get rid of him without triggering him into leaking the story to the press. I have *got* to shut him up with shame."

For an hour we mulled it over. Gradually it came to make a certain foolhardy sense, no matter that the odds were recklessly high it would fail.

And if it did fail, where was I worse off than now? At least I would have tried.

The ethics of it were as clear to Susan as to me, even with her residual Catholicism: Conyers was using all his powers as a prosecutor, all the FBI agents he had at his command, to carry out a personal act of revenge. He was perverting his oath and his duties to nail Susan and me. My long-shot idea was at worst, I rationalized, self-defense.

We talked and the future became bearable, for I carefully excluded any thought about how it could be in jail. When the fire burned down, I pulled the screen on it. The house was warm.

Before we slipped into passion again, the dark outside now bringing with it the cold, and us secure in bed, I thought of a poem about love and time by Auden: "from this night, not a whisper, not a thought, not a kiss or look be lost . . ."

Not a whisper lost. We made such fine, desperate, and

free love, such a thrilling touching of parts and of tongues and of lips that I was sure the baby, if it were not conceived in a moment of love and passion, must have now absorbed those emotions within its innocent casing.

At dawn, we lay a while longer in each other's arms. Then we got up for our individual reckonings. I fixed breakfast.

"Maybe we could mark last night up to time and circumstance," I said. "It was never that good before and you not lugging around a kid inside."

"Remember that bug man in South Carolina, you told me what he said about the gypsies and the bugs sensing . . ."

"Susan," I stopped her. "I swear I hadn't thought of that guy until a day or two ago, not since we were down there, and here you are thinking . . ."

"So," she said, domestically getting up, her stomach carried cautiously around the table, to get me another cup of coffee. "So, we were made for each other. So what else is new?"

There was a catch in her voice and I looked up at her, still in my bathrobe, and she was crying, the tears running down the cheeks and she making no effort to get them, because she had a coffee cup in each hand.

"But why not?" I burst out. "We're crazy not to!"

For reply, she only shook her head "no" and went on into the kitchen.

By the time we reached Union Station, I had caught the spirit. We stood there, she big as a house and me in my executive tweed tailored topcoat, hugging each other until the train was called.

Each time we looked at each other, the tears welled again. And well they might, for neither of us wanted to go where we were going and if this wasn't good-bye, it was the next thing to it.

"I could tell you I'd marry you," she said. "I could do it if you wanted me to." I did want her to. And yet . . . Did I want to surrender to that bourgeois life with Susan? Even now, really, with the mark of the beast on my chest, did I want to leave off entirely my selfishness, the egotism that had led me out of the basement with Athanor and into that sunny Cabinet room with the mighty?

"I do want to," I told her. But she sensed my thoughts.

"Oh, my God. My God," she groaned. The practicalities

overwhelmed us even as my poor mind played with jettisoning Cabinet room and all, and clinging to Susan. Marrying the doctor made such perfect sense. Marrying me now, or waiting until we knew what was going to become of us, made no sense.

I walked by the window, making little awkward waves at her, until the train pulled out, leaving me with the memory of a loving, anguished face streaked with tears. Then, I drove to work, the Ellipse snow so bright when I parked that I could hardly see, the gutters running heavy with cold, clear water.

At the White House, I stared at the bowl of the table light. I could see the dark irregular spots through its translucence, the insects that had flown in there, died and been cooked black, a small dry semicircle of them. The entomologist in South Carolina was right about insects and the shortness of life.

Of course, Susan and I must marry. But the gloom hit me. I put my head in my hands. Suppose the worst happened? I to prison and she to wait? Wasn't that a good possibility considering the craziness of my scheme? No, let her have the doctor.

I muddled over my bills for Congress. Finally, I called Anita. Drop by tonight, I told her guardedly.

"I've thought of an easy way out," she said almost as soon as she came in. She wore a dark plaid suit, the octagonal watch pendant on its jacket. Her face was agitated.

"Susan is already in a mess," she began, "I mean with the baby and all."

"No," I interjected, "forget it."

"Why? Why?" she said tensely, staring into my eyes. "Look, she's already in the soup. We can get out the story that she did it in a misguided effort to protect me from something that wasn't really illegal. My God, Susan can carry off a story like that. Don't underestimate her."

"Oh, bullshit, Anita," I said. I had made up my mind.

"No, let me finish." She was almost in tears. "Conyers won't do anything to her. Do you think a man as ambitious as that is going to put a poor little pregnant girl in jail? Why, all Susan has to do is say she refused to marry Conyers. She'd only have to tell the Attorney General that. My God, the AG would drop that case like a hot stone. Susan could leave who the father is up in the air and automatically the AG, everyone, no matter what Conyers said, would think Conyers was the father. It would finish him."

She was building her case. Did I feel a flutter of hope? She must have sensed it. Where was my resolve to meet Conyers on his own filthy grounds?

"Listen, I've thought it all out," she went on.

I walked from her to the window and put my brow against its cool.

Oh, we could try something like that. Maybe Conyers didn't have enough to hang us without Susan's help. And Susan, now that she loved me again and could see a way of keeping me out of jail, might go along with that kind of conspiracy. I could see her now, her decent voice low and serious, talking to the Attorney General. He might believe her, even over Conyers' rock-honest Irishness—because sex was involved and men were a little different about truth and lying when sex was the crucible.

For Susan, it would be a sweet way of getting back at Conyers. And for Anita and me, it would be a reprieve, a total reprieve, and so goddamned easy.

Yes, it might work, the nasty business might work for a time. If by will and force of love, I could manipulate Susan into lying. Ah, but to compel her that way to imply Conyers was her child's father, and to coat that shabby lie with other deceitful icing. No, I couldn't do it, even I.

And would Conyers, despite all that, give up? Wouldn't we have to confront him again at some other time? And would the Attorney General really disbelieve Conyers? Wouldn't he scratch deeper himself before throwing out such a case against Anita and me? In a few years it might come back to blacken his name forever as a cowardly Attorney General, afraid to push on because the malefactors were in high places.

The panes on my front windows were cold. Outside the day was gray. The cars, so bright earlier with the melted snow on them and the sunlight, huddled dully to the curbs. I thought of long ago, looking out Anita's windows for the first time at that cathedral tower in the foreground, and then on down that long, bosky sweep through the park down Massachusetts Avenue past the embassies and on past the Jockey Club—ah, Buffi—and into the thrilling corrupted heart of Washington, the Capital City.

There had been fine things, yes. For mistresses I had

possessed Anita and the wild moments when I thought her lovemaking was a gasoline fire to sear me and warm me forever. And I had Susan, served up to me, really, in an almost medieval way by Anita, my mistress.

And Anita had given me power.

But all these things, save perhaps Susan, had done for me what? Exhilaration, sweating palms, anxieties brinking more and more on panic, a life of running too fast, scheming too much. Anita had given me pain and anxiety, in the end.

I tried to focus on her idea for saving us, she sitting behind me in the dim living room. But it was no good. I was wearied. I was climbing into the decomplication chamber all by myself.

I sat down opposite her, a stranger in a way now in spite of it all, of Tapir and Buffi and the Spanish fly, of our incredible loving satisfactions—even now I could taste the passion faintly—of our plots, of blue movies, of the comic obscenity of the Black Mass.

"No, Anita," I said. "We're going to do it my way."

"That's melodramatic horseshit," she said aloud. Then her face, its bones still so perfect and her puffed lips apart with the hope not entirely dead on them, crinkled up and she pitched her head forward into her hands. When she looked up, her face was older than I had remembered, and because the age was more pronounced, it was all the more open to hurt.

"I want to give Roger Conyers the kind of royal fucking he's trying to give us," I told her quietly.

"Even if I get caught in the middle," she said, knowing now that there wasn't going to be any easy compromise that would keep her world intact. But she was almost resigned, waiting.

Since trying out my plan on Susan, I had thought it out in more detail. In a low voice as if even in my own home I had to fear being overheard, I laid it out:

First, I was going to buy myself one of those mini-recorders, the kind you can put in your pocket to record everything that's said. I had seen them in catalogs, no bigger than a deck of Tarot cards. They could be actuated manually, or by voice, to keep them from recording long gaps of silence.

Then, I would make an appointment with Conyers this Friday if possible. He had told Susan that if I had information, he would welcome a talk. Well, I would be there, nasty little recorder in my pocket. Conyers saw me as a sort of boob. He would not expect the recorder. On Saturday, the day when he confessed, I would have the little machine taped inside his confessional booth somewhere. That would be the rub. That would be the dangerous part of it.

If it worked, I would have a showdown meeting with Conyers. I would play him a retape of the meeting in his office in which he agreed to let me plead to a crime I never committed—grounds for disbarment. The bugging of the confessional, if it worked out, would catch him acknowledging guilty intent, the most vital element in any crime.

The audacity of the plan made me giddy. "Anita, can I carry it off?" I murmured.

She was in no mood for reflecting on the pilgrim's progress of Martin Dobecker.

"Are you saying you think you can get him to drop the whole thing?" she said, ignoring my question. I laughed.

"Madam Secretary," I chided her gently, and her face, for the first time that day, crinkled into smiles. Her fabulous power to bounce back always gave me a resiliency by contagion.

The next morning, I called in sick, which was true enough in its way. Then, an attack of dread struck me so hard I had to sit. When the spell passed, I called the Justice Department.

Conyers made me wait on the telephone.

"Conyers here," he said crisply at last.

"When can I see you," I asked, not trusting myself much farther than that. "Tomorrow?" That would be Friday.

"Fine," he said.

"About four?"

"Fine." So it was sealed.

I found the mini-recorder at a shop in Arlington. The clerk ran me through its simple, insidious workings twice. It had a thirty-day guarantee and cost me $387.50, an outrageous rip-off. But even I could see it was the best he had. At the same time, I bought a cassette recorder into which I could plug my little machine for transferring voices from the tiny wires to a more conventional device.

On Friday, downtown was gray, cold. The first staggering regiments of civil servants straggled onto the sidewalks and queued unhappily at the round yellow bus stop signs along Pennsylvania Avenue. I snaked through their ranks, a nonworking interloper, and into the Justice Department. I passed through seedy corridor after seedy corridor. The names on the standardized doors with their glazed glass panes menaced me with their unadorned block lettering, Julian, Sheridan, Goldwein . . . D'Orfeo, Conyers.

I knew he would keep me waiting again. This was the unimaginative sort of meanness that he could carry off. A government-issue metal chair was directly in front of the secretary. I wiped my palms on my trousers: from the secretary no hope. She was over fifty and beneath her mussel-shell nose she wore like a flagellant's welt an incipient moustache of black hairs. Finally Conyers buzzed her and she signaled me in. I pressed the mercury action piston switch in my coat pocket and I walked in wordlessly. The room was the size of my old *Labor Notes* office. A Pan Am calendar was on the wall and a picture of the Attorney General. On the other wall were some attractive seascapes. I wondered if Susan had got him to hang them up.

"Sit down," he ordered. In those blue Irish eyes there was so much hate that I thought in momentary panic that everything I had done up to this moment had been some sort of unserious game. Unnerved, I waited for him to speak again. But he was not going to let me take that defensive position.

"You wanted to see me," he reminded me after a moment of silence.

Oddly, his hatred and need to destroy me, now I had perceived it and was getting my panic under control, strengthened me. It was a fuse which I could light to explode him. He had no such personal hold on me.

"You had Susan before your grand jury," I began. "She made a statement which you think conflicted with what your investigation has turned up. You believe you have some evidence she perjured herself."

"Are you acting as her lawyer?" he said, a cutting sneer in his voice. "You sound like it."

"I am acting as hostage for her. I want to get her off the hook, to be blunt. You knew *that* when I called you. You knew it when you suggested to her that you weren't interested in her, but in her employers."

"You seem to know a great deal about what I'm interested in and what I'm not interested in." He was evasive, almost as if he knew I were recording our talk. But the blade was still in his voice. I was dying for a cigarette.

"I came here to make a deal with you," I reiterated. "I know you only have enough to make a case on Susan and to drag Mrs. Tockbridge and me in by inference."

"Ah?" he said, noncommittally. He went into his pocket for his cigarettes. I took one when he offered it to me.

"No, if you had something on us, you'd have asked her more questions about us in front of the grand jury."

"That's not my way," he replied cautiously.

"Oh, your way is to drag a pregnant woman into a grand jury and mousetrap her?" I challenged him.

Conyers flinched. Would it trigger him? No.

"She mousetrapped herself," he said. "She mousetrapped you or you wouldn't be here." His anger had not flared, now it hardened into threat. "I don't have to deal with you, Dobecker. I know damned well you helped buy off Doolittle and I think I can prove it."

His words pierced me. Had he tapped some call? Had Doolittle talked? I fidgeted, trying not to lose my calm.

"Come off it," I said. "You have Susan. For the rest, you've got your cop's intuitions . . ." I drew heavily on my cigarette now. "Look, if all you're interested in is putting Susan in jail, then why did you give me this appointment?"

"I thought you wanted to make a statement."

I ignored him for a moment and he went on.

"I thought you might want to make a statement about Mr. Fred Pauhafen's death." I felt suddenly faint. "You were with him when he died. Mrs. Tockbridge was with him at least shortly before he died, in the Mayflower bar."

Conyers was boasting now, about the thoroughness of his investigation. But in it also was a warning. Do it my way, he was saying, or these are the avenues I will follow.

"You were also with Baron de Plaevilliers when he died after that gravedigging caper in Virginia." I started to interrupt, but he shook me off with his big football tackle's head.

"Oh, I'm not saying I can prove it all, not yet. You checked into the Capitol the night a maniac in human skin cape attacked a secretary. A human skin! And we knew that it was the body of a man exhumed illegally, also in Virginia."

I was morbidly interested in how he identified Krals' skin. Had the FBI softened up the fingers with some chemical? My God, they had been like leather, and had they gotten a fingerprint? I was in a panic now. It was I, not he, who was being tape-recorded into destruction.

"You were assisting the attacker of that girl to escape and he would have been"—Conyers paused as if he expected me to finish his sentence for him, but I was struck dumb by his omnipresence—"a Mr. Krals, who came to this country with the help of Baron de Plaevilliers and who conveniently left his prints all over the Senate carpenter shop. Luckily for both you and him, Mr. Krals is now in Austria."

I was steamrollered by him, underestimating his diligence and his ability. Yet, how easy, in a way, it must all have been. He would have checked out Anita's contributors and found Tapir, then checked Tapir's death and discovered my statement to the local police. The bar waitress would have identified Anita's picture, mine, too, and Tapir's. He would surmise the rest.

"You are very imaginative," I summoned up weakly.

"I wanted you to know that you are not uninvolved in our investigation," he said. "Some of this stuff I can make on you now," he said harshly.

"If you could, you would," I sighed. "I came to make a deal."

"Um," he said. "No deal."

"Now you're being coy," I managed. "If you don't want to talk business, I'll go. We'll get our defense together, including your unsuccessful relationship with Susan as your revenge motive, and we'll lay it all out on the record. Let the jury have the whole damned thing."

I shakily pressed out the butt in his tray and stood, brushing an ash onto his uncarpeted floor. He was pinching his lips together, knowing I would not walk out, but unsure what to do. Like that damned pair in Dante, we were locked in the same cake of ice.

"You know there's no use leaving," he said at last. "If I don't have you today—I'll have you tomorrow, or the next day or the next." I could see he was having a tough time with his temper.

"I'm trying to make it easy for you," I murmured.

"Okay, sit. What will you do, exactly?"

"I'll plead to something cheap. In exchange, you let Susan off."

"Noble Dobecker. What else?"

"And you leave Mrs. T. alone."

"She belongs in jail," he said flatly.

I stared at him now, square-headed, a terrible throw-back of a man, witch prosecutor, a young medieval avenger.

"They all do," I said quietly.

"They all what?"

"They all belong in jail. All politicians."

But he turned off my philosophy.

"That's not my affair right now. What will you plead to, specifically, just for the sake of argument." He smiled slightly now. This was the part of the conversation he understood, perhaps enjoyed.

"A misdemeanor, say a false official statement. I'll make one for you right now under oath," I said with pretended jauntiness.

"I can do without the bullshit," he squelched me.

"What do *you* want?" I asked.

"A felony."

"So you can get me for five years." Now I truly feared, tape or no tape.

"The judge sentences, not me."

The judge, I thought. The judge will do pretty much what Conyers wants. If I plead to suborning, the judge will know damned well I'm copping a light plea as part of a deal. And suborning could carry five years.

"If I plead, is that the end of it?"

"Mrs. Tockbridge will be mentioned," he said. "Not by me, but you know damned well if you plead, the fact of the grand jury is going to leak out somehow and the fact that she's involved. If you plead to conspiracy to bribe . . ." I stopped him.

"Let's say I plead to suborning Susan to testify falsely even though I didn't suborn, you understand."

"Well, whatever you plead to, the newspapers are bound to draw conclusions," he took me up. My chest panged: Conyers had not directly balked at the idea of my making a plea to a false charge. Was that enough for my little recorder? No, of course not. But clearly he was so consumed with shaping his case, the craftsman whistling as he beveled the edges of his gallows platform, that he was neglecting to make it out of good wood. The bastard: I'd hang him from his own noose.

"Okay," I said. "For the sake of argument, I plead to suborning Susan. What then?"

Suddenly, surprisingly, the hate was back in his eyes. "Then you do some time, Dobecker!"

"On a first offense? You said the judge . . ."

"The judge will do what we ask," he snapped with vicious honesty. So there it was out, part of it.

"For *suborning* . . . a crime I didn't even commit?"

"Then plead to something else you did commit. You're the one who suggested suborning. If you say you suborned . . . Mrs. Bieber, then who am I to argue."

"No, suborning it is," I said, I hoped not too hastily. It was on this theme that I must spin enough variations to entrap him. "So if I plead to this phony charge, Susan's off, right?"

He nodded. Goddamnit, I thought, I've got to have sound.

"Right?" I repeated.

"Right."

"You back off on Anita."

"No criminal charges, but something leaks out."

"And me?"

"You give me a statement I can submit to the judge along with your guilty plea."

"You mean I say that at such and such a time I told Susan to tell the grand jury such and such and such a whopper . . ."

"Something like that." I could see him tasting it and finding it good.

My palms were wet with sweat. I thought wildly that the wetness might short circuit the damned recorder when I tried to turn it off. He was getting closer, closer to my trap.

"Okay, so I dictate this phony statement and you witness it and give it to the judge. The maximum on this is five years."

"Yes. I won't ask for the maximum."

"You'll promise in writing?"

"You'll just have to take my word for it."

I paused, tried to look defeated. I was so nervous I thought I would lose bladder control. The string had only to be played a little longer.

"Well, so that's that," I sighed. "I have to trust you."

Conyers looked almost pleased with me. He picked up

the telephone to call in Miss Moustachio so I could dictate my false confession. "Just one minute," I said. He cradled the phone. "Just as a point of information. I'm done. I've agreed. But how can you ethically take a plea to a crime I'm innocent of, even if I'm willing to go along with it? How can I trust you to keep your word to me?"

The thrust got him in the vitals.

"I wanted you badly, badly," he gritted through his teeth, the anger loose in him now. "Only you and I know that charge is phony, and both of us know that you're the sort of snake who *would* suborn her, right?" He smiled with all the warmth of a glass eye. "The only reason you're not guilty of it is that you didn't think of it."

Well, I thought, if that $387.50 machine didn't work for the statement, then God is up there pulling the strings against me for my perfidy. I felt almost relieved. He had gone a long way toward stringing himself up.

"Maybe in that case, I should plead guilty to false pretenses," I said. "Then you can just pretend to send me to Lewisburg."

The light tone infuriated him. Perhaps in some recess of his mind, he had decided that Susan had left him because he was humorless. I had never really put myself in his shoes—assuming I could—to try to discover how he had rationalized her leaving him. Whatever it was, I could see the wrath in him pressing up from his chest almost as if it were a physical flooding, a levee breaking. His face went red.

"And what would you do if you didn't go to jail, Dobecker?" he hissed angrily. "Marry Susan and give your bastard a name?"

I could feel myself blowing now, feel a rush to slug him, big as he was. But some blessed control that I had built up from the pressure-cooking days since I left *Labor Notes* held me in—and the tape recorder whirred silently.

Now I wanted to give him back a little sac of poison that would secrete into his system for time to come, case or no case.

"Ah, Conyers," I said to him. "You're right. It is my little bastard. It's a little bastard that you weren't quite man enough to figure out how to make, huh?"

Sweet jealousy. His rancor engulfed him. His eyes bulged with outrage. I'd given him a good one, right in the balls.

"Yes," he said, barely under control, "and you're going

to have a long time to think about it. You're going to be able to spend two or three years thinking about how making that little bastard got you into a federal penitentiary."

"I thought it was my offenses against Title Eighteen," I said, I hoped with quavering bravado.

Conyers must have been thinking in that split second after his anger imploded that if I had my day in the bedroom, he would have his in the courtroom.

"You know better," he said grandly, and I heard in my mind the jaws click shut on him.

There was even a minor note of pleasure in his voice as he said to his secretary, "Could you come in, Mrs. Bates, I'll have to keep you a little overtime, as I told you I might, to type up Mr. Dobecker's statement."

When I got home, weary, agitated, I kicked off my shoes and dropped my clothes on the floor. For hours, I replayed the interview, making three extra cassettes of it for safety's sake.

It was good enough. Or was it? Couldn't he explain away much of what he said as bragging, or the normal reaction of an angry man, or simply as sparring for more information?

My spirits sank. I played it one last time. Yes, it was good stuff, good enough surely to get him a roasting from his boss, but maybe no more. I had only scotched the snake.

There is no way to avoid Confession, I thought with remnant humor.

CHAPTER

17

Confessions

Gloomy Saturday. Nervous as I was, I looked up St. Bridget in my *Lives of the Saints*. Man without firm belief in gods turns to omens, and I was heartened by St. Bridget's venom for political fat cats, including a Pope or two, and her no-nonsense backing of underdogs. If a church were going to be bugged, better hers than most.

I put on gloves and did my best to wipe the smooth little recorder clean of prints in case it should be discovered. On its back, I pressed one of those furry stick-um pads, keeping its mate to affix in the confessional where I could attach the bug. I drove to the old neighborhood where St. Bridget's was located; the church and parsonage sat well back from the three-story houses on either side.

Inside the church, I was in luck. There was only one other three-o'clock worshiper. Confessions, I had already determined, did not begin until five. I knelt and prayed dubiously but hard, waiting for the pious lady to leave.

Was I on the side of the righteous in what I was doing, I wondered. Yes, conditionally. Was I genuinely penitent? Yes. Yet, in my stomach the dragon's tail of my colon threshed around, grown spastic with my ascent to power.

Who needed such malaise? Once done with all this, could I live a life sufficiently guilt-free to spare me these hideous physical and mental symptoms of spiritual mal-
298

feasance? Or was dirty work built into my job? Did it go with the territory?

My co-worshiper left. With a quick look around I eased myself past the confessional's curtain. In the small booth, the underside of the triangular kneeling bench offered the only possible place for the recorder. My heart shuddered with fear.

I depressed the voice-actuating plunger. It would only run now when someone was talking. Blessedly, I would not need the stick-um to attach it. I shoved the recorder fairly far under the bench, and left the booth.

Well, the device was in place, as I had heard intelligence people say. Still, it was a long troubled wait until six thirty when I would go into the church to pull the thing out. I could not risk leaving it there until next day when some verger might sweep it out. To be sure, at six thirty or seven, I would likely have to confess myself to get it out. But it was a sacramental rite I had read of often enough to parody.

As I waited, my superstitious dread of the sacrilege contorted me. I knew I was being neurotic, but I imagined that because I was toying with God now and had blasphemed him at the Black Mass and the grave digging, he would pay me back by letting the damned recorder break down or, worse, squeal electronically.

I had first planned to watch Conyers go in and out, but dismissed the idea as too dangerous. By seven, confessions would be over and either he would have come or not come.

It was five now. I imagined him getting out of his car, which he had parked so many times in front of Labor to await the docile approach of Susan. He would walk fast, athletically into the church. Or would he be skipping this Saturday. No, he couldn't. He would genuflect at the aisle, make his way to the confessional. Would the line be too long? Might he put it off until next Saturday? Please, God, no, I thought. Let him move straight into the booth. But would he say it, say those damning words? Would my little sneak-ear go on, function correctly? Had I set the thing right? Suppose Conyers by some fantastic fluke dropped something, a coin say, and it rolled beneath the bench?

Dear Lord, surely they would all be waiting for me: the priest and Conyers, and local police and FBI men, all anticipating an arrest for violation of the federal electronic surveillance statute?

At last, six thirty came. If only Conyers had been as punctual as Susan said. The street was dark now. Still, I parked four blocks away. The Morgan was too recognizable.

Not a police car was in sight in front of the church. Nevertheless, I paused at the church door, wiping my sweating palms on my trousers. I could still turn away, not risk that catastrophic moment when I opened the door and faced my assembled enemies.

With a shake of my head, I pushed open the padded door and saw all was at peace within St. Bridget's.

There were a number of parishioners in the church, one waiting near the confessional. Now, to retrieve the bug! I was dizzy, sure I was going to faint. Heart attack! I thought with spectacular panic: see a doctor tomorrow!

See a priest tonight, I steadied myself.

The matronly woman ahead of me went into the booth and was swiftly shriven of sins I would hear of later, if I chose.

I entered, knelt, looked at the colander-like screen from which the faceless priest's voice would come, then knelt even deeper. My hands fluttered frantically for the minirecorder. It was gone!

I sagged lower and pawed further under the bench. Finally, I touched it. Oh, Jesus! I thought as I popped it into my coat pocket.

"Is there anything wrong?" I heard the youngish voice of the priest say through the colander holes.

"No," I said. "Just a little nervous. I thought I dropped something." I was giddy with both relief and apprehension.

"Father," I began, "I have sinned . . ."

Quickly, I confessed myself. It was surrealistic. There was not an explicit word in anything I said. Without naming anyone, I told him I had betrayed two women, lied to my bosses and to the authorities, but not in a way that would hurt anyone but me, committed numerous blasphemies and inferentially sold my soul to the Devil.

The poor man must have been overwhelmed by this gush of vague, generalized sin. Getting his thoughts together, he replied: "You've been away from the sacrament for a long time?"

"Yes," I said. "But believe me, I am sincerely penitent."

"I would like to go over these things in a little more detail, if you don't mind, before I can absolve you," he said dubiously.

I could tell from the decent doubt in his voice that the mini-recorder remained undiscovered. He really was concerned about me. I felt shame, still buoyed by relief.

"Father, it was hard enough for me to cough it out this way." Suddenly, I cared profoundly about what he was going to say to me. Oh, if the taped confessional were there, no matter how ugly its use against Conyers was going to be, I was going to use it.

Yet, I yearned, my nerves strung like a harp now, for someone to absolve me. However unreal, this episode before a stranger-priest, it had emotional meaning for me.

"Can you absolve me? This is all I can confess right now. I promise I will work to bring myself honorably out of this mess. I swear, I am truly penitent."

I could feel him sorting things out, even as I clutched the recorder wetly in my sweating palm. I marveled at my own craziness.

"Yes. You've taken the first step," he said finally. "Can you come back?" Panic hit me. "You're not a Catholic, are you?" he asked.

"No," I murmured so he could hardly hear.

But the priest was not interested in exposing me.

"The need that brought you here was therefore all the stronger," he went on. My tarnished pendulum emotions swung between shame and gratitude. "You know that I cannot absolve you in the sense that you asked me originally," he continued. "After all, you asked me under false pretenses." God, how right he was.

"But if your penitence is genuine," his voice lifted, "then you are on the way out of your trouble." He paused again. "Come back if you like, when you like, okay?" There was firm hope in his voice. "Go in peace." I left the booth, tears in my eyes.

I can only say in my defense that I listened to no one's confession from the tape but Conyers'. The others I erased after I had methodically put Conyers' on three more cassettes.

The prosecutor's voice was so different from the snap-and-snarl I was accustomed to that I knew from the outset

Susan was right about his one confidant being his priest.

"Bless me, Father, for I have sinned," Conyers began. The priest's answer was more fraternal than clerical, coming out distinctly from the recorder's tiny remarkably pure speaker.

"All right, go ahead."

"I committed the sin of impurity." I was jolted; put down my bourbon on the rocks and replayed what he had said. "Impurity" was hardly what you would call accepting a false plea. I listened in astonishment as he explained.

"The girl I was going to marry. She's caught in the switches in a case . . . in my case. I saw her the other day. She was a witness. She's pregnant. By a guy I mentioned before, a screwed up intellectual fake. A rat, for my money," he said with vehemence. Damn it, he was overdoing it. "Anyway, I saw her . . . Susan and . . ." He looked for words.

The priest waited so long that the time-lag on the voice-actuator clicked off and then clicked on as Conyers recommenced.

"I am still in love with her." His voice lowered. "I lust after her. I got smashed last night and went to a prostitute."

"*Umphf*," I could hear the priest grunt. His exclamation of surprise meant that I had surmised correctly in believing Conyers belonged to that old school who kept themselves pure for marriage.

"Yeah," said Conyers, acknowledging his confessor's astonishment.

"Is there anything else?" asked the priest.

"Yeah, but I'm not sure it's a sin. I'm bothered by it."

"Okay, go ahead."

Well, here it was. I turned up the volume. Conyers was putting himself in the best possible light, but he was getting the facts into the Church, all the same. Because he was making my case for me, I half admired his honesty.

"This guy talked me into letting him plead to suborning. Or let's say he let me talk him into it. He's plenty guilty of a lot worse things, including conspiracy to bribe, probably bribery itself. But I'm not sure I can make it stand up in court. Here was a sure bet for a plea to something he must have thought of, even if he didn't do it."

"Suborning? That would be . . ." interjected the priest.

"Suborning. That means getting Susan . . . the woman

in question . . . well, to be technical about it, to induce someone to give false testimony."

"Did she give false testimony?"

"Yes."

"But . . ."

"Right, but he didn't induce her to do it. She did it herself. The point is, that I have let the guy plead to it, at least I got a statement from him and witnessed it and plan to let him plead to it in front of the judge."

"So that you can avoid the uncertainties of a trial."

"Right."

"So you are accepting a false plea in order to be sure you get him." Conyers paused. Like an unseen cheering section, I was rooting him on to answer this one honestly.

"Yes, I suppose that's what you'd have to say."

"And how much does Susan, your . . . the girl . . . figure in?"

God, I thought, this damned priest was relentless. I could believe confession was good for the soul, anybody's soul. But, in this instance, between the two of them, Conyers and the priest, they were destroying Conyers. Then I thought of the cruel, brutal man as *I* knew him and felt a little better.

"I don't know."

"Would you have gone after this man if she wasn't involved, that is, if the jealousy element wasn't involved?"

"I'd have gone after his boss."

"His boss?"

"Yes. She's the real crook in all this."

"But you took the plea from him. What about her?"

"Father," Conyers said at last, seeing what he had done. "I am letting both women off in order to get him." I could hear some shuffling around on the tape. Then the priest said, a little tensely:

"Can you withdraw from this case, Roger?"

"I don't think so. I don't think I would."

"You see the problem?"

"Yeah."

"It's the problem of revenge in addition to compounding a serious lie."

"Yeah." Poor son of a bitch, I began to feel.

"So you realize that you are fully intending to commit what you yourself believe to be a serious sin?"

That was too much for Conyers to swallow.

"Look what he did to me, to the country."

"*He* took your girl. It was his boss who wronged the country."

Conyers said nothing.

"Roger, I can't absolve you. Can you see me at the rectory next week?"

"Monday?"

"Sure." Roger Conyers knew better than anyone but me that he had a heavy sin on him until Monday.

"Go in peace," sighed the priest.

"Not likely," I said to myself, gulping heavily on the raw whiskey as I carefully turned off the dirty little device. Again, I thought of calling Anita. But this time, my avoiding her had something to do with my own ignominy.

Clearly, the time to get to Conyers was as soon as possible. Whatever his talk with the priest Monday, at best, from my point of view, it would put off the day of reckoning on Anita, and on me, too.

Conyers, I suspected, would get right with God by reneging on our deal and then would go on with his probe, or turn it over to some other equally remorseless Justice Department inquisitor.

Now, while his guilt was still fresh, I must strike a conclusive bargain. I called him at home Sunday at 11:00 A.M.

"I want to talk with you," I said briefly.

"What about?" He was cautious, perhaps warned by my brusqueness.

"The deal's off on the plea." There was a long pause.

"I have your statement."

"Bring it with you. I want to see you this afternoon. Near the Mall somewhere, so we can walk. About two."

"Look, that's not convenient." He toughened up. "I don't think I need to talk with you anymore. I have your statement. We are proceeding on that basis." My old hate came back for him.

"Let's not crap around, Conyers," I told him. "You're as guilty of criminality as I am or Anita and a helluva lot more than Susan." I feared he would hang up. "Just listen."

I had the tape recorder set on a section of the interview at Justice. I turned it on and held the cassette speaker up to the phone: "I thought it was my offense against

Title Eighteen," it said. Then there was his voice. "You know better."

I talked into the mouthpiece again. "There's more. I've run off a copy for you."

"You motherfucker," he shouted, slamming down the phone in my ear.

Good Lord, I thought, suppose he just refuses to talk with me, lets me blast him—and all of us—out of the water. But that would not be the way of the man I had heard in the confessional. I waited ten minutes and called him back.

"I was hoping you would call me," I said. "You win that one."

"There's not that much was said in there," he said tensely, but I had him. He knew he had said something he regretted in his office.

"Two in front of the Jefferson Memorial?" I said. "There's always a place to park there."

It was still overcoat weather and we stood inside the marble rotunda to keep off the wind. I assumed he was recording me and I had my little machine turning in my coat. He was calmed down and I was weary.

"Look," I said. "You know I've got a machine going and I assume you have. We're like two humans out of some crazy paranoid world of the future."

"I don't need any speeches," he said.

"I do." For better or for worse, we were locked into a mutual horror story. "If I pull this damned thing out of my pocket and hand it to you, will you do the same? At least we can get that far toward trusting each other." I pulled the bug out of my pocket and gave it to him. He looked at it curiously.

"Not bought with government funds," I said.

He smiled crookedly at that and put it in his pocket.

"Here's the kind of junk they supply us with." He dug into an inside pocket and pulled out a contraption almost the size of a flashlight. Then the menace was back in his voice. "I'd already decided not to use this statement when you called." He drew a sheaf of paper from his pocket: the original and four carbons of my statement. "I don't even want it in the office."

I sought for words that would not make him blow up. "You agreed to do something that will get you in trouble at Justice and with the bar association," I murmured. "I have proof of it. You admit you went after me because of Susan. That's selective prosecution. I'm sorry, but it is."

Angry as he was, he was listening to reason.

"Mrs. Tockbridge?" he asked, looking to save his case.

"If you ever do get her, you will be able to drag me in so it comes to the same thing. Besides, she's not the worst crook in this administration."

"You're asking me to drop the whole thing?"

"Yes."

"No cheese," he said. "I'd rather quit and hand it all over to somebody else. You may have quite a little tape there, but it's not enough really to hurt me—if I get out of government. You can still wind up in Lewisburg. You plead to a misdemeanor. Susan gets off. That's my limit."

"No," I said. "I'm not pleading to anything, not even some misdemeanor I *did* commit. You could still put me away for a year."

Conyers thought a moment. Again, he was the bargainer, trying to salvage what he could of his wares. After a minute, he looked at me, the hate back in his eyes, along with a nascent hope.

"I can pass my talk on your recorder off as boasting or anger, take a reprimand, let my associates pull off this case and maybe I can even stay in Justice. You just don't have enough, Dobecker. No deals." There was no compromise in his voice.

Well, I thought. That's that. More or less as I had expected. Yet, I knew I would never fully forgive myself for what I was about to do.

"Let's walk to the car. I want to tell you something else," I said. Conyers was uneasy now as I tried to figure out how to say it. I looked out over the gray Tidal Basin, then back at him.

"I know you went to church and confessed yesterday."

His eyes bugged, unbelieving.

"You . . ." he gagged. "You . . ." He perceived it all in my eyes.

I never even saw him swing. I felt the tremendous shock on my cheekbone and fell sprawling backwards onto the moist, cold grass. It could only have stunned me for an instant, for when I looked up he was struggling in his coat pocket to pull out something, and finally he got out my mini-recorder. Like the outfielder he must have been when he wasn't playing football, he heaved the little machine in a great arc toward the Basin's choppy waters.

I felt my broken face. The pain was enormous. I could see people running toward us. My God, if a policeman, I had the wits to think. I struggled to my feet.

"The police," I said in agony. His wild eyes settled for a moment. Then, grabbing me by the coat, he half helped, half dragged me to his old car.

"Oh, you motherfucker. You motherfucker," he grunted in anguish as he hustled me along. I willingly followed. Whatever else was to happen, I had done what I could. It was all up to the man who had knocked me flat, now. My head was shot with pain. He drove rapidly away from the monument.

"I ought to make you take me to the hospital," I groaned.

"I ought to kill you," he gasped, still barely in control of himself. Terror struck me. His blow had made me feel he might.

"I want out. Now!" I considered screaming out the window for police.

"Ah, you fuck," he said. "I'm not stupid enough to kill you."

I touched my face. I guessed he had fractured my cheekbone from the pain and the way my head throbbed. But I had lost no teeth. And, thank God, no police. Without them, we could still patch something together. I thought of using an assault charge against him as one last counter. But that might well be suicidal.

"I don't believe you," he said at last, about the confession.

"If you want to hear it, a tape is in my car," I muttered, far enough back in my throat so I didn't have to open my lips much.

"Ah," he gasped in anger again. He drove aimlessly toward town. "What do you want for all the copies of everything?" he said.

"No," I said. "It's not going to be that way. You can't give me all your files on us. It wouldn't matter if you did anyway. You know enough about us to start the whole thing going again. So I'm not going to give you all the tapes. It's a stalemate. We're like Russia and America. Trust won't work. It's the practicalities. If you bomb me with a prosecution, I bomb you with the tapes. We both had better just keep our weapons."

"You get out of government. At least that," he said. I took offense, my face now aching steadily and mightily.

"Me? *You* get out. You're damned well more of a danger to good government than I am. Look," I said, "I've got to go to a doctor. I don't want the police in on it. But I'm going to my personal doctor."

The tears of pain were flooding my eyes.

But I could feel him yielding, like those fish at Sint Maarten, flicking, fighting still, but caught. Despite the jolts of agony in my face, I was going to win, win the whole game, myself, my job, Susan, Anita.

"I'm staying," Conyers said, as if to preserve some thread of pride by holding on to his job at Justice. I had him at boatside.

"Then it's agreed," I said, hiding my exultation. "Stalemate." If ever need be, Anita could take care of him at Justice with those damned films and Harry. I'd won! I had beaten him!

I was already thinking how I would explain my shattered face at the White House, when I felt, more than saw, a tightening in the man next to me. Unbelieving, I stared at him.

"I'm not going to sit by paralyzed and watch you become Labor Secretary and her . . ." he didn't have to say "Vice President." I froze, feeling nothing but the face pain: agony in a block of ice. Was he balking, balking when I had it all won?

"Aw, come on," I managed. "You know chances of that are . . ."

He interrupted, staring now with those eyes of blue hate.

"I'd rather bring the whole temple down on all our heads," he said harshly. Good Jesus! I thought. Here it was, the one thing I had not bargained for. I had assumed either I would fail completely or that, mirabile dictu, I would come out whole. I had assumed, above all, that Conyers would protect himself, his good name—that there was not a suicidal cell in his whole body. For a moment I was too shaken to speak. Sure, I had pondered increasingly about how long I wanted to stay in government. But never, now with victory as real as the pain in my cheek, had I wanted to stay so badly.

"That's crazy," I muttered. "Look. The way I suggested makes some sense, bad as it is for both of us with pipe bombs up our asses. You go on and do your job of catching real criminals. I go on doing my job . . . believe me, I'm burned enough now not to fool around with crooks."

I was pleading now for both of us.

"God, man, look at what you have to lose." I did not have to review for him the tapes. He recognized anew the dangers to him. It would finish him as a lawyer.

But for answer, he only tightened up his lips and shook his head. The bastard had put himself in a noble position now, and I felt myself morally the weaker for the first time.

"You wouldn't even have a case anymore if you tried to prosecute us. You realize don't you that these tapes taint your whole case so much that you couldn't even get me into court? We've got a selective prosecution case against you that's out of this world, not to mention the bar's ethics committee."

"You'd have to quit," he said bluntly, not even angry anymore, reconciled.

"*You'd* have to quit," I answered him. He turned now for an instant as he pulled up at the turnoff to the Jefferson Memorial.

"Right. We'd all have to quit. It's no deal, Dobecker, not if you stay in the government." Well, there it stood. For a few moments, in silence, I ran the possibilities through my frenzied mind. Was he bluffing? No. What did I lose: ah, the feeling of power. The long vista from the executive offices, on across the Potomac to the blue hills of Virginia and beyond. The power to do things. And what did I gain? I smiled inwardly with rue. I gained a little peace of mind, a nonspastic colon if I were lucky. Maybe Susan.

"Goddamnit," I said sadly.

Now, almost without rancor, but with a vicious satisfaction, he stared at my face. "Damn, that felt good," he said, recalling, as I did, the smack of his fist on my face. Then, he was all business. "I want a copy of those tapes. I want to hear them before I agree to anything. The one . . . at the church."

"Drop me here," I said. "If you pull up, somebody will see your car and call a cop maybe. I'll get the tapes and drive back here." I pulled his tape recorder out of my coat pocket where I had almost forgotten it and laid it on the seat. "We're clear on the terms of the bargain, right?" Be sure, I thought.

"I'm clear enough," he said. "You leave government and I lay off the rest." He shrugged.

"You ought to be thanking me," I said, wanting to get in one last lick for the broken face. "I solved your moral dilemma for you. You'll have good news for your friend Monday."

But he didn't take it the way I thought he would. Without answering me directly, he looked at my face, swollen so much now that my eye was jammed shut. Perhaps the sight of what he had done to me, perhaps his recognition that he could now more easily make his peace with his God, had calmed this choleric man.

"You sure you can make it over to the car?" was all he said.

When I drove back to where he was parked, he got out of his car and silently I handed over to him one of the cassettes on which I had transferred my talk with him and his talk with God.

I would have to quit, I thought as I drove toward my doctor's home. I would have to quit. Goddamn it, that hurt far worse than the cheek. Objectively, I could see I had carried off almost the impossible, even with the terms I had gotten. But all I brooded on now was the end to my rise, to my hopes. Power is addictive, people said. The withdrawal symptoms proved it.

Anita came to my house in answer to my call. She was duly impressed by my mutilated face. I told her the whole story and she was jubilant.

"He should have hit you harder," she laughed. "Now I stay, right?" I almost hated throwing ice water on her.

"Conyers will stick to his bargain personally, but as long as he's in, there's always a danger he'll get it out indirectly, through some aide. You're going to have to get Frieden to get rid of him."

"That means the films."

"Won't he do it for past favors?" I said mildly. She ignored the sally and shook her head.

"If I use the films, I'll probably have to quit." But she was so upbeat about the criminal threat disappearing that this prospect didn't depress her for the moment. And with my own mind made up for me by Conyers, I didn't feel sorry for her. I had saved her from jail at the cost of my job and my cheekbone.

"You're getting off easy. After Harry agrees to ease out Conyers . . . make sure it's done slowly, in a half year, no sooner, huh . . . then give him the two reels."

"He'll never trust me again," she sighed. "He'll know I had to cooperate with Buffi and Krals to make those goddamned things." A freshet of lust ran through me, thinking of that day in the chapel. Animated as she was, she looked young and desirable.

"Well," I said, pushing back the thoughts, "You said the films were your ultimate weapon. Now you *need* an ultimate weapon."

I could see she still thought she could survive in government. She sensed my thoughts. "Even if he lets me stay, it's finished for me as his Vice President."

I looked at those sunny pale blue eyes.

"And if you have to quit, what then? Go away?"

"For awhile, maybe to France. To the Riviera or someplace. That would be Buffi's way. Why think about it?"

"He'd pick the Dalmatian coast."

She smiled, jarring me with a mannerism, a caught breath between words that held a tender whiff of remembrance. Uncomfortable as I was, I wanted her.

"Well, I wish Buffi were still here," she said.

"To take care of you?" I joshed her.

"Yes. If he hadn't been so crazy I could have grown old with him." She laughed. "When he wasn't doing something peculiar, you know, he was really, well, just nice."

"You mean, as a . . ." It was odd how chaste, how delicate our talk had become now that we were parting forever. She read my thought again and smiled.

"Yes. Mostly normal and even loving."

"That's funny. And touching." I, too, missed him now, poor dead Buffi.

I rose and went to where she sat. She looked up, her eyes unfaded, youthful, spectacularly blue. It was at just such a moment that we might have reconciled our alienated ways.

Her hair had fallen over her ear, and I brushed it back in an old gesture. She took my hand away from her head and kissed it. For an instant, I thought of letting that great wave I could feel behind my brain sweep over me and catapult me into her arms. But no, I was flying away, centrifugally off another way. Dizzy almost, I went for her coat.

I helped her on with it. She stood in the opened door, the chill, darkling day behind her. It left her features indistinct, wiping out the lines and leaving her face young and pure.

"What about you, Martin?" she asked.

"Practice law someplace. I'll die both a good and a bad Christian." The instant I said it I wondered where it had come from.

"I'll let you know how it goes with Frieden," she said. Oddly, I didn't really care that much. I kissed her lightly on those full, spoiled lips.

"A bientôt, baby," she said, leaving me always to wonder from what new lover she had learned the phrase.

That night I rummaged around for my own forgotten quotation.

I found it in Palmer-More's *English Faust Book,* buried in the boxes of books from my Nostradamus period.

"I intreate you, if you hereafter finde my dead carcasse, convay it unto the earth for I dye both a good and a bad Christian; a good Christian, for that I am heartely sorry, and in my heart always praye for mercy, that my soule may be delivered: a bad Christian, for that I know the Devill will have my bodie, and that would I willingly give him so that he would leave my soule in quiet."

The memory of the foolish old necromancer's death was oddly consoling. Faust has always seemed a sympathetic character to me, a failure of a human being, a tinkerer really, hyped up by Goethe and Berlioz and Gounod into a mythic giant. Yet, what had he really done except to save Marguerita?

I thought now of calling Susan. She would want to know what had happened, of course. But to call her was to try to lure her away from her doctor, from a future that had some balance to it. We had made our good-byes. Awake with my pain that night, I dwelled on her. But I did not call.

Finally, there was Athanor. Next morning I telephoned around for gold. The first jewelry shop told me to try Fort Knox. The second man, as suspicious as the first, loosened up a bit when I lied about some handicrafts.

"Save a little trouble for yourself. Buy an ounce of wedding rings from a pawnbroker."

The silver I located at an artsy-craftsy shop.

By eleven I was out. The day was warm again with a breeze from the southwest, the sort of balmy streak in late winter that forced reluctant buds from the feeble downtown street saplings and, in Georgetown, where I walked for my merchandise, tapped the few sunlit lawns for crocus spears.

The hydrochloric and nitric acids for my aqua regia were easy to come by, although I had to drive to Southeast Washington to get them from a metal wholesaler.

I put two gold wedding rings in a Mason jar of aqua regia, wondering vaguely whose initials these were on the inside and what pawned lovers had worn them. I thought gloomily of Susan and her doctor. The rings were ghastly white in the fuming, oily-looking yellow of the acid.

The chip of silver in the nitric acid began to dissolve almost at once, throwing off its tiny bubbles of disintegration like a petillant wine. Athanor! I had chased these worthless bits of knowledge for so many years, hiding behind them from life. I had wrestled with life my season or two, and here was I again, taking consolations from my recluse oddities.

I had been to the future, and I had found that for me, in any case, it did not work. But if nothing else, and how much it was, I had come back with a sort of balls. Conyers had not won it all. At worst I had tied him. I had, I reminded myself, protected my womenfolk.

Smoky old Athanor. What in God's name would the next occupant of this house think on finding such a furnace in his basement? Would he discover what it was. Easter Island on the Potomac?

It was fumy, smelly work. I drank spritz and tried not to think of Susan as she had been on that long ago day, or of Conyers.

In Athanor I heat-dried the silver nitrate and the gold chloride separately. The lumpy grainy substances had a medieval charm to them. I looked at gold and silver there through the isinglass peephole, sooty and mysterious, and knew something of the thrill of those old *souffleurs*— "Maybe," they must have thought, "maybe this time . . ."

I distilled the distillate as prescribed seven times: seven

for the seven rings of Hell, the magic number for craps. Seven for good luck, the seven magical words of medieval occultism, the seven last words, the seven planetary ages of man.

Chronocrators! It was fun, letting the old thing-for-itself knowledge clatter around in my head.

I mixed the liquid with the dry metallic compounds and melded in the three parts mercury, pasting the poor, corrupted metals with the quicksilver.

Was it precisely at this point that the alchemists had recognized failure, even before the paste was locked into its "egg"—the two china egg cups I had bought to simulate the Aludel?

Yes. Surely here, the chemists aborning had separated from the philosophers. The chemists, wondering where their formula went wrong, the philosophers recognizing at last that there would be no gold from dross. And which was I?

My cellar was a menace to safety with its half-filled acid jars, its charcoal underfoot and the hearth of Athanor beginning to crack from my inexpert cementing and the constant fire.

The egg cups wired together behind the isinglass blackened but did not split apart. I cooked the "egg" as prescribed, let it cool and fished it out. With long-nosed pliers I unwrapped the wire. I had gone through the ritual.

When I gently pulled apart the two egg cups, a little granular nugget fell to the hearth and broke into three pieces. It was an interesting if uncohesive creation, tints of gold on the leaden, blackened surface, and the bright gold within.

That was the end. Athanor's work was done. This was the Philosopher's Stone: nothing.

I looked at the mess around me. Was I the only man in the twentieth century to follow the rules for turning metals into the Philosopher's Stone? Perhaps. Had it worked? No.

I took the lumps upstairs. I emptied the cuff links from a square, lined box and put my creations inside.

Well, now I would do it. Susan wasn't here to hush me with her words or tears and I would try her one more time. I looked at the odd pieces of "jewelry" in their bed of cotton. How Susan had laughed when we stoked up Athanor for the first time.

To be sure, she had a good thing with the doctor now that she was free of Conyers. But if she did not love the doctor, her marriage to him had no wisdom to it at all.

It was late afternoon before I finished the letter, trying to keep it short and straight, knowing as I did my inclination toward hyperbole and dishonesty.

"Dear Susan," I wrote, resisting the temptation in my first two drafts of saying, "Dearest Susan."

"I made the Philosopher's Stone as you can see. My recipe wasn't right—it didn't turn lead into gold for me and it didn't make me wise.

"I saw Conyers and agreed only to quit government which I was quite ready to do anyway. You and Anita are off scot free. That gives me a chance to ask you to think about things one more time. When I said goodbye to you at the station, it was all very romantic to give it a 'farewell forever' quality. It seemed then that your marrying the good doctor was a good idea. It would make an honest woman of you, give our little fatso a name, provide a father for Ems and give you all the benefits of a respectable Roman Catholic marriage to a professional and undoubtedly decent man.

"But there is this other side. Even admitting I am prejudiced, we have loved each other. We fit emotionally and, clearly, physically. I love Ems and would be sure to love the new kid and any other kids, too. You'll have to grant my track record with kids is better than with adults.

"And although God knows what I will do, whatever it is, I do work hard.

"Simply stated, I'm begging you not to marry the good doctor. Instead, I am asking you to wait at least until you are sure that *I am not* the man you want to spend the rest of your life with. That shouldn't take you too long to decide, one way or the other.

"Susan, I am not going to blame you if you turn me down or even if you decide not to wait at all. But I do love you. And I don't want to say to myself in the future I didn't try.

"Above all, no decisions based on 'duty' to me for bailing us all out! You know I have done some seedy things, some things I am honestly ashamed of. But you know that even these were done in the course of my becoming something I wasn't before. And what I did become was a stronger man than you saw at the riot at 8th and H so long ago."

I wrapped the letter around the cuff-links box and put them in an envelope with fifty cents worth of stamps on it, to make sure it had all it would need.

My alchemy was finished. And had I changed any more than the elements in those coarse nuggets? Had the leaden life I once led become more golden, more worthy? Yes. Somewhat.

Tonight, face injury or no face injury, I would go to the Jockey Club. God, I was hungry. When had I last gone there? I would drink Moselle with the soup and fish and a Haut Brion with the beef tartare, then—half bottles all—I would drink a Chambertin with the cheese.

I showered, washing away the residue of my alchemy. I painfully shaved off the two days of beard and got dressed in my Saltz worsted and my fine tweed topcoat.

Outside the foehn lay heavy on the soft night. The Morgan started and gasped with a fine roar. There was no need for the heater.

There was going to be, no doubt, a hell of a lot of cold weather. Now it was like spring. Was it useful, I wondered, to let my imagination stray forward, and backward to spring? What a good, free time it had been when Susan and Ems and I had gone driving in the Morgan along George Washington Parkway, the towers of Georgetown and the brown, beautiful, polluted river over our shoulders.

Well, I had laid out my case fairly to Susan. I thought of her delight when she saw the fragments of Philosopher's Stone. She would look up from those fragile encrustations, wanting someone—me—to laugh with over them. "Fairly?"

At the next filling station, I screeched in and pulled up to the telephone booth. Susan's mother answered the call and greeted me with all the enthusiasm of Madam Defarge over a postponed guillotining. Up hers, I thought.

"Martin, damnit, I've been worried . . ." Susan began.

I was laughing at myself despite the lingering pain. There was her voice, concerned, excited by my call.

"Susan," I interrupted her, "I wrote you a fair letter about how you should consider marrying me. But fairness: it's bullshit. I'm coming up."

She tried to butt in, but it was no use. I could always talk her down if I had my heart in it.

"No, I'm coming up. I got us off. Got us off clean, Susan. I'm quitting government. I'm coming up to get you and bring you back in the morning."

Only then, did I hesitate. For a long moment, there was no answer. Sane Susan, weighing the consequences. When she spoke, it came in a rush, but ordered, just as she was.

"What about Ems? Is she safe in your car, coming all that way? Should I be staying at your house, I mean until . . ."

"Yes," I said to everything. "Look," I broke in at last, "I have got to get on the road. It's three hours."

"Well, be careful," she cautioned, then, before I could say goodnight for the time being, she added rapidly, "Listen, are you sure you want to do this?"

"Yes," I said one last time.

I wheeled the sports car through the ant hill city, on past the Capitol's lighted dome and toward the north, reflecting. I had asked Susan to marry me and she had asked me questions about children and cars and lodging. Was that what I wanted? Yes, I thought, most of me. At least her questions all had real answers. I accelerated. Three hours. The warm night began to roar into the open car and through my hair.